Acclaim for
THE STORY PEDDLER

"Lindsay A. Franklin is a fearless storyteller. She weaves a colorful fantasy of light, darkness, and the many adventures in between. *The Story Peddler* is a perfect blend of humor, heartache, and healing."

— NADINE BRANDES, author of *Fawkes* and *Romanov*

"*The Story Peddler* is like nothing I've ever read. Lindsay A. Franklin weaves a magical and one-of-a-kind tale packed with danger, treason, and forbidden stories. A girl who wants to escape her mundane life. A king who harbors dark secrets. A princess in search of truth. *The Story Peddler* has it all.

Filled to the brim with mystery and intrigue, this stunning debut will transport readers to a realm from whence they'll ne'er desire to return. Save a spot on your TBR list for this beauty! *The Story Peddler* is a binge-worthy read sure to be treasured by peasants and kings alike."

— SARA ELLA, award-winning author of the Unblemished trilogy

"Traitors, rebels, and the most original magic system I've seen since Patrick Carr's *A Cast of Stones* make Lindsay A. Franklin's *The Story Peddler* a unique and engrossing debut! I read through the book in two days. Did not want to put it down."

— JILL WILLIAMSON, Christy Award-winning author of *By Darkness Hid* and *King's Folly*

THE STORY RAIDER

The Weaver Trilogy

The Story Peddler
The Story Raider
The Story Hunter

THE STORY RAIDER

THE WEAVER TRILOGY

BOOK 2

LINDSAY A. FRANKLIN

Published by Enclave Publishing, an imprint of Third Day Books, LLC
Phoenix, Arizona, USA

www.enclavepublishing.com

ISBN: 978-1-62184-078-7 (print)
ISBN: 978-1-68370-204-7 (eBook)

The Story Raider
Copyright © 2019 by Lindsay A. Franklin

Edited by Steve Laube
Cover design by Kirk DouPonce
Interior typesetting by Jamie Foley

Printed in the United States of America

For my parents, Doug and Gina.
Thank you for loving your little wanderer,
even as she struggled to find her way.

CHAPTER 1

NAITH

Naith Bo-Offriad hurried down the main thorough-fare of Afon. Of all places.

How had it come to this? The High Priest of the Tirian Empire skulking down the cobblestoned streets of some peninsular town, praying to the stars not to be noticed by the provincials, should they still be milling about at this hour.

Cethor's tears.

At the sound of voices, Naith slipped into a shadowed alleyway. Just in time, as two men rounded a nearby corner. One said, "Tide's turnin'. I'm tellin' you. Won't be long afore Urian falls."

Naith pressed himself against the building.

"A season ago I would've told you the monarchy couldn't fall," the other responded. "Two moons ago, I'd have sworn she and her ilk were too powerful. But Gareth fell, didn't he? If the father can be toppled, so can the daughter."

Naith held his breath as the men passed in front of his hiding spot.

The first man laughed. "Too right. Much too right. Usher in the new era, I say! Down with the nobility!"

"You're drunk."

"I'm drunk on the potentials!"

"And the ale."

Their laughter faded into the distance.

Naith's whole body trembled. Fear, anger, dismay.

How could the Master have let this happen?

Naith slunk back onto the street and shuffled the last two blocks to another deserted alleyway. But this one backed up to the temple.

This is what it had come to—the high priest sneaking in through the back door. The Master had much to answer for, but even now, Naith dared not call the Master to account.

He felt along the wooden doorframe, and a splinter stabbed into his palm.

Blast.

He tried the doorframe again.

There it was. He slid the false piece of wood from its place and plucked the key from within the concealed compartment. He fumbled for the keyhole and then inserted the key.

The door squealed on hinges rusty from disuse.

Naith paused. Listened. But nothing stirred. He opened the door just enough to squeeze his bulk through.

The black of the room swallowed him, pulled him into its depths. He shut the door behind himself and said a silent prayer.

If there was anyone to hear it. The goddesses? Foolishness. The stars? Perhaps. Or perhaps even deeper foolishness. Naith only knew his heart longed to cry out to someone or something, now that he had seen the Master falter. The Master had always maintained perfect control. And now . . .

"Naith."

The High Priest of the Tirian Empire gasped. "Who goes there?"

"Naith."

And then the voice registered. He had heard it hundreds of times—cold, smooth, neither male nor female, all around him at once. "Master."

"Come in, Naith. I have been waiting."

Naith obeyed and moved deeper into the room. He squinted,

for a moment unable to see anything. But there—in the corner, seated and shrouded in shadow thicker than midnight.

"Master." Naith bowed low to the ground.

"Yes." The Master paused. "You do not look well, Naith."

"No." He wondered how the Master could see in the darkness. "I have come at your beckoning, Master. Please tell me how I might serve."

The plea tasted sour on Naith's tongue. It might not have a moon ago. But now that all was falling apart, how could Naith be expected to grovel as in the days when the Master's power seemed unmatched?

"Yes, you have come." The Master paused. Naith could practically feel a dagger-sharp gaze upon him. "And I shall give you your new orders."

Naith's hopes quickened. "New orders? You have a plan, Master?"

"Always."

"I live to serve you." He bowed again.

"Gareth is dead."

Naith's body went cold. "Dead?"

"As of an hour ago."

"It . . ." Naith fought to find his voice. "It must have been the rebels, or perhaps Braith's operatives."

"No. It was I."

Naith blinked.

"Come, Naith. Are you truly surprised?"

"Master, why? Gareth was your most loyal servant, aside from the one who stands before you."

A soft chuckle emanated through the room. "Gareth was only useful because he was king. As he was no longer that, he was no longer useful. And a Gareth who is no longer useful is a dangerous liability."

Unease sprouted in Naith's stomach.

"I see your hesitation, Naith," the Master murmured. "You are still High Priest of the Tirian Empire, are you not?"

"Yes, Master."

"Then I can still use you."

Naith swallowed. "But without Gareth, how shall we proceed?"

"You must return to Urian."

"Urian?" Naith wrung his hands. "But I've barely made it out alive. The rioters are calling for Braith's head. When news of Gareth's death spreads, it will only foment more unrest."

"Yes. And you shall use that unrest to our advantage."

"Master?"

"In due time, the plan will be revealed to you, Naith. For now, you will obey me and return to Urian."

Naith paused for a long moment, then lowered himself in a bow. "Yes, Master."

CHAPTER 2

TANWEN

MY BODY SLAMMED TO THE STONE FLOOR HARD ENOUGH TO knock the wind from my chest. I struggled to draw air, but my ribs felt two sizes too small.

Squeezing. Pinching. Strangling.

I pressed my hands against the stone and forced myself to flip over—to see what was happening around me. Only blackness met me. Blackness thicker than velvety midnights in the grain fields of Pembrone. Blackness deeper than the moonlit waves of the Menfor Sea when Brac and I snuck down the rocky cliffs to press our feet into the pebbly sand and share childish whispers about our dreams.

Brac. Where was he?

"Brac! Are you there?" Hadn't he been beside me a moment ago? Where in Tir was I?

"Hello?"

Brac didn't answer, but my body did. It jerked against the stones—lifted me up and slammed me down, robbing my chest of its air again. And then again.

A memory pricked me.

I had seen this before, except from the outside. I had stood helplessly in the Corsyth forest hideout and watched as Gryfelle's body jerked and writhed. I had listened as she screamed and growled and whimpered. I had watched the others try to protect her body and bring her mind back to us. Yes, I had seen all this before.

But now I was on the inside. Now it was happening to me.

"Mor!" I cried out, but the blackness swallowed it. "Father? Help me!"

No one answered. My mind scrambled, clawed its way back to them, even if my body wouldn't obey. Were my memories leaking from my mind at this very moment, like they had with Gryfelle? Were they swirling off into the air like lost story strands, never to be reclaimed?

Stars above. The curse had found me after all.

Another jerk of my body and the air flooded into my chest, the light rushed back into my eyes, and familiar surroundings pushed their way into my sight. The couch under the windows overlooking the palace gardens. Father's heavy writing desk. The small dining table. The many bookshelves, slowly filling up again after thirteen years spent empty.

I was in my family's palace apartment. And someone was banging on the door.

I forced myself to set aside the horror of what had just happened and respond to the knocking. Set it aside; deal with it later.

"Just a—" My own cough cut me off. My mouth felt like it was stuffed with cotton sprinkled in sawdust. I tried again. "Just a minute."

I peeled myself off the floor. Another series of thumps sounded at the door.

"Coming." I stumbled to the door, unlatched it, and threw it open.

Brac's frown greeted me. "Sakes, Tannie. You look a fright. Everything all right?"

"Er . . ." I rubbed my temples, then stepped back to let him in. "Of course."

"Aye?" He frowned at me again, a shock of straw-colored

hair falling across his forehead in that way it always did. "You don't look it. I just stepped out to get some tea, and now I come back and you're lookin' like you had a run-in with a mountainbeast."

I scowled and plopped into a chair. "I'm fine, thanks."

"You didn't really look well afore I left."

"I'm fine."

"Then you ready to finish our talk?"

My stomach lurched. "Not especially."

"Tannie, this conversation's happening whether you want it to or not." He rubbed his side where he had been wounded in battle just a moon ago. With the help of Queen Braith's physicians, it was mostly healed up now, but it seemed to bother him most when he wanted me to agree to something.

"I don't have the head for it today, Brac."

"You never do." He glanced at my wrist, and his face darkened. "Not wearing it again?"

I slipped my hand to my lap so my wrist wouldn't be visible to him. "I hadn't finished dressing when you showed up. Not all of us see fit to rise with the sun." True, but that wasn't the reason I'd failed to put on the leather wristband Brac had given me—the leather wristband that signified our engagement.

"Tanwen En-Yestin, will you stop dodging this?" His voice rose. "We're having a discussion about this here adventure of yours. Or that *pirate's* adventure, more like."

My gaze darted through my open bedroom door to my nightstand where I'd placed the sailing hat Mor had created for me out of story strands. Black, tricorn, with a silky white band, fluffy plume, and sparkling blue pin. A hat fit for an adventure on a ship, which was exactly where Mor had invited me. "I wish you'd stop calling him a pirate. He's a proper sea captain with his own ship now."

Brac glared. "If the eye patch fits."

"Fry it, Brac!"

A puff of shimmering blue mist burst from my right hand. Not on purpose, certainly. Not in front of Brac. Not when that blue was the exact color of Mor's eyes. I squashed down my anger for fear of what else might be revealed through my blasted story strands.

Brac watched the blue mist dissipate. He pressed his lips together so hard they turned white. The rest of his face flushed red. "Sorry," he finally spat.

It had plainly cost him to say it, and for some reason, that made me all the angrier.

"Excuse me." I rose. "I'm feeling a little faint. I'm going to splash some water on my face."

"Knew you wasn't well. Let me help you."

"Aye, that would be real great. My father returns from breakfast to find you in my private bedroom, alone with no chaperone." I shook my head. "I'll be fine. Just give me a moment."

Brac didn't look pleased about it, but I slipped through my bedroom door and closed it behind me. I crossed to my vanity table but didn't bother with water. My reflection in the looking glass stared back. Was it my imagination, or did she look to be mocking me?

You're sick, Tannie, she seemed to say. *You're sick, just like Gryfelle.*

"Not just sick like Gryfelle," I whispered back. "Dying like Gryfelle."

CHAPTER THREE

BRAITH

"WOULD YOU CARE FOR MORE TEA, YOUR MAJESTY?"

Queen Braith pulled her gaze away from the window. "No, thank you, Cameria."

Braith's trusted maid poured herself some instead. "Is your breakfast satisfactory, my lady?"

"Yes, of course. Thank you, Cameria."

Cameria sipped her tea—slowly, like she was swallowing her thoughts down with it.

Braith raised an eyebrow. "Is something bothering you, my friend?"

"No, my lady." Cameria replaced her teacup in its saucer. "I wondered if something was bothering *you*."

"Oh?" A flicker of a smile played at the corner of Braith's mouth. "And why would you suppose that?"

"It is your third morning in a row taking breakfast in your private chambers. I believe you would dine only with me for all your meals if I'd allow it." Cameria hastily added, "Forgive me, Your Majesty. No impertinence intended."

"You know I prefer it when you speak freely with me. You are perhaps the only one who will these days."

"That is not true, Majesty. You have many friends—many supporters and excellent advisors."

"You're right. I'm sulking."

Cameria's dark eyes searched Braith. "Please, tell me what troubles you."

Braith inhaled slowly, then released her breath in a long, deep sigh. "I have held this title scarcely a moon, and already I grow weary. Four short weeks of this, and I feel ready to shut myself in my room forever. I hoped being queen would be easier than being princess in some ways. As princess, I had always to tiptoe around my—" Braith's words died on her lips. It was still too difficult to give voice to the awful truth.

"Around your father," Cameria finished gently.

"Yes."

"Have you visited him lately, Majesty? I know it vexes you to do so, but . . ." Cameria shook her head. "I know not why I continue to suggest it."

Braith looked away. "I saw him two days past. He was unchanged. The only word he says to me is *traitor*."

"I am sorry, my lady."

Braith shrugged. "My troubles with my father must be left in the past. At present, the peasant riots throughout the empire are more pressing."

"Indeed."

"And perhaps there is no hope there, either. Perhaps they will never accept me on the throne of Tir. I am my father's daughter, after all."

"In name, not practice." Cameria paused. "My lady, would you forgive a very forward suggestion from me?"

"Really, Cameria." Her faithful Meridioni maid never would dispense with formality, it seemed.

"Majesty, I believe it's time you hold your first official council meeting. You have appointed your councilors at last. It's been nearly a moon since your father fell. It is time. Perhaps this return to the normal order would ease the peasants' ire and make them feel as though Tir is once again under firm control."

"I'm not sure the rioters will feel fully settled until they see my head on a pike alongside my father's. But I believe you are right. It is time I start acting like a queen, even if I don't much feel like one."

A small smile broke across Cameria's face. "And perhaps make it to the royal table for breakfast tomorrow morning?"

"Yes." Braith laughed. "I suppose I can manage it."

A knock sounded at the outer chamber door.

Cameria rose. "I sent the other servants down to dine. I'll answer it."

Braith tidied her place setting, then rose. She brushed her hip-length hair from her shoulders and sighed. She would have to take Cameria's advice about hiring new beauticians soon, since Trini and her assistants, along with half the servants, had fled the palace when Gareth was deposed.

"My lord!" Cameria's voice, surprise evident, floated back to Braith.

Braith recognized the man's soft, raspy tone.

"Forgive me." His speech was getting easier and freer with each day that passed, but a few weeks couldn't undo thirteen years spent hidden in secret passageways within the palace walls. Yestin Bo-Arthio, former First General of Tir.

"My lord, what are you doing here?" Cameria's voice had risen to a scandalized pitch. "Her Majesty is not yet dressed!"

"Forgive me. This could not wait."

"My lord?"

"We received news. Royal table." He cleared his throat. "At breakfast."

Braith hurried into the outer chamber. "News? What news, Sir Yestin?"

At the sight of Braith, Yestin turned away. "Forgive me, Your Majesty."

Braith glanced down at her nightclothes and dressing gown. "Please don't trouble yourself over my state of dress if there is urgent news, Sir Yestin. I should have been dressed hours ago."

"Yes, Majesty." He turned back to Braith, and his eyes brimmed with sympathy. "Majesty. I'm sorry to be the one."

"The one?"

"To deliver such news."

Braith gripped the back of a chair and braced herself. "Please do so quickly."

Yestin drew a full breath. He seemed also to be bracing himself. "Your father."

"Yes?"

"He was found dead in his cell this morning."

Braith's knees buckled beneath her.

The others rushed to the queen's side. "Your Majesty!" Cameria cried.

Yestin looped his arm around Braith's waist and held her as she swayed on her feet. "Shall I take you to your room?"

"No." Braith swallowed hard. "I'll just . . . sit here."

Yestin eased her into the chair, then crouched before her and took her hand. "My deepest sympathies, Majesty."

"Did he . . . I mean, how did . . ." Her words faltered.

"I don't know, Majesty. The night guard swears he did not sleep. No disturbances, except the usual muttering. The morning guard found him."

"Was he . . . was he murdered?"

"There's no way to say yet, Majesty."

Braith drew a deep breath and steadied her voice. "Cameria, please order the finest colormasters you can find to examine the cell."

Yestin's face registered surprise. "As in the days of Caradoc?"

"Yes. It is time to reinstate the weavers to their former positions," Braith said firmly. "If any remain. My father's regime sent most of them into hiding, but I believe he kept a few weavers in his employ. See if you can find them or any others who might still be around, and have them do this task. At least two of them, Cameria. Four or five, if you can manage it."

Braith turned to Yestin. "Sir, I have a favor to ask of you."

"Anything, Majesty."

"The young captain who requested a ship from my naval fleet."

"Mor Bo-Lidere."

"Yes. He has quite a quest marked out, I understand."

"Yes. The four corners of the world."

"Accompany him. Bring this news of my father's death to the outlying areas of the Empire—Haribi, Meridione, Minasimet, and the Spice Islands. Act as my official envoy, and bring a letter marked with my seal informing our neighbors that I now sit on the throne of Tir."

"Of course, Majesty."

"And also this—tell them they are once again our neighbors and no longer our subjects. As my first official act as queen, I am reestablishing the sovereignty of these nations."

Yestin stared. "Majesty, I . . ." His words trailed off, unfinished.

"My lady." Cameria dropped to her knees before Braith's chair. "Do you mean this? Freedom for my people and the others enslaved under Gareth?"

"I have never meant anything more in my life."

Cameria's response was swallowed in a teary sob.

Braith squeezed her friend's hand. "This isn't how I wanted to tell you. I wanted a joyous celebration and a grand announcement. But this will have to do."

Cameria paused, and a shadow crossed her face. She glanced at the window. The sound of peasants shouting only just carried into the room from the palace gates.

"Ah, yes," Braith said. "The peasants."

"The riots will double," Cameria said. "Triple, perhaps, if you give back all the land your father conquered."

"Yes, I expect they will."

Yestin rose and collected himself. "I'll leave you now. I must prepare." He bowed. "Majesty. Lady Cameria."

Cameria saw him to the door. Braith stared at the wall until the sound of the heavy latch dropping back into place caused her to jump.

Cameria hurried over to her. "Majesty, please, let me help you. Do you wish to lie down? More tea, perhaps?"

"My mother used to believe tea could solve everything." Braith's tone was bitter. "I wonder where she is now. If she lives, she will hear of her husband's death with the rest of Tir, I suppose."

"One never knows, Majesty," Cameria replied. "Perhaps she cannot return to the palace. We do not have to assume the worst of Lady Frenhin."

"We knew her well, so we might always assume the worst." Braith sighed. "Forgive me. That was unkind. I'm . . . upset."

"Understandably." Cameria helped Braith to her feet. "Do you require some water? Something to eat?"

"No. I shall ready myself for the oncoming storm." Braith smiled wryly. "Or at least for council. Please send messengers with the news that we shall hold an evening council. Today. It's unorthodox, to be sure, but what isn't these days?"

"Very well, Majesty. I'll prepare your gown, if you wish."

"Thank you, Cameria."

With Cameria's worried gaze still fixed on her, Braith retreated to her private bedroom. She closed the door behind herself and leaned against it, staring up at the ceiling beams.

And then Braith wept.

CHAPTER FOUR

TANWEN

"I DON'T CARE WHAT YOU AGREED TO. I AIN'T LETTIN' YOU go, Tannie!"

"Letting me? Letting me!" My voice carried all the way down the palace hallway, and I cared less than a hathberry in a hailstorm. "Since when do you have that sort of say over me, Brac Bo-Bradwir? Letting me, as if you were my . . . my . . ."

"Your father?" Brac folded his arms across his chest, triumph scribbled all over his handsome, sunburned, stupid, bearded face. "Aye, that's an idea. Let's ask your father what he thinks about this whole thing. I doubt he's keen to let his daughter go gallivanting around the globe with a pirate."

"He's not a pirate! He's the captain of a ship!"

"Well, now you're just sorting sniffler fur."

"There's an enormous difference between a pirate and a ship captain. When was the last time you captained anything except a wax-bean cart down a Pembroni alley?"

He recoiled. "Oh, so that's it, is it? You think he's better than me."

Oops.

"That is not what I said, Brac."

"You didn't have to. It's there, plain as pie on your face."

I rubbed my eyes and sighed. "Can we talk about this later?" I glanced around the hallway. "I'm sure we're disturbing . . . someone important."

"No, we'll talk about this now, and I don't give a flying fluff-hopper who we're disturbing. You wouldn't talk to me in your private chambers, and I practically had to chase you out the door, you left so fast."

Aye, that had rather been the point of leaving. To avoid this conversation.

I took off down the hall again. "Don't you have to report for guard duty, or something?"

"On medical leave until next week, earliest. I was stabbed in the gut, you'll remember. Guess you would have liked to see that job finished, eh?"

"Oh, shove it. If I'd wanted to, I could have poisoned or maimed you just about every day of your life. I knew exactly where you slept, *you'll* remember. And I still do, so how about you mind your nibbles and nackles?"

In spite of everything, Brac chuckled.

But I didn't want matters to get confused with warmth and nostalgia. "There's nothing you can say to change my mind, Brac. I'm going with Mor and the others, and that's the end of it."

He flared right back up. "It ain't the end of nothin'!" His Tirian got worse when he was angry. "I'm your betrothed, and I have some say here if anyone does."

"Aye, about that . . ." But my objection stopped in my throat. I eyed that blasted spot on Brac's tunic, under which his bandages had been just a few days before. Was he ready to have *that* conversation yet? Would he ever be healed enough for me to tell him I didn't love him like a wife should love her husband?

Blazes. How had I gotten myself into this mess?

Because he was dying. I had thought I was giving him a final moment of joy and peace before he slipped from this life. Instead, Warmil and Karlith saved him, and now we were engaged. I was glad they had saved him, of course. My heart would break to lose my best friend in the world since as far back as I could remember. But my acceptance of his proposal hadn't been genuine. It had been borne of pity—rash and foolish.

And if I ever told him so, I didn't think he'd recover from it.

"Tannie! You listening?"

I jumped. "Oh. Not really."

He rolled his eyes. "Figured." He stepped toward me, grabbed my hands, and looked into my eyes in a way that wouldn't have made my skin crawl a couple moons ago. But now I felt like I was covered in scuttlebugs. Everything was so mixed up.

"Tannie, ain't no one has loved you better than me your whole life. Ain't that true?"

I thought of Father. He had loved me, truly, but he'd been locked away for so many years. Cut off from everyone, including me. I hardly knew the man.

Brac *had* been there. Always.

"Aye, Brac. I know." I glared steel at him. "But that doesn't mean you get to make my choices for me."

An image of Brac hog-tying me and plunking me before an altar popped into my head.

Creator preserve me.

He sighed, but it by no means signaled defeat. "Tannie, honestly. You're the most impossible lass who ever breathed. If I don't have say over your life, who does?"

"Me, possibly," a new voice intruded.

Father. And the sound of his voice nearly sent me jumping from my skin. I whirled around to see him leaning against the stone wall of the hallway, all gray-bearded and solemn.

"Father. What are you doing here?"

"Coming to see you. But I heard you a league off."

Heat rose in my face. "Just having a discussion with Brac."

"So I heard."

Hotter heat. Why did his piercing gaze make me squirm? "Having a bit of a disagreement."

"Aye, that's right," Brac cut in. "Maybe you can talk some sense into her about that pirate, sir. We respect your thoughts on everything, o' course."

I spun around and glowered at Brac. Kissing up to my father? The sniveling, dirty tactic didn't suit him.

Father didn't respond directly. "Tanwen, Bo-Bradwir. I have dark news."

I turned back to him. "Dark news? What's happened?"

"Gareth was found dead in his cell this morning."

"Dead?" I stared at him, sure I had misheard. "Dead-dead? As in, no longer living?"

"Aye." Father made to reach out to me, then hesitated and pulled his hand back.

A hundred questions tumbled through my mind. "Was he murdered? Who did it? Does the queen know? She must. Is she all right?"

Father shook his head as if my questions buzzed around him like flies. I forgot. He wasn't used to human company yet, let alone my league-a-minute rambling.

"I'm sorry," I said.

"Quite all right." But he didn't look all right. He looked like he was sifting through my questions with effort. "Not sure what happened. Guards saw nothing. Queen Braith has her people investigating."

"And the queen . . . is she . . . ?"

"Not well. She is pretending, though."

And there it was. That was why Father's piercing gaze made me so uncomfortable. Because the man didn't just look at you. He looked right through you. There was no hiding anything from him.

Which was why I cringed at his next question.

"Tannie, what's the trouble with Mor?"

Truly, I had much to hide. How could I say two words about Mor without Father seeing my feelings for him ran deeper than mere friendship? Father had probably already guessed I didn't harbor a shred of romance in my heart for Brac.

"Nothing is the trouble with Mor," I said. "It's Mor's ship. Brac doesn't think I should go with the other weavers."

"I see no reason for it," Brac added. "It ain't safe. And it's all for the sickly one, ain't it?"

"Gryfelle." I gritted my teeth. "Her name is Gryfelle. And Mor knows what he's doing. His father ran a shipping company, and Mor was practically raised on a ship."

"I don't care if Cethor herself is captaining the ship. It ain't safe to go to the four corners of the world, no matter who's at the helm!"

Brac invoking the name of a goddess. That was rich.

"Mor has captained ships before."

"Pirated, you mean."

"Forced into it by Gareth!" I felt like I'd aged twenty years since Brac and I first started having this conversation. "How many times do I have to remind you of that? A lot of decent people were pushed into indecent situations by that tyrant. Mor was just trying to survive." I turned to Father. "Tell him I can go. Please."

"Well." Father looked at us both. "I am going."

My mouth fell open. "What?"

"The queen has commissioned me as her royal envoy."

Hope blossomed inside me. "So . . . if you're going, then of course I'll go. Right?"

"Well, I—"

"It's safe. It is. Warmil will be there. He's a former king's guard captain. And you don't really know Aeron yet, but her skill with a blade would make the swordiest swordsman blush. And Dylun will be there in case we need to fend off anyone with a book. And Mor wouldn't let anything happen to me."

Heat flushed my cheeks again. Because that statement was true enough, but unless I was totally daft, Mor wasn't only about friendship with me, either.

Brac huffed. "I can't believe you're trying to make this sound reasonable. You ain't that pirate's first priority, Tannie. He'll be about that sick lass, you know. You're extra window dressing, far as he's concerned."

"Gryfelle. Her name is Gryfelle!"

"Aye, so you've said. Whatever her name is, that's who Mor will be paying attention to. Not you."

I could have thrown him out the palace window.

"Are my ears burning?" A *fourth* voice, and not a welcome one at this exact moment.

At least not in front of Father and Brac. For the fourth voice belonged to none other than the smirky captain in question.

Brac crossed his arms. "Burning your ears?" he muttered under his breath. "That could be arranged."

I shot him a look, then turned to face Mor. My stomach tightened at the sight of him—cropped dark hair, twinkling blue eyes, the scruffy smatterings of a beard, a gold ring punched through his ear. I didn't know quite what to say with him standing there, in the flesh.

And then my gift betrayed me. A silky red ribbon poured from one of my hands and curled through the air toward Mor. One heartbeat of pure mortification stuttered in my chest, then I lunged for the strand. I waved the ribbon into mist. And just in time, too. Fry me if the blasted thing wasn't about to curl itself into a heart right around Mor's head.

I steeled my will and determined no more strands would come streaming out of me in front of these three. "We were just talking about the trip," I said quickly to fill the awkward silence.

Mor's gaze lingered on me—impassive, impossible to

read—and then he turned to my father as if I hadn't spoken. "I understand you'll be joining us, General Bo-Arthio."

"Please." Father held up a hand. "Yestin."

For some reason, their polite conversation irritated me. "Hey!" I snapped. That got their attention. "Gryfelle is my friend and she's desperately sick. I want to go. It could just as easily be me."

If only they knew.

Mor glanced at me again, but I still couldn't read him. First time that had been the case since I had known him. He turned back to my father. "The queen's orders have moved up our timeline a bit."

Brac's tone was vicious. "Well, we wouldn't want anything to foul up your precious timeline."

"I'd accept your kind words if they weren't laced with venom, guardsman," Mor replied coldly.

"Enough." Father sounded like he was scolding a couple of farm boys. "I'll be ready before the afternoon's out, Captain Bo-Lidere. We'll travel via the king's road—that is, the queen's road—I assume?"

"Aye. Queen's road to Physgot. The queen's navy has prepared the ship for us, and we'll set sail from that port."

"Very good. As I said, I'll not hold you up."

"Um . . . anyone?" I waved my hands. "Anyone care to speak to me? Because we seem to have a problem here. I say I'm going, and that's tha—"

Never finished my thought. Next thing I knew, I was on the stone floor of the castle hallway.

"Tannie?" Brac's face appeared over me. Then Mor and Father beside him. All brows furrowed; frowns everywhere.

I couldn't find my voice to answer him, or to address Mor or Father.

And then the room splintered into pieces.

Rips opened up in the fabric of reality. Mor's face wavered

and then disappeared. Brac, Father, and the walls of the palace hall ribboned to shreds and vanished.

I wasn't on my back anymore. I stood alone in an empty, black room.

"Hello?" I took a step forward but stumbled in the darkness. "Is anyone here?"

No reply. No echo. Only the sort of black silence that swallows you from the inside out.

"Where am I?" I called out.

Nothing. Just dark. And silence.

But then silvery strands began to trickle down around me from the ceiling of blackness above. Pale light emanating from the strands struggled to break through the pitch dark. I stepped toward one of the strands.

"There are words in them," I said aloud to no one.

And true as the moon, the strands weren't wisps of story. They were actually made of words themselves. I watched them scroll by.

Yestin Bo-Arthio, First General under Caradoc II, was the sole witness to the confession of Gareth Bo-Kelwyd.

Tanwen was a lonely little girl who found solace in the company of her best friend, Brac Bo-Bradwir.

In the deepest, most honest part of her heart, Tanwen had to admit that Mor Bo-Lidere was something special.

Tanwen was a gifted storyteller, but she often doubted her ability to create something truly worthwhile—something all her own.

I stared at the dripping silver words. Puzzled. Confused.

Who was this Tanwen? And what was a storyteller?

All at once, light exploded around me—crashed down onto my head and body. I blinked against it. Blinked into several faces, all peering over me like I was a prize grazer being auctioned at market.

"Are you all right?" The oldest of the faces, covered in a close-trimmed, grizzled beard.

"Sakes, Tannie, what were you on about? You was havin' a fit, or somethin'. You all right?" A young, sunburned face. Blond hair.

The third face had gone pale as a noonday cloud, and I couldn't place the expression in his eyes. Horror?

I sat up, only then realizing I'd fallen over at some point.

Stone walls. Tapestries. Arched windows, torches in brackets along the wall. "Where am I?"

Looks passed between the men.

I frowned at them. "And who in the blazes are you?"

Father passed me another cup of brisk-leaf tea across the table in our front room. "Are you sure you're well, Tannie?" The concern hadn't left his eyes since I collapsed.

"Of course." I buried my face into my cup as best I could.

It had only taken a few reminders—their names, who they were to me, what we were doing in the palace, what we'd been talking about—and then I'd come back to myself. I told them I must have fallen and bumped my head. They were worried, of course, but seemed to take my word for it.

At least, Father and Brac did. Mor pretended to.

I got the sinking feeling Mor had witnessed such collapses far too many times to buy what I was peddling.

How long before he would corner me and force me to admit what had truly happened?

I sipped my fire-hot tea and barely noticed the roof of my mouth scald.

"It seemed we lost you for a moment." Father was staring at me, no matter how I tried to hide my face behind my cup. "And you look shaken now."

"I'm fine." The lie tasted like a pile of ashes in my mouth.

Because, truly, there was no question about it now: Gryfelle En-Blaid's mind wasn't the only one that had begun to slip away inside these palace walls.

CHAPTER FIVE

TANWEN

I shoved an extra tunic into Father's traveling trunk. "There. You're done."

The lid banged closed, and I flopped onto Father's bed beside the trunk.

"Tannie." He gave me a look. A look that said, *Grow up, little one. This is for the best.*

A look that made me want to scream in his face.

I immediately regretted the harshness of my thoughts. Maybe I should try one more time.

"Father, if we could just—"

"No, Tannie."

"But—"

"Tanwen." How did he make his voice so firm and uncompromising without raising it? "I don't think it's safe for you. You need to stay in Urian."

"Because it's safer with rioters banging down the front door?"

He gave me another look.

I tried again. "Gryfelle is my friend. I . . . I want to help."

"I know, my girl."

I hopped up from the bed. "Then why won't you let me go?" I had not inherited his trick of keeping my voice calm in an argument.

"I think you are ill."

My heart tripped. "What do you mean?"

He stared hard for a moment. "Your episode."

What did he suspect? My stomach pinched, and I squashed down whatever truth wanted to rise and explode out as story strands. Almost immediately, dizziness overtook me, and I had to sit back down.

If I didn't want to end up next to Gryfelle in the infirmary before suppertime, I was going to have to stop keeping so many secrets from everyone.

"Tannie?" Father's eyes were like swirling gray pools of heartfelt concern.

"I just . . . swooned, is all," I offered lamely.

"Swooned?"

"Aye, you know. Fainted." I flopped back onto one of his feather pillows. "It's a thing ladies do, I'm told."

"Tannie . . ."

"No, it's perfectly fine." I jumped up and strode for the door. "I'll stay here, do what I'm told, just like everyone wants. But no matter what you say, I'm coming to Physgot with you. I *will* see off my friends, even if I'm being kept captive in Tir while you get to go around the world with them."

I moved past him, through his bedroom, and toward our front door.

"Tanwen!" His voice followed me, but I didn't turn around. Even though he sounded wounded and I already wished I could take back my barbed words. Even though I knew I was making a greater mess than everything already was.

I did my utter best to slam the heavy front door like I meant it.

CHAPTER SIX

TANWEN

IT TOOK THREE SECONDS OF RUNNING DOWN THE PALACE hallways for the tears to start.

Frustration. Anger. Hurt. Remorse.

And fear.

They coursed down my cheeks in a muddle of conflict.

I should turn around. Apologize to Father. We were both dumber than difflesnouts at this father-daughter thing. It didn't sit comfortably. We weren't used to it. He didn't need my poisoned-dart words. He needed my compassion—my love—just like I needed his.

But I didn't turn around. I didn't go back and tell him I was sorry. I wanted more than anything to be on that ship when it set out from Physgot, and he wouldn't allow it. For some reason, I found myself unable to defy him.

And that infuriated me.

A strand of crackling lightning shot from my hand and exploded with a *snap* on the stone floor.

Blast. I needed to get control of myself.

Suddenly there was only one place I wanted to be. One person I wanted to talk to.

I turned into a stairwell and took the spiraling steps two at a time. Down, down to where I knew he would be.

The palace libraries.

"I can't work like this, Mor!" Dylun Bo-Ino's frustrated voice met me before I reached the library door. "How do you expect me to create a proper route when you cut my timeline in half?"

I eased to a stop beside the doorway, just out of view.

"Dylun, I don't know what you want me to do about it." Mor, equally frustrated. "Should I tell Queen Braith to hold her royal horses?"

A big *thunk* sounded—like a heavy book dropping onto a wooden table. "I don't care *what* you tell her. Just give me more time! You understand what I'm up against. This is like trying to nail color strands to the wall. I have scraps of rumors, pieces of a story that may or may not be a myth. And most of it in languages no one speaks anymore. I'll remind you that Tirian is my second language. Old Tirian is my fifth, and I'm barely proficient by scholarly standards. Have you ever seen Ancient Meridioni? There's a reason it's a dead language, Mor!"

Mor sighed. "I know, mate. I'm sorry. You have been doing an excellent job. I don't mean to push. But we have the queen's orders. And Gryfelle had a bad episode today."

"How bad?" Aeron En-Howell's voice. I hadn't realized she was there.

"Very." Weariness drenched Mor's words. "She wasn't fully back yet when I left her with Karlith."

"Dylun, look at this." Another voice. Warmil Bo-Awirth, former guard captain. "It's the Ancient Meridioni symbol for 'cure,' isn't it?"

Dylun grunted. "I believe so. If only Master Insegno were here. He would know for certain."

"An old friend of yours?" Warmil again.

"Yes. Well, my teacher from Meridione. A scholar. My

father had me educated here in the palace by Tirian tutors for many things, but for Meridioni customs, history, and languages, I learned from a true Meridioni. I never knew if Insegno got out before Gareth's crackdown. Probably dead now."

Dylun said it matter-of-factly, but I had felt enough loss in my life to hear the pain behind his words.

"If he lives still," Warmil said, "would he know about this ancient cure? Seems we're traveling in circles here."

"He would know if anyone would. It is finding Insegno that would be the challenge. Unless . . ." Dylun's voice brightened. "I suppose it could be as simple as that. He may have just returned to Meridione, peaceful as you like. He came from the capital, Bordino, like my family. It's right there on the coast. He could be living there still. Reading books on the beach while we breathe dust here in the library."

"Then that will be our first stop," Mor declared. "We'll see if we can't find your old friend."

"Ho, Tannie!"

Stifling a scream, I jumped at the hand on my shoulder. I spun around to face the intruder. "Zel! Zelyth Bo-Gwelt, you scared me half to death!"

"I see that." He grinned. "If you wasn't sneakin' about the palace, eavesdroppin' on conversations, you wouldn't be so prone to a start."

You could have fried an eaglet egg on my face. "Aye, thanks for the advice."

He waggled his eyebrows, then pushed past me into the library. I had more than half a mind to slink back down the hall without facing the others, now that they knew I was there. But Zel grabbed my hand and pulled me into the library after him.

"Tannie's here." Like it needed to be announced.

Dylun barely glanced up from his stack of dusty tomes. "Hello, Tanwen."

Warmil nodded. "Tannie."

Aeron seemed to be biting back a small grin—a grin that knew far too much about the swirly turmoil in my heart these days. I shot her a look—half pleading, half irritated, with just a dash of amusement. Like *she* was one to throw stones about awkward non-romances. She'd been pining for Warmil since he was her captain in the guard, ten years past.

And then there was Mor, the one I'd come to see in the first place. The one who would comfort me about my banishment from the trip. The one who would tell me how to apologize to my father. The one who would soothe the ache in my heart.

But I found none of the warmth I expected. Instead, Mor's face might have been carved of marble, hard as it was.

"Tanwen," he said, and his voice was ice. "Can we speak privately?"

I nodded. Numb, unable to form words.

Mor led me into a nearby room. There was no door on it, so it wasn't exactly private. But I guessed it was good enough for Mor's designs.

He turned toward me. "Tanwen, I—"

"Stop calling me that." I frowned at him. "You never call me that."

He held my gaze for a moment, then dropped it.

"Mor, what's wrong with you? You're acting strange."

"No. Just focused. Ready for my task."

A few days ago, he might have said *our* task. *Our* quest. "That's what I came to talk to you about."

"Me first, please. If you don't mind."

"I do mind. What's the matter with you?" My stomach pinched again. Whatever emotions simmered just below the surface were going to boil over.

"Nothing is the matter. I'm just anxious to get underway. Gryfelle doesn't have much time left." And then he met my eyes again. The ice had melted, but he looked . . . angry?

"My father says I can't go," I blurted.

I don't know what I expected or hoped for. Understanding. Comfort. Outrage on my behalf. Something that mirrored all the frustration and disappointment I felt. Something that let me know I wasn't utterly alone in the world.

Instead, Mor nodded. "I don't think you should go, either."

I stared. "Wha . . . what?"

"You should stay here. With your betrothed. I was going to tell you so, even if your father hadn't."

"With my . . ." I spluttered around the words. "Mor, are you serious?"

"Staying home with your engaged beau is strange to you?" He arched an eyebrow. "I don't think it is, Tanwen."

"Stop calling me that!"

"Unless, of course, you have no intention of marrying the lad. Then, naturally, staying home to be near him might be a strange concept."

And now we'd gotten around to it, finally. Mor was angry about Brac.

"Is that what this is about? Are you jealous of Brac?"

Mor snorted. "Hardly."

His words pierced my heart. He might as well be throwing ice daggers.

"I know you well enough to see what's going on, Tanwen." He ignored my dark glare. "You have no intention of marrying him, but have you told him so?"

"Um . . . there . . ." I fumbled. "It hasn't been the right time yet."

"But you thought you would leave on a journey—one that could take weeks or months—without finding that right time? You thought you might escape to the sea, is that it?"

"Look who's talking about escaping to the sea! I guess you don't like me stealing a line from your play."

For the second time in the space of an hour, I wished I could suck my words back in. I had hit Mor in the tenderest spot beneath his armor, and his hurt was plain in his eyes. For he had escaped to the sea instead of going after his little sister, Digwyn, when Gareth had taken her away and turned her into a slave. Mor had spent the past four years regretting it, trying to erase it, trying to redeem himself.

That was part of what his tie to Gryfelle was all about. Mor had decided to stop choosing what was best for him—to stop choosing what he wanted and instead think of what was best for others. So no matter how sick Gryfelle got, no matter how much of her mind was erased, no matter how little she even remembered of the adolescent romance she'd shared with him, Mor would never leave her. He would never stop trying to save her.

And he would never choose to be with me because of it.

The air between us heated—warmer than a summer midday. Strange and out of place in the dank, dark palace library. After a moment, I could make out nearly invisible strands swirling around us—the source of the warmth.

But fried if I knew what these strands were. Once I might have guessed they were the feelings Mor and I shared. Now I wondered if it was only anger.

The impassive mask slipped back over Mor's face. The strands evaporated. "Quite right, Tanwen. I suppose I do have experience escaping to the sea. And maybe that's why I don't want you to do it."

"Or is it just easier when I'm not around?" Tears stung my eyes, and I tried to force them back. Last thing I needed was to dissolve into a blubbering mess right in the middle of Mor casting me out.

"Tannie . . ."

I looked up, and the tears spilled. But he had called me Tannie.

He lifted his hand like he might reach for mine, but then he let it drop. "I think it will be easier for everyone if we are not around each other. Don't you?"

"I . . ." I hiccupped through my sobs, like the proper lady I was. "I don't want to not be around you." And I almost told him, right then and there, that I feared I was getting sick like Gryfelle. But something stoppered my mouth. Something told me he might collapse under the weight of that truth.

Mor swallowed hard. "The fact is, you are engaged to Brac. You accepted his proposal and you haven't taken it back, whether you see a future with him or not. I'm bound to Gryfelle, whether or not she has a future to give. Best we begin to accept that."

Before I could say anything else, he turned and strode away. I had a sinking feeling he was walking away from more than the room. I stood there for several moments, as if I had sprouted roots.

"Tannie?"

I turned to find a sympathetic look in Aeron's eyes. "Ho, Aeron."

"Are you all right?"

I sniffled loudly. "Aye. Brilliant. Why wouldn't I be?" The bitterness in my voice was plain.

"It will work out, Tannie. Mor is . . ." She waved her hand. "Well, he's under a lot of strain right now. It's wearing on him, and he's not himself."

I wanted to scream. I wasn't myself, either. I was getting sick. I needed *someone* to understand. Someone to care. Someone to help me share my burden.

Maybe I could tell Aeron.

But before I had a chance to form the words, she extended a slip of parchment. "Would you do us a favor? Dylun would like this list delivered to Karlith. He found some new recipes he thinks might help Gryfelle—herbs and such. Maybe make her more comfortable while we search for the cure. Would you bring this to Karlith? She'll need to stock up before we leave."

"Aye." I took the list from her.

"It will all work out, Tannie," Aeron said again. "You'll see."

I forced a nod and trudged out of the library.

Aye, it would work out. It would work out with me in the infirmary, losing my mind, Brac's wedding band on my finger.

CHAPTER SEVEN

TANWEN

I STOPPED BEFORE THE DOOR TO GRYFELLE'S CHAMBER. THERE were no interesting conversations floating out of this room. Only the labored strains of a girl fighting for every breath.

I leaned against the stone wall and closed my eyes.

Stars above. I prayed the Corsyth weavers would find the cure. Gryfelle wouldn't hold out much longer. How could she possibly? She had been sick so long already.

And I would be lying to suggest I was only thinking of Gryfelle. I needed the Corsyth weavers to find the cure, too. Otherwise, I was listening to my fate in those labored breaths.

I gathered my strength and entered the room. "Ho, Karlith."

Karlith Ma-Lundir looked up from her seat beside Gryfelle's bed. She smiled, heavy-lidded eyes crinkling at the corners. "Ho, Tannie. How goes it?" She dabbed a wet rag across Gryfelle's forehead.

My voice was lost somewhere in my stomach. I hadn't seen Gryfelle in at least a week, and she barely looked to be living. If not for the rattling rise and fall of her chest, I would swear she was dead already.

Her skin was pale on the healthiest day, but this was beyond pale. This was ghostly white. Her lovely jade-green eyes had sunken into her skull, and her fair hair lay stringy and matted on the feather pillow beneath her.

Karlith smiled sadly. "Aye. She's not lookin' her best, poor Elle."

I had often imagined what Gryfelle must have looked like when she was a teenaged noblewoman at court. Before she'd suppressed her songspinning gift and succumbed to the curse. Before she had gotten so ill. She must have been the most stunning girl ever to dance in the palace ballroom.

And now . . . now she was a wasted shell.

I swallowed down my tears. "She's looking . . . comfortable as could be expected. She is well cared for, Karlith."

Karlith patted the extra chair beside her. "I appreciate that, my girl. It's no easy task caring for them who's so sick. But I don't mind it. Especially not for our Elle."

Gryfelle twitched in her sleep, and Karlith swiped the cloth across her brow again. "Poor dear. You know, Mor's usually found in that seat right there. But last Gryfelle woke and was lucid, she told him to leave. Thought the lad's heart would bust."

My heart felt ready to bust too. But it was because it split right down the middle between breaking for Mor and wanting to rage at him.

Why was everything such a mess?

"Tannie?"

"Huh?"

Karlith was studying me. "Did you have a purpose in coming here, lass? Not that I mind the company."

Guilt washed over me. "Oh. Right. I have something from Dylun. He found some recipes, it seems. Something to help Gryfelle, maybe, while you all search for the cure."

"You all? Are you not coming with us?"

"My father won't allow it." I slumped back on the chair. "And I think Mor uninvited me."

"Did he, now?" Karlith didn't take her eyes off Gryfelle, but there was something in her voice that made me feel she was looking right at me.

"You don't sound surprised."

"Aye. I'm not."

"I was."

"Don't trouble, Tannie. It'll work out."

I resisted the urge to spit something angry. "Why does everyone keep saying that? Things don't always work out, you know. Of all people, we should know that."

Karlith gave a sad laugh. "Aye. Reckon I know that."

I wanted to sink into the floor. Of course Karlith knew it. She had lost her family—her husband and two wee ones—to Gareth's wrath.

I glanced at Gryfelle. There was also the whole life-and-death matter of a curse weighing on my mind. Literally.

Perhaps I should confide in Karlith.

But before I could tiptoe into those waters, Gryfelle groaned. Then her eyelids fluttered open, and her eyes were lucid this time. First I had seen them so in a while.

Tears and laughter both wanted to bust from me, but I restricted myself to a huge grin. "Ho, Gryfelle!"

A tiny smile drew her cheeks up. "Tannie."

"Well!" Karlith beamed. "How's my girl, Elle?"

Gryfelle's smile drooped, and her words came out in a slow whisper. "I have been better. At least, I believe I have." A wry twinkle in her eye. I think she tried to wink my direction.

"You're teasin'," Karlith declared. "Don't think I don't know it when you do. Incorrigible, all you young ones." But she was still beaming. "Can I get anything for you, my dear? Broth?"

"I've no taste for it, but yes. I should while I'm awake."

"Aye, that's my girl." Karlith rose and nodded to me. "Tannie'll look after you while I steal away to the kitchens. Be back as quick as a flash."

And truly, she would. We all knew Gryfelle could lapse back to sleep any moment. If Karlith wanted her to eat, she would have to be quick about it.

I lowered myself into Karlith's seat closer to Gryfelle's bed. "How do you feel? Truly."

"Weak. Like I could never sleep enough to recover."

I took her hand. "You feel cold."

"Inside I feel like I'm on fire."

Fear tightened my stomach. I wanted to ask her what it was like. Did it hurt? What did I have to look forward to?

But, for once today, perhaps I could think of someone other than myself. Maybe whatever goodness I possessed had been leaking out during my episodes.

"The others?"

I started.

"How are the others?" Gryfelle asked again.

"Oh." I looked down at her pale hand in my sun-browned one. "They're fine."

Gryfelle stared at me. Waiting for more, obviously.

I swallowed. "They're getting ready to go. I've been banned from coming along. But my father will be there, so . . . close enough?"

I tried to chuckle. Quiet, thoughtful Yestin Bo-Arthio and bubbling, impulsive Tanwen En-Yestin. The only thing we shared was a name.

"I'm sorry you've been banned."

"Me too. But the others will do their utmost for you."

"Yes, they will."

"I probably couldn't have offered much, anyway."

"That isn't true, Tannie."

Tears stung again. Blast them. I shrugged. "I don't have anything to offer that isn't covered by the other storytellers. Zel and . . ." I couldn't force his name out.

"And Mor." Gryfelle turned toward me, a fraction of an inch closer.

"Aye. Mor, too."

"Tannie, please don't trouble about Mor on my account."

My heart tripped. "What?"

"You're hardly able to say his name in my presence."

"We . . . we had a fight today. That's all."

"Is it?"

My, she had a way to shoot straight at things. "I . . ."

"Tannie, I'm cursed, not blind. I can see what has happened between you and Mor."

"What?" I popped to my feet, quite involuntarily. "Nothing has happened between me and Mor."

Gryfelle breathed out a laugh. "No, I meant the attraction between the two of you."

"Oh." My skin felt too small for my insides. "Um, well, there might have been, if things were different."

"If I weren't around. But that is precisely what I told Mor. I won't be around for much longer."

"Oh, Gryfelle!" More burning tears. "Don't say that! Please don't. Even if it were true, I can't . . . I don't want to . . ."

"I know, Tannie. You and Mor both. I keep trying to tell him—"

"No," I cut her off. "You mustn't try to tell him anything about this. The only thing Mor wants is to save your life, and that's just as it should be. They're truly searching for a cure for you, Gryfelle. Besides, I . . . well, I guess I'm technically betrothed. So I'm not even free." As Mor so kindly reminded me.

"Tannie, I understand the situation is complicated and strange, to say the least. But if I could only explain what it's like to you both." She sighed. "I can't remember my feelings for Mor. And he isn't my husband. I want you both to—"

"No," I said again, not even sure why I didn't want her to finish.

"Tannie, if you would just—"

"Here it is." Karlith bustled into the room, stopping Gryfelle's plea short. "All nice and hot."

I took my chance and brushed past Karlith and her steaming bowl of broth. "Excuse me. I'll leave you to it. I hope you feel better soon, Gryfelle."

I stepped into the hallway, resisting the urge to run as I hurried away. The staircase that led to our apartments came into view, but I dropped onto the bottom step instead of climbing them.

Why couldn't I even bear to let Gryfelle speak her mind? Perhaps her words would release some of the guilt—some of the responsibility—that hung over the situation for me and Mor. Then maybe we would be free to open up our hearts just a little. Maybe then I would have the strength to speak to Brac.

But I knew. It didn't matter what Gryfelle said or how she tried to make us understand. Mor would never abandon her. And if I were being honest with the best part of myself, I didn't want him to. It was good and right for Mor *not* to give his heart to me.

And that truth smarted like I had been slapped a thousand times across my face.

I dropped my head into my hands and allowed the tears to flow.

CHAPTER EIGHT

BRAITH

BRAITH STOOD BEFORE THE THRONE ROOM DOORS, STARING straight ahead at the pattern of the wood.

"Your Majesty?" The guardsman manning the door leaned down to catch her eye. "Are you well?"

Braith closed her eyes and swallowed hard. "No, I am not. I think I might be sick."

"My lady." Cameria's voice came from Braith's left. "Please, how can I help?"

"There is nothing," Braith said faintly, her eyes fluttering open. "I simply must . . . enter." She pressed her hands against the unforgiving oak door. "Can I do this, Cameria? Can I be Tir's queen?"

The guardsman knight and Cameria shared a glance around Braith.

"How can I possibly? They don't want me—Braith, the daughter of Gareth the Usurper."

"Braith." Cameria's voice carried an urgent note.

Braith turned to her friend. "I don't know if I can do it, Cameria."

"You must." She forced Braith to meet her eyes. "Do you remember what Yestin said to you at luncheon?"

"He told me not to let them out-shout me because I'm a woman."

Cameria smiled. "Yes, he did say that. Do you remember what else?"

Tears glittered in Braith's eyes, and her breath rattled. "He said my name is Braith En-Gareth, but I will reign like Caradoc—with strength, kindness, and goodness."

"Yes. And you shall. You have it in you—and you always have."

Braith drew a deep breath, pulled herself up to her considerable height, and nodded to the guardsman.

He and one of his fellows pulled open the door and announced her arrival. "Her Royal Majesty, Queen Braith En-Gareth, presiding over Queen's Council, session one."

A hundred pairs of eyes stared back at Braith. Repairs to the throne room were still in progress—repairs rectifying the damage incurred during the battle that had unseated her father. Her father, who was never meant to be king in the first place.

Braith lifted her chin, looking past the scaffolding and fresh paint and new wood.

"The committee chose you," Cameria whispered as they entered the room.

Some of the two hundred eyes looked friendly. Others curious. Still others glared. Glowered.

Braith steeled herself and strode down the silver carpet before her. New, just like her reign. She had walked on this carpet a thousand times before, but then it had been green. And purple before that, when Caradoc II reigned.

She glanced at Yestin, seated at the council table.

Reign like Caradoc.

She passed the table where she once met with her father's councilors. Now, seated around it were nine men and one woman Braith had appointed but two days ago, including the former First General. Her gaze roved to Sir Fellyck, an underlord of some of the villages surrounding Urian.

Fellyck had a reputation for his outspokenness, but he was

popular with the people. Perhaps the only reason he never landed in Gareth's dungeons. Gareth would have had unrest on his hands if he had removed Fellyck.

Braith needed his support now.

She reached her throne, the one in which she had always sat, now moved to the center of the dais and standing quite alone. No throne for her father. No throne for her mother.

Braith claimed her seat and met the eyes of her people. The court bowed as one, as they always did for their monarch.

A good sign? Mere habit? Who could say?

"Thank you. And welcome." Braith cleared her throat. She pulled herself straighter, as if the point of a blade were at her back.

In a way, it was.

But when she spoke again, her voice rang out true and strong. "Let us begin. Forgive me for the novelty of holding my first council at evening. After all we've experienced recently, I trust we will survive the oddity of this as well." She smiled, and a ripple of laughter rolled through the court. "I have called the council because urgent news has broken today, and I did not wish to delay in sharing this with my people. It is grave, indeed, but I trust in Tir's resilience, even in these dark times."

Braith paused.

"This morning, Gareth Bo-Kelwyd was discovered dead in his cell."

Three seconds of absolute silence followed her declaration. Braith's fingers whitened around the arms of her throne.

Then the room exploded in a roar.

A few rogue shouts rose above the din. "Justice!"

"Murder!"

"Who has done it?"

"Lies! Produce the body!"

Braith's face did not change. This was expected. They had prepared for it, she and Cameria and Yestin. The loyalties of the courtiers were revealed by their shouts—those who had been struggling to accept Gareth's dethroning shouted curses; those who had been loyal to the true king celebrated and cheered. More than a few courtiers looked lost, unsure whether they should say anything.

Wisdom in these times.

After a long while, Braith held up her hands, calling for silence. "I know this is troublesome news for many of you. I know some will view this as justice, but I remind you the Tirian justice system requires a trial. Gareth Bo-Kelwyd, knave though he was, ought to have been afforded the same rights as any Tirian."

There was muttering among some of the nobles.

"We must launch an investigation into Gareth's death. If he was murdered, the responsible party will be held accountable."

She held up her hands again. Yestin Bo-Arthio caught her eye from the council table and offered an encouraging nod.

"I understand some may view this as a waste of resources," the queen continued. "But Gareth Bo-Kelwyd was a poor king because he thought he was above the law. He did not respect Tir. I do. If someone dies under suspicious circumstances, the law demands that death be investigated. I plan to obey Tirian law. Just as I expect my people to obey Tirian law."

"Majesty?" Sir Fellyck said from the council table. "May I speak?"

"Yes, Sir Fellyck."

Fellyck rose and addressed the court as much as his queen. "Of course, we all respect the laws of the land. But perhaps this latest occurrence is an answer to our prayers."

"*Our* prayers?" Braith's eyebrow lifted.

Fellyck bowed. "Of course, Majesty. I only mean that trying Gareth for high treason would have been a great source of heartache—for you, my queen, and for Tir, and a great drain on our resources besides. Perhaps, with the avoidance of such a public affair, Tir can begin to heal from her wounds."

"Death is a poor salve to bind a wound, Sir Fellyck. Especially murder." Braith rose and descended the dais to look Sir Fellyck squarely in the eyes. "Please hear me, as I'll not repeat myself again. I know what kind of man my father was. But he was under the care of the palace—under my care—until such a time as his trial could be held. We shall hold an investigation to determine if Gareth was murdered. If so, we shall discover who is responsible for Gareth's death, and that person will be held to account. Am I clear?"

Fellyck lowered himself into his council chair. "Unavoidably, Your Majesty."

Yestin offered another slight nod. Braith returned it.

But just as she reseated herself on her throne, Fellyck's voice sounded again. "I apologize for my impertinence, Queen Braith. But I suppose your desire to hold a trial for the party responsible for Gareth's death, if there is one, proves Her Majesty does not have an aversion to trials. I had wondered."

"Aversion?" Braith frowned. "Why would you wonder such a thing?"

"Do we not have another important prisoner languishing in the dungeons at this moment?"

Braith sucked in a small breath but said nothing.

Fellyck showed convincing meekness. "Oh, have you forgotten, Your Majesty? Surely not. I know the business of the queen is varied and weighty, but surely she has not forgotten about Dray Bo-Anffir, her father's closest advisor."

"No." Braith's voice had lost half its strength. She well remembered his pitiful, wasted appearance last she had seen him. She remembered what sounded like remorse in his voice. Remorse, and perhaps a deep longing for redemption. A longing for something other than who he had been.

And a longing for Braith that she would never fulfill.

Yestin rose from the council table. "Dray remains in the dungeon. Perhaps Her Majesty will set a date for a trial." His eyes were sympathetic but firm. This was right. This was necessary. Inevitable.

Braith found her voice again. "Yes. Dray will stand trial. As soon as the investigation into Gareth's death is complete."

"And the charges for Dray Bo-Anffir?" Fellyck was relentless.

Braith swallowed. "High treason."

Braith shifted on her throne and turned to Sir Ethyn, the noble who had just been petitioning her. "I understand your province has been hit hard by the riots."

Ethyn inclined his head. "Majesty, we need soldiers immediately. Aid. Something."

Braith measured her words. She did not wish to reveal that at least half her army had deserted when Gareth fell. Stars, some of them were leading the rioters.

"I understand your plight. I will do all I can to aid my stewards, governors, and lords. You have my word."

Would it be enough?

Sir Ethyn bowed, though he offered none of the wheedling thanks the lords were so prone to offering Braith's father.

"Is that all for petitions?" Braith asked.

Yestin glanced at a piece of parchment before him, then nodded to the queen.

"Very well. I should like to begin our investigation, then." Braith signaled to a guardsman at the back of the room.

Two men entered the throne room. Just two. It had been all Cameria could manage to round up on such short notice.

Murmurs sounded.

Fellyck watched as the men approached the queen. "What is this?"

"Colormasters," Braith said. "I know Gareth enforced deeply restrictive policies on such weavers, but I intend to restore them to the positions and functions they once held." Braith nodded to the two colormasters. "If you please, gentlemen, you may begin to recreate the scene you observed in Gareth Bo-Kelwyd's cell this morning."

One colormaster, an aged man dressed in peasant clothing, hesitated at the tabletop. The other, younger and wearing the finer garb of one who lived in the palace as the second son of a courtier, allowed his fingertips to light.

Braith stood and walked down the dais. She put her hand on the arm of the older colormaster. "It is all right. You will not be harmed. You have my word."

The man nodded once, then his fingers, too, lit up.

The younger colormaster was already sweeping his hands above the table. Strands like paint spilled out, and he directed them with ease. Before many moments passed, an image took shape—a dark cell with a large man's body lying in the middle.

Braith closed her eyes. After a short breath, she opened them again and began to examine the evidence.

The older colormaster swept his fingers over the image on the council table. He added detail the younger man missed. A particular shade to the eyes, a clump of straw clustered in one corner of the cell, markings on the body.

After a few moments more, both colormasters stepped back and bowed. It seemed their work was complete.

Braith nodded slowly. "Thank you very much, indeed." She stared at the image they had created—so real, it was as if they were standing before the scene in person. "This." She pointed to the markings around her father's throat. "Was he . . . strangled?"

"I believe so, Majesty." Cadwyth Bo-Balas, captain of the palace guard, had joined the councilmen at the table and was examining the picture alongside the others. "Do you see his eyes? The broken vessels there." He cleared his throat.

How awkward he must feel to have this discussion with the dead man's daughter.

He glanced sideways at Braith, then continued. "That suggests strangulation."

"Indeed." Braith leaned closer, and sure enough, the older artist had filled in that detail.

"Majesty?"

Braith sighed a little. "Yes, Sir Fellyck?"

"This is all well and good." He held up the piece of parchment he had brought to the council meeting. "But if it pleases you, I have other items I'd like to discuss."

"Oh? And what be they?"

"Well, I'd first like to address the sticky matter of Sir Dray Bo-Anffir."

Braith's voice hardened. "Oh? I thought we had already discussed that matter."

"The council is well aware that you and Sir Dray had a relationship of a personal nature."

"Indeed!" She fought for control. "I was unaware of this personal relationship."

Of course, Dray had made no secret of his desire to wed her, but that was not her fault.

General Bo-Arthio cleared his throat. "Sir Fellyck, may I point out that Her Majesty has given us no reason to suspect she would not be fair and evenhanded with any prisoner who stands accused, no matter who he is? Let us not forget she stood against her own father when he was in the wrong."

"Indeed." Fellyck's voice sounded full of icicles. "And what do you know of this, Bo-Arthio? Could you hear council meetings from your hideout? Have you been eavesdropping at court these last thirteen years?"

"That's enough." Anger laced Braith's words. "General

Bo-Arthio has been appointed to this council the same as any of the rest of you, and I will not tolerate disrespect. Disagreement and discourse are encouraged, but disdain is not. Now, in answer to your original question, Sir Fellyck, Dray will be brought to trial before the council and myself, just as any other prisoner. But we will see to this matter you have interrupted first." She returned her attention to the art on the table.

"And my other matter?" Fellyck insistently held forth his parchment.

"Yes?"

He pursed his lips. At least he seemed to be choosing his words carefully. "Your Majesty, I mean no disrespect, but your unorthodox succession to the throne requires some discussion."

Braith stared at him.

"Tir accepted your father's own rather unorthodox succession because King Caradoc's will seemed explicit and clear. But that was the first time Tir has been ruled by a man of no royal blood. And this . . ." He gestured to Braith. "Again, no disrespect. But not all the riots in the streets are on account of your father, Majesty. If nothing else, further inquiry would protect you from speculation, coup attempts, and a whole host of other unsavory possibilities I'm sure Your Majesty would not like to face."

Braith's gaze dropped back to the table. She stared at the image of her father's body. "Very well. I will remind you I was chosen by the committee. But we shall open such investigation and discussion *after* the case of my father's murder has been looked into to my satisfaction."

Fellyck bowed. "Thank you, Majesty. And do make haste. The oak doors of this palace are only so strong."

Braith waited until the throne room was mostly clear before

she sat and dropped her head in her hands. She lifted it at the sound of approaching steps.

Yestin bowed. "Majesty."

"Yes, General. How goes the preparation for your voyage?"

"I believe the captain and his, ah, *crew* have it well in hand."

Braith smiled. "Never fear. I have commissioned a naval commander and his men to accompany my rogue weavers on their journey."

"I'm glad of it. I'm sure the Bo-Lidere boy is a fine sailor, but the others . . ."

"Yes. I suppose they are the greenest sailors a queen ever commissioned." Braith's smile fell. "My first council was a disaster."

Yestin's eyes were kind. "I've seen far worse in my time."

"I just thought . . ."

"It would be easy?"

"I suppose I thought it'd be easier without having my hands tied by my father and his whims. I thought when I had more authority . . ." She sighed. "Foolish, I know."

"Optimistic."

She gave a short laugh. "Well, General Bo-Arthio, I'm afraid that after one council meeting on this throne, I'm beginning to understand my father's iron rule more than I ever did sitting in that chair." She nodded to her former seat at the council table.

"Yes, Majesty. Understand, perhaps. But not support."

"No, not support." She glanced at him wearily. "Let us never hope so."

Yestin offered his arm to Braith. "I have no worries about that, Majesty."

Braith rose and accepted his arm. The two strolled toward the throne room door. "You have more faith in me than I do in myself, General. But I shall endeavor not to disappoint you."

A guardsman opened the door for the queen and her advisor.

Yestin remained silent as they walked for a moment.

"General, might I ask a favor?"

"Of course, Majesty."

"Would you escort me to the palace gardens? I long for the days when I was freer to wander there. Even then, I felt like a bird trapped in a cage. But now . . . I cannot recall when last I enjoyed the sunshine and fresh air. Would you mind terribly staying with me?"

"Not in the least, Queen Braith. It's my honor."

Braith smiled. "No need to stand on ceremony, General." They descended the palace stairs. "I know you're busy with your preparations, but somehow I cannot bear to return to my chambers. Preparations for our next council are all that await me there."

"It will come easier in time."

"Is it strange that I rather hope not?"

Yestin lapsed into silence as they cleared the stairs and crossed through the crowded palace foyer toward the front doors.

"It will become more familiar," Yestin said at last. "You were born for this."

Braith's eyes misted. "That is kind of you to say, General."

"I mean it." He led Braith toward the palace doors. "Your blood may not be royal, but it is diplomatic, and I think that is better." He gestured Braith forward.

But before they could take another step, a shout sounded nearby.

"Down with Gareth's line!"

Braith spun just in time to see a dagger flash toward her.

I WAS SITTING HALFWAY UP THE FIRST FLIGHT OF STAIRS LEAD-
ing off the foyer, feeling extremely sorry for myself, when I
heard the commotion.

A muffled shout, a rustle. And then Braith screamed.

I flew down the stairs.

"Braith!"

I bolted toward the front doors of the palace, barely pro-
cessing the blur of bodies and shouts and chaos around me.
"Braith!"

My feet skidded against the stone floor as I pulled to a stop
in time to see my father reach up and disarm a dagger from a
shouting peasant's hand. In another moment, he had the peasant
pinned to the floor, face down, arms secured behind his back.
Father spun the dagger around in a swift motion so that the
blade rested against the back of the peasant's neck.

The whole thing lasted about the span of a single breath, and
Father didn't even look to be sweating.

I stumbled back a step.

His calm, quiet voice somehow carried over the panic in the
foyer. "You, soldier." He nodded to one of the guards who was
supposed to be manning the door. "Arrest this man for treason
and attempted regicide."

"Yes, General." The soldier motioned to two of his fellows,

and they had the peasant on his feet and secured in a few moments.

The man bled from a cut on his forehead, I guessed from his fall to the stone floor, but otherwise he seemed unharmed. He screamed as the guardsmen led him away. "Gareth's line will end! Down with the pretender queen! Down with the monarchy!"

One guardsman delivered an elbow to the peasant's gut. "Shut up, you!"

The crowd thinned as some of the onlookers padded after the struggling prisoner and palace guard. Braith came into view. She sat crumpled on the floor, eyes wide and mouth slightly open.

"Braith!" I rushed to her side and dropped to my knees. "Are you hurt?"

"No." She shook her head like it was full of fog and fluff. "No, just . . . startled."

I checked her over anyway. "Cameria is going to explode when she hears. She leaves you alone for half a moment . . ."

"Indeed." Braith allowed me to help her to her feet—not an easy task in her queenly corset and gown.

"Tannie," Father's voice cut in, maddeningly calm and soothing. "It is the palace guards' job to protect the queen. What are you doing down here?"

"Well, *you* seemed keen to jump in."

Father paused. "The guardsman in me is slow to retire, I suppose. I am technically still a soldier."

I bit back any further argument. He was right, of course. "Aye. I need to get back, anyway. Need to finish packing. Just for the trip to Physgot," I added before he could misunderstand me. If this very long day had beaten one thing into my head, it was that I would not be traveling on Mor's ship.

"All right, Tannie. I will see you up there shortly."

I nodded to Father, curtsied to Queen Braith, and took my leave.

I trudged back up the stairs. Father didn't even want me going to Physgot. I could tell by the look he gave me when I mentioned it. But I had to see my friends off from the dock. Stars, it was probably safer for me in Physgot than Urian right now, with assassins breaching the palace doors.

A shudder rippled through me.

I took a right turn toward the tower housing our apartments and ran bodily into a solid black wall.

"Tannie En-Yestin, there you are!"

The wall knew my name.

But then the voice registered, and I moved past my mental hiccup at his attire. Still wasn't used to that blasted palace guardsman uniform, even though he wore it all the time, on duty or off.

"Ho, Brac." I moved to sidestep him and continue toward my room. I had packing to attend to and wasn't keen to let him know about it just yet.

But Brac put his hand on my arm and pulled me back. He wrapped me in a hug. "I heard there was an attempted assassination in the foyer. So glad you weren't down there."

"Oh." My voice was muffled as he pressed my face into his chest. "I was down there."

He held me at arm's length. "What?"

"Aye, I heard the shouting and went to see if Braith was all right."

"Tannie! What's gotten into you? Are you tryin' to get yourself killed?"

I glared at him. Ironic. His overprotectiveness—and my father's—might *actually* get me killed, if I really was getting as sick as Gryfelle.

"No. Course not. I just reacted."

"Like always."

I rolled my eyes and pushed past him. "Excuse me."

He pulled me back again. "I'm sorry."

I didn't look up.

"Did you hear me, Tannie? I'm sorry. I didn't mean to yell. Just been so worried about you. Everything seems so dangerous these days. And now that we're betrothed, I feel a special need to protect you. You understand that, surely."

Discomfort rose in my throat. "I really need to go."

He didn't even seem to hear me.

Next second I was wrapped in another hug, and he may as well have been trying to wring the air from my chest for all the breath I could manage.

I needed to get out of there.

"Brac, I must go. Please."

"Aye, my girl." He released me at last. "I'll check on you later. Shall I have dinner sent up to your room?"

I looked at him like he'd dropped through the ceiling.

"Dinner sent to my room?"

"Aye. Thought you might want a quiet meal after your fright."

"I'm fine," I mumbled.

"I'll have dinner sent."

"Aye. Whatever you want."

"It'll be all right, Tannie. I promise."

I forced a thin smile and nodded, then I fled for the stairs.

Nothing was all right. Nothing at all. Brac used to feel like home, and now? Now when I was with him I felt . . . alone.

And he was going to lose his mind when I told him I was going to Physgot.

CHAPTER TEN

TANWEN

I COULD TELL YOU ALL ABOUT THE ROW BRAC AND I HAD over Physgot. I could tell you how my father finally stepped in and said I had permission to see him and my friends off, and how I just about keeled over with shock. And about how Brac insisted he would travel with us as part of the guard and see me home, safely to Urian. Or about how I screamed Urian wasn't home and then a story strand made of fire shot from my finger and singed my curtains to a blackened crisp.

But really, it's all more of the same. It felt like my whole life had turned into one long argument, and I was sick to death of it.

Maybe if I could have had peace with Father *or* Brac *or* Mor, it would have been bearable. But I had peace with no one. I was truly alone.

And I hated it.

But no matter how I felt about the turn my life had taken, when our heavily guarded wagon train rolled up to Physgot, something in my spirit lifted. It wasn't Pembrone, mind. But it was so like it in many ways. And what I'd once considered a town a fair distance away—south and across a wide bay—now seemed downright local. My world had grown since last I set foot on this peninsula.

I breathed deep of the coastal air, heard the Menfor Sea crash against the nearby shore, and watched the provincial bustle of Physgot's main thoroughfare—not exactly like the feel of

Pembrone's farming village, but similar enough. Just geared toward merchants and small-time fishermen. My heart hummed with the sights, sounds, and smells of it.

Home.

"That's pretty." Aeron nudged my elbow from her place beside me in the wagon.

I glanced over and saw what she saw—a strand I hadn't meant to create. It was glittery gold and just barely visible in the full sunlight. "Huh." I smiled at the dancing strand and sent it over the eave of a candle shop to swirl above the crowd of shoppers and sellers.

A few children squealed in delight, and I grinned to recall the days when I'd entertained hundreds of peninsular children just like these. Seemed so many moons ago.

I watched the shimmering gold ribbon twirl through the air. "I wonder what it means. I didn't intend to create it."

"Looks like a little sliver of happiness, maybe."

My gaze tripped over Brac, riding beside the wagon on the horse he'd earned from his commander under Gareth—for turning in my weaver friends from the Corsyth. He was looking at me, too, like he could sense my joy at being so near home. The home he'd wanted me to make permanent with him and which I'd always resisted.

Absolutely everything felt so upside down these days.

The gold strand vanished. I sighed. "Aye. A very little sliver, I guess."

Aeron squeezed my arm. "It'll—"

"Be all right. I know." My tone softened the words—I hoped. "Thanks."

"I know it doesn't always feel like it will. But it will."

We both watched a few children chase after our wagon, then give up and go after the wagon just behind us, where Warmil rode with Karlith and Gryfelle. I didn't let my mind linger too long on Gryfelle. Traveling hadn't been kind to her. I could only guess how awful the bumpy ride felt on her tired bones. I hoped she might find some relief on the ship. But would it be any better? I'd never been on one myself—only little riverboats and tiny rowboats. I could've asked Mor what the ship would be like. If only he were speaking to me.

"Hey, that's the queen's seal!" The shout of a passing peasant drew my attention. The man's shoulders were loaded with strings of fresh fish. "They travel under Queen Braith's banner!"

I tensed. The guardsmen had made a fairly obvious showing of their presence as we traveled, though we had kept to the less populated paths as we were able. There had only been a few moments of unease so far. But something about the way this man shouted Braith's name signaled he was no admirer of Tir's new ruler.

"Greetings, sir." It was my father, astride a large horse like he'd been born there. He reined in next to the peasant.

The man with the fish drew away a bit, his hesitation written on his face. Perhaps he was afraid Father would trample him. I'd never exactly seen a guardsman under Gareth do that, but they'd certainly threatened it before.

The man spoke again. "You're traveling under the queen's banner."

"Aye, sir. We are." Father's gaze never left the man's face. "Our good queen sends her well wishes to her people."

The fish man frowned. "She's Gareth's daughter."

"Aye. But she is not Gareth."

A long moment passed while the peasant seemed to consider this. Finally, he looked up at my father again. "Who are you?"

"General Yestin Bo-Arthio."

The man's fish flopped to the ground. "Nay. It's . . . impossible. The general's long dead. We heard rumors, o' course. But . . . no. It can't be."

"I am he."

The man squinted, then shook his head. "If you say so."

He truly didn't seem able to believe Father was who he said he was. But in his confusion, it seemed he had forgotten his anger. He picked up his strings of fish, spared our party one last suspicious glance, then went on his way down the road.

Father watched him go. We had drawn a crowd now, and disquiet surfaced in his eyes. He signaled the train to resume its rumble toward the docks.

Aeron shook her head. "I sure am glad to have your father here."

Humph. Easy for her to say. Although I couldn't deny his presence seemed to act as a salve on the smarting wounds of the peasants.

In a moment, the procession was on its way again, passing the curious onlookers, and Father was riding alongside my wagon.

"I thought you didn't like that old title anymore," I said.

I wouldn't have blamed him if there had been annoyance in his eyes when he looked at me. But, of course, there wasn't. "My name and that old title are useful tools. As you saw." He cleared his throat. Speaking so openly and so often was still uncomfortable for him, I knew. "I will never escape the title, however much I'd like to." He smiled slightly. "Queen Braith won't let me."

"Aye. That's true. Can't say I blame her. You're a bit like a wizard, you know."

Now he looked annoyed. "Don't be silly."

I grinned. "Warlock Bo-Arthio."

He rolled his eyes, then chuckled. It was the first time I'd heard him laugh. That I could remember, anyway. The sound filled my heart deeper than the coastal air filled my lungs.

But the humor quickly faded into that perpetually solemn state I'd grown accustomed to. "My name is a tool, Tannie. Just as your story strands are tools to be used wisely. And carefully."

"Story strands aren't *just* tools, Father. They're art."

"Aye. And that art is more powerful than you realize."

I couldn't see him do it, master rider that he was. But he must have signaled his horse to pick up the pace, because he rode off after he said that, leaving me to stew like a hunk of grazer meat. Or maybe a watta root.

How could he say that I didn't understand the power of art? If anyone knew the power of the weaver gifts, it was me. Wasn't it? I'd seen Zelyth fill Gareth's throne room with wild strands of sweet-root-colored hair like Ifmere's. I'd seen those strands knock men dead. I'd created a halo-head made of story that ate half a dozen men. Quite by accident, but it'd happened, hadn't it? I'd seen Dylun make colormaster's fire and Mor spin objects out of thin air, all with their weaver gifts.

Of course I understood the power of our gifts. Father couldn't possibly be right.

Could he?

The crashing waves of the Menfor grew louder, and our wagon train slowed to a crawl. I barely waited until the wagon stopped to hop down, cast my traveling boots aside, and head for the beach.

The sandy shore of Physgot slipped between my bare toes. I let all thoughts of Father and Brac and Mor, all worry over Gryfelle's illness and my illness and Braith's unstable empire slip from my mind as I padded through the sand toward the gentle waves licking the shore.

Eastern Peninsular water was only warm this time of year, and I didn't want to miss my chance. I hiked up my skirt and splashed in up to my knees. Salt and surf wrapped around my legs. I cheered. "It's summertime!"

A deep, unfamiliar laugh sounded from behind me. "Aye,

it's summertime, lass. You needed the Menfor to tell you, did you?"

I turned and met the grin of a man who looked to be about Warmil's age—younger than Father but older than me. A shock of sweet-root hair and his freckle-smattered face spoke to Tirian heritage. But he had that quirked accent that Mor carried—like he'd been raised everywhere and nowhere at once.

I grinned back at him. "Aye. I'm a coastal lass, so I suppose I do need the Menfor to tell me when it's summer."

"Where do you hail from, girl?"

"Pembrone." I hiked a few steps back in his direction so we wouldn't have to yell to each other. "You're a sailor, aren't you?"

"Commander Jule Bo-Kwyrm"—he bowed—"at your service."

"Oh!" My grin grew as the others finally made their way down the beach toward us, grim-faced Mor among them. "I think I found your naval commander, Captain Bo-Lidere."

Mor didn't acknowledge me but turned to Jule. "Commander Bo-Kwyrm? I'm Mor Bo-Lidere." They shook hands, and I fought the urge to *harrumph* at Mor. He could at least pretend we were on speaking terms in front of strangers.

The commander bowed again. "Please, call me Jule. While we're aboard your ship, I'm not commander."

Mor smiled, and I was pleased to see he was still able to manage it. "That's generous of you. I think you have a few more years at sea than I do."

Jule laughed. "No doubt. But Her Majesty gave me fair warning you were a pup." His eyes twinkled, and it was clear he meant no malice. "An experienced pup she trusted for this task."

"Just the same, I'm glad to have you on my crew. It's been a fair few moons since I sailed. My father always said you couldn't forget, especially when you grew up aboard the way I did. But I never tested his theories. Until now."

Something inside me twinged. Mor was apprehensive. The nerves rattled in his voice, showed in the creases around his mouth. Had he been able to share that fear, that unrest, with anyone? No, because he was too busy thinking about his mission, worrying over Gryfelle, fighting with me.

I wished we could at least be friends. Maybe I could have shared his burden somehow.

But Jule seemed equal to the task, now that Mor had voiced it. "Aye, your father was quite right, least in my experience. My sisters and I were raised on our father's fishing boat, and the lasses didn't serve in the navy like I did, but whenever they set foot on deck, no matter how long it'd been, they knew just how to pull their lines. As the saying goes."

Mor laughed. Actually, truly laughed. "Well, let's hope I'm a sailor to equal your sisters."

Jule bowed again.

It was good to hear joy in Mor's voice. But as soon as he caught my gaze, his posture stiffened. "Right, then. Good to meet you, Jule. I'm sure we'll have much to discuss after I help the others unload these wagons."

The whole group turned back to the wagons then, and Mor's introduction of Jule to the others was lost in the crashing waves. I was left behind, which seemed fitting somehow.

"Oh, don't mind me!" I shouted after them. "I'll be along to help in a minute."

No one turned.

"I'm just going to soak my feet awhile. If you miss me, don't worry! I'll be back soon."

They kept walking.

I sighed and let the sea swallow up my legs again. I turned toward it, the great blue expanse of adventure stretching before me like a challenge. "Wish I were going too. Wish I got to feel those waves through the deck of a ship."

"Who're you talking to, Tannie?"

I sighed and didn't turn to face Brac. "The Menfor Sea."

He snorted. "Well, you let me know if that there ocean answers you back, will you?"

"Very funny. Think I'm losing my onions, do you?"

"Think you never had 'em in the first place."

I spun and made a face at him, but he was grinning. Something about Brac grinning with his feet planted firmly on the Eastern Peninsula beach made me less annoyed with him than I had been in weeks. I could almost forget the black guard uniform that looked an ugly blemish on the sparkling shore.

"I like the Physgotian beach," I said. "It's sandy. Isn't it nice? The Pembroni beach is so pebbly."

He glanced down. "Aye, I guess."

"You'd know what I meant if you'd take those heavy boots off."

Brac frowned. "Nah. Don't want to get dirty."

"Dirty?" My brows shot up. "Since when did you give a fluff-hopper about getting dirty?"

He paused. "Since when didn't you?" Then a whisper of disdain crept across his face. "You're ruining your dress, you know."

Indignation boiled up inside me. This, from the boy who shoved me into a hay mow when I was wearing a brand-new dress it had taken me six moons to save up for? This, from the boy who once tried to trip me into the mud pen where his father's snort-snouts frolicked? Now he was going to scold me for letting a little ocean water onto my skirt?

"You pompous . . ." Anger stole my words, and I dropped the rest of my skirt into the water, just to spite him.

He folded his arms across his chest and smirked. "Careful.

That big dress'll get heavy. Pull you right out to sea. But I guess that's what you want, ain't it?"

With that, he spun and began the march back to the wagons.

But I didn't hesitate. I threw all my anger into my hands and sent a deluge of water strands at Brac's back. The force of the water smacked him hard, and he went down in the sand, face first. Heavy though my "ruined" dress was, I paraded past him before he had a chance to wipe the sand from his face and collect his wits.

"Now who's the one who's all wet?" I called.

I might have felt completely satisfied, at least for a moment. Except I caught a very stern glance from my father. A glance that told me he had seen the whole display.

Shame flickered inside me. But I ignored it and grabbed some bags down from one of the wagons.

Jule was addressing the whole lot, including the soldiers who had traveled with us and some men I didn't recognize but who must be Jule's sailors. They wore those curious shiny boots I'd noticed on Mor back when I'd first seen him in Gwern while on a tour with Riwor.

"We'll set sail tomorrow," Jule said. "This will give you time to unpack and rest. It won't be a pleasure cruise, that's certain, and I expect Captain Bo-Lidere will make sailors of all of you by journey's end."

Karlith chuckled, and Dylun looked a bit apprehensive. Didn't suppose either of them were any more experienced on a ship than I was.

"You'll have time to eat, sleep, and pray, if you wish," Jule continued. "The Physgotian temple is that way." He pointed back the way we'd come and west a bit. "I'll not join you there, mind, but feel free to ask the favor of your goddesses or stars or whatever you like. Priests still attend this temple, despite the unrest."

I was half tempted to ask what had been happening in the

villages out here. We'd not heard much news from the country-side. Had the priests been under fire since Gareth fell?

Strange. I'd always felt like I knew nothing about the big, wide world because Pembrone was so small and dinky and closed off from the "real world." But really, it hadn't been much different in Urian. Wherever you were, it seemed you could really only understand your own troubles and the trials of your little spot on the world.

Sad thought, that.

"The *Cethorelle* is ready for sea, Captain." Jule nodded toward the dock. "It's a fine ship the queen has given you from her fleet. The crew and I will sleep there, and anyone who wishes to join us and get settled may. Otherwise, we've taken rooms at this inn for you. Do as you will, and meet us at the dock, just after sunrise."

"And then we'll make way," Mor finished. "My thanks to you, Jule. You're a better first mate than I deserve, I'm sure."

"At your service." Jule bowed, then he and the men continued helping us unload the wagons.

A slightly sandy, still dripping, and very grumpy-looking Brac took the bags from my hands. "Here, let me. Your Highness."

I couldn't decide whether to apologize or douse him again. That engagement band burned a stripe on my wrist.

"Ho, Aeron." I sidled up next to her. "Are we sharing a room at the inn?"

She winced. "Oh, I'm sorry, Tannie. I'm staying on the ship with the crew tonight. Mor thought it best so we might get used to the sea a bit before sailing."

"Aye. Course."

"If we were staying in the inn, of course I'd—"

"It's fine. Don't worry." I tried to force a smile. "I'll be fine."

"Maybe I can tell Mor I'd rather—"

"No, don't. If you mention me, he'll just turn to stone, anyway."

She winced again. "Sorry, Tannie. I really am."

I did manage a real smile then, albeit a weak one. "You're a good friend, Aeron. I'll be wishing you well the whole time you're away."

She smiled back. "Thanks. We're going to need all the luck in the world."

We both eyed Gryfelle then, for the men were passing right by us, carrying the pale, limp girl on a litter. Gryfelle didn't appear to be conscious.

"Aye," I said softly. "She'll need it too."

And so will I.

CHAPTER ELEVEN

TANWEN

MY SUPPER OF ONION SOUP AND FRESH BREAD HAD TASTED good at the time, but now it settled in my stomach like a stone. What time was it? Still hours before sunrise, judging by the black square that served as my window to the outside world. But I felt I'd been lying awake for days, unable to sleep.

Brac's snores weren't helping matters. I could hear the lad through the inn's thick walls. Matter of fact, I'm pretty sure all Physgot could hear him. He would make the town crumble if he wasn't careful.

I sighed and swung my legs out of bed. The bare floor chilled the soles of my feet, summer though it was. Must truly be the middle of the night.

I pulled the strings around the top of my nightdress a bit tighter, then grabbed the shawl Karlith had knitted for me during her long hours beside Gryfelle's bed. Karlith had knitted half the wool in Tir into sweaters and scarves in the past moon.

My feet slipped into my soft leather shoes, and I wrapped the shawl around my shoulders. Didn't bother grabbing a candle. We were right in the middle of the village, and the street was dotted with oil lamps. I'd be able to see enough to make it to the docks.

The shops and storefronts felt familiar as I crept along, even though I'd seen them for the first time earlier that day. I supposed every peninsular village had some commonalities. The sign I tiptoed beneath read "Patty's Pub," but it might as well have said, "Blodwyn's Tavern."

Wondered if I would ever get back to Pembrone to see Blodwyn. Would I ever taste her grazer stew again? And if I did, would I remember it?

I shoved the thought aside. No use dwelling on that. Right now, I just needed to soothe my anxious heart so I could get some sleep.

The rhythmic song of the waves reached my ears, and I knew I was close. Sounded so like the waves lapping at the cliff below my cottage in Pembrone. I'd fallen asleep to that sound most nights of my life. Maybe it was what I needed now, on the eve of saying good-bye to my father. Again.

It hadn't really struck me until I reached the docks, but I was angry with him for leaving me after we had just found each other again. Angry and terrified.

It hadn't been easy to adjust to our new life together, but . . . what if he didn't return from this voyage? The sea was no man's friend. It seemed sailors entered into a tacit agreement with her that might be revoked at a moment's notice. Pembrone had boasted a proper dock once and nearly as much shipping trade as farming. But half those boats had been lost to storms, while half the merchandise to ship had been swallowed by famine. Pembronis respected the sea enough to fear her.

And Father was gallivanting off on a mission for the queen before we'd even had a chance to get to know each other properly.

Though I had been rather quick to do the same. Not a moon ago, it had been me planning for this adventure and he the one remaining in Urian. I closed my eyes against my own hypocrisy.

I plunked down onto the planks of one of the smaller jetties. Didn't really want to go sit on the pier next to the *Cethorelle*. It would be like sitting next to a pie you weren't allowed to eat. No, this jetty would do just fine, thanks.

I stared out at the water. Should I tell Father I couldn't bear it if he left? Should I tell him I needed him to stay? Ask him to put me before the queen?

No. I couldn't do that to him. I didn't think he'd know what to do if I shoved him between that boulder and anvil.

There was no clear answer, except to let him go. Pray he made it back and I could learn how to be a daughter.

I wrapped my shawl tighter.

"Are you cold, Tannie?"

I barely stopped myself from screaming. But it was only a moment before I recognized his voice and the way my name sounded on his lips.

"Mor." My heart felt lodged somewhere around my throat. "What in the name of mountainbeast milk are you trying to do? Make me keel over into the sea?"

By the sound of it, Mor might have chuckled. I couldn't be sure, so dark as it was out here on this little fishing jetty. He settled in beside me. Not too close. "Sorry. I thought you heard me."

"No. I was thinking."

"About?"

I paused, and he cut in before I could respond. "No, don't answer. I . . . haven't earned that."

"What do you mean?"

He turned toward the water. "I've been pushing you away, haven't I? Making sure there's nothing shared between us. So why should you talk to me now, even if we're just speaking as friends?"

"You're right. I shouldn't." We let the silence settle, then I asked, "But do you think I could talk with you? Just as a friend?"

Mor waited a moment—too long for my liking. "Five minutes. I can be your friend for five minutes."

"I hate you a little bit right now, you know."

"Hey, is that any way to talk to a friend?" Even in the non-existent light, I could see his wry smile.

I resisted the urge to laugh. "I don't want my father to go."

"Because you just got him back." He answered so quickly, clearly this had occurred to him long before it had to me.

"Aye."

"The general is unlike anyone I've ever known. If anyone will survive this voyage, he will."

He had a point. Father had lived in the walls of the palace for thirteen years, making friends with rope-tails and writing journal entries in the dark. What was a little trek around the world compared to that? "Aye, I suppose. But . . ."

"If something happened, you'd regret the way you left things between the two of you."

"Been prancing around in my mind again, Captain?"

"I try to avoid prancing when I can. Plus, we only have five minutes. No time to waste cutting to the point."

"Indeed."

He looked down. "I'm sorry for the way I spoke to you in Urian. That's not really how I wanted to leave things when I'm not sure I'll return."

My breath caught. "You can't tell me my father will make it back safe in one piece and then tell me you might not!"

"I'm not your father. Have you seen the way he handles blades and bows? He's like a walking weapon."

Tears rose. "I hate this. I hate that you're both leaving me, just when I—" I broke off before I confessed my sickness. That was the last thing I wanted to say in this moment.

Mor didn't press for me to finish. "You'll be all right, Tannie. You'll have Brac."

"Stop."

"I'm not trying to yell at you again. Or make you feel guilty. I mean it honestly. Brac has been like a brother to you. You'll have him by your side while we're gone, and all will be well.

You're not alone, even though things have . . . changed between you."

"Changed?" My voice rose. "That's an understatement, don't you think? The lad thinks I'm going to be his wife!"

"And now you'll have plenty of uninterrupted time to tell him you don't plan to marry him. Or you'll have plenty of time to decide if you *do* want to marry him."

"Mor, it's not even a—"

But Mor cut me off by rising to his feet. "Five minutes are up. Good night, Tannie."

And before I could say another word, he vanished into the pre-dawn blackness.

CHAPTER TWELVE

TANWEN

THE WAVES HADN'T HAD THE EFFECT ON ME I'D HOPED. I LAY awake all night until the light of dawn slanted through the window in my room at the inn. Though perhaps the waves had done their best and Mor had made a mess of whatever peace I might have been able to claim.

I could only imagine the puffiness of my eyes and the drawn, haggard look on my face as I stood to the side of the dock and watched the sailors and the Corsyth weavers make the last of their preparations before setting sail. In a moment of defiance, I'd brought along the tricorn hat with the white feather and sparkling blue pin Mor had made for me when he had invited me to come with them. A sailor's hat and an invitation for a time that felt much simpler. I clutched the blasted thing in my hands—a reminder to Captain Bo-Bumplelump of *his* broken promises.

A hand brushed my shoulder, and I turned to find my father gazing at me with his steady gray eyes. "About ready to leave, Tannie girl."

"Yes, I gathered." I looked down. "See you later, I guess."

He was quiet, and I didn't look up. "Aye. I'll see you when I return."

I could feel him moving . . . getting ready to make his way down the dock and onto that ship for goddesses knew how many moons.

I closed my eyes and drew up the best part of myself, determined not to be an utter mountainbeast to my father. My eyes popped open in time to see him halfway down the dock already.

"Daddy?"

He halted. Turned slowly.

I let the tears fall and ran to him. "Daddy, I'm sorry."

He wrapped me in a hug, just as he might have done when I was small. He stroked my head. "All is well, Tannie."

"I'm sorry I'm such a mountainbeast sometimes."

He tightened his hold on me.

"I'm sorry I can be awful. I don't want to be. Please stay safe. Come home so I can be a better daughter."

"Tannie . . ."

"Please."

He squeezed me tighter. "I'll return home to you, my girl." Then he gently pried me from his chest and looked me in the face. "And will you be well while I'm away?"

I swallowed hard. Should I tell him? Should I spill my fearful heart to him right there as he was getting ready to leave? No. It would only make him fret. "I'll be well."

A frown creased his brow. He didn't believe me. He knew something was wrong.

I opened my mouth to venture some honesty because I had to tell someone. But just then, an arm wrapped around my shoulders, and Brac's voice intruded. "I'll keep her safe, sir."

Father glanced at Brac and then back at me. He let a long moment pass, then nodded. "Very well. Creator be with you both." He kissed my forehead, then turned and walked down the dock.

I stood, Brac's arm wrapped around me like a tether. I watched the last of the crates, the last of my fellow weavers, make their way aboard. Mor had been out of sight all morning, and I wondered if that was by design. Somewhere belowdecks, Gryfelle rested in a bed.

Please, let them find the cure.

And I truly meant it for Gryfelle's sake, not my own. But then I wondered . . .

If they did find the cure and they were able to save Gryfelle, would it do me any good if I wasn't with them? Would they be able to return home with the cure to help me too? What *was* the cure?

I hadn't thought any of this through. I'd been so clouded by frustration and heartache and the desire to go with them, I hadn't given reason a space to breathe. Was I not only saying good-bye to my father and friends but to my only chance at healing? I realized I knew less than nothing about this cure they sought. Was it an object? A person? A potion? An incantation? Could it even be brought back to Urian for me?

I glanced up at Brac. He looked pleased enough to see the *Cethorelle's* ropes begin to be loosed.

"Brac?"

He didn't seem to hear me. "They're just about underway. Nice ship, eh? Queen Braith was generous with the pirate."

"Brac . . ."

"Hope they can help the girl. She didn't look well at breakfast. Her skin's the color of turned milk."

"Brac!"

He started. "Eh?"

"I'm sorry."

"For wha—?"

But before he could finish, I slipped the leather engagement bracelet from my wrist, pressed it into his hand, and stood on tiptoe to kiss his cheek. "I have to. Please forgive me."

I yanked the hat onto my head, hiked up my skirt, and then sprinted down the dock. Toward the ship pulling away into the Menfor Sea. Toward the deck growing farther out of reach by the second.

My heart hammered, but I pushed harder. The gap between

the dock and the ship widened—impossibly far. I'd never make it. I'd be daft to even attempt it.

I jumped.

Next moment, I clung to the side of a moving ship, the breath knocked from my chest by the unforgiving wood.

But thank heavens for those decorative bits of railing, or whatever they were called. If not for them, I'd be sinking to the bottom of the bay by now.

"Man overboard!" The unfamiliar face of a crewman came into view above me. "Well . . . sort of." He appraised me. "Need a hand, lassie?"

My eyebrow arched as I fought for breath. "Aye, if it's not a bother."

He laughed and grabbed my wrists. Then his hands found my underarms, and he hoisted me onto the deck. I collapsed in a heap, and he shook his head over me. "I dunno what you were thinking, but the captain doesn't look pleased."

"Tannie!" Mor thundered across the deck toward me. "Tannie, what in the name of the taxes are you doing?"

He dropped to his knees beside me and twisted my face this way and that. Checked my arms and any bit of me that wasn't covered by my dress, as if the answer to my moment of daftness might be written there. "Are you hurt?"

"Bruised a little." I worked to draw a full breath. "Your ship beat the air out of me."

"Well, you hit *her*, after all." He was still frowning. "What in the world, Tanwen En-Yestin? What in the wide world of watta roots were you thinking?"

A shadow from above fell across us both. "She's ill."

Father.

I looked up at him. Tears pricked my eyes. He didn't look angry. Only concerned.

"Am I right, Tannie?" he asked.

I let Mor help me to my feet and stole a glance around at the curious crew and my weaver friends. Aeron, Warmil, Zelyth, and Dylun made no pretense of trying to hide their shock. Zel's mouth actually dangled open.

I lowered my voice so that only Mor and Father might hear. "Yes. I'm ill."

Mor took a step back. "I don't understand."

But his eyes told me he did.

"What you saw back in Urian. When I collapsed . . ."

"Then it's true." Mor's eyes pleaded with me to take it back. "I convinced myself I was being too anxious. Reading into things. You would have said sooner if it were true."

Now was the time for honesty at last. "It's true, Mor. Whatever is killing Gryfelle, I have it too. I need you to save us both."

CHAPTER THIRTEEN

NAITH

NAITH STOOD IN A DESERTED ALLEYWAY OF URIAN. HE SPENT so much time in alleyways of late.

Disgraceful.

The sun had barely made its presence known, and the city had not yet woken. Except the rivermen on the docks. Naith had paid one of those wretches handsomely for his silence after he ferried Naith to the docks nearest the palace.

Naith would not be able to travel anywhere in Urian without being recognized. What was the Master thinking, sending him back? What could they possibly stand to gain? All was deeply unstable, and it seemed this place where he might face the wrath of some emboldened peasants at any moment was the last place in Tir he should be. If the goal was to keep him alive, at least—and Naith wasn't sure that was what the Master wanted at all.

He frowned. The back entrance to the palace—the one favored by kitchen servants and deliverymen—was visible just down the lane.

How undignified. Was this what the Master expected of him? To slink around the city like a four-legged critter? To duck into service entrances like a common slave?

After the care he had taken to escape the capital in the first place . . .

"Blast it all."

Not cursing me, are you, Naith?

Naith stifled a scream. He had been so focused on the palace, he hadn't noticed the smoky strands swirling nearby. And if he hadn't been so familiar with those strands in the first place, he would have taken them for morning mist.

"Master," Naith whispered to the strands. "You startled me."

You should know I'm always with you.

"Forgive me, Master. I was trying to strategize. But you have not shared your plan with me." Naith prayed the Master would give him grace in this moment of danger.

No, I did not share my plan with you. In fact, I never told you to return to the palace at all.

Naith froze. He replayed the Master's instructions over in his mind. *Return to Urian.* Naith had assumed that meant his former home, the palace.

"Master, I thought—"

You assumed. Nasty habit, that. And you nearly ruined everything with your assumptions and your haste.

"Forgive me, Master. Where shall I go if not to the palace? To the temple?"

Stay, Naith. Watch.

Naith stood in the alleyway as the Master's smoke strands curled lazily through the air around him. The sun peeked over the tops of the cityscape. The palace now glowed around its edges in the early-morning light.

The city wakes.

And indeed, it had. The sounds of doors closing. Of shutters being opened. Of vendors and merchants calling their morning wares—hotcakes and fishing supplies and fresh milk. Soon the fabric and dress shops would open for business. Milliners and haberdasheries. All seducing Urian's middle class to try to pass for nobility with a new hat, a few fine buttons on last year's dress.

But Naith had heard these sounds thousands of times before.

Why had the Master brought him all the way back to Urian to listen to the sounds of the citizenry? What did he care for them?

Wait for it.

Yes, there it was. A less pleasant sound. Less familiar to Naith's ears and his years of experience in the capital city. Shouts of treason. Calls for the queen's head. Demands to see Gareth's body. Cries against the monarchy. The sounds of heavy pounding on a heavier door.

Listen to the sounds of unrest, the cries of peasant rage.

"Yes, I hear it, Master." Naith hesitated. "But surely you know they would see me as one to overthrow. I sat at Gareth's court. I had a seat on his council. They would well remember my fine robes, the temple taxes."

Indeed. So you must make them believe you are beyond such things. Remind the peasants of a time when the priestly class served the goddesses more humbly and were not so concerned with lining their pockets.

Preposterous. Unravel two or three centuries of history . . . how? How could he possibly change the well-earned reputation of the Tirian priests? And why would he bother? "Master?"

We need them now, Naith. Make them believe in you.

"They'll kill me. If I take one step out there, they'll have my head."

Then perhaps you ought not act so brashly. Craft a plan, you fool.

"Yes, Master."

Of course, I have already crafted a plan for you. I know my game pieces well enough to know I cannot trust you with this.

He lowered his head. "Forgive me."

I shall. Because I need you. Do you know what I've just witnessed, Naith?

He didn't even know where the Master's body was at this precise moment. "No, I do not."

I've just watched a ship set sail.

"From . . . the river?" A riverboat was hardly a ship, but Naith couldn't follow the Master's train of thought. Hadn't they just been speaking of Urian? Urian had no ships, only river vessels.

No, Naith. Out into the great, wide Menfor Sea. I thought I would be watching this ship set sail, charting its course, then meeting you back in Urian so that we might work together. But things have changed.

"Changed?"

Yes. I cannot meet you in Urian now, for my quarry has departed and now I must wait.

"I don't understand."

No, you do not. Not yet. But you will. Listen to the peasants, Naith.

He obeyed. They had grown louder and angrier with each passing moment. "I hear them."

It is time to leverage their rage. It is time for you to create your weapon while I chase mine.

CHAPTER FOURTEEN

TANWEN

Mᴏʀ ʟᴏᴏᴋᴇᴅ ᴀᴛ ᴍᴇ ʟɪᴋᴇ I'ᴅ ᴍᴜʀᴅᴇʀᴇᴅ ʜɪs ꜰᴀᴠᴏʀɪᴛᴇ fluff-hopper. "How could you not tell me?"

Despite the state of things—that I'd just forced my way onto his ship and demanded he save my life—I glared at him. "Is that a serious question? Take a moment, Mor, and consider when I might have told you. When you gave me any inkling you wanted to hear about my burdens."

He blinked, looking properly chastised, but that didn't make me feel a bit better. "Still," he said softly. "You could have told me. It might have . . . changed things."

"Really? How, exactly?"

"I . . . don't know." He glanced at Father. "If we had known, we could have . . . done something."

"Aye. Like we've been able to 'do something' for Gryfelle?"

"That's enough," Father interrupted. "It doesn't matter anymore. She's here and we know now."

I glanced at the others. Most of the crewmen had returned to their work, including orange-haired Jule, who I now saw at the ship's wheel. But the weavers stared at me, and something told me that even if they couldn't hear this hushed conversation, they knew. They knew this was no longer "Gryfelle's quest" but now was "Gryfelle and Tanwen's quest." And their knowing I'd squashed down my storytelling gift enough to land myself with a curse made me want to hurl my breakfast overboard.

"Yes. She's here." Mor's voice had lost its confusion, hurt, and concern. It hardened to stone. Again.

Maybe I should toss *him* overboard instead.

"Excuse me, General. Tanwen." And then he stalked away, like my illness personally offended him. Or like he had a ship to captain, or something.

"Easy, Tannie girl."

Father touched my fingertips, and I looked down at them. They were glowing red-hot.

Oops.

I sucked in a deep breath. "Sorry. He's just . . ."

"I know. Give him time. This isn't easy on anyone, and he's just a lad."

"He's not just a lad. He's captain of a ship and fully of age, far as the law is concerned."

Father smiled. "Aye. You're right. But you're all children from where I sit."

"Nearly of age myself, you know. Will be before this journey's done, if I make it that long."

Father frowned but didn't argue. "I'll see to a cabin for you. I hope Aeron's brought extra clothes." He eyed my traveling dress. "That won't do."

"Trousers? You want me to wear Aeron's trousers?"

He shot me a look. "You're part of the crew now. This is what you wanted, and you'll need to dress for the work. I'll see to that cabin."

And then I was alone on the deck, feeling exactly like a bumplelump that had fallen off her favorite log and into some very deep water. I didn't quite know what to do with myself.

"That was pretty brave, you know."

I turned toward the sound of a vaguely familiar voice. It was the crewman who had helped me on board after I'd jumped like an idiot. He was younger than I'd realized at first. Barely sporting blond beard stubble on most of his face. His hair was shorn, as sailors favored. His friendly smile felt like a ray of sunshine after Marble-Face Mor's cold departure.

"Brave, huh?" I challenged. "If you say so."

"Well . . . brave or daft. Depending on how you look at it."

"And how do *you* look at it?"

He grinned. "A little of both."

"Aye, that about sums it up." I chuckled and held out my hand. "Tanwen."

He took my hand and shook it. "Wylaith Bo-Thordwyan."

"That's a mouthful."

"Call me Wylie."

"Call me Tannie."

"I will." He tipped his hat. "So, you going to explain that little fit of brave daftness? Or will you leave us to wonder what was so important on board that it couldn't wait for our return?" He glanced toward Mor at the wheel with Jule. "I suppose the captain knows already."

The last thing I needed was the crewmen making jokes and jabs about something between me and Mor. "I'm Tanwen En-Yestin."

Wylie's eyebrows rose. "The general's daughter?"

"That's what they tell me."

"I guess I see it there. In your nose a bit."

"Are you saying I have the nose of an old war hero?"

"Aye. Exactly that."

I laughed. "It's nice to meet you, Wylie."

"Likewise. You looked like you could use a friend."

He meant it kindly, but somehow it felt like a dart of ice to my chest. "My misery's been well spotted."

"Sorry. Didn't mean to poke at you. It was just an observation." He paused, looking around the deck. "Have you sailed before?"

"Never."

"Never?" His eyes widened. "Oh, lass, are you in for a time!"

"Good or bad?"

"Yes."

"Brilliant."

"Don't worry. It'll be fun. Do you know anything about ships?"

"I know they're made of very hard wood that's likely to bruise a girl's ribs when she smashes into the side of them." I rubbed the sore spot on my ribcage.

"See now? You're teaching me things about ships I never knew."

My laughter felt good, all the way to the depths of my soul.

"Want me to teach you about knots?" Wylie offered.

I hesitated. "Why do I need to know about knots?"

"We use them a lot in sailing. You've really never been on a ship?"

"Just a boat with oars. And riverboats. A ferry or two."

"Well, sails need ropes. Ropes need knots."

"In that case"—I grinned—"I'm ready to learn."

CHAPTER FIFTEEN

BRAITH

BRAITH STOOD AT THE END OF A LONG ROW OF CELLS. THEY had been emptied, most of them, but one remained occupied. The one nearest the door. The most torturous location—so close to freedom one might smell it, yet its prisoner remained just as caged as the others.

The queen nodded to Cameria beside her. "Give me a few moments, please, Cameria."

Cameria curtsied. "As you wish, Your Majesty," she said, then she slipped from the dark hallway.

Braith held a single candle close. It flickered at Cameria's departure, threatening to blow out.

Braith shielded the flame and stepped forward. "Dray?"

The straw lining the floor of the cell stirred. "Don't come too close." His voice, but hoarser than it used to be.

Braith took another step forward. "Why not?"

"Because I look dreadful. I can't bear you seeing me like this."

"Honestly, Dray. Are you so vain?"

"I always have been. I don't know why you should be surprised. But do you blame me for feeling out of sorts in here?" He stepped into Braith's candlelight.

Braith gasped. Dray was cleaner than she'd expected. But ever so thin. Gaunt.

"Are they not feeding you?" she asked. "I have ordered humane treatment for all prisoners."

"They are. They bring me soap to wash with and a cloth to clean my teeth. Your orders have been observed." Dray leaned his head against the bars. "Why have you come, Braith?"

Braith did not answer. She regarded him through his cell bars.

"Braith?"

But she couldn't seem to find the words. She looked down at the flickering flame. "I needed to see . . ."

"Me?" Dray frowned quizzically.

"I needed to see how you were. What you were like. When we last spoke—"

"I spilled my heart to you, and you told me I didn't have one."

Braith eyed him warily. "I think I told you it was made of stone, actually."

"Close enough."

"And?" Braith stepped closer so that the light might spill over Dray's face. "I came to see what lives in your eyes now. Are you still made of stone? Has your time here changed you? Are you the same man who committed treason and regicide and used my father, a man of weak will and abominable character? Are you the same man who tried to steal me and the throne of Tir? Or are you someone else?"

Dray was quiet for a moment. "You came to see if I found that redemption we spoke of." He smiled a little. "They are calling for my trial at last."

"Yes."

"And duty will demand you execute me."

Braith's tone sharpened. "I did not say that."

"No, you did not. But do you think you'll have a choice?"

"I don't know."

Dray nodded to the jewel-studded circle of gold once worn

by Queen Frenhin, now resting atop Braith's head. "That crown weighs on you. I'm not sure it suits."

"The crown or the title?" Braith asked.

"Either."

"Nor I." Braith took another step toward Dray so that they were inches apart. "Dray, your crimes must be examined in the full light of the law."

"Harsh light, that."

"Yes. And yet we are all bound to it. Especially me."

"Because you must prove to everyone—the peasantry, your council, the nobles, and most of all yourself—that you are not your father."

Braith lowered her head again. "Perhaps. But also because it is right."

Dray's voice lost its sarcasm. "Release yourself from guilt, Braith. It is not because of your deeds that I find myself in this cell. Those crimes were mine, and I'm ready to answer for them. My soul is mine to trouble over."

Braith's eyes welled. "Yes."

"Do what you must to secure your position, Braith."

Braith's hands trembled. "Very well, Dray."

Then she slipped away from the bars. She hurried from the dungeon, and the flame of her candle snuffed to smoke.

Dray was right, of course. She must bring him to trial, and surely he would die for his crimes, as the law demanded. But his words haunted her. For they were the words of a man whose heart had perhaps changed—a man who cared for her peace of mind. A man who spared a second thought for his own soul.

And now she must sentence him to die.

CHAPTER SIXTEEN

TANWEN

I PLACED MY HANDS ON THE SHIP'S RAIL AND WILLED MY stomach to stop roiling.

Nope. Didn't listen.

I heaved my breakfast—if you could call it that—over the side of the ship. Again.

"Ah, Tannie. Not better yet, eh?"

I couldn't spare Wylie a glance. Because here came another round of fire-roasted fish and biscuits. For the third day in a row.

"You say it'll get better." I wiped my mouth on the back of my hand. "But I don't believe you. Why do you lie to me, Wylie?"

"For laughs?"

"Ugh." I eased down onto the deck and leaned my back against the ship's side. "Wouldn't mind so much if I felt any better after it was over."

"The ship would have to stop rocking, I guess." Wylie sat beside me.

"Also, this food doesn't taste any different coming up than it did going down. How will I possibly manage for weeks on fish and biscuits?"

Wylie smiled. "We've had favorable wind. Meridione was sighted during my watch this morning."

"Truly?"

"Truly."

"I've always dreamed of seeing Meridione. I wonder what they eat for breakfast there."

"Fish."

"Ha." I winced. "Ugh. Wish I had some brisk-leaf paste."

"We all do."

"Sailor Bo-Thordwyan," Mor's voice cut in.

Wylie clambered to his feet in an instant. "Aye, Captain Bo-Lidere."

"Don't you have work to do?" Mor asked. "Surely there's a deck to be swabbed somewhere."

"His watch just ended," I said, glaring up at Mor. "Thought you'd know that, seeing as you're the captain."

Wylie cleared his throat. "I've got things to attend to below-decks." He nodded to us in turn. "Tanwen. Captain."

Then he disappeared. It wasn't the first time Mor had chased Wylie away.

"Well," I said, peeling myself off the deck and collecting my unsteady legs beneath me. "Are you happy? He's gone."

"He's being paid to work."

"And he is working! You act like he neglects his duties to play skipstones with me, or something. He works his watches, then takes breaks, just like everyone else. You're only hassling him because he's my friend."

Mor looked away.

"But I guess I should feel lucky you're even talking to me," I shot.

"Best I steer clear. You know that."

"Yet here you are."

My stomach lurched again just then. I put one hand on the rail and the other over my mouth.

Mor's brow crinkled in what looked like mingled sympathy and amusement. "Still seasick?"

I waited a full minute, until the roiling of my stomach settled. "Aye," I choked.

"Not keen on our ship food, are you?"

I glared at him. "What I wouldn't give for a bowl of porridge right now."

"Well, perhaps you'll get your wish sooner than later."

"Meridione was sighted. Wylie told me."

"I expect we'll make port before nightfall. Or maybe Wylie already told you that too."

A thick silence hung between us.

After a long moment, Mor said, "Well, I best be back."

Then he was gone.

But I couldn't stay too cross, no matter how annoyed or seasick I was. By evening, we would make port in Meridione.

I only hoped Wylie was kidding about fish for breakfast.

I was curled in a ball like a paranoid prickle-back, knees drawn up to my chest as I huddled on deck, wedged between a couple of barrels. My stomach felt better in that position, somehow. It was evening, and I was keeping myself busy with a length of rope Wylie had given me for practice.

"Nice bowline."

I glanced up to find Dylun watching me. "I didn't know you knew how to tie knots, Dylun."

"I don't. I mean, not exactly. I've studied them, of course."

"Of course. Because why wouldn't you study knots you have no intention of ever tying?" I softened my jab with a grin. "Barely seen you for days. How goes the tome-combing belowdecks?"

"Slowly. I only hope we'll be able to find Master Insegno alive and well. And quickly, if possible. He would be able to help."

I untied my bowline and began to practice again. "And what is this cure we're looking for, exactly? No one's told me."

"That's because we're not really sure. I read a number of dead languages, but not fluently. Not like Insegno. This is old stuff we're dealing with, Tannie. Ancient stuff."

"I don't care how old it is, as long as it works." The image of Gryfelle's ashen face popped into my head and stayed there.

"Indeed." Dylun cracked half a smile. "That's the hope."

"Port Bordino!" one of the crewmen shouted from high above.

I could practically feel Dylun suck in his breath. "Port Bordino."

"Home?"

"Yes." He wrung his hands. "In a manner of speaking."

"Dylun." I nodded to his fingers.

Red colormaster paint dripped from his fingertips onto the deck. "Oh. Forgive me." He traced his fingers over one of my barrels instead, and in three seconds flat, crimson flowers like none I'd ever seen covered it. He stepped back, then flicked his fingers toward the barrel. A silver-scaled fish splashed onto the wood in the middle of the flowers.

It was lovely. A colormaster's ten-second masterpiece.

Dylun grinned wider than I'd ever seen him grin. "Home."

Warmil and my father jogged by us.

"Right on schedule!" Warmil declared.

"Tannie, you should go belowdecks," Father added.

"What? No! I'm not going below. This is the first time I'm spotting soil outside of Tir. I can't miss it!"

"Belowdecks, Tannie," Mor said as he strode by.

"No." I glared at him. "I'm part of your crew. I can help up here, Mor."

He met my gaze. He looked resolved but not hostile. "If you're part of my crew, then consider it an order."

"But—"

"Tannie." Father spared me a backward glance. "It's not safe. We don't know how we'll be received."

"No arguments," Mor insisted. "All the women have been sent below."

"I see Aeron in the stern right there!" I pointed. I felt my voice rise shrilly, and I knew it wasn't helping my case. "If Aeron is staying, why can't I? She's no more sailor than I am."

"Aeron is a trained soldier," Mor pointed out. "And it's battle we're concerned with, not sailing."

"Battle?"

Dylun frowned at me. "Tannie, don't be obtuse."

And the way they all looked at me, it told me that's exactly what they thought I was.

My frustration burst from my hand in a silver strand. In another heartbeat, the strand hardened to steel. The blade clattered to the deck at my father's feet. "I'm not useless!"

He didn't even blink. He bent down and picked up the sword. It was a little wonky—bowed slightly, not fine and straight like the guardsmen's. But I'd only made it out of anger, and it'd taken me less time than a sneeze. So there was that.

Father seemed to be considering my blade, and I didn't know if that was a good thing or not. "I don't think you're useless," he said at last.

"Then may I stay?" I glanced at Mor, wondering if the word of the general would override the declaration of the ship's captain. Probably not, strictly speaking, but I guessed in this case, Mor might relent.

Father glanced at Mor and handed the blade to me. "Stay above, but stay close to me. You understand?"

"Aye."

And I would obey. Truly, I would. But guilt pricked at me. Because I should have felt some of the tension crackling in the air. I should have been on my guard, readying for battle, preparing myself for a hostile foe on the shore. We were flying the banner of Tir, after all, and Meridione had no reason to love us.

Or even trust us.

But all I could see was the watercolor sky. The sun setting in pinks and purples and golds over the waves. All I noticed was the turquoise ocean and the way the sunset sparkled off the sea—like the glittering diamonds off the chilly waters of the Menfor back home. But here those sparkles flared seastone-blue and green and violet where the Menfor warmed itself along the Meridioni coast.

And the sand milk-white with not a pebble to be seen.

The only interruption of the natural beauty was the occasional dock jutting into the ocean. And Bordino was supposed to be the Meridioni capital? How could that be? Tir's capital was a flurry of noise and trade and the relentless crush of many people. Bordino's docks were deserted.

Except that knot of armed men over there.

And now I finally came round to what the others saw. What they had feared. For surely those men had seen our Tirian banners, and they crouched ready as our ship glided closer.

Mor and half his crew fussed about the lines and ropes while my father, Warmil, Aeron, and the rest of them fussed about those armed men. Aeron pulled a bowstring taut, and she wasn't alone.

Part of me wondered if this was all necessary. If we only told them we didn't mean harm. That Queen Braith had sent a message of liberation . . .

But I supposed we needed to live long enough to deliver that message. Maybe I should have gone belowdecks.

"Run up the flag of peace," Mor called to one of the sailors.

I had wondered what that plain white sheet was.

"Approaching the bay!" another sailor shouted.

I lost myself again for a moment. I even forgot my

seasickness. I leaned over the rail and gazed straight down to the bottom of the ocean, so clear was the water. Fish glided in schools of hundreds. And not the silver and gray fish we saw back home. Those were here, too, of course, but also bright fish. Fish like flowers.

And then there was something else that nearly made me tumble over the edge into the water.

I stumbled back a step into something solid. The "something solid" was Dylun, for he hovered about, same as me, without a specific job to do just now. "Careful, Tanwen. You'll fall overboard."

"Dylun. What is that?" I pointed to the creature. It circled beneath the ship, then popped up alongside us, then disappeared to the other side. Like it was playing tag.

Dylun cracked another smile. "Trygoni. They like to keep boats company in the shallow water of the bay."

I caught another glimpse of the creature as it passed by our side of the ship. "It's like it's flying in the water."

"It is, in a way. Sailing is what it's called. They're friendly enough with ships, but if you're ever out in the water, mind your toes. They'll sting you." He pointed to the long tail trailing the trygoni. "That's barbed, and it smarts worse than you can imagine."

"Truly?"

"Yes. Well, and the poison will kill you."

"You're always so cheerful, Dylun."

He shrugged. "Facts cannot be cheerful or somber. They just . . . are."

"Well, thanks for the warning. I suppose I'll mind my toes in these Meridioni waters."

"You should mind your toes in all waters."

"Is that a Meridioni proverb?"

"No. Common sense."

I wanted to take a moment to laugh, but just then, the dock

came within spitting distance of the ship, and a fierce shout split the air.

"Chiva ala, smelti!"

I stared blankly, for the words meant nothing to me.

But I didn't need to speak Meridioni to know the men on the dock weren't happy. A moment later, Meridioni swords rang from scabbards and arrows nocked into bowstrings.

It didn't escape my notice that one of those arrows was pointed straight at my heart.

"Tanwen, I said stay close!"

I had never heard Father's voice so loud. I slipped behind him without complaint. He had an arrow in one hand, his bow in the other.

I'd seen him shoot once before, and I knew he could have that arrow nocked, aimed, and released before the Meridioni soldier even thought about loosing his arrow at me.

Still.

It didn't settle my empty stomach to have a pointed missile aimed straight at me. Or my father.

Dylun stepped forward. His words flowed so rapidly I couldn't make out one from the next. Meridioni was a strange, rolling sort of language. But it sang nicely in my ear, even if Dylun was firing it off faster than the beating of a hover-bird's wings.

If those words were meant to have a softening effect on the men on the dock, it didn't seem to be working. The men continued to scowl. Worse, the arrows stayed aimed, ready for loosing, and the swords remained drawn.

I couldn't help but stare at these men. I knew it showed my provincial roots, but I didn't care. Dylun was the first Meridioni I'd ever seen. Those dark-haired Tirians like Mor usually had mixed heritage of some kind, if they could trace it back far enough, but even they were rare enough on the peninsula.

I'd seen Cameria and plenty of palace servants of Meridioni blood since meeting Dylun, of course, but something about this cluster of warriors was striking.

Their uniforms were black and blood-red, their crest a glittering, silver fish. I knew that fish. It appeared in the crowned story I'd once told about Meridione. But it seemed funny to me now, having seen their bright fish, painted in the many colors of the rainbow. Why choose the plain silver for their emblem?

Another shout from the dock sent all thoughts of fish swimming from my mind. The fiercest-looking of the bunch was hollering something to Dylun. Dylun shouted back.

Then he turned to my father. "General, they won't accept our letter from Queen Braith until we prove we mean no harm."

Father nodded. "Aye, I heard."

I was bewildered for a moment. But then I realized of course he spoke Meridioni. He was former First General to the king, after all. He probably spoke half a dozen languages.

Father turned to Mor. "Captain, with your permission, I would like to speak to them."

Mor nodded. "Of course. If you think you can help."

Father's Meridioni sounded as good as Dylun's, though his voice still rasped when he raised it. And I didn't exactly know if the words were correct. It rolled off his tongue the same as Dylun's. I could only make out one thing he said: Yestin Bo-Arthio.

It was those words that seemed to change things. The man at the front and center of the knot of Meridioni warriors held up a hand. "Yestin?" he said in thickly accented Tirian. "Can it be?"

"It is I, Gerrio. You were captain once, but is it commander now?" Father nodded to symbols on the shoulder of the man's uniform. "You have done well in these . . . fifteen years, is it?"

"Fifteen, yes. But you have aged thirty, my friend." The

commander lowered his weapon, and his fellows followed. "I thought you were dead."

"I nearly was. Often."

My heart squeezed at his words.

Commander Gerrio hesitated, and who could blame him? Seeing my father must have been like seeing a ghost.

"I bring you glad news, my friend," Father said. "From Queen Braith."

"Queen, is it?"

"Aye." Father produced a folded piece of parchment with the queen's signet pressed into the wax seal. She'd had her own crest drawn up, and it looked nothing like her father's.

Wise move, that. And besides, the velvet-petal symbol she had chosen fit her perfectly. Much better than Gareth's family crest of a frightening serpent.

Gerrio nodded, and one of his men saw to accepting our ramp as the crewmen lowered it to the dock. I noticed Wylie and Jule at work, and I prayed everything would stay calm. My friends were awfully close to those Meridioni swords just now.

I was fairly useless with the lines and the process of securing the ship. It was the first time we'd made port, after all, and it's not like I was handy with those things in the best of circumstances. But it didn't take long with our crew and the soldiers on the dock working together. Once we were tethered and the ramp secured, Father stepped forward to deliver Braith's letter into the hands of the commander.

Gerrio broke the seal and unfolded the letter. He skimmed it, peered closer, then read it again. Slowly this time.

He glanced up at Father, a hint of shock edging his features. "Is this . . . ?"

"Authentic? Yes."

"But is it . . . I mean, is it true? Gareth has fallen?"

"Aye."

"And his daughter reigns?"

"Aye."

"And she wishes to give us our freedom?"

"Yes. Queen Braith wants you to be Tir's free neighbors again. No longer her subjects."

"I shall . . ." He shook his head, as if that might clear the unbelievable news from it. "I shall have to take this to the Senate. They've had little enough to keep them busy these past thirteen years. But if we are truly free again, Meridioni rule falls into their hands once more."

"Yes." Father nodded once. "Gerrio, our business is not purely political."

"No?"

"We have a sick girl aboard ship. Our Meridioni lad here thinks he knows someone who might help. Do you know a Master Insegno?"

"I have heard his name. A scholar at the *atenne*, is he not?"

Dylun nodded. "That sounds right. And he's alive still?"

"True as I know."

I glanced at Father. "Atenne?"

"University."

Gerrio whistled sharply, and the next thing I knew, Meridioni warriors were climbing aboard our ship.

But not in hostility. They were helping us carry boxes and bags and trunks, barrels to refill with fresh water, and anything else we needed help with.

Including a barely conscious Gryfelle on her mat.

Commander Gerrio continued to stare at Father. "I can hardly believe it. But here you stand. And with this letter."

"The world has turned sideways, has it not?"

"*Se*, my old friend." Then he turned to me. "Welcome to Port Bordino, *ragizzi*."

CHAPTER SEVENTEEN

TANWEN

I PRACTICALLY TRIPPED OVER MYSELF ALL THE WAY INTO Bordino. Who could keep her eyes on her own feet when there was so much to see all around?

Commander Gerrio led us up the white-sand beach, and my feet fairly sank with each step. If I'd thought the sand in Physgot was fine, I'd been dead wrong. This sand melted around my shoes. I resisted the urge to crouch down and feel it between my fingers. Maybe I'd get the chance later. Didn't want to remind everyone just how poorly traveled I was.

Gerrio walked beside Father. They spoke quietly, but per Father's command, I was nearby. Gerrio's brow knitted. "This news of the Tirian queen . . ."

"Hard to comprehend, I know."

"How did Gareth fall? And what is this treason Queen Braith's letter spoke of?" He leaned closer to Father. "It has been confirmed?"

"I was a direct witness to Gareth's confession. He murdered Caradoc and claimed the throne for himself."

Gerrio shook his head, as if in shock. "Gareth has been no friend to Meridione, to say the least. But I did not suspect . . . this."

"Few did."

"Yestin, my friend. Your name is enough to gain access here in Port Bordino because I am here. I do not think you should expect a warm reception elsewhere. Gareth conquered his empire some years ago. Unrest has been growing. His name is reviled the world round, and your banner is Tirian. I would expect hostility."

"I'm counting on it."

He nodded to me. "You would bring your daughter on such a journey?"

Father frowned and glanced at me. "It's complicated. I did not bring her, exactly."

My face burned.

Subject change, please. I cleared my throat loudly. "What's that up ahead?"

Red-rock cliffs rose ahead of us, beyond the beach. Atop the ledges and peaks, I could make out some white structures.

"Meridioni villas." Gerrio pointed out the architecture. "See those columns? That's how you know it was built by a Meridioni. And the arches there. You'll see the designs when we are closer."

He led us to the base of a wide staircase of the same white material as the villas—not marble, as was all over Urian, but like stone covered in thin white plaster.

"Follow me." Gerrio led us up the steps.

Hundreds of them, it seemed. The stairs cut into the red-rock mountainside and up, up, deep into the cliffs.

I glanced over my shoulder at the men and the weavers, everyone loaded with packs and boxes, or else helping carry Gryfelle. At least poor Gryfelle was sleeping through it. I could only imagine being dragged up this cliff on a wobbly litter by a bunch of tired sailors.

"Where shall we stay tonight, Gerrio?" Father asked. "We have coin. It's imperial coin, of course, but it is gold. It could be reminted into Meridioni *solidis*."

"Se." Gerrio nodded. "Your gold will be welcome, even if the stamp on it is not." He paused and seemed to be collecting his breath. We were nearly at the top of the cliffs. "There is an inn near my villa. I can arrange rooms for you there."

"Many thanks." Father nodded back toward Gryfelle. "The girl is very unwell. We will need to find Master Insegno as soon as possible."

"Morning," Gerrio said simply, then continued his trek.

I just about collapsed when we reached the last stair. I didn't have a bag like the others, but I did have a bundle—a blanket, the clothes borrowed from Aeron, and my own traveling dress all rolled up so that I might carry them.

I dropped the bundle on the ground and plunked on top of it. The world swayed before me. I closed my eyes and tried to lean away from the edge of the cliff.

"Tannie?"

I cracked one eye open and found Wylie's concerned face in front of me. "You all right?"

"I thought the seasickness would wane after we got off the ship. In fact . . . my body seems to think we're still on the ship."

He chuckled. "Give it a bit. Takes time to adjust to solid land again."

"Scaling cliffs right after disembarking doesn't help matters."

"Not especially."

I averted my gaze as Mor walked by—purposeful, discussing matters with the men. With my father and Commander Gerrio and Jule and Warmil. Seeing him there made me feel . . . small. Young. Insignificant. Though I couldn't say why. Probably wouldn't have bothered me if things were settled between me and him.

"I usually try to mind my own onions," Wylie said. "But if you ever wanted to talk . . ." He glanced at Mor, then turned back to me.

"Aye." I smiled. "Thanks for that."

He returned my smile. "Come on," he said as he pulled me to my feet. "A little food in your stomach will help."

I grabbed my bundle and followed after him and the others. "As long as it's not fish."

Wylie was right. Food helped, and bless the stars, it was *not* fish that night. Instead, we ate thick pieces of oven-baked maize-meal flatbread piled with sweet tomatoes, shaved pink onions, herbs I'd never tasted, and ribbons of salty cheese and cured meat. It was impossible to eat that and not feel better.

Sleep helped too. So did the feel of the solid earth beneath my feet for a few hours.

An extra couple hours of sleep might have been nice, but I woke with the rising of the sun, as had become my custom on the ship. Used to be my custom in Pembrone. I was raised on a farm, after all. But I'd grown used to slower mornings and breakfast magically appearing at the queen's table in Urian.

I'd become downright citified.

But this morning, I allowed the pink-gold sunshine to rouse me from my dreams. Karlith had knitted me a new shawl on board the *Cethorelle*, for knitting time was still something she had aplenty and I'd left my other shawl back at the inn in Physgot. I wrapped the new one around my shoulders, then slipped into my leather shoes and tiptoed out the curtain-covered doorway of the room where I'd slept.

They weren't so keen on proper doors in Meridione. Instead, their open doorways were covered in long sheets of fabric or leather.

Strange. But they also slept on mats on the floor and cooked in small clay ovens. Things were just different in other parts of the world.

I'd noticed an open courtyard near the inn, which wasn't a

proper inn the way I thought of inns. Just a smattering of rooms laced throughout the plaster-covered buildings that made up the city. Many of those rooms circled this courtyard, where there were benches and flowers and things I wanted to see. I had lacked the energy the night before.

The morning light was still dusky, but I could see the flowers clear enough. Red, and much like those Dylun had painted on the barrels aboard ship. I smiled. They were shaped like bells and unlike any plant I'd ever seen in Tir. I touched the waxy petals, and as I watched, a furry, purplish beetle crawled out of the bell.

"*Coletto* beetle."

I gave a small shriek, and a strand of purple glitter shot from my hand. The strand smashed into the flower bush. About forty coletto beetles scattered from the red bells with an angry buzz and flurry of wings.

I spun around. "Mor!"

He held up his hands and took a step back. "I'm sorry."

"You scared me!"

"Aye, and you scared the colettoes, or so it would seem." He cracked the smallest of smiles. "I really didn't mean to frighten you."

My heart took a moment to return to its normal rhythm. I looked back at the flowers. "Blast." Purple glitter covered the leaves and petals.

"Need to get control of that."

"Aye, thanks." I moved to pass him and return to my room. Didn't need a lecture from him about my story strands or anything else.

"Hey, Tannie."

I skidded to a stop beside him and stared. "Stop it."

"Stop what?"

"What you're doing. You don't get to be Captain Ice Man aboard ship in front of everyone else, then get all squishy when we happen to meet up in the wee hours of the morning next to a bush full of beetles. Or the middle of the night on a fishing jetty. Or any other time. And anyway, what are you doing here? Were you watching me? Spying? Seems strange we keep meeting up like this."

Mor's voice was quiet. "No, of course I wasn't spying on you. I expect it's because neither of us is sleeping well."

"Aye, I suppose there's that. Excuse me." I passed him and prepared to march away.

"Wait. Please."

I stopped but didn't face him. "What is it?"

"I wanted to show you something. If you want to see."

I turned back around. "Where?"

"The atenne. When I couldn't sleep, I decided to go scout it out. When the others are up, we'll go see Master Insegno there. But I found something else." He could barely contain his grin, and seeing him smile made something inside me sting like a million trygoni barbs. "I have to show you."

In spite of myself, I followed him through the courtyard out onto a stone-paved lane that cut through a field filled with wild grass and lots of flowers.

"Try not to murder the rest of the fauna, will you?" he called back to me.

I fought the urge to punch him. "That was *your* fault, not mine."

"It was your strand."

"It was your scare."

He chuckled. "Look. That's the atenne."

A large, white, stone-and-plaster building stood at the end of the pathway. There were the columns Gerrio mentioned as the mark of Meridioni architecture and a lovely arch over the wide doorway in front. It was pretty, sure enough. Quintessentially Meridioni, if Gerrio's descriptions were right. But . . . why did Mor want me to see this?

As if he could hear my unspoken question, Mor nodded up to the top of the building. "See them working up there?"

I hadn't noticed them before, but as we got closer, sure enough, I could see two men toward the top of the building working on the piece of roof that sat atop the columns.

"Are they cleaning it?" I squinted, trying to make out what was happening. "You trying to tell me something? You want me to learn how to clean the tip-tops of the masts aboard ship?"

"Look closer."

And now that we were just beneath the men as they worked, I could see they weren't cleaning at all. They touched their fingertips over the stone—grazing, flicking, swiping. Shaping. And all twenty of their fingertips glowed hot orange.

"They're sculpting the rock," I realized aloud.

"Stoneshapers."

"I . . . I didn't know this was a thing."

"Aye, but you barely knew colormasters or songspinners were a thing a few moons ago."

I stared as the men carved true-to-life images into stone. A scene unfolded beneath their luminous fingertips. A battle with men on horseback on one side of the panel, and ships rolling along the high seas on the other.

"We don't have stoneshapers in Tir," Mor said. "Not that I've heard of, anyway. Meridione has a long history of stoneshapers and colormasters, though they seem to have a lot of weavers in general. Stoneshaping is called *intagli de fascinzi* in Meridioni—literally 'the weaver's glory,' according to Dylun."

"It's beautiful."

"Se," a thickly accented Meridioni voice agreed. An old man stood in the doorway of the atenne smiling at us. He wore what looked like a fine linen bedsheet draped over his body instead of trousers or a shirt. His hair was white as snow and cropped short. "It is beautiful. And no one stoneshapes better than the Meridioni." His gaze wandered over to Mor. "I believe you are looking for me." The accent was thick, but his Tirian was perfect.

"Master Insegno?"

"Yes, Captain Mor Bo-Lidere." He shuffled down the steps to bow and clasp Mor's hand. "And this is?"

"Tanwen En-Yestin."

He took my hand and bowed to me also. "Two storytellers."

He didn't explain himself further or clue us in as to how he could possibly know that, but he retreated back into the gaping doorway. "And where is my old pupil? He is not with you."

"He's back at the inn," Mor said. "I'll fetch him."

"Se. You do that. I will show Tanwen En-Yestin things she has not seen before."

I blinked, startled.

"Follow me, Tanwen En-Yestin."

Mor was already gone, and I supposed that meant he thought I could trust this strange little man. I followed Master Insegno into hallways made of the same material as the rest of the buildings around Bordino—stone and plaster. Lamps filled with golden oil dotted these halls and cast glimmering light on the walls.

I don't know what I expected, exactly. Perhaps a dank little study like the libraries in the palace at Urian. Dust and tomes and firelight. But instead, Insegno brought me through the hallways and into a wide-open room, circular with a domed ceiling ringed in carved sculptures. The top of the dome was cast in frosted glass, and morning sunlight poured through, all over a circular, polished-stone table beneath it.

"Sit, Tanwen En-Yestin."

I obeyed, still unsure what I was doing here.

"Tell me what troubles you."

"I . . . what?"

"You are troubled, are you not? Tell me what is the matter and perhaps I will help."

I stared at him. "Are you some kind of wizard?"

He chuckled and took a seat across the circle from me. "No."

"You knew Mor and I are storytellers. And now you know something is troubling me. Seems like magic to me."

"I was told you are a band of weavers. You are Tirian and so unlikely to be stoneshapers. Your fingers have not taken on the characteristic tinge of a colormaster. You could have been a songspinner except I saw your interaction with a swarm of colettoes as I returned from my prayer walk on the beach this morning. You did so with a purple strand of story. What appears to be magic is mere observation and logical deduction."

My eyebrows rose. "And how do you know something is troubling me?"

"I overheard you and Mor Bo-Lidere fighting."

I laughed. "If you already know what's wrong, why did you ask?"

"Because it is rude to eavesdrop." He folded his hands on the table. "And because I believe something else troubles you."

"I'm ill." Something about this gentle, wise man made me blurt out the truth.

"Like the young lady you have come here to cure."

"Aye."

"And does your captain know?"

"Yes. He knows now, anyway."

"Secrets eat at the soul, Tanwen En-Yestin."

"That's true enough."

He paused. Considered me. "I will share all I know about this cure you seek. I hope it will help you and your dying friend."

I didn't care for his phrasing, but I could tell he meant it kindly. Strange though he was. "Thank you."

"Master Insegno!" Dylun and the others appeared in the circular room just then.

Insegno's smile was warm, but he did not rise. "Navilto Giligato. Sit, my pupil."

Warmil followed Dylun into the room. "Navilto?"

"My birth name," Dylun said as he sat. "Or, my Meridioni birth name, anyway. Dylun is Tirian, you know."

"Yes, I know." Warmil eased into a seat around the table, brow furrowed. "It's just I never thought about you having a Meridioni name. You were born in Tir."

"Yes, but I *am* Meridioni. Surely you didn't fail to notice." Dylun indicated his ink-black hair.

"No, of course. But . . . Navilto? Shall I call you that now?"

Dylun snorted. "Please don't."

"But I shall," Insegno cut in.

Dylun smiled, which was a rare enough sight. "You always did."

Insegno nodded. "And are we all here?" He eyed the whole company.

Mor, Aeron, Warmil, Jule, and Father took seats around the table. A moment later, Karlith bustled into the room.

"I'm sorry." She panted and took one of the remaining seats. "Had to get Zel settled looking after Gryfelle. She had a bad spell this morning."

Gloom fell over the room, sunny though it was, and Mor was most somber of all. This wasn't an idle quest. This was life-or-death, not just some grand adventure, and it was best treated as such.

Master Insegno folded his hands and placed them on the table. "You have come for my help."

"Yes," Dylun said. "Our friend is ill, and I think there might be a cure, if the ancient texts are to be believed. But my knowledge only extends so far. I can't tell what I'm reading anymore. Or if I'm translating correctly. It's been too long."

"Too many years camped in your forest hideaway."

All the weavers from the Corsyth stared at him, for none of us had mentioned our Corsyth hideaway, tucked deep in the Codewig Forest back in Tir.

Insegno smiled. "Do you think gossip does not reach us in Meridione? You are famous, my friends. The weavers who defied a tyrant and lived in secret for ten years."

Father turned to Warmil. "If the weavers of the Corsyth are known, perhaps this helps us make port elsewhere. If others know of your deeds, they may trust our message."

"It may help," Insegno said. "But do not forget the long years of oppression under Gareth Bo-Kelwyd. The Tirian banner is an unwelcome sight the world over."

"Has news of the liberation been told in Meridione yet?" Dylun asked. "It didn't seem so when we spoke to Commander Gerrio yesterday. Queen Braith's emancipation is genuine. I know the queen myself and would not vouch for her if she were anything like her father."

Insegno leaned back and looked at his former pupil. "These are matters for our Senate to ponder. You always did love politics, Navilto, and I see time has not changed you in that regard. For me, I care little for such things. The matters of the past concern me more than the present."

"And this is why we have come to you, Master Insegno. Please, tell us. Is there hope for our ailing friend? Help me understand the texts I've found."

Dylun placed several old tomes I recognized from the Urian palace library onto the table, but Insegno made no move to open them.

"I do not need your books, Navilto Giligato. What I have to tell you is stored here." He pointed to his temple.

Then he rose and began a measured stroll around the circular room, his fingers tented and his eyes straight ahead, as though he were alone, speaking to himself.

"The whispers of a cure you have found are real enough. They hearken back to the time of the ancients—a time when the weaver gifts were much changed from what one witnesses in Tir or Meridione today. A mere thirteen years of suppression has altered the landscape of Tirian weaving in ways you could not possibly recognize, so young were most of you when Gareth Bo-Kelwyd rose to power. So how could you fathom the days of the ancients, when the gifts were truest and purest?"

Mor opened his mouth as if to answer, but Father held up a hand.

Insegno went on. "Weavers were held in great esteem in the ancient days. The gifts they practiced were prized. Revered. Respected. Master weavers from all around the world held council each year. They created together and used their gifts to solve many problems plaguing the world. Disease. Blight. Ailments of the heart, mind, and body. The master weavers were powerful, to be sure, but they used their gifts with respect to the Source of such treasures. Acknowledgment of the Source has been all but lost today, but then . . . yes, then they understood.

"There was an ancient curse much like the one you describe in the young ladies."

I held my breath, then, for he had spoken in plural, and I wondered if anyone would notice.

But no one seemed to. Or if they did, they didn't interrupt him.

"I do not know for certain if it is the same, but it *sounds* the same. *Vashtith*, the ancients called it. It has not been seen in the world for some time, but if anything could return ancient curses to the world, it is a king like Gareth Bo-Kelwyd the Usurper."

Insegno stopped walking a moment, but still he didn't look at any of us. "Gareth Bo-Kelwyd is not the first to disrupt the natural order, of course. You understand? There is a reason the gifts do not exist as they once did, for power cannot keep company alongside man and not become corrupt. In the ancient days, some weavers became drunk on their own abilities. And other people sought to exploit the weavers. The council convened, and the masters voted to dim the glory of the weavers. And to obliterate the world's cures."

Mor rose to his feet. "Then they're gone?"

Dylun pulled Mor down by his shirtsleeve and shot him a look. "Don't interrupt. Trust me."

Master Insegno continued. "The master weavers knew better than to try to destroy the cures. The release of that power could be catastrophic. If such a thing could even be accomplished in the first place. No, instead they broke up the cures."

I bit down hard on my tongue. I wanted to ask the scholar what the cures were. It sure sounded like he was talking about a physical object of some kind—something tangible to be held or broken apart or put back together. But I heeded Dylun's warning and held my peace.

"The masters scattered the pieces of the cures to the corners of the world. They no longer practiced the arts as they once did. 'Dimmed the glory' was the way they phrased it, as they had decided was best for humankind. But though they did this, they retained the basics of their crafts and still passed on that knowledge to their apprentices.

"Storytellers still sought to capture the narrative of life, to make connections between events of the past and the present and to speculate about the future. They sought to make sense of the world around them and of human experience and immortalize those truths in sparkling crystal."

Insegno resumed his stroll, but now his hands were not tented like a dignified scholar's. He waved them as he spoke about the weaving gifts, and colored ribbons of story swirled from his fingers.

"Songspinners still sought to express the deepest, truest, rawest emotions of the human heart. Though the ancient powers were diminished, the spinning of songs still brought light to the soul, comfort in times of sorrow, hope to those who despaired."

Insegno's strands collected together in a swirling mass of dancing lights above the circular table. I didn't even need to strain to hear whispers of music coming from the lights, unlike any music I'd ever heard in Tir. Was it Meridioni? Was it some ancient melody Insegno had pried from his crumbling scrolls? When I watched the flashes of purple, green, blue, gold, pink, and orange, my soul soared.

"Colormasters still taught their young ones the triumph of self-expression—the importance of capturing a moment, whether as it looked or as it felt. Apprentice colormasters learned to see beauty where no one else could and to ensnare that beauty in paint and pigment—a single moment of truth and expression turned static. Permanent."

Insegno's strands of story and music froze in midair. After a pause like a breath, the strands collapsed to the tabletop in a splash of glorious color.

I gasped and leaned back in my chair, struck by the beauty. And half expecting to be doused with paint.

But spanning the entire table was a Meridioni sunset like the one I'd seen the previous night. This time, I was viewing it from above. The setting sun was cast upon the tile-roofed houses clustered among the red-rock cliffs of Bordino. Purple and pink, orange and yellow bathed the white walls. Liquid-gold oil lamps glowed here and there, and blue shadows swallowed the farthest cliffs.

It was breathtaking. Perfect. And he had made it from . . . a story and a song?

I looked up to find Insegno smiling at me, the childlike delight of a weaver whose work is truly appreciated. I knew that delight.

Jule let out a low, slow whistle. "These weaver gifts still look pretty powerful to me."

"Ah," Master Insegno said, holding up a finger, "you only think so because you know nothing of the ancient gifts." He gestured to his creation. "This is human expression—beautiful, yes. A gift, assuredly. But in the old days, there was power in the strands, direct from the Source. It was a reflection of the Source, true and perfect. And those strands looked like—"

"Blinding white light," I realized aloud.

Insegno spun toward me and stared. "Yes," he said at last, his eyes narrowed.

"Master Insegno," Warmil cut in. "Is this sorcery you're speaking of? I've never heard of anything like it in my studies."

"No, not sorcery, Captain Warmil Bo-Awirth. It is power from the Source, as I told you. Of a different realm—spiritual, though not evil. But make no mistake. This is a dangerous, dynamic artifact you hope to recreate. You are meddling with something much deeper, much more real, than sorcery."

"So it *is* a physical object," I said. Insegno seemed to be done with his solo lecture and open to answering our questions now, so I took my chance.

"It *was* an object," he corrected. "Now it is broken apart in living strands. Scattered. Each piece buried and concealed. The masters did not want them to be found, so seductive was their power. You will have a difficult task to locate each and bring them together once more. It will stretch even my abilities to create a map for you."

Mor hopped up again. "But you'll try?"

"Se. I will try. We begin today. But first"—he rubbed his hands together—"we shall eat."

Warmil grunted. "Just like a Meridioni. Always about their stomachs."

"Warmil Bo-Awirth," Insegno answered, "if I had to eat Tirian food every day, I would not wish to recline at the table long, either."

Father stifled his laugh with a cough. "Yes, let's eat and then we will begin."

Everyone filed out of the room, but I lingered, gazing at Insegno's sunset.

"You have seen the power of which I speak." Insegno's voice was quiet.

"I . . . think so. Art has a way of revealing truth, Karlith said. I always thought of the white light as truth."

"Se. Something is stirring. Power that hasn't been seen in many centuries."

"And we're poking it with a big stick." A dull ache pulsed at the base of my skull and spread like ink over the back of my head. "Master Insegno, are we . . . that is, are we making a mistake?"

Insegno never pulled his gaze from my face. "Everything from the Source is good, including this power. But the sad truth is that all good things are corrupted by weak men."

"Aye." I knew he was right, and it sure didn't settle my spirit. After a moment of silence, I turned to leave.

But Insegno reached out and gripped my arm. "Beware, Tanwen En-Yestin. Where there is great light and true power, always nearby lurks the darkness."

Then he released me and strode from the room. Just in time for a bubble to pop in my head and remind me of my curse.

Darkness, indeed.

CHAPTER EIGHTEEN

NAITH

Naith waited in the cold, still temple. Master said it would be any day, any moment, but Naith felt he had been waiting forever. Nearly a week now.

Not that Naith doubted. Not anymore. The Master knew their business better than he, and Naith was beginning to feel the familiar comfort of complete trust in his shadowy Master again.

Naith brushed a speck of dust from a carved stone idol of Noswitch, the goddess of the night.

He had been a faithful servant. Far more faithful than Dray, who never really believed in the Master. That man believed in nothing. Naith had been more faithful even than Gareth, who had truly thought the Master divine. A god.

Or . . . goddess? Naith eyed the feminine curves of Noswitch's statue but shook the thought from his mind. He'd long ago given up trying to figure it out. The Master wished secrecy of identity, and secrecy the Master would have. Naith was powerless against the Master's magic, and he knew it.

Just to test the new trick, Naith flexed his fingers as he and the Master had practiced all week. Wisps of inky smoke curled from his fingertips—power by proxy. Not his own ability, but a borrowing of the Master's, so to speak. He had been warned not to practice often. Such careful manipulation of idea strands had taken years for the Master to perfect, and still it drained the Master. Having to proxy it to Naith? Doubly draining. But Naith had been given some allowance. After all, to pull off the deception, Naith's performance would need to be flawless.

The door to the sanctuary flew open.

The priest calmed his heart with one long, slow breath.

"Oh. Sorry." The lad in the doorway scratched the back of his neck. "Didn't know someone would be in here."

"Sit, my son." Naith gestured to a padded bench on the opposite side of the altar.

The boy sat like a great boulder coming to rest after a long trip down a mountainside.

This might be easier than Naith had thought.

"You are troubled."

The lad looked up. "Aye. You could say that."

"A broken heart."

The lad's eyes widened. "How'd you know?"

Naith pushed as much warmth into his smile as he could muster. "The goddesses reveal things to me."

The lad's gaze dropped. He fumbled with something in his lap and was silent for several moments. "Can I tell you something, Your Eminence? Something secret that might've got me in a mess of trouble a few moons ago?"

"Of course, my son."

"I'm not sure I've ever believed in the goddesses."

Naith didn't bother feigning shock or outrage as he would have done a few moons ago. "Ah, yes. Many peasants have felt the same and have not dared say anything until now. Now that our world has been turned upside down, most unpleasant."

"Is it unpleasant?" The lad frowned. "Seems like a false king being overthrown ain't a bad thing."

"Does your life seem better since Gareth was deposed?"

"No, but that's something else entirely." He folded his arms across his chest. "That ain't got nothin' to do with royalty."

Naith smiled again and produced a loaf of ceremonial bread from the shelf beneath the table. "Eat, my son."

The boy looked concerned. "Are we supposed to?"

"I am High Priest of the Tirian Empire, son. If the food sacrificed to the goddesses is not for me, who would it be for?"

"High Priest?" The lad's throat bobbed. "Flying fluff-hoppers. I didn't know, Your Holiness."

"You have nothing to fear. Shall I show you something? Perhaps it will restore your faith in the power of the unseen."

Naith made a great show of flexing his fingers again. Black smoke curled from Naith's fingertips once more, and this time, Naith pretended as though the smoke were speaking to him.

"You loved a girl."

"Still do."

"She . . ." Naith trailed off, leaned his ear toward the smoke. "She has used you badly."

"Don't know if it's fair to phrase it like that, exactly . . ."

Naith paused. Closed his eyes, pretending to divine the truth from the smoke. Really, he gave the Master a moment before the finale of this charade.

Then came the loud, dramatic cry. "Anwyl's heart!" Naith threw one hand forward as he called a goddess's name, and the smoke turned to lightning.

A bolt zapped the lad's wrist. Two leather engagement bands sizzled and dropped to the floor. The boy nearly fell backward off the bench.

"She's left you," Naith said, as though the smoke, the lightning, or the goddess herself had spoken it to him. "Your betrothed has left you . . . for another."

The lad's face crumpled. "It's true, then. I knew it, of course. Why else would she jump aboard that ship, last second. She *has* left me for that . . . that . . ."

"Sailor."

"Pirate, more like!" There was such pain and rage in the

boy's words, it was all Naith could do to keep his satisfaction in check.

Far, far too easy.

"Oh, my son." Naith came around the altar, and though it cost him a bit of pride, he lowered himself beside the boy. "We shall set it all to rights. Your heart, the pirate, and this upside-down world."

The lad frowned. "What do you mean?"

"Do you think it coincidence you came here this afternoon?"

He shook his head, as if it were full of chaff. "I don't know why I came. I felt . . . pulled here, somehow, though I never visit the temple. I can't explain it."

"You do not need to. I understand. For you *were* pulled here by something quite a lot bigger than yourself. Something . . . divine."

"Divine?"

"Indeed. If you did not believe before, you will soon. Trust me, Brac Bo-Bradwir."

He gaped. "I don't understand. How did you—?"

"Ah, Brac." Naith put his hand on top of the lad's blond head. "You do not understand yet. But you will come to see the truth soon."

"Wha—?"

"You, my son, are the Chosen One, and you will save Tir."

CHAPTER NINETEEN

BRAITH

QUEEN BRAITH SAT LIKE A STATUE ON HER THRONE BEFORE the council table.

She had put it off long enough, and now it was time for the most dreaded of announcements. Nothing in her newborn reign had been so potentially explosive as this—not her father's murder, not even the announcement of her ascension to the throne of Tir.

"If we are through with our court business for the day, I have something I wish to say."

Sir Fellyck and the other councilmembers fell silent and stared at the queen. If only Yestin Bo-Arthio's kind, fatherly gaze were among them.

"As you know, I have sent my councilman General Yestin Bo-Arthio on an ambassadorial mission. He and those accompanying him set sail from Tir over a week ago, and I would like to tell you what their business was about."

Braith took a deep breath. Her voice was firm.

"I have emancipated the countries and territories my father conquered. Meridione, Haribi, Minasimet, and the Spice Islands are free. We are no longer the Tirian Empire. We are simply the Kingdom of Tir, as we once were."

Half the council jumped to their feet. Raucous shouts arose from every corner of the room.

"Why, Majesty?" a councilman called. "Why would you do such a thing?"

Braith rose and held up her hands. "Your queen commands silence."

The clamor died down.

She turned to the councilman. "It is because my father's conquests were not right. He spilled Tirian blood and the blood of our neighbors to satisfy his lust for land. And what has it brought us? What has it brought *you*, my fellow Tirians? Wealth? Fortune? Health? Happiness? Our peasants are starving. Our own territories are unstable. My call as your queen is to address these problems for you—for *us*—not to fill my palace with slaves, my table with imported foods, and my treasury with foreign gold."

She lowered her hands and scanned the room. "Do not let my father's affinity for conquest become your own. Realize that he gained much while Tir's people gained little and our neighbors suffered greatly. We get to decide what the Tir of the future will look like. Let this be the first step toward a better way of living—the first step toward a better Tir."

Braith stood in silence now, as though awaiting a hail of arrows from an execution squad.

But the arrows did not come. The court did not form a mob. They did not rush her throne or arrest her.

One by one, the councilmen sat. The ladies at court resumed fanning themselves, and the lords stood silently and expectantly, as though simply waiting for the next agenda item.

Braith pondered them. Could it be they truly heard her? Could it be that, for once, they understood her heart and didn't find it wanting?

Perhaps there could be a different Tir—something better than had ever existed before. Something that could reflect the values Braith had always longed to see her countrymen hold as dearly as she did.

Perhaps she would get to be the queen she had always dreamed of being.

She lowered herself back onto her throne and turned to one of her governors. "Orellwin."

The Governor of the Western Wildlands bowed. "Yes, Majesty?"

"How are the silver mines of Clofay yielding these days?"

"Oh. Ah . . ." He shook his head, obviously surprised by her query. "Tolerably well, Your Majesty."

"Good. I should like to commission a new circlet." Braith removed the jewel-studded gold crown that had belonged to her mother. "This was Queen Frenhin's, and it's the crown of an empress—the empress of an ill-gained empire. I should like something simple and fine, something that befits the Queen of the Kingdom of Tir."

Orellwin bowed low to the ground. "It would be my honor, Your Majesty."

Braith was surprised as others began to bow. Not all, and some perhaps because they felt pressure to do so. But many nobles and officials around the room lowered their heads to her. The peasants might riot when they heard of the emancipation, but it seemed perhaps she had won over the nobles. At least for now.

Braith smiled, relieved. "Thank you. Together, we shall dream about what the future of Tir might hold."

And she prayed that it might be so.

CHAPTER TWENTY

TANWEN

I LEANED BACK AND DRUMMED MY FINGERS AGAINST THE plaster wall outside the room where the others spouted opinions around a half-finished map.

"Yes, I agree," my father's voice carried to where I stood. "It's definitely the Ancient Meridioni word for Haribi, but see this character here? I think that means north."

"Northwest, I think." Warmil's frown could be heard in his words. "Unless that mark changes things."

"It does," Master Insegno said. "Northeast, and lucky for you. If it were northwest, you would be docking in Haribi and traveling many leagues overland to Haribi's western coast. The sea north of Haribi is too rough for most ships."

"Traveling overland takes longer. That's time we don't have to spare," Mor said.

"Nor do we have the proper supplies for such a journey." Dylun sighed. "That is one bit of luck in our favor. It appears the ancient masters kept largely to the coasts when hiding these strands."

"Perhaps they did not have the threat of death looming over them," Insegno said, "but they did have threats of other kinds. It would not surprise me if the strands are located in places you find convenient."

"Convenient would have been if they'd not destroyed the

cure in the first place." Mor. Angry. Frustrated. The sound of a heavy book smacking shut punctuated his sentence.

"They did not destroy it," Master Insegno reminded him. "They only broke it apart. It, and many others like it, for the abuse of the weavers' power was great. You do not understand how dangerous it was because you have not seen the full measure of the ancient strands. And you are bitter and frustrated about your personal situation with these two sick *ragizzis*. It is clouding your perception of this journey."

Heavy silence followed that observation.

"Two sick girls?" Dylun cut in. "Then it's true that . . ."

He didn't finish his sentence. I wanted to step into the room and change the subject. But my head still ached. Three more little "bubbles" had popped since the one that morning with Master Insegno. I didn't know what it meant, exactly, but all I could think of was the time I saw Gryfelle have a full-blown fit in the Corsyth, when treasured knowledge of the healing arts slipped from her mind before my eyes.

What was I losing when those little bubbles popped in my head? Or when I had full-blown fits? And would I even know enough to miss it? Gryfelle always said it was sadder for us to watch it than for her to live it, because she didn't remember all she had lost.

"Yes, Tanwen is cursed," Mor finally spat.

And his words stung like drops of poison all over my skin. As if he hated me for complicating his already-messy life.

I pushed myself from the wall and rounded the corner into the stifling air of the gathering I'd stepped into the hallway to escape.

"Aye." I tried to keep my voice firm, but it was shaking. "It's true. Seems I didn't meet you all soon enough. Apprenticed under Riwor too long, practicing those blasted crowned stories too often, and it was too late by the time you got me to the

Corsyth. And now I have what Gryfelle has, and I guess we'll both die if we can't figure out how to finish drawing this map."

"Is there an indication of a landmark?" Mor spoke as though I hadn't just mentioned my death and Gryfelle's death or admitted to the room I was sick. "If there's a landmark of some kind, that would help a lot once we get to the Haribian plains."

Warmil shared an uncomfortable glance with Dylun, and my father's eyes remained steadily on me. Commander Jule's brows rose, and Aeron looked like maybe she wanted to give me a hug. I just glared at Mor. My warm, smirky sea captain who told me never to change had been replaced completely by this cold, unfeeling man on a mission.

"Yes," I said, hopping back up to my feet. "Let's see about that blazing landmark, and then maybe we can plot out a course directly off the edge of the blasted map while we're at it."

I spun toward the door, ready to make a big, flouncy exit. Instead, the room around me ripped to shreds. I inhaled to scream, but my cry was choked off by a blanket of darkness, wrapped all around me in half a heartbeat.

My body dropped to the floor. The impact jarred my bones, but I didn't feel pain.

It was happening again. I lay on the ground and wondered if I could control it, somehow. I knew what was happening. I had accepted that this was what those fits of mind-wiping looked like from the inside.

Could I choose what I lost?

I rose and turned a slow circle in the blackness. I tried to take a step, but everything wobbled. It was like I was back on the ship, except worse. Like the world was made of pudding. I didn't venture another step. I waited for the silvery strands of memory to begin spinning by, out of my head forever.

Apparently, it wouldn't be my choice. Of all the memories that might have zipped by me, the one the curse chose was from my childhood.

A silver strand snaked toward me, ribboned around my body, and swirled over the top of my head.

Tanwen En-Yestin was a very lonely little girl without her nursemaid's company, until she made friends with her new adoptive sibling.

As the words swirled around me, a picture unfolded, like I was watching back the memory. Two little blond heads bounced by as we ran through the fields—me six years old, he eight.

The shadowy image of me giggled and pushed harder to keep up. Were we racing?

No. Chasing a fluff-hopper. A tiny white one we'd stumbled upon in Ma-Bradwir's garden. It had been eating her greens while it stalked a larger snack—one of the Bradwirs' new puppies. We'd tried to catch it and it had bitten me, a tiny nibble, for this fluff-hopper must have been a very young baby.

Then it had taken off, and we after it, through Farmer Bradwir's grain fields.

"Got it!" the boy shouted, and he held the tiny ball of curly white fluff in cupped hands.

I squealed in delight, and a strand of pink light burst from my palm. "If only it were pink, it would grant all your wishes!" As I said these words, the pink light bunched together and popped into a clear pink-crystal fluff-hopper figure.

A little lopsided, I could see now. But the boy looked impressed.

"Sakes," he said. "You did that."

"Aye." I stroked the head of the real fluff ball, snatching my fingers away just in time to escape another bite. "So?"

"It was like magic."

Little me laughed. "Race you back!"

Then I took off, and the boy after me.

What was his name?

Only blankness answered me. No recollection, no

recognition. I knew I had known this boy once—and that I knew him still. But in that moment, I couldn't grasp his name.

The image of the boy ran past me in the blackness. He laughed and tossed his blond hair from his eyes.

"Brac," I said aloud to the ghost boy. "Brac!"

A wave of sorrow hit me. It was my accidental betrothed, the one who had been so frustrating and thickheaded and controlling lately but with whom I had shared my lifetime.

"No!" I cried. "I don't want to forget him." I reached for the shadowy image, but it was too far away. And not solid, in any case. "I don't want to forget this Brac—the boy who was my brother. Please!"

But the images of me and Brac as children and the silver strands of memory were gone. Darkness swallowed me, and my tears were my only company.

A pinprick of light invaded my senses. Then it grew to a streak and widened until the whole room came into view, and then finally into focus.

I won't lie. I expected to see Mor's face, first thing. I expected him to be crouched over me, calling my name and cradling my head so I might not slam it against the ground, same as he had done for Gryfelle many times.

Instead, my father was there, and so was Aeron. It was she who held me with Warmil beside her, his arm around her shoulders. I could see then that Aeron was crying. How long had I been fitting? Had it been gruesome to watch, whatever my body had been doing?

Master Insegno must be near, for I heard him speaking in rapid Meridioni.

I sat up slowly with Father's help. My head spun and threatened to split in two. But I looked around anyway. Mor was nowhere to be seen. He had left the room at some point.

At that moment, it truly sank in. Not only was I going to die, but when I did, Mor might not even notice.

CHAPTER TWENTY-ONE

TANWEN

I traipsed down the white steps onto the Bordino beach. I needed to see something other than the inside of the room I'd been trapped in for a week now. Something other than the inside of the atenne, actually, because if I had to hear Master Insegno, Dylun, Warmil, and Father argue over the curvature of this character or the description of that landmark for one more minute, I was going to scream.

Mor had been scarce all week, and I couldn't decide if I preferred it that way or not. Probably for the best, as the captain himself would say.

But now I wanted air and light and some pleasanter company. So, I padded across the white sand to where the crewmen worked along the shore among scattered shells, driftwood, and clumps of beached seaplants. They had set up a collection of crates and boxes and barrels to sit upon, and it seemed they had almost created a proper workshop.

"Ho, Wylie." I sat on an unoccupied barrel beside Wylie.

"Ho, Tannie." He grinned. "Barely seen you in days."

"We've been busy." I dragged my toes through the sand. "I thought this whole journey-mapping thing would take a day or two with all the progress they made the first day." I picked up a coil of rope. "Turns out they were just 'rough-sketching' things, and now they get to argue about the finer points, exact locations, and specifics of long-dead languages until we grow old and our teeth fall out."

"That long, eh?"

"Gryfelle is running out of time."

It didn't need saying. That dark cloud hung over us all the time, a constant threat as we worked to make progress. And still, I needed to voice it. To vent my frustration.

I glanced down at the rope I'd picked up. "Hey, what are we doing with these?"

"Cleaning them." He dipped his rope in a bucket of water. "We rinse off the salt in fresh water and lay them out to dry in the sun. Keeps them nice and healthy."

"Maybe that would work with me and Gryfelle."

"Dunk you both in buckets of water and lay you out in the sun to dry?"

"The cure of the ancients!"

Wylie laughed, but then his smile faltered. "How have you been feeling?"

I shrugged. "Fine, I guess. Haven't had any more . . . spells or fits, or whatever you want to call them."

"Captain seems worried."

"Aye, Gryfelle's his lass," I answered, a little too quickly.

Wylie didn't press matters further. Bless that lad. He just leaned over and adjusted the way I was dunking the rope.

I sighed. "Can't I even wash rope right?"

"Apparently not."

"Hey, Wylie?" I said suddenly.

"Hmm?"

"I'm glad you're here." I meant it with all my heart.

Wylie leaned back and looked at me.

"Aeron really tries," I continued. "She tries to be there for me, but I think it's hard. She watched Gryfelle get sick, so it seems like she's keeping her distance with me. It's too much to watch it all over again, I suppose. And besides that, Aeron is . . ." But I didn't really know how to phrase it.

"Aeron is Captain Bo-Lidere's friend first?" Wylie suggested.

"Aye. Aeron belongs to Mor. They've been friends a hundred times longer than she and I have, so if Mor and I are at odds, it puts her in a spot. I guess." I shook the rope gently in the water, trying to copy Wylie's easy movements. "I'm just saying I'm glad to have a friend. A friend who's fun and doesn't mind me hanging around."

He smiled. "Glad to be your friend, Tannie. Truly." Then he looked down at my rope. "Really, you're terrible at that."

"How can I possibly be doing it wrong? I'm doing it just like you."

"You're agitating it too much."

"*You're* agitating it too much."

We settled into a comfortable silence where I watched him wash the ropes and didn't bother trying to help, and he didn't get offended that I wasn't helping.

After he'd gotten through several more lengths of rope, I said, "I think I'm ready to be back aboard ship."

"Tired of Meridione?"

"No."

"Miss the roasted fish?"

I wrinkled my nose. "No."

"What, then?"

"I just want to feel like we're *doing* something."

He nodded. "That makes sense."

"I need to go see her."

"Gryfelle?"

"Aye."

"I'm sure she'd like that. See you later, Tannie." Wylie nodded to me once, then returned to his ropes in silence.

Gryfelle's room was through an old stone archway where the white plaster had crumbled who knew how many centuries before. I wondered why they didn't replaster it, but I was glad they hadn't. The stones were beautiful in their own way, and they reminded me of Tir somehow.

A breezy curtain made of nearly sheer, pale-green fabric covered the doorway. Karlith hummed just inside. After a pause, I drew the curtain aside and went in.

"Tannie!" Karlith's eyes lit up, and she set her knitting aside. "It's good to see you here."

Gryfelle stirred slightly, but her eyes didn't open.

"Ho, Karlith. How goes it?"

"Gryfelle's morning has been good."

I looked at the still, ashen body before me and couldn't fathom Karlith spoke truth. "Has it?"

"Aye. She's not had a spell in a full day now, and her fever is down."

"That's good." And it was, of course, but it pained me that the bar for health was so low for Gryfelle these days. "Has she been awake at all?"

"A little. She took some broth earlier."

"I wonder if she's as glad as I am to have something other than fish."

The sound of a slow, labored breath startled me. "I think it was fish broth this morning," Gryfelle said, her eyes fluttering open. She smiled slightly. "Hello, Tanwen."

"You're awake!" I sounded too bright. Too falsely cheerful. But I didn't know how to act. How are you supposed to be around someone who could pass from this life at any moment?

"Yes," she said slowly. "Mostly."

I sat beside her bed. "Sorry they're bringing you fish broth. Least we could have real broth if we're to be stuck here so long."

"It was shellfish, I think. Tasted like the sea. But I didn't mind."

"I always thought shellfish looked like the bugs of the ocean."

She smiled. "Yes, they do. Quite."

If it were possible, Gryfelle had gotten paler than she was when we arrived in Meridione. She'd had light golden hair and fair skin as long as I'd known her, but now her hair was white and her face almost green. What had once been high, delicate cheekbones now looked like sharp peaks above the sunken valleys of her cheeks. She looked to be a living skeleton.

"Gryfelle . . ." I bit back my tears. "They're trying really hard. We all are. They're working on the map every second."

"I know, Tanwen."

"They're going to find these strands and put them back together and make the cure."

She took another long, slow breath. "I do hope they will find the cure."

After a moment, Gryfelle was asleep again.

Something inside me began to boil. It started in my gut, then spread throughout my whole body. I felt my fingertips begin to warm, but I willed the wild strands not to shoot from my hands.

Still. I was fired up.

I didn't give Karlith a proper good-bye. I flew from the room and stormed toward the atenne, toward those scholars and learned men and world travelers who couldn't seem to make a proper map in a timely manner.

I burst into the discussion room like I meant it. Conversation ceased immediately, and I didn't give anyone the chance to ask questions. "Look. I know you're doing your best."

Many pairs of eyes snapped to me. Including Mor's. He was sitting at the table beside Dylun.

"You simply have to move faster," I continued. "Gryfelle can't get sicker while we argue about this word or that, fuss over the different interpretations of one Old Tirian phrase or another Ancient Meridioni proverb. Enough. Let's finish this map and *go*. Surely I'm not the only one who can't endure another minute of waiting."

Dylun spoke up. "Actually, Tanwen, the map is complete. We believe we've identified the locations of all the strand fragments."

"Oh." I shifted my weight awkwardly. I sure did know how to make an entrance. An exit? Not so clear.

"But we're puzzled by this one phrase, and until we get it, we won't be able to start. This phrase holds the key to our first strand, here in Meridione." He frowned and shook his head at the scroll before him. "None of us, with all our combined learning, can figure out these words. And I don't know where else to turn."

Even Master Insegno looked a little ruffled. "I believe my Ancient Meridioni to be fluent. But this phrase puzzles me."

I don't know why I did it, for I'd not been any help in the work of translation or map reading, or really anything else except fetching bitter-bean brew and tea all these days. I hadn't had any proper schooling, after all. But I walked over to the table and peered over Dylun's shoulder to get a look at the troublesome phrase.

"Rock pile," I said immediately.

Everyone turned to look at me once more.

"I mean . . ." I trailed off, suddenly self-conscious. "I'm not sure if that's what it means here. But that phrase. That's *rock pile*."

Warmil stared at me. "How do you know?"

"There's a saying we use in the country. I guess it must be Old Tirian, though I never thought about it. *Un lail napil craig*. It means, 'You're dumber than a rock pile.' I must've said it to Brac a thousand times. Isn't that the same thing here? *Pil craig*?" I pointed to the words that looked to me like they could be nothing other than *rock pile*.

"Se." Master Insegno's eyes lit up. "I know the place of

which this speaks. A day's journey northwest, in the foothills of the Orlos, there is a grouping of stones thought to be a place of worship for the ancients—an altar of sorts."

I shrugged. "Sacred rock pile. That works."

"Then that's where we begin," Dylun said, rolling up his scroll and turning back toward me. "Extraordinary."

My cheeks heated, but at least it wasn't my fingertips.

"I said she would do nicely when we first met Tanwen, didn't I?" Dylun's eyes twinkled. "I guess sometimes a Tirian farm girl is just what's needed."

CHAPTER TWENTY-TWO

TANWEN

AN ENTIRE DAY OF TREKKING NORTHWEST TO A PILE OF ancient rocks didn't sound like a party, but at least we were moving.

Or . . . would be, once we found Mor.

We had spent a whole day preparing. The *Cethorelle's* crew had helped us pack several donkeys with bedrolls and food and water, and anything else we might need for our journey. We lined a cart with cushions and blankets and hitched a donkey to it, since poor Gryfelle had to travel with us. Karlith protested at first, but something about the way we had to retrieve this living artifact strand required a songspinner, and she was the only one we had handy.

Master Insegno said the rock pile was a day's journey one way, so we would have to spend a night out in the Meridioni wilderness. Surely that seemed unkind to Gryfelle, but we didn't have a choice. So sleeping under the stars it would have to be.

And I'd forgotten to ask if they had mountainbeasts around here.

Commander Jule was coming with us, and I'd convinced my father it would be a great idea to have a handful of crewmen around to help care for the animals and set up camp, which was certainly true. But mostly I just wanted to have Wylie along for his easy company.

All was ready, and the sun was up, but Mor was nowhere to be found.

Zel shrugged and popped the last of his steamed maize cake into his mouth. "Tannie, Mor ain't hardly been sleeping. He's barely eating. He's twisted up bad—about all of this. I guess he just needed a moment away. He'll be back."

Memories of Mor's steely glares and hard words snapped back to me.

I rubbed my temples. I couldn't tell anymore which of us was less reasonable, me or Mor. Was I in the right? What were we even fighting about? Sometimes it all blurred together into a soupy fog of bitterness and strife.

I hated it.

"I'm going to go look for him," I said to Zel.

"Are you?"

"You sound surprised."

"It's just—"

"We've been avoiding each other. I know. But we really need to get going. And since I'm not otherwise occupied . . ." I let the rest of that sentence die and rose to my feet. "I'll be back."

I selected one of the stone-paved pathways at random. They all wove through the hillside streets of Bordino in such a way that everything was connected. No matter which I chose—and no matter where Mor was—I'd be able to cover the entire city. The pathways sprawled like the web of a thread-spinner.

Pathway led to alleyway and then back to pathway. I poked my head into open doorways, peeked behind a few curtains, and softly called Mor's name. No one answered me except a few friendly Meridionis and the sounds and smells of breakfast.

"Ragizzi!" An elderly Meridioni woman stuck a tray of hot maize cakes under my nose as I passed her doorway. My mouth filled with saliva. "*Mamanjia*, ragizzi!"

I swallowed my mouthful of gluttonous desire, since I'd

already eaten about twelve of those beauties not an hour before. "Oh, I've eaten, thank you. You're kind."

But after living in Bordino for a week, I had learned you don't say no to a Meridioni grandmam. Or rather, you *can't* say no to her.

The sweet lady practically hand-fed me three maize cakes before she would let me go on my way. Seemed strange, but somehow these cakes from a clay oven in a modest, one-room dwelling in Meridione were better than the maize cakes the palace cooks put together back in Urian.

Meridioni grandmams knew what they were about.

"Mor, where are you?" I mostly mumbled to myself. I had crisscrossed Bordino and not seen any sign of him. Now I stood on the edge of the city and stared across the field where the atenne stood.

I didn't want to return to those white plaster walls, and something told me Mor wouldn't want to either. We'd been trapped there all week, hunting for every scrap of information, chasing down every lead. The atenne was a place of worry and pressure and exhaustion. Mor wanted escape.

I let my eyes drift closed and listened for . . . something. Something in my gut that told me where he might be.

If I wanted to escape, where would I go? Perhaps down to the shore, except the crew was always there. He would be bombarded with updates about the state of the ship and questions from the men.

No, not the beach.

Somewhere away from the city. Removed. A place to be alone and not have to look at Gryfelle getting sicker. A place where he would have a break from glaring at me.

I turned left through the field. Off the path. Toward that grove of trees further away from the crash of the ocean and the warm Meridioni sounds of Bordino.

The trunks of the trees were like rope—corded, as if many

strands of bark had clumped together, then twisted a quarter turn and frozen there. The leaves fluttered in a mild breeze, glittering silvery-green. Most of the trees bloomed with white flowers, and I wondered what another few weeks might bring. Fruit? Nuts? I'd forgotten to ask, and I realized we wouldn't be around to see it. A twinge of regret tweaked my heart.

I picked through the grove, treading over a blanket of fallen white petals, and came out into the field of solitude.

Except not complete solitude, for there Mor stood, his back to me. I stumbled back a few steps, because I hadn't at all expected the scene that met me.

Mor's hands were raised, and strands poured from them, flowing from his palms and ribboning from his fingertips. Seastone, violet, pearl, aqua, midnight. The strands didn't dance the way mine did but waved before their creator, interlacing themselves like they were threads of wool yarn and Mor was at a loom, weaving them into cloth.

But the cloth was alive. It moved in response to Mor's silent commands. The colors found order, organized themselves to reflect their creator's imaginings, and before long, the roiling sea stretched before us. Mor had created a moving picture, a tapestry of story strands.

He thrust one hand upward, and an earth-colored strand burst from his palm. It wove itself into the center of the scene, and I realized it was not earth but wood. Mor had made a ship and set it in the sea.

But this wasn't a scene of tranquility on the deep-sea waves or even a grand sailing adventure on the high seas. The ship listed sideways and took on water. A wave crested above the mainsail then crashed on deck. Masts cracked, sails ripped, and the water turned black and swallowed the vessel whole. As the ship splintered and blackness engulfed it, whispers of faces appeared, some familiar and one not.

Mor, Gryfelle, a young girl with dark hair and blue eyes. And me.

And then the wispy story faces were gone, lost with the ship in a sea turned to ink. In another blink, the strands vanished entirely. Mor's hands dropped. His head sagged. Before I could gather my wits, he turned around.

His face was wet with tears.

We stared at each other a moment, him with shock written plainly in his eyes, me with a strange defiance, almost like I was steeling myself against an accusation he hadn't yet leveled.

But he didn't accuse me. He didn't ask me if I'd followed him or yell at me for seeing him pour out the fear and heart-break and self-hatred I'd just witnessed in that story.

All he said was, "I can't . . ."

He never told me what he couldn't do. He just walked to me and took my head in his hands. Next second, his chin was resting on top of my head, and I was almost sure he was crying again.

I froze. Closed my eyes. Prayed to the Creator that some-thing in this world could soothe Mor's aching heart, because I was almost sure I could only bring him more pain. There was no solution, as I saw it. There was no good answer that could set everything right and bring healing to Mor and Gryfelle and me and Brac and everyone else all at once. If someone won, others lost. And right now, it felt an awful lot like we were all losing.

We were on a fractured ship in the middle of a blackened sea.

I opened my eyes to find glowing golden strands surround-ing us like a cage—the fine-barred, intricately wrought cages the ladies in Urian used to house their pet birds. Mor and I were like the birds inside. I had no idea if he'd created the strands or I had, or if they had somehow created themselves when we touched.

"Mor . . ."

He pressed his lips to my forehead. "I'm sorry."

Then he broke our connection and disappeared into the grove of twisted trees. I didn't know whether to laugh or cry. Or to sit down and give up.

I did none of these things. I waited until all the golden cage strands had disappeared, then slowly returned to the city and our waiting party.

I expected the cold mask to be back in place on Mor's face by the time I returned to Bordino. But it wasn't. He just looked tired—tired of trying to manage everything he was feeling while redeeming himself from past wrongs while also saving a couple of lives. That was a lot.

We were all dealing with a lot, but perhaps I could find a softer spot in the back of my heart for the weary pirate.

"Ready, Tannie?"

I turned to find Wylie's grin and a collection of maize cakes, still wrapped in their leaves from steaming. He was holding the offering out to me.

"Why does everyone keep trying to feed me today?"

"Because you look sad."

"And food helps?"

"Aye." He unwrapped a cake and popped it in his mouth. "It does when the food tastes like this."

I shook my head and took one of the bundles, in spite of myself.

Master Insegno stood at the head of the group, though the old man would not be traveling with us. He raised his hands and allowed a solemn smile.

"Questers, I bid you the blessings of the ancients." He bowed to Karlith. "And the favor of the Creator."

Dylun approached and kissed his teacher on each cheek, as Meridionis did. "Thank you for your help, Master Insegno."

And then we were off, traveling to the stone altar of the ancients. It was mostly a lot of walking. We stopped for lunch, and Wylie and I made a game of tossing some small round fruits into our mouths.

"*Uvillini.*" Dylun nodded at our handfuls of bluish-purple projectiles. "They are pressed and fermented to make wine."

I choked on one that had gone too far back into my throat.

Dylun shook his head like we were hopeless, which was probably true, and took his leave.

Truly, that was the most exciting thing that happened on the journey, except a couple scares where the path roughed out and Gryfelle's cart nearly tipped over. We rushed to right it and calm the donkeys, and so it didn't topple, thank the stars. She slept most of the day, but when she was awake, she tried to offer encouraging smiles. None of us liked that she had to ride along in that bouncy cart under the sun all day.

At last, we reached the base of the Orlos mountains, and a wide field of flowers stretched before us, basking in the setting sun. I stopped and let the sight wash over me. Delicate petals of flame-orange lit beneath the final rays of the day, like the grass was on fire.

"Pretty, isn't it?" Father stood beside me.

"We're not camping on the flowers, are we? I'd hate to crush them."

"You always were sensitive about flowers."

I looked at him blankly. "What?"

"It's true. You used to pluck flowering weeds from between the cobblestones of the palace courtyards and bring them to your mother as gifts. You always cried when the petals wilted."

"I don't remember that at all." I looked back at the field. "I can't even see Mother's face in my mind."

"I see you both, clear as the field before us."

Before I had time to talk myself out of it, I looped my arm through his and leaned my head on his shoulder. "You won't let me die alone, will you, Father?"

I could imagine his startled gaze, aimed at the top of my head. "What do you mean?"

"Promise me."

He paused. Waited. "Tannie, you will never be alone."

I fought my tears until they retreated from my eyes.

"Those are the monuments Master Insegno told us to watch for," Dylun said to the group as he pointed up toward the mountains.

And sure enough, I had been so captivated by the flowers, I'd failed to see what looked like ancient stone buildings, teetering on the edge of the mountain face, like a good strong rain might be the end of them.

"The *pil craig*, so the Old Tirians called it, should be that direction." Dylun pointed again. "At the base of that little waterfall next to that old temple. Shall we wait until morning?"

"No," at least ten of us, including me, said together.

"We've come so far, and we still have some light," I said with a quick glance at Gryfelle, whose eyes were closed. "Let's see if we can get that strand out tonight. If Gryfelle is up to it."

"I don't know that I'm 'up to it,' as you say." Gryfelle's voice was tired but firm. "But I'm not likely to be any stronger tomorrow morning."

And that settled it. We trekked the short distance to the base of the waterfall, and sure enough, there was a rock pile there.

But it wasn't a rock pile like stones that had been discarded on top of each other with no care or thought. Instead, a circle of large stones had been thrust deep into the earth. They leaned toward each other slightly, and on top was a slanted capstone— flat and smooth, like stonecutters had sanded and polished it down.

Or . . . stoneshapers, I realized. Perhaps this smooth stone table had been shaped by hands, not tools.

"If they wanted to hide the strand, why make it so spectacular?" Aeron was staring at the mossy stones with reverence. "This must have taken them some time to create with their limited tools. Why draw attention?"

"These rock piles were common once," Warmil answered. "Priests and kings and warriors would be buried in them. It would not have appeared to the ancients the curiosity it is to us. It's simply that very few still stand."

"Do you think the strand holds it up somehow?" I peeked through the gaps in the circle of stones. "Is that why this one is still standing?"

"Who knows?" Warmil completed his circle around the barrow. "And who knows if the strand is even still in here."

"So, what are we supposed to do?" I asked Dylun, who was poring over Master Insegno's map and notes.

"We need a colormaster, songspinner, and storyteller. Insegno says it will probably be best if the afflicted participate, so . . . Gryfelle, Tanwen, take your places." He indicted where he wanted us, me on the far side and Gryfelle directly opposite so she might have the least distance to walk.

Karlith and Zel supported Gryfelle on either side, and everyone else hung back.

"I'll act as colormaster," Dylun went on. He stood on one of the other sides of the barrow.

"Now what?" I looked up at the strange capstone. "Is something supposed to happen?"

"We have to create something. Tanwen, tell a story."

"Does it matter which?" I peered around the corner at him. "Surely there's some particular story I'm supposed to tell."

"It's not a magic spell, Tanwen." Dylun sounded irritated. We'd had a long day. "It's more like a key."

"Or a knock at the front door," I ventured, "letting the strands know we're here and asking if they'll come out to play."

"Er . . . precisely."

Warmil was holding Dylun's notes now, and he frowned over them. "This won't work."

Dylun swiveled on the spot. "Excuse me?"

"The colormaster can't be you."

"Oh, I suppose you want a go at the ancient ritual?"

Warmil shot him a look. "No. Not unless I look like a woman to you."

"I don't know how to answer that." Dylun snatched his notes back. "Oh."

"Aye. That word for triangle there is in the feminine form. We ought to have noticed before, but we were so focused on the map."

"Right." Dylun stepped away from the stones. "We need a female colormaster. Apparently this one works better with female weavers."

"Let's get on with it," I said. "Karlith will do it, then?"

"No," Warmil said suddenly. "Karlith should stay with Gryfelle."

"But she's our female color—"

"Aeron will do it."

And then I remembered that Aeron *was* a weaver, though she didn't like to admit it for some reason. I had never seen her create anything. I suppose I had never asked, but she must be a colormaster, like Karlith, Dylun, and War.

"Me?" the swordswoman squeaked.

I almost laughed. She charged into battle without hesitation, but this was frightening?

"You," Warmil said. "It's time you stopped hiding your gift."

"I use it. Sometimes."

"You use it when you're fighting," I realized aloud. "I saw a purple glow around your hands once when you crossed blades with a guardsman."

Aeron smiled wryly. "Took me years to be able to channel my colormastery that way and not leave paint all over my weapons."

"And that's why you don't have the curse. You use your gift enough that you're not squashing it down, but it's hidden. Secret."

"There's no reason for it to be a secret anymore," Warmil said. "Go ahead, Aeron."

Aeron moved into Dylun's place, and the triangle was complete again. I could see her swallow hard, even from my distance. "What story, Tannie?"

My mind jumped to the list of crowned stories I'd been allowed to tell under Gareth's regime. Blast that man. I supposed it would take some time to undo the training that had been hammered into me.

"Do you know the one about the forfynin?" It was one of my favorite fairy stories from my childhood—a very old tale about a sea creature called a forfynin, half human, half fish.

"Aye, I know that one," Aeron said.

"Gryfelle?" I couldn't really see her around the barrow.

"Amazingly, that story is a memory that remains. My mother used to tell it to me when I was young."

Dylun nodded. "Very well. Tanwen, you start and the others will join with song and color, and we'll see what happens."

I drew a deep breath and began.

"Once upon a time, a young man lived by the sea." A glittery aqua strand rose from my hand and swirled above the barrow. "One day while he was fishing with his brother, he saw a woman in the water. He rowed over to her, for he thought she was drowning."

A brown strand that might be the wooden boat or the young man's hair, for all I knew, swirled out next.

"When the boat reached the drowning woman, whose hair was rose-gold and shimmering like the water, the young man reached over the side to help her out."

A shimmering rose-gold ribbon undulated from my left hand and began a lazy circle around the other strands. Closing them in. Entrapping them.

I opened my mouth to speak the next line, but then I heard a sweet sound—Gryfelle's voice. When we first met, she often sang in Old Tirian, and I imagined if any story had some sort of ballad version, this one would. But she didn't sing words now, only a melody. When Gryfelle sang, it was so beautiful that just the melody was enough.

Wispy song strands joined my dancing story strands. They swirled together, and somehow, the colors of my strands were more vibrant when Gryfelle's airy whispers of music played alongside them.

"But just as the young man leaned over the edge of the boat to grab the woman's hand, his brother pulled him back and said, 'No! Do not touch her, for she is a forfynin. She will drown us both.' The young man resisted his brother's grip, for he had been entranced by the sea maiden's seductive magic."

The rose-gold ribbon slithered through the aqua strand.

"His brother begged him once more to resist the charm of the forfynin, and lo, he heeded the warning. He pulled back his hand and moved away from the edge of the boat. The sea maiden's cries for help died on her lips, and her face contorted in rage. 'Fools!' she cried."

As I said this line, a strand of painted fire from Aeron's direction joined the story above the barrow—the forfynin's rage.

"'I should have liked to eat you for breakfast,' the forfynin said, 'but now I shall go hungry. For this, you will pay. I will watch you always, stalk your shores, sink your boats, and drown your children in the sea.' Without another word, she dove beneath the waves with a mighty flick of her golden fish tail.

"The young man and his family lived with great fear for many years. He married and had children, but never did he allow them to play near the sea. They lived in poverty, for they could not fish as they once had."

A stream of fog from Aeron covered the rest of the strands like a dome—the lingering threat of the forfynin over the man's life.

"Then one day, the man went down to the seashore, praying some clams might have washed up on shore so that he could feed his children. Instead, he found the forfynin, golden tail and shimmering pink hair, beached and dying. Helpless."

The vibrancy of the rose-gold strand faded now, as the forfynin's life slipped away.

"'You have won,' the forfynin said. 'I got too far ashore, hoping to snatch one of your children, and I did not mind the tide. And now here I am, helpless, and you may kill me as I have tried to do to you for so many years.' But the man was kindhearted and gentle, and he did not want to kill the creature. Instead, he scooped her up into his arms and carried her down the beach. He walked into the water as far as his waist and released her into the sea.

"The forfynin was whole after a single moment back in her beloved salt water. She looked at the man. 'Why have you done this? Surely you know I will just kill you now.' And the man said, 'If this is what you wish to do, so be it. I am not responsible for your actions, only my own. And I could not let a living creature die before my eyes if I had the strength to save her. Now do what you will.'

"The forfynin paused a moment longer, and her face softened. 'I will guard these shores for you and your family as long as I live. I will make sure you have plenty of fish in your nets and food on your table the rest of my days. You shall always have a friend in these waters.' And then she disappeared beneath the waves. The man never saw her again, but for many generations to come, his family stayed safe at sea and were the most prosperous fishermen in the region. And even were it not so, the man felt peace over his actions. For what is honorable does not change with the tides, and when one acts with honor, he need not fear the consequences."

At my last words, the strands came together and crystallized. For one glorious moment, I saw the forfynin figure I expected—pinkish hair and shimmering golden tail—but also waving strands like the sea rolling inside the crystal figure and the light, sparkling mist of Gryfelle's song hovering about the outside.

Then the story dropped onto the flat stone atop the barrow and shattered.

"Oh!" I watched it splinter to pieces and had to fight my urge to climb atop the ancient stones and collect the bits to try to put them back together, so pretty the figure had been.

But before I could try any such fool idea, the barrow rumbled. The ground shook beneath me, and I nearly lost my footing.

"Tannie!" Father's voice cried out, but I barely heard.

I stumbled closer to the others and saw Karlith, Zel, and Mor getting Gryfelle back to the cart, away from the chaos. Then a royal-blue strand poked out from between the stones. I couldn't help myself. I turned back toward the barrow and moved closer to get a better look.

"Tanwen!"

In another breath, the strand had emerged fully and the ground stilled. It was a solid ribbon, but within it swirled other strands, as if within the fabric of every single piece, a million more lived. The inner strands floated the way a drop of oil dances on water.

As I stood, the blue strand rose up. Like it was looking at

me. Its head cocked to the side, and it seemed to be studying me as I studied it, almost as if to say, *Was it you, storyteller? Are you the one who woke me?*

"Here." Dylun appeared beside me and put something in my hands. A box—wood with metal at the corners and a metal latch with a keyhole. "It's for the strand."

I took the box and looked back at the strand. But this wasn't *my* strand. I hadn't made it and couldn't command it to go where I wanted. And it seemed to be thinking things all on its own. I couldn't force it into a box. Could I?

"Um . . ." I unlatched the box, opened it, and held it out. "Would you like to go in here?"

The blue strand paused, tilting its head to the other side.

"Dylun . . . I'm talking to a strand."

"Try again."

"I feel like a crazy person."

"Yes. Try anyway."

I offered the box again. "It's . . . er . . . nice in there. It's lined in velvet."

The strand shrank back a little.

"We need your help," I said. "We need to put you back together with the other strands—to remake the cure. Please. My friend is dying."

The strand didn't pause another moment. In a royal-blue flourish, it whirled into the box, curled up like a fluff-hopper at nap time, and stayed there.

"Close the box," Dylun said.

"Look at those swirls! Have you ever seen anything like it?"

"Indeed, no. Now close the box before it flies away."

"I don't think it's going anywhere. But if it wanted to, I'm quite sure I couldn't stop it." I gazed a moment longer, then whispered, "Thank you," and closed the box.

Suddenly I felt like I could sleep for a week.

Dylun patted my shoulder. "Good work, Tanwen. One down. Only three more to go."

CHAPTER TWENTY-THREE

TANWEN

At least a hundred Bordinis waved from the beach as the *Cethorelle* pulled away from the dock.

"If not for the pressing need to keep moving on this quest, I think I could've lived here," I said to Wylie as he secured lines and I leaned over the rail to wave at the Meridionis.

"It's the maize cakes, isn't it?"

"Even better than porridge for breakfast."

"And now you get fish again."

"Don't remind me."

"Sailor Bo-Thordwyan," Mor's voice cut in. "You're needed astern."

"Aye, Captain." Wylie nodded to me and took his leave.

I resisted the impulse to speak first—to fire off some kind of smart remark. I just waited for Mor to say whatever he wanted to say, if indeed he had sent Wylie astern so we could be alone.

But now that we *were* alone, he just stood at the rail and looked back at the Meridioni shore with me.

After a long minute, he said, "Tannie about what you saw . . ."

"Forget it." I don't know why I said that, because I sure would never forget the first story I saw Mor weave.

"No, I can't forget it. I feel like I need to explain . . . that is, you should know what I was . . ." He didn't seem able to complete his thoughts.

"It's fine. You were upset."

"Aye. I was upset. I've been upset. I can't even remember a time when I didn't feel like my insides were tied in knots."

"You're worried about Gryfelle."

"I'm worried about all of us."

"Aye." I looked at the water. "But that's why we're trying to find the pieces of the cure." My thoughts jumped to the royal-blue strand coiled in the box belowdecks.

"Yes, but about the way things are between you and me, I wanted to—"

"No. Don't." I surprised even myself by saying, "Let's not have any discussions of 'you and me' right now. It just distracts and destroys, and I'm sick to death of it."

"But Tannie—"

"No, see, you're calling me Tannie again, and what will happen is I'll get all melty inside and remember when we first met and the way you helped me grow as a storyteller and how you helped me rediscover who I was supposed to be and where I belonged. I'll think about the time you told me never to change and I considered for the first time that being a farm girl from Pembrone was maybe something I could accept about myself. Not only accept, but appreciate. And then I'll think about the laughs we've shared and your smirky smile, and I just can't. I can't right now, and maybe I can't ever. So let's not. Let's not talk about you and me."

I pushed away from the rail and moved past Mor, tears streaming from my eyes.

"Tannie, wait." He reached out and grabbed my arm.

The moment he touched me, a spray of sparks burst from our connection. Instinctively, I grabbed his hand and pulled it from my arm, but when our hands touched, a strand of fire sailed out and into the ocean.

We stepped back and stared at each other. His wide eyes told me he didn't understand what had happened any better than I did.

"Links." I hadn't noticed my father's presence nearby until he spoke. "You're starting to create links."

I faced him, too bewildered to blush. "What? What do you mean?"

"It was something that happened in the old days before Gareth stole the throne and suppressed the weavers. Sometimes when weavers had certain . . . ah . . . strong feelings between them, they would create . . ." He trailed off and waved his hand, as if to shoo away all the wrong words to describe it. "Sparks."

The color drained from Mor's face, but he didn't speak.

"I've never seen such a thing." I shook my head, trying to clear the fluff from my mind. "How does it work? And why? Why do these links exist?"

"I don't know much about it," Father said. "Except that two together are stronger than one alone."

Then he walked away without further explanation. Mor and I were left with a million questions, heavy awkwardness between us.

And a few sparks still sizzling on the deck.

CHAPTER TWENTY-FOUR

NAITH

"Try again, son." Naith forced his voice to sound patient. After a solid two weeks of working on the boy.

Bo-Bradwir frowned. "I just don't understand. I ain't never produced anything like a story strand. I've seen Tannie do it a thousand times, and I'm telling you, I don't have that gift."

"Or the girl made you believe that about yourself. She made sure to hold you down, convinced you that you were nothing more than a farm lad beneath her notice."

The boy's frown deepened. "Tannie's not like that. She would never make me stop telling stories if I had the gift. It was always *me* trying to get *her* to stop."

Naith paused and ran through the Master's instructions again. Don't use her name. Strip her of identity and dignity and humanity whenever possible. Distance the boy from his feelings for her. Slowly stoke his jealousy over the sea captain's gift. Convince him the storytelling brat who started it all had never been on his side.

And above all, patience and persistence. It took time to unravel almost twelve years of friendship. Unravel, but not destroy, for they needed some bonds to remain so that they might be later leveraged.

"My son, please listen. You have seen the power of the goddesses through me. They bestow secret knowledge upon me.

How else could I have known what troubled your soul when you first came to me?"

"Yes, that's true." Bo-Bradwir looked down at his calloused hands. "But I'm just a farmer."

"No, you are a soldier."

"Barely. I mean I only got that position because . . ." He didn't finish his thought but looked away, as if ashamed.

"Because you traded information about the rebels to Gareth." Naith didn't need the Master's inside knowledge or information collected through spy strands to know that. He remembered well enough from his days on Gareth's council that this was how the boy rose to the palace guard. But he would certainly play it off as more divine knowledge from the goddesses.

"Aye. Those goddesses don't leave nothing out, do they?" Bitterness tinged his words, and Naith knew he needed to address it.

"Son, the goddesses do not judge you. They chose you. You are the one who will save Tir."

"I thought Tir was already saved. From Gareth. Wasn't he the enemy?"

"Gareth was a knave, to be sure. But everything is just as backward as it's ever been. More so, even. The usurper's daughter sits on the throne. The peasants have lost their faith. They have been pressed down, hemmed in, used and abused. The nobility and the priesthood abandoned their people and sought their own interests. Have you not spent half your life starving due to blight on your crops? How hard must your father work simply to feed his children and maintain his land? And still, the wealthy demand more."

"That's true." The wheels of the boy's mind seemed to be turning. "But Braith is not like Gareth. I think she's going about setting some of that right."

"Even with her bad blood? Was Gareth not her father? Was she not reared by a usurper and a deserter? Where is Frenhin

Ma-Gareth, now that her husband is dead? Gone. Hiding. For she was no better than he. These are our new queen's parents. This is the line from which she descends."

"But Braith is different."

"How do you know?"

Bo-Bradwir's face reddened. "Well, because Tannie and the others told me."

"Precisely. The girl who broke her engagement with you to adventure on the high seas with a pirate—a pirate who has the weaving gift."

"She's more than just that. I've known her most her life, and she's more than just some girl who broke a promise and jumped on a ship. You can't sum her up like that, as if that's all her life's been. She's more than that." Defiance edged his words.

Time to back off it.

"My son, let me tell you what I know to be true. You have been chosen by the goddesses to restore order to Tir. You are gifted. You have power beyond your imagining, and the peasants will follow you. Through you, a golden age for the Tirian people will dawn. I will help you. Together we will nurture your gift. It will grow, and so will you."

Bo-Bradwir shook his head. "I'm confused."

"Of course you are, my dear boy. But in time, your destiny will feel surer, as it does for all of us as we grow into our calling."

How often had he and the Master repeated the opposite refrain to the puppet king, Gareth? How often had they said that those with strength and the will to lead made their own destinies? But Naith had decades of experience speaking whatever "truth" he needed to in the moment—whatever words his listener most desired or needed to hear.

Naith held Bo-Bradwir's hands out, palms facing up.

"My boy, Tir is your destiny. Look at your hands."

Bo-Bradwir looked down.

"Now make the strands. Show your power."

"I . . . can't."

"Believe you can. Have faith that the goddesses are not wrong about you."

He drew a deep breath.

"Believe!" Naith cried.

With that, strands like tongues of fire coiled from Bo-Bradwir's hands. Slow and deliberate, not like the wild, willful flickering of an actual fire. Naith felt the Master using him as proxy, the power flowing from Naith's body to Bo-Bradwir's. This must be draining the Master tremendously, but the moment was crucial.

Bo-Bradwir stared at his hands. "How . . . ?"

"They are not wrong, my son. You are powerful. And you are the future of Tir."

"Master?"

Naith waited. He had seen the boy to the priestly chambers of the temple and told him he should rest and prepare to make the room his new home. Bo-Bradwir had been meeting Naith in the evenings when he was off duty from the guard, but now it was time for the boy to stay in the temple permanently. His superiors would miss him, but that would be of little import soon enough.

"Master?"

A misty smoke strand appeared in the air before Naith, and in it, the Master's voice. "Naith."

The Master sounded tired.

"I'll not keep you. You must be exhausted."

"Yes, I am. This has been quite a test of my abilities."

"But it's working, Master. The boy rests in his new chambers. I will have him here with me now at all times—no more long, lonely watches to sit with his thoughts and question the things I tell him."

"We have been fortunate to find such a malleable piece of clay to work with."

"Everything seems to be falling into place here in Urian." He dared not ask how things progressed elsewhere. The Master did not appreciate uninvited queries.

"Good," the Master said. "The situation is rather more dynamic here."

"Oh?"

"I have kept pace with our band of rebels. They were docked in Meridione for some time."

"Meridione? Part of the general's ambassadorial journey for the queen?" Naith no longer held a seat on the council, but he caught bits and pieces of politics from his subordinate priests who traveled more freely throughout Urian.

"Yes, I believed that to be the reason at first. But they have the dying girl with them."

"Yes, Bo-Bradwir mentioned."

"And I think they're seeking a cure for her."

"A cure?"

Naith paused. He had seen many weavers succumb to the curse in the months after Gareth's ascension, before they came up with the idea of crowned stories. Dray's idea, actually. Control the narrative, he said at the time. Use the weaver gifts to the king's advantage by allowing weavers to tell stories that glorified the king and their Tirian heritage.

Naith had been quick to insist stories of the goddesses be included, of course. Without a passing belief in the goddesses— or at least a fear of the priesthood—Naith's power and that of the priesthood would be greatly lessened in Tirian culture. Naith had always fought for a balance of power with Sir Dray. The Master had agreed to crowned stories of the goddesses, and it was supposed these stories would give weavers enough of an outlet to prevent their deaths.

The plan had only met with marginal success.

But through all of that, Naith had never heard of a cure for the curse.

"Yes. We have stumbled into something a bit broader than I anticipated."

"Broader?"

"Naith, must you repeat my words back to me?"

"My apologies, Master."

"In my studies and the development of my arts, I have run across suggestions of ancient weavers—whispers of the way strands were once used and the power contained therein. And I had some reason to believe I had in my possession . . . that is, I should have realized . . ."

The Master paused for a long moment, and Naith scarcely breathed.

"No matter now. The scrolls and manuscripts were in long-dead languages," the Master continued. "The rebels must have a linguist. Or a scholar. Perhaps both. If I had realized the significance of those whispers I heard, we might have acted many years ago."

Naith didn't respond. He had never before heard the Master admit fault or weakness.

"I am very tired just now, Naith," the Master said. "But it is time you know about these pieces of the puzzle."

"Of course, Master. I shall give you my full attention as long as you desire it."

"Good servant, you are. I believe the rebels have uncovered some history about an ancient cure. I have been too far away to listen closely or for long, and it drains me so. But I saw a strand."

"A single strand? Is that of import?"

"This strand is, yes. It was made back in the days when the Creator wandered more freely along the earth."

Naith sat heavily. "Did you say *the Creator*?" The Master had been so decided, so exacting about outlawing even the mention of the Creator's name. It was one of the first things Gareth did as king, and he was glad to do it, for Gareth was a faithful servant of the goddesses.

But now the Master spoke the Creator's name as though his existence were a fact?

"Master, I don't understand."

"And it is not necessary that you do. Only believe me when I tell you these strands are powerful. If we might collect some and learn how to use them . . ."

"We would be unstoppable," Naith realized.

"Precisely."

"Then you must destroy the rebels and take their strand."

"No. So rash, Naith. Always so impulsive."

Naith stayed silent, thoroughly chastened.

"They are now on their way to Haribi to gather another. And then after that, Minasimet, if I guess correctly."

"And you'll kill them then?"

"Not all of them."

"Master?"

"That is enough for now. You continue with your 'chosen one.' You build your army of peasants, and I will pursue my weapons."

"Weapon or weapons?" Naith was puzzled. When had weapons become plural?

"The strands must be mine. But I will need some weavers powerful enough to wield them."

CHAPTER TWENTY-FIVE

TANWEN

"Dylun!" I squealed. "Look!"

I pointed toward the long, flat, sandy coastline. It sloped slowly up to rolling green hills. Totally different from the white sand and steep red cliffs of Meridione but also different from the rocky formations and pebbly beaches of the Eastern Peninsula. It was as if everywhere the land touched the sea, it claimed its own unique appearance.

"Yes, I see."

I gestured again. "*Look*, Dylun! It's the west coast of Tir!"

"Indeed, it is."

"Have you seen the Wildlands before? I've always wanted to."

"Well, you will have your chance. We're staying in port for three days to restock our supplies."

My stomach twinged. Could Gryfelle spare three whole days? Could I?

"But I wouldn't make too many plans," Dylun added. "You know what Mor said. No one is to be traveling. He'll need all hands."

Blast. If we were forced to stop for three days, at least I might have made the most of it by having an adventure. It might be my only chance to see the Wildlands.

But it wasn't worth the fight. I knew Mor wouldn't relent and no one was going to undermine the captain of the ship.

"Have you been to the western coast?" I asked again.

"No, I haven't."

"And still you're so calm as you glimpse it for the first time? Does nothing excite you?"

Dylun paused. "History excites me."

I laughed. "You are a truly bizarre individual, Dylun."

"Oh." He blinked.

I studied him another moment. It hadn't occurred to me before then, but he hadn't seemed quite himself since we left Meridione almost eleven days prior. "You seem a little sad, Dylun. Are you all right?"

"I suppose."

Realization dawned. "Oh, Dylun, I didn't even think of it. We were back in your homeland. You've been captive in Tir so long, and you'd finally come home. Of course you wanted to stay in Meridione."

"Well, I thought I would want to stay. I thought I would feel at home in Bordino. And then I found I didn't really belong there."

"But you and Master Insegno seemed to pick up right where you left off all those years ago."

"In a way, yes. But in other ways, I felt very out of place. I've lived in Tir my whole life. I'm not as Meridioni as I thought I was. I have no country and no people, Tanwen."

"No, don't be silly. Of course you are Meridioni. You're just a Meridioni who had to live away from your home country a long time. And you're *also* Tirian. You're every bit as Tirian as I am. You just need some blond braids and freckles."

He actually laughed at that.

"So, how about that adventuring in the Wildlands, huh?" I flashed a big, hopeful grin.

He raised an eyebrow, and a hint of a smile crept onto his face. "Maybe we can arrange something."

"The wood looks darker. Is it darker?" I gazed around the Wildland pub, simply called Mho's. An afternoon in a pub wasn't exactly the adventure I had been envisioning, but I was grateful for it anyway. At least I was getting to see a bit of Tir's west coast away from the ship.

Warmil raised an eyebrow at me. "We have different trees here."

"I forgot you're from the Wildlands, aren't you?"

"Aye." Then he took a drink of something that smelled like it was made to strip the bark off Wildland trees.

I wrinkled my nose at the barmaid. "Got any tea?"

She stared at me.

I tried again. "Hathberry tea?" Silence. "Brisk-leaf? Anything?"

The barmaid looked at Warmil. "She with you?"

"She's fine." He smacked a few copper bits on the counter-top. "Just bring her whatever you brew with your breakfast."

The barmaid shrugged and disappeared through a set of swinging double doors. I guessed that must be where they kept the tea.

"Why did she look at me so funny? You don't drink tea in the Wildlands?"

"Not usually in pubs, Tannie. And besides, that lass has probably never had a hathberry in her life. They only grow on the east coast."

"Oh." I sniffed at his glass. "Ugh. If that's my other option, Captain, I think I'd rather drink fish juice."

"That could probably be arranged." He glanced at me wryly, then took another sip of the bark-stripping concoction.

"You know, you could cheer up a little. You're home, after all."

Warmil drained his glass. "Nah. Home is still three hundred leagues inland for me."

"Oh. Well, you could at least enjoy your afternoon off."

"I'm not off. I've been assigned to watch you."

I glanced at the sword at his hip. "Aye. I guess my father wouldn't let me come in here without some accompanying steel."

"Wasn't your father, though he has been on edge of late. Says he feels like we're being watched."

I shivered but didn't comment.

"It was the captain who insisted I stand watch over you."

"Mor?" I rolled my eyes. "Honestly."

Warmil signaled the barmaid to bring him another drink just as she returned with my tea.

The scent of a rich black tea filled my nose, and I closed my eyes at the heavenly smell. But then I looked at Warmil's second drink. "If you're on duty, you shouldn't have any more."

"Last one." He drained half of it.

"Something bothering you, Captain?"

He shrugged and stared into his glass. "I tried to have that talk with Aeron last night."

I sputtered into my mug, then reeled back and looked at him. "Just now? Took you long enough!"

"I needed to collect my thoughts."

"For three moons? Goodness. How do you stand yourself?"

"Not sure."

"So. How did it go?"

"Great. Can't you tell?" He took another drink.

"What happened?" I was almost afraid to ask.

"I choked up. Told her she was nearly as good a sailor as she was a swordswoman. I might have said something about the 'mighty fine knot' she was tying."

I made a valiant effort not to snort into my steaming drink. "Well . . . that's nice?"

He glared at me. "It's the least romantic thing any man has ever said to the woman he loves. I'm . . . not cut out for this."

"Well, this isn't the end of the world. Maybe in another twenty years, you'll work up the nerve to have another go."

"Not funny."

I sipped my tea, despite my grin. "Look, War, Aeron knows you. You've lived side by side for . . . what, ten years? I'm sure you didn't offend her with that knot-tying business. In fact, I'm pretty sure she took it as you meant it and is just waiting for an appropriate time to tell you she feels the same way about your sailing skills. Like when she has an afternoon off, say."

"How can you possibly know that?"

"Because she's standing right there. She looks beautiful . . . and very much like she wants to speak to you."

Warmil swiveled on his barstool, and then he saw what I saw behind him: Aeron had just walked into Mho's. Though she wore trousers and a blouse like always, she had taken care with her hair. Her shoulder-length black locks were sleek and shiny. A tiny braided circlet wove around the crown of her head.

She strode toward us, then stopped before Warmil, looking like she didn't know quite what to say.

"Um, I'll be going now." I slipped off my barstool and abandoned my tea. "Meet you both outside in a few."

I hurried away from whatever conversation was about to take place. A little strand drifted from my hand before I could stop it—a rope that swiftly knotted itself into a perfect heart between them.

CHAPTER TWENTY-SIX

TANWEN

After half a moon of nothing but ocean as we crossed from the Western Wildlands of Tir to the Haribian city of Paka, you would think the sight of land would have thrilled me. Instead, I was puzzled.

"It's so flat," I said to Wylie as I gazed over the rail. "It's like a field that's been cleared for grain but never planted. Where are the mountains? The hills?"

"They don't really have them. At least, not in this part of the country." He pointed. "Those are marshlands along the coast, but when you get further in, the ground's much drier. They do grow some kinds of grain there."

"Oh! That means they have porridge!"

Wylie shot me a look but didn't comment.

"Come about!" Mor's voice cut through our conversation like a sword. "Bo-Thordwyan, all hands!"

Wylie shrugged. "Duty calls. See you, Tannie."

I turned toward the approaching Haribian coastline. "All hands" didn't mean me, and I knew it. I could tie knots better than before and help out with cleaning, but actually lowering sails or belaying lines? Not so much. Still, I donned my tricorn hat like the rest of them. Like I belonged.

They let me pretend.

And it didn't sting to pretend, as long as I avoided Mor. Which I'd done with success since Meridione.

"Better get ready to disembark." Speak of the blue-eyed devil. "There's no proper port in Paka. We're dropping anchor."

"What does that mean?"

Mor nodded toward land. "We'll get close, then we'll let down the anchor to secure the ship. We'll lower our rowboats and pull the rest of the way to shore."

I eyed the rowboats as the men loosened them from their secure holds. They looked rickety, now that I'd been aboard ship so long. "Is it safe?"

"Not really." Mor shrugged. "What choice do we have? We won't linger in Haribi."

I cast another mistrustful glance at one rowboat as Mor strode away. Then I sighed. He was right. What choice did we have?

The men got the ship anchored and boats ready to lower alarmingly fast. They were rather like huskbeetles building a colony. It made me wish I could do more than pretend to be a sailor. It would be nice to be part of that bustle—that efficiency.

Gryfelle was already loaded in one boat, Karlith with her. Mor and Jule conversed about the ship—Jule would stay back with most of the crew while we went ashore.

I caught Wylie's gaze some distance away, and he shrugged apologetically. I guessed he had been ordered to stay behind.

"Tannie?" Mor's voice from the other boat startled me. He had climbed over the side and now offered me his hand. "Ready?"

But I wasn't. I stared at his hand, then met his gaze. What if we made sparks or fire or a golden cage of sadness when we touched in front of the whole ship?

Horrifying.

But then I realized he was wearing leather gloves. Maybe it wouldn't work if his hands were covered?

I placed my fingers in his outstretched palm. Stillness. No

strands. Just the tiniest bit of heat beneath the leather. Our eyes met, and I could see that he had been wondering, too.

Well, at least we knew how to stop it from happening, even if we couldn't really control it. That was something. And yet, somehow, it felt like a loss.

I settled onto the bench of the rowboat next to my father.

"Ho, Tannie girl."

I scooted closer and leaned against his arm.

But I didn't have long enough to settle into anything that felt like comfort.

"General?" The worry in Zel's voice carried across the waves from the other boat. "What's that?"

Father craned his neck toward the shoreline. "We have a welcoming party."

I wasn't sure what a Haribian welcoming party usually looked like, but the line of warriors taking their places along the marshy coast didn't look much like they wanted to welcome us.

I knew I was staring, but it was hard to look away. For one, these men barely wore clothes by Tirian standards. They stood bare-chested with long, colorful cloth skirts hanging down to the ground. Some had spears and small stone blades fixed to leather straps across their bodies. All of them held bows as tall as they were, and each man seemed to match Zel in height. What looked like white ink markings stood out on muscled, umber skin that glistened like it was covered in oil.

But I supposed it wasn't the time to be admiring how impressive this party looked. Seeing as there looked to be about a hundred of them, and every bow had an arrow nocked. Especially since all those arrows were pointed in our direction.

"*Hu!*" The sharp cry from shore almost startled me overboard.

Several of the men had moved forward enough to meet our boat—and their bowstrings were pulled taut, their spears pointed at our throats.

"*Wew ninani? Yaki ninini ni lengo?*" one of the warriors shouted.

I stared at my father a moment, then glanced at Warmil. I sure hoped one or the both of them spoke Haribian. Or maybe Dylun? Was there more than one dialect of Haribian? Surely so, though I'd never thought of it before now. Father had said that Haribi was made up of about three hundred clans.

"*Sisi kuju amani.*"

I swiveled to look at Father again, for those Haribian words had come from him. How strange to hear this foreign language out of my father's mouth.

He spoke to the Haribian with the harsh voice again. "*Jumbe kwa malika.*"

"*Mwong!*" The man pulled his bowstring tighter and aimed his arrow straight at Father's head.

My heart shot into my throat and stuck there. "No!" I choked out.

Several pairs of eyes turned toward me. Would their arrows and spears follow?

Tears stung. I wished for the first time in my life I spoke Haribian. I gripped my father's arm.

"*Mwongi.*" The one who seemed to be the leader nodded toward Father. But didn't lower his bow, I couldn't fail to notice.

"We're not liars," Father said in Tirian. "I do carry a message from the queen. Queen Braith En-Gareth."

"Ah! Gareth!" The leader spoke in rough, clipped Tirian.

Mention of the usurper king might have been a bad idea.

But Father kept speaking in a reassuring voice. "*Sisi kuju amani.*" He held up his hands. "We mean you no harm."

From the line of defenders came a thickly accented voice, but the Tirian words were clear. "I know this voice."

While the Haribian warriors didn't budge or lower their weapons, I saw Father's breath release in a slow stream that sounded like relief. A smile broke over his face. Though the rest of us could have been carved of stone for all we dared to breathe.

The Haribian man who had spoken appeared at the front of the throng. He was tall, glistening, and every bit as fierce as the others. Just as armed, too. The polished-stone head of his spear was longer than any of the others, and I noticed with a leap in my chest that he wore a necklace of beasts' teeth. But the moment he saw my father, his face split into a wide grin, revealing the whitest teeth I'd seen in my life.

"I knew this." He laughed, lowered his spear. "Yestin. The old general of Tir."

Father nodded, seemingly delighted. "Askari." He addressed the rest of us. "Askari is a local warlord. His village is that direction, if memory serves. The village of Kiji." He motioned left, toward the southwest.

"Yes, this is right. General Yestin." Askari shook his head. "You were . . ."

"Dead?"

"Yes. How? How do you stand here?"

"Long story." Father's gaze shifted to the other warriors, whose weapons were all still trained. "I'm going to reach into my tunic and get the letter from the queen. Is that all right?"

Askari spoke to the others in Haribian. Most weapons lowered, but the harsh-voiced one paused.

"Gareth." He glared at my father. "Gareth."

Askari spoke in Haribian again, rapidly. I frowned. That language sounded to me like a hail of arrows hitting a stone turret. I didn't think I'd ever be able to learn one word of it.

Askari turned back to us. "He fears this name. Gareth."

"Gareth is dead." Father held out the letter. "Here. Askari, you know I was loyal to Caradoc II, not Gareth. Please, I beg you. Give Queen Braith's words the consideration you would have given to Caradoc's." He bowed and stretched across the distance to offer the letter sealed in wax with Braith's signet pressed into it. "Upon my honor, Braith is cut from Caradoc's cloth."

Askari looked puzzled. "What is this 'cut from cloth'? You make no sense, old friend."

"Forgive me," Father said quickly. "She is a ruler like Caradoc. Or she will be, if she can gather enough support to keep her throne. You understand?"

"Yes." Askari stepped into the marsh and took the letter, then he handed it over to the harsh-voiced man. He looked at Father. "Is this why you have come? To deliver the Tirian queen's letter?"

"Yes. But we have another purpose."

It took Father a minute to explain the situation with Gryfelle and me. It may have irked the others that Father made a point to say, "My daughter is in danger," when Gryfelle was so much worse off. But he knew what he was about. What would inspire compassion more, a Tirian stranger near death or the sick daughter of an old friend? I was beginning to realize Father was strategic in everything he did, every word he spoke.

Though truly, Askari didn't seem to need the extra shove, even if the others might have. As Father spoke of Gryfelle, Askari's face grew graver and graver. He eyed her in the other boat. Finally, he said, "We have our legends here. I know the help you seek." But then he shook his head. "I do not know where it may be, my friend."

Mor spoke up. "Please, sir. We have a map, and our situation is desperate."

Askari cast his gaze back to Father, clearly amused. "*Mwanume?*"

Father laughed. "He is not a boy. He is the captain of

that vessel." He nodded out to sea where the *Cethorelle* was anchored.

"Ha! They give ships to younglings now."

"Or perhaps we have grown old, my friend."

"Perhaps." Askari turned toward the harsh-voiced one and spoke in Haribian. After a moment of arguing, he turned back to Father. "Katili is warlord of Paka. This is his land here, and he does not want you. But I have told him he must, as a favor to me."

"We will not stay," Father assured him. "Our ship can't be tethered too long."

Askari nodded. "The village mother will look after you."

I glanced up at Father. Village mother?

"A female elder," he explained.

"She will look after the dying one." Askari took another long look at Gryfelle. He didn't speak his question, but when he turned to Father, I could see it in his eyes.

Is she not dead already?

"She is very sick," Father said quietly. "But we must do all we can for her."

"*Haki*," Askari responded. "Indeed. I hope your map is a good one."

CHAPTER TWENTY-SEVEN

TANWEN

I HAD NO IDEA WHAT THE PAKAN VILLAGE MOTHER WAS saying. I just knew it would be unwise to interfere with her. She reminded me of Karlith, but fiercer. The two of them together, guarding Gryfelle's limp body, were more frightening than the hundred Haribian warriors had been.

Zel and I sat on a flat rock with one young warrior. He didn't speak a word of Tirian, and of course Zel and I couldn't understand anything he said, but he showed off the designs on his skin with a big grin and obvious pride.

"Tattoos," Dylun said as he glanced over top of his map.

"What?"

"Those are white tattoos."

"What's a tattoo?"

That flicker of annoyance crossed Dylun's face—the one that always showed up when the rest of the world proved itself less educated than he. "Permanent art markings on skin. Common practice in much of the world." Then he wandered away from the other men, eyes on his map.

I looked closer at the designs. "Beautiful, of course. But . . ."

The young warrior said something to the Haribian men standing nearby, then laughed.

"He says they would not show on you," Askari translated.

I looked down at my pale skin and grinned at the warrior. "True enough."

"I am sorry you will not see our great cities," Askari said suddenly.

My eyebrows rose. "Great cities?"

"Haki. We have great cities in Haribi."

"I believe you." I frowned. He seemed defensive. Like I had attacked him.

"Tirians believe we are uncivilized," he explained, even though I hadn't voiced my question.

Oh. I fought the urge to avert my eyes. "Not us," I said at last, pointing to myself and Zel. "Zel and I come from small farming towns. I only saw my first great city this year. We grew up under thatched roofs."

Askari tilted his head toward the south. "That way is Jila. Filled with sandstone temples and statues of great beauty."

"You have stoneshapers," I mused. "Seems Tir is the only place in the world that doesn't."

"We have many *mwama*."

"Weavers?" I asked.

"Haki. Weavers."

"I wish we could stay to see your cities." I thought of Gryfelle lying in a hut with Karlith and the village mother, barely clinging to life. "But our friend is very sick."

Just then, Dylun interrupted.

"I have a course plotted," he said. "It's not far, if I've done this properly. Tanwen, I'll just need you and Mor."

"What?" A note of panic crept into my voice.

"Just you two. You'll do for this one. Again, if I've read it right . . ." He wandered off again, still staring at his map.

I found Mor a few paces away. He was looking at me intently. Then he turned away and gave his full attention to my father, who was saying something important, it seemed.

Aye. Just me and Mor for this one. I sighed.

Perfect.

My fingertips grazed the tops of long, wild grass as I walked through it. Sunshine warmed my face. A couple weeks remained of summer's third moon, and Haribi was holding on. The air seemed twice as dry as a steamy Eastern Peninsular midsummer day, and I let the glow heat me all the way through.

"There!" Dylun's voice sliced into my reverie. "That's it, straight up ahead."

"Already? No. We've only been walking an hour. Took us a whole day through the rocky Meridioni wilderness. Couldn't we have at least half a day in the Haribian sunshine?"

Dylun looked personally offended. "Excuse me, but Meridione is not rocky, nor is it the wilderness. At least not the part we walked through."

"All right, but this is so warm and lovely." I closed my eyes and tilted my face toward the sun again. "A little while longer?"

"No." Dylun couldn't be dissuaded when he was on a mission.

Zel and Father had traveled with us, even though Dylun said it was just me and Mor he needed. It never hurt to have a couple extra swords about.

"Here," Dylun said. And he pointed to . . . a rock.

"Really?" I squinted at it. "It's just a big rock."

"No, it *appears* to be a big rock. Come on."

The five of us moved closer. It still looked rather like a big rock, but the nearer I got, the easier I could see an opening within the boulder. And then we got even closer, and I felt the gentle breath of hot air exhaling from it.

"What . . . ?" I peered toward the hole. "What in the world?"

"*Pum yakoj*—the breath of the beast," Dylun said.

"Great." I eyed the rock warily. "So, what are we supposed to do? We tell a story and the strand comes out?"

"No, we go inside."

I turned and stared at him. "Pardon me?"

"We're going inside."

"Into the breath of the beast?"

"Yes."

I looked elsewhere for help. "Father?"

"I'll go first," was his response.

"No!" I said it louder than I meant to. "You can't go in there."

"Tannie, if that's where the strand is, that's where we have to go."

My mouth opened and closed twice, but I couldn't drum up an argument. "It doesn't seem safe."

"It might not be," Dylun admitted. "But it's not safe for you or Gryfelle if we don't try."

Blast.

"All right." I sighed. "Then what's the plan?"

"I'll go first," Father repeated. "I can help the rest of you inside."

"Let me go first, General," Mor insisted. "It could be a long drop. Or maybe there's a literal beast in there. None of us is exactly an expert in reading these runes."

Dylun squinted at his map. "That's true enough," he said absently.

Brilliant.

Father examined the rock a little closer. "If there is a real beast in there, my sword would be of use."

He was too polite to come right out and say he was a better fighter than Mor, but we all knew that to be true.

Mor nodded to his own sword belt. "I'm armed." He gave a lopsided grin. "I'm no Yestin Bo-Arthio, but I did help take down a mountainbeast once."

I turned to look at him. "Are you jesting?"

He shrugged. "My crew and I needed money, and

mountainbeast furs sell for a fortune up north. We only did it the once, and once was enough—both for our treasury and our nerves."

I stood in stunned silence, and before I regathered my wits, Father was lowering Mor down into the gap.

"Mor, wait—"

But Father released Mor's hands, and he disappeared completely. I waited for the *thunk* that would signal Mor had arrived at the bottom of whatever we had just dropped him into.

But it never came.

Without pausing to think, I tumbled toward the warm stream of air flowing from this strange rock formation. "Mor!" I shouted into the gap. "Mor!"

"It's all right," his voice carried back softly, as though through water. "It's not far."

"You next, Tannie," Father said. "Mor will help on the other side." He grabbed my hands, and not for the first time, I was very thankful to be wearing Aeron's extra trousers.

Father and Zel lowered me into the narrow gap backward.

I suppose Father, Zel, and Dylun jumped in after that, but I couldn't say for sure. Because once I was down, my mind was bedazzled by the beauty of the place.

"It's a cave," I whispered aloud, and the walls did strange things with the sound of my voice.

"Aye." Mor nodded to the ground. "Look at that."

Water traced a path through the bottom of the cave, like a small creek. It caught the light through the narrow opening above us and tossed it back onto the cave walls in shades like a sparkling amber-brown gemstone.

"Wow." The word danced off the walls, then died in the cave creek. I laughed and just barely resisted the urge to say more so I could hear how the cave toyed with the sound.

"I don't know where the warm air comes from," Mor said, turning slowly. "Something about the water, maybe."

Dylun didn't seem keen to speculate about the natural won-ders of Haribi. "The strand is in here, or so the map tells us," he said. "And we need you two to link."

Mor and I looked at each other across the space. Then I glanced down. His hands were still encased in leather gloves.

"You'll have to take those off," I said.

"Aye."

I held his gaze as he took off his gloves and handed them to Zel.

He cleared his throat and nodded to Dylun's notes. "What are we supposed to say?"

Dylun shrugged. "Not sure you're supposed to say anything. It just says link."

"All right, then," I said. "Are you ready?"

Mor looked like he was considering saying no, even though he smiled a little. Then he simply held out his hands.

And I took them.

A shock of energy raced through me and grasped my breath. Ribbons spilled from our connection—every shade of green you can imagine, from deepest evergreen to palest waterlily, sea foam to emerald, fern to moss.

Without meaning to, I giggled. Something about the spill-ing of so many strands at once tickled my palms and made me giddy.

It didn't help any when Mor leaned over and said, "Tannie, this is serious," though he himself had a smile on his face.

In this moment, the rush of creating whatever we were making was enough to erase all the cares and troubles so weigh-ing on us. We both relaxed in the peacefulness and let the link do its work, whatever it was.

I closed my eyes, just to bask in the feeling and to imagine that perhaps someday Mor and I might be able to link like this without shame. That I might be able to tell stories without fear, without the weight of a curse or a tyrant king or a harsh mentor pressing against the creativity that wanted to spill out.

A long moment passed. When I opened my eyes, I knew the creation was done. I looked around, but Mor and I did not release our hands.

"Look at that," he said.

There, in the middle of an underground cave on the golden, windswept plains of Haribi, Mor and I had made an exact image of the Corsyth—trees, moss, clear-water marshes, glowing lanterns, and splashes of color. I inhaled the scent of Tirian pines.

"Missed home, did you, Captain?" I asked with a grin.

"Or you did."

"Guess we both did." I breathed in again. "It does smell nice."

"General." Dylun's voice barely registered through my happy haze. "Do you have the box?"

"Yes, I have it here."

I watched a sparkling gold strand dance out from one of our Corsyth lanterns. "Oh. That's why we came here, isn't it?"

"Aye," Mor said slowly as he followed the path of the strand with his gaze.

Did he feel as sleepy as I did? Sleepy, happy, and hazy.

Father held open the box. The blue Meridioni strand still lay coiled up there, like it was napping.

Father inclined his head toward the strand and extended the box. "If you please."

The gold strand jumped as if startled, then ribboned into the box, coiled itself up, and lay still next to its blue fellow.

Mor and I held the connection a heartbeat longer than necessary. I knew—and maybe he did too—that as soon as we broke it, the weight of the real world would return to us.

I held his gaze one more moment. Then I unlaced my fingers from his.

The Corsyth vanished into a puff of green smoke.

Golden-brown light sparkled from the walls again, and the warm air of the "beast's breath" lingered all around us.

Mor's expression fell, painfully slow, so that I could see every single worry return to his mind, every care burden his heart.

My face must have mirrored his.

Father put his hand on my shoulder. His grip was sure, but his eyes were kind. "Let's get back, Tannie girl. For Gryfelle's sake, we need to make haste."

Aye. For Gryfelle's sake.

CHAPTER TWENTY-EIGHT

TANWEN

Askari insisted we spend the night in Haribi and give the villagers time to make enough bread to last us a couple days. It had taken two full weeks to sail from the Western Wildlands of Tir to Paka, so we weren't going to refuse a nice stock of fresh bread. Or their hospitality. Father said it would be very rude in Haribian culture for us to refuse the woven mat beds in their huts.

And to tell you the truth, those mats were more comfortable than I could have imagined. Between the squishy mat and the warm summer night's air, I slept like a swaddled sniffler.

The next morning, I worried our rowboats might sink under the weight of the bread they loaded us up with.

I waved to the Haribians who stood among the marshes to see us off.

"Someday we'll go back," Father said to me. "I'll show you Haribi's great cities."

"Askari mentioned them. He said they have statues and temples."

Father nodded. "Exquisite stoneshapers in Haribi. Some of those temples are thousands of years old."

Hard to imagine a building standing for a thousand years. We had some old castle ruins around Tir, or so I'd been told. I wondered if I would ever get to see them.

Best not to pull at that strand. Better to focus on finding the cure and doing what we could, especially for Gryfelle. We had left Physgot about seven weeks before, and she had barely been alive then. I didn't know how she clung on, but I was glad for it.

Jule, Wylie, and the crewmen had been busy during our night away. The *Cethorelle* sparkled. The men looked mighty happy for the haul of bread we brought along with us.

"Have porridge for breakfast?" Wylie asked with a grin.

"No, even better." I handed him a piece of bread. "I had this, fresh off a hot stone."

Over Wylie's shoulder, I spotted Mor finishing up a conversation with Jule, then Jule beginning to give the men orders to get underway.

"Excuse me a second, Wylie."

He nodded and shoved another piece of bread in his mouth.

I walked up to Mor, keenly aware it was the first time I'd intentionally done so since I stumbled on him pouring his heart out in strands back in Meridione.

"Ho, Mor."

His face registered surprise. "Ho, Tannie."

I steeled myself and spoke quickly. "I just wanted to say I'm sure that retrieving the gold strand was a little awkward for you. It was for me. That we had to link, and all that. If you think it's better if we avoid each other for a while, I promise not to be angry about it. I don't really understand this whole linking business. It's a bit mortifying when it happens."

The corner of his mouth twitched. "*Mor*-tifying?"

I stared at him. Then I laughed and felt a bit of sorrow vanish from my heart. This was the Mor I had been friends with in the Corsyth. The one who had helped me learn to use my gift in new ways. It felt nice to talk to this Mor and not the one who had gone all twisted up inside on account of Gryfelle and me.

"Well, I just wanted you to know," I said.

"I don't really understand linking either, if it makes you feel better."

"No?" I thought a moment. "I don't know why that surprises me. I guess it's been squashed out of existence for most of your life too."

"Aye. It seems there's a reawakening of sorts happening."

"And we get to be in the middle of it." I raised an eyebrow wryly. "Hooray?"

"My father talked about linking. He thought it was happening with me and Diggy once."

"Your sister? Was she a weaver?"

"I don't think so. Usually a weaving gift would be apparent by age thirteen, though I suppose not always. She didn't seem to produce strands. But my strands would do strange things around her sometimes. When we were children, I'd be telling a story to the crew, she would laugh, and suddenly my strand would burst into a puff of glitter." His eyes softened at the memory. "My father mentioned something about weaver gifts connecting at times, and maybe that's what it was, but her gift never really showed itself. So I always supposed it must have been something else."

"It makes you wonder what things would have been like without Gareth in power. How our gifts might have flourished differently," I mused. "Maybe Diggy was a weaver but it was suppressed out of her."

"I'm not sure that's possible, Tannie. Look what's happened to you and Gryfelle."

"True. But Gryfelle and I both embraced our gifts from a young age and then tried to control them. Maybe it was different for Diggy if she didn't discover her gift until later. If she never realized it was there to begin with, maybe everything was different for her."

"Maybe so." He paused. "I'd give anything to find out. To see what she's like now, at seventeen."

"*Is* like?" He had spoken in the present tense.

He shook his head. "Would have been like, I mean."

I paused. "You miss your family terribly."

"Aye."

"I'm sorry for all the loss you've suffered, Mor. I truly am."

"Same to you, Tannie. We have both lost much. I . . . don't want to lose you, too."

My heart tripped, but my voice was cautious. "Well, we're sailing the world, raiding strands from ancient monuments so you won't have to."

"That's not really what I mean. I don't want to lose"—he gestured between us—"this. Your friendship."

"Aye." I swallowed hard. "We'll figure it out."

"Sure."

"Maybe when we get back to the Wildlands, we can grab a drink in Daflin. Warmil took me to a great pub."

"Aye, we'll go to the pub and grab some tea."

I narrowed my eyes. "Warmil told you about my pub tea. Are you mocking me, Captain?"

"Never." He smirked. "I best be back to work now."

"Right. See you around."

His smile tightened. "Aye." He nodded once, then strode away.

I watched him go, praying my declaration that we would "figure it out" was true.

Just as I began to feel the lift of a breath of hope, a bubble popped in my head. An utter void blackened my mind, then I came to myself. And I was disoriented, disjointed, and left wondering what I'd just lost.

CHAPTER TWENTY-NINE

TANWEN

Strange how the roll of the ship put me to sleep now. It had made me ill once, but at this point, the creaking boards, the lap of the sea on the sides of the *Cethorelle*, and the constant rocking were the best sort of lullaby. The only thing that felt comfortable and normal.

Except when I was startled awake in the middle of the night by the shouts of the watchmen.

It hadn't even been a full day since we'd left Haribi.

I flew from my bunk and nearly crashed into Aeron, on her way to the cabin door. She strapped her sword belt around her hips. "Stay here, Tannie."

"But—"

She cut me off with a look. "Thought you'd join in the fight?"

I hadn't realized it before, but now that she mentioned it, footsteps were pounding above deck. If I strained hard enough, I could hear the ring of swords being drawn and the clash of metal against metal.

There was some kind of battle happening up there.

For some reason, I still followed Aeron out of the cabin, down the hall, and toward the stairs.

"Tannie, stay down!" Aeron didn't bother turning around to shout her command.

"I can help." I thought feebly of the wonky sword I'd made to convince Father I wasn't useless.

Maybe I couldn't help with *that*, but surely I could do something if we were under attack.

I ran up the stairs after Aeron and met an explosion of chaos.

The crewmen swarmed the deck amid a mob of total strangers—strangers in piecemeal sailing garb with glittering rings upon their fingers and more weapons on each of them than any one person had a right to carry.

Pirates.

Their ship rested alongside ours, and their grappling hooks were secured in our railing. We'd been boarded and attacked in the middle of the night.

Stars above.

Aeron crossed blades with a blond man about as wide as he was tall and carved from a solid block of muscle.

The man grinned as Aeron blocked another of his strikes. "You're good! Pleasure to spar with you."

Oddly, he looked as if he meant it.

Wylie fought amidships, and he looked bleary and mussed, like he'd been woken from sleep. His opponent was a Meridioni woman who looked to be about Cameria's age and was nearly as beautiful.

Wylie's strikes were hesitant, unsure, and the black-haired woman laughed. "This will be easy," she said in accented Tirian. "Perhaps you will just hand over your spoils to me now?"

"Sailor!" Father blocked the woman's sword stroke just before it would have cleaved Wylie. He then launched a counterstrike. The pirate lass blocked it but winced and drew back her hand.

Father spared Wylie a quick glance. "They're playing for keeps, lad, and your chivalry won't save your life."

The Meridioni smiled again. "Ah, a true soldier."

Father crouched a bit lower. "I don't want to hurt you," he said. "But I will if you force me."

"Tell me where your captain keeps his spoils and I will not force you. Unless you want me to." She winked.

Was this woman flirting with my *father*? I resisted the urge to shoot a strand of fire her direction.

Father's instinctual glance toward the stern led my gaze that direction, and sure enough, there was Mor. He squared off with a sandy-haired pirate, and I thanked the stars he'd ended up with this opponent and not the block of muscle Aeron was fighting. Because both Mor and the pirate had been disarmed and were trading blows with their fists.

Fire sparked in my gut as I watched Mor take a hook to the jaw. Before I could question if it was wise, a strand shot from my hand, so bright it lit up the deck like it was midday. The beam of light hit Mor's assailant squarely in the legs, and he toppled to the deck.

The Meridioni crossing blades with Father froze. "What is this magic?"

"She's just the creative one in the family," Father replied as he exploited his opponent's momentary confusion. He disarmed her swiftly, kicked her sword out of reach, and pinned her in a stranglehold.

Another woman's voice cut through the din. "Schiva! Croy!" Tirian, not accented.

I found the voice's owner—a blonde woman whose hair was a shocking shade of purple on the ends—and it seemed she had been about to go belowdecks. Maybe to look for treasure we weren't carrying.

Unless, of course, the pirates were after our ancient strands.

The idea hit me like a block of ice. Could they be? Were they strand thieves, here to steal our cure?

But no, I realized. The Meridioni had been shocked by my beam of light. These pirates didn't know anything about weaver gifts, let alone ancient cures. They were simply after gold we didn't have. What would they do when they learned that fact?

Though Mor had been standing over his downed opponent with a dagger pointed toward the sandy-haired man's throat, he suddenly abandoned his prize and approached the purple-and-blonde woman, disbelief written all over his face.

Her sword was drawn now, and still he moved toward her, his dagger useless at his side.

"Mor!" I shouted. What was he thinking?

But the purple-and-blonde woman lowered her sword. "Mor?"

He was now within striking distance of her. His face broke into a grin. "Venewth? Venewth En-Gorgyn?"

"Mor Bo-Lidere." She laughed. "In the name of the taxes, I never thought I'd see the likes of you again." Then her smile fell. "And certainly not sailing under Tir's banner! Cethor's tears, Mor, what's happened to you?"

"Son." Father was still holding the Meridioni woman—Schiva, I assumed—awkwardly around her throat. "Perhaps some explanation first?"

Mor raised his hands and told the crew to stand down. "It's all right. These are my friends."

"Friends?" Venewth raised an eyebrow as she placed a hand on her hip. "We're his old crew." She sheathed her sword. "Until he left us to chase after a lass."

"It's a bit more complicated than that," Mor said, and I could swear I saw his ears turn red, even in the dark. "Hey," he added, turning toward his downed opponent. "You're new."

The sandy-haired man climbed to his feet. "Croy Bo-Wyryck. I've heard a lot about you from Captain Venewth."

"Captain?" Mor's eyes went wide. "Well, look at you. What happened to Freith? Thought I left him in charge."

Venewth snorted. "Aye. Caught him stealing from the

plunder less than three moons into his stretch as captain. You should've known better than to hand him the captaincy."

Mor sighed. "True enough. But I'd hoped for more. What did you do with him?"

"Shoved him overboard." Venewth shrugged at my scandalized expression. "We were close to land. He swam to shore. Most likely."

"Mor!" The blond block of muscle embraced Mor like they were brothers. "It's been too long."

"Gyth!" Mor turned to the rest of us. "Gyth was my first mate."

"And now he's my first mate," Venewth cut in, "and this reunion has been swell, but it's time we collect and be on our way. No need to shed blood or any more sweat."

Mor's expression hardened a little. "Venewth, we aren't carrying any gold."

"That's a Tirian banner, isn't it? Princess Braith's by the look of it."

"Queen Braith."

Venewth cocked her head to the side. "So the rumors are true?"

"Aye, they're true. And we're sailing under the queen, but I assure you, this is not a typical royal commission."

"Oh, come Mor. Surely there's something aboard you might share." Venewth held a dagger now, though I didn't recall seeing her draw it. "For old time's sake."

Mor sighed long and low through his nose. "We have bread from Haribi."

"That'll do. Think of it as a tax on the queen."

Mor held Venewth's gaze, then signaled the crewmen to begin collecting some bread.

"What kind of royal mission is this, Mor?" Venewth asked. "Never took you for a queen's man, so it must be important."

"It's not really a royal mission. It's a personal one."

"Should have guessed." Venewth's expression softened. "I really am glad you're alive. You dropped off the map for a while there. We thought you dead."

"Not yet."

"Sorry to be pillaging your ship. Especially now that you've turned legitimate, and all." Mischief danced in her eyes.

"It's just bread."

"And what is it you're seeking on this mission? I doubt it's bread."

"Strands," he said simply. "Important strands necessary to save someone."

"Noble." She glanced at her crew, the five she'd brought aboard the *Cethorelle* now laden with Haribian bread. "Well, we'll be out of your way now. Sorry for the wake-up call." She cast a sideways glance at me and winked. "Happy raiding, Mor Bo-Lidere."

CHAPTER THIRTY

BRAITH

"YOUR MAJESTY, IT HAS BEEN HALF A MOON SINCE DRAY Bo-Anffir was found guilty of his crimes," Sir Fellyck said. "Can we expect his execution anytime soon?"

Braith sat at the table with her council. She folded her hands and looked at Fellyck. "Do you have a personal vendetta against Dray, Sir Fellyck?"

"Majesty, you know full well Dray made many enemies during his time at this table."

"Indeed."

"It is not bloodlust but the desire for justice that prompts my questions."

Braith drew a deep breath. "Yes."

For once, Fellyck's voice took on a kind note. "Queen Braith, I am not an unfeeling man. I know this must be difficult for you."

Braith smiled sadly. "Thank you. I appreciate that acknowledgment, at least. I do not wish to forestall justice. It's only . . ."

"It's the first time you have sentenced someone to death."

"I rather prefer mercy to justice."

"Yes." Fellyck pressed his lips together. "However . . ."

"I know." Braith rose and ascended the steps of the dais. She lowered herself onto her throne and sat there a moment, thinking.

Then she spoke. "Dray Bo-Anffir has been sentenced to die, and his sentence will be carried out on the—"

But her words were cut off by a commotion at the back of the room. Muffled voices, a shout, then the throne room doors banging open. The room full of courtiers turned at the disturbance.

Braith had remained seated. "Captain?" she said to the guardsman at the other end of the silver carpet. "What is this?"

The guardsman assigned to her personal security already had his sword drawn. He barked at the intruder, "Who goes there? In the name of the queen, declare yourself!"

A man slipped free of the knot of guards clustered around him. "Forgive me," he said, his unarmed hands raised. He strode calmly down the carpet toward Braith. "I did not mean to cause a ruckus."

"Halt! Sir, I order you to halt!" Braith's captain didn't seem sure whether he should cleave the unarmed man in two or not. "Halt there, and speak your purpose!"

The man stopped at last, nearly at the council table now. He smiled up at Braith pleasantly. He was young still—not much older than Braith herself.

Braith watched him, puzzled. This intruder was at ease as he disrupted her court, defied her guardsman, and smiled brazenly at her. She scanned him head to toe. He was well dressed in fine leather, though with none of the frills and baubles the titled lords favored. In that way, he reminded Braith of Sir Dray.

But in all other respects, he was the opposite. Young with blond hair and the close-cropped beard the palace guardsmen wore. But he was unarmed, without even a sword belt at his hips. His hair was pulled into a tail, as was the fashion for most Tirian men.

The son of a wealthy merchant, perhaps? The son of a knight? But Braith did not recognize him.

He bowed low at the waist. "My lady."

The captain now stood beside the man, and he looked ready to remove the intruder's blond head. "You will address your queen properly, cur, or I'll have you in irons before another smirk crosses your face."

The man's gaze was still fixed on Braith. "Forgive me. It has been so many years . . ." He smiled again, but then he glanced at the fuming guardsman. "I will address my lady with the respect due her, for all I know of her character does command respect. But I cannot address my lady as queen."

The captain looked ready to spew fire, but Braith raised her hand to calm him. She held the intruder's gaze. His eyes were a stormy blue-gray. There was something vaguely familiar . . .

"Sir, I don't believe we have met, but you seem to know me."

"It has been a great many years, Lady Braith."

She narrowed her eyes. "Who are you?"

"We were children last we saw each other face-to-face." His gaze turned significant. "Thirteen years ago, to be exact."

Braith inhaled sharply. Thirteen years ago, when her father staged a "plague" and murdered King Caradoc II. This was a boy from Caradoc's court? But who?

"Sir," she said at last, and her voice shook, "I must demand your name before my guardsman makes good on his threat."

The young man spared the captain half a glance, then spoke to Braith. "Kharn Bo-Candryd, my lady." He bowed again. "At your service."

A roar erupted from the room.

Some of the newer nobles seemed confused. "Who? Who is this?"

Others clearly knew the name. "Impossible! He lies!"

"Kharn, did he say?" Sir Fellyck asked. "I know no noble by that name."

But Braith knew.

She held up her hands to quiet her people and addressed the

intruder. "I thought all Sir Candryd's sons died in the supposed plague."

"The appearance my family wished to put forth, my lady. I'm sure you can understand why."

Indeed, she could. It was no small wonder half the room had never heard the Candryd name. Braith's father had done his best to extinguish the memory of many noble families that represented a threat to his unscrupulously gained rule.

Braith realized she did know those eyes. And his voice and smile and even his walk. He had grown into a man these past thirteen years, just as she had grown into a woman. But she knew he spoke the truth.

She lifted her voice that the whole room might hear. "This man is the youngest son of the late Sir Candryd, youngest brother of Caradoc II." Braith looked slowly around at those gathered there. "He is Caradoc's nephew, blood heir to the Tirian throne."

Cameria stared blankly at Braith. "I don't understand what you mean, Majesty."

"Kharn Bo-Candryd interrupted council today. He was the youngest son of—"

"Caradoc's brother, Candryd. I remember who he is. But I don't understand what you're saying to me, my lady."

"He is alive, apparently."

"Are you certain?" Cameria was obviously concerned. "Should we order an inquiry? It could be an imposter."

"I recognize him."

"But thirteen years have passed. Surely he is much changed. How can you be certain?"

"I just remember him. His eyes and his smile. Everything about him. It took his name to recall the memories, but once he said it, I knew. We played together as children, and one doesn't forget one's playmates so easily."

"I suppose, but—"

"It is he, Cameria. I'm certain."

Cameria bit her lip. "He has been in hiding all this time?"

"Apparently."

The maid lowered herself to one of the padded benches in Braith's front room. "Unbelievable. What does this mean?"

"That is the question of the day, I suppose." Braith sat next to her friend, a little harder than she meant to. "He is the heir."

"Your Majesty! You're not considering handing him your throne, are you?"

"I don't know what to do, Cameria. I don't even know what to think."

Cameria rose and began to pace the room. "Well, *if* he truly is Kharn—"

"He is."

Cameria ignored her comment. "Then he is the blood heir of Caradoc II. But does that really make him king? Thirteen years have passed. And whatever means your father used to claim the throne, the fact is, he did."

Braith sighed. "That is true enough."

"And he ruled Tir for over a decade. He ought not to have been king, but he was."

"Also true."

"And you were princess. You sat on his council. Whatever your father's character was, *you* have served Tir faithfully."

The only agreement Braith could muster was silence.

"And you were appointed queen."

"By a few. It was not a vote of the people but of a tiny handful of representatives. A mere committee."

"That is no matter. They chose you. You are queen."

"Cameria." Braith rose and strode to the window. She flung it open. "Do you not hear them?"

The sounds of the peasants banging at the front gate floated up to the palace rooms, just as they had every day since the first week of Braith's reign.

"They hate me."

"No, they do not hate you. They don't know you. They are angry about your father. They are weary from his oppression. And half of them are starving. This will settle once they see the sort of ruler you mean to be."

"But Kharn . . ."

"Make him Lord of Wax Beans, since surely he has been hiding on some distant farm all these years while you helped rule Tir."

Braith turned and shot her friend a look. "Cameria. That was uncharitable."

"Forgive me. I just don't understand what he hopes to accomplish, appearing suddenly when your rule is barely established."

"I believe he means to reclaim the throne my family stole from his."

"But that isn't fair!"

Braith laughed, but it held no mirth. "None of it is fair."

"You cannot just hand it to him. I won't let you!"

Braith shook her head. "You are so loyal, Cameria."

"You earned this! You are the ruler Tir needs. At last there is some hope for the people, even if they are too blind to see it."

Braith swallowed. "You have more faith in me than I have in myself."

"That is my point!" Cameria insisted. "When was the last time Tir was ruled by one humble enough to admit to not knowing all the answers? The reason I know you will not falter is because you will listen to your people. You will listen to your councilors. And you will listen to that iron-rod moral center you have been blessed with."

Braith looked fondly at her. "You trust me too much."

"Stop. Please, Braith, I beg you to stop convincing yourself that Kharn would be better for Tir. You don't even know the man."

"I don't know what else to do, Cameria."

Cameria grabbed her hand. "We will work through this together. And you will consult your council. Do not agree to anything until you have spoken to them. And wait until Yestin returns from sea."

"The general? He could be away for a year."

"Then send a letter. Perhaps the carrier birds could intercept them at some port or another. And if not, we will stall this intruder, for that is what he is. Don't do anything rash until you have heard from Yestin."

Braith laughed, and a few unbidden tears spilled out. "That may be the first time in my life anyone has accused me of being rash."

Cameria quieted. "Forgive me. I am not accusing. Merely cautioning. I know you, and I know that as soon as Kharn Bo-Candryd starts in on you, telling you why it is right that he sit on the throne, you will agree."

"Am I that spineless?"

"No. But you do feel that much guilt over what your father did to Caradoc. And if Kharn is half the politician Dray or Naith or any of your father's councilors were, he will exploit that guilt. And you will sign away your throne to him before supper time."

"You are right. And you are right that I don't know the man. Childhood playmates do grow up, do they not?"

"Indeed. Do everything you can to stay well away from Kharn Bo-Candryd."

"Yes, Cameria," Braith responded with a smile.

"Good." Cameria nodded, appeased. "Shall we get you out of this heavy dress, Your Majesty?"

"A soft dressing gown sounds heavenly. I feel I could go to sleep for the night and it is not even supper time."

"Let's start with the dressing gown, at least."

A knock sounded on the door.

Both women froze.

After a moment, Cameria went to the door.

Braith picked up the book she had been reading before bed the previous night. She had read it before—some long-dead general's musings about military tactics—but it never hurt to brush up on such things.

Cameria's voice took on an angry note. "No, you may not— excuse me!"

Braith sat up straight as an arrow.

For Kharn Bo-Candryd stood in her front room, a small bouquet of snow-white velvet-petal flowers in his hands and two armored guardsmen holding either elbow. He offered the bouquet to her with some difficulty, a wry grin on his face. "Good evening, Braith."

"I . . ." Braith stared at the flowers, then at the guardsmen. "What?"

"Majesty," one of the guardsmen said. "We caught him just as he forced his way into your front room."

Kharn eyed the man. "I did not force. I knocked like any respectable visitor."

Braith looked past the velvet-petals. "I do not usually receive visitors in my front room, sir."

"Of course." Kharn winced as the guards tightened their grips. "I did not think you would accept a written invitation to meet with me. So I thought I'd try this."

Braith raised an eyebrow. "It isn't working out much better, though, is it?"

"Not especially." He winced again.

Braith paused to consider the situation. She glanced at Cameria. "I will meet with you at my council table in the throne room with my guardsmen and my maid present. You may have thirty minutes."

"Excellent!" Kharn's eyes were bright. "I'll have tea sent."

"Excuse me? You'll have tea sent to *my* throne room from *my* kitchens?" Braith took the bouquet from his hands. She passed it over to Cameria. "Please put these in water." Then she glanced at her guards. "And if Sir Kharn misbehaves, perhaps we'll put him in water too. Let's go then, shall we?"

She passed by the others and exited her private chambers, relieved that her voice hadn't shaken.

Braith eyed the man who sat across the council table from her. A kitchen servant placed a silver tea tray before them.

"I hope you'll forgive the intrusion," Kharn said at last.

"The intrusion of you visiting my chambers uninvited? Or perhaps the intrusion of you showing up at my council meeting this afternoon?"

"Both." Kharn waited as the servant set out three cups. Then he glanced at Cameria. "Do you often take tea with your maids?"

Cameria stiffened.

"She is my lady's maid," Braith said tersely, "but she is also my friend."

"Oh." Kharn turned his pleasant smile toward the Meridioni woman. "Most excellent. That is the ideal combination, is it not? And might I have the pleasure of your name?"

Cameria did not look at all happy about it, but at last she said, "Cameria." The single word was clipped and annoyed.

"Cameria En-Benatti?" Kharn's face showed genuine surprise.

So did Cameria's. "Yes, Benatti was my father."

"I knew him." A shadow of grief crossed him. "I'm sorry for your loss. He was a fine man."

Cameria's mouth opened, then closed. But no words came out. Such sentiments had not been offered in the months after Benatti's death when Cameria was grieving his loss.

"That is kind of you, Kharn," Braith spoke into the silence.

"Benatti was excellent at cards," Kharn said. "We played often, and he must have earned a year's wages off my foolish bets. I was just a lad, and the other nobles would let me win. But not Benatti. He said it taught me nothing to reward me for my foolishness."

In spite of herself, Cameria laughed tearfully. "Yes. That sounds like him."

Braith glanced at Cameria, who had gone from a block of ice to a puddle of sentiment in the space of a breath. She turned back to Kharn. Kharn Bo-Candryd, who seemed to be kind and was certainly charming.

"You have twenty-four minutes, Kharn," she said at last.

"Ah, yes. This is a difficult position we find ourselves in, is it not?" He watched as the servant poured boiling water over three linen sacks filled with tea leaves. He took a deep breath. "I smell burnt sugar, fine black tea, and coconuts all the way from the Spice Islands. Coconuts are a bit indulgent, don't you think, my lady?"

Braith frowned. Of course, he would find her *one* indulgence. Her *one* weakness. She did so love coconut. "It was a tea sommelier's suggestion. He knows my fondness for those fruits. There is only a little in there." She frowned at Kharn again. "I do not need to explain my tea to you."

He chuckled. "Forgive me, Braith. I was only teasing."

Kharn added grazer cream to his cup. "A princess is allowed some indulgences, is she not?"

"I suppose." Braith added cream to her own cup. "But you do not really believe I was a princess."

"Of course you were. You sat on the princess's throne for thirteen years. The only question is the legitimacy of your reign as queen."

Braith stared at him. He said it so casually. So carelessly. "Not everyone finds my reign questionable." It didn't come out as forcefully as she would have liked.

"But when they hear I'm alive, I think it will be a question for everyone." He held out a small bowl. "Sugar?"

"No," Braith snapped. She paused and forced herself to draw a calming breath. "No, thank you, Kharn."

"I don't take it either. The tea is delicious enough. And besides, that burnt sugar in your blend"—he inhaled deeply of the vapor rising from his cup—"is sweet enough on its own, I'd wager."

"Yes. Would you like to spend your remaining nineteen minutes discussing tea blends?" She looked down at her cup, suddenly wary that her rival had handled it.

Somehow, he read her thoughts plainly. "Braith. Please give me more credit than that. I would never poison anyone in the first place because it would be dastardly. And foolish, besides. My uncle was murdered with poison, and it seems a very unwise thing to try to reclaim his throne by poisoning the people's queen with her evening tea."

Still, Braith would not touch her cup.

He smiled. "Shall we trade? I'll sip from both, if you like, but then I will have sipped from your cup, and I'm not sure that's proper."

"Kharn!" She rolled her eyes. "You are just the same."

He laughed. "You expected I would have changed?"

"I don't know what I expected. Certainly not any of this."

Kharn's face grew serious. "I'm sure that is true, and I am sorry for your situation. This is awkward and unpleasant, and you don't deserve it." He regarded her for a long moment. "You are both changed and the same."

Braith sniffed her tea one last time, then glanced at Cameria and took a sip. "Oh? How am I both changed and the same?"

"You always were so grave. So serious. But something else has been added over the years. You seem sadder."

The word struck like a dart. "Of course. Much has happened in the thirteen years you've been away. Much has happened in the two moons since Gareth fell."

Kharn's tone was gentle. "You have suffered much, Braith. And yet you served Tir well."

Braith found herself softening. "Thank you. I did try, though it was not always easy."

"I doubt it was ever easy with your father on the throne."

"Stop," Braith said sharply.

"Drinking tea?" Kharn took a sip. "But I rather enjoy it. Your sommelier has done well."

She glanced at him, then dropped her gaze to her cup. "No. You should stop talking to me about my father. It . . . isn't right."

"Why not?"

Braith had no answer. Instead she said, "You have twelve minutes to tell me what you're doing here."

"Here in the throne room? I'm having tea."

Braith shot him a look. "No, in Urian. Where have you been all these years?"

"Hiding. On a farm."

"Cameria was right, then. Shall I make you Lord of Wax Beans?"

Kharn laughed. "Lord of what?"

"Nothing." Shame heated her cheeks. "I was being rude. I'm sorry."

"I love bean salad. Can I be Lord of Bean Salad?"

In spite of herself, Braith chuckled. "Honestly."

"The farm I lived on belongs to a relative of my father's most trusted servant. It was quite prosperous. At least, as prosperous as a farm can be during years of war, blight, and famine."

"You never fought, did you? In the expansion wars?"

"Indeed, no. The last thing I needed was for someone to recognize me."

"No, of course." Her father would have seen Kharn's head on a chopping block faster than he could toss a bean salad.

"I stayed on the farm. I won't say exactly where, just in case, but it was across the Endrol River in a sleepy little area beyond the Codewig."

"Just in case?" Braith's eyebrows rose. "Just in case what?"

"In case you might arrest those who housed me. They became my family and treated me like their own son. I would not want to see harm come to them."

Braith was horrified. "How could you think that?"

"Forgive me if I've offended you. I don't believe you capable of such a thing. You are a woman of character. But I am still readjusting to court life. I suppose spending half my life in hiding has made me mistrustful."

The funny thing was, he didn't really look mistrustful. He looked like the young lad she knew once. His easy smile, his slightly irreverent sense of humor, his warm eyes. He didn't look paranoid and irritable the way her father had become.

"I only want to protect them," he said again. "They are all the family I have left."

"Of course. I'm sorry. I should be more . . . that is, I understand." She met his gaze. "And you didn't deserve it either."

His attention lingered on her for an extra moment, and a hint of a smile played on his mouth. "Thank you, Braith. I appreciate that from you."

She nodded, then lifted her teacup and allowed a somewhat

awkward silence to fill the room. Now what? Kharn acted like they were two old friends catching up. And, in some ways, they were.

In others, they were anything but.

"Shall we take a stroll in the garden?" he asked.

"Excuse me?"

"The sun is beginning to set, and gardens are lovely at sunset."

"But you only have six minutes left."

"I thought perhaps I might request an extension."

"There are rioters. It isn't safe."

"I'll be there. And so will your guards. Perhaps that's more to the point."

She looked at the remnants of her tea. "You are rather unnerving company, you know, Kharn."

He smiled. "Am I?" Then he rose and offered his hand. "Perhaps I'm less unnerving in the fresh air."

Braith stood and warily accepted his arm. "I rather doubt it."

CHAPTER THIRTY-ONE

BRAITH

CAMERIA TIED OFF THE END OF BRAITH'S COMPLICATED PLAIT. "There. Finished at last."

"You have gotten quite good at this, Cameria. Keep it up, and I won't have to replace my beauticians."

Cameria shot Braith a look. "I will make sure to do more poorly tomorrow."

Braith laughed and rose from the vanity table. "The court will want an update on the investigation into my father's death. One of my generals has a plan, I'm told, about how to handle the uprisings. I shall be interested to hear that, as long as it doesn't involve slaughtering the people. We have a governor of a Wildland province—I've forgotten which—who is here with a petition. I can only assume the famine has worsened. Perhaps the eastern farms will be able to provide some aid." She sighed. The farms had little enough to spare. "I would dig into the treasury if only it would help."

"Yet the peasants cannot eat money."

"No, indeed." Braith frowned. "Fish? Could we pay the fishermen to hire some extra hands? There is never a shortage of fish in the sea."

"That is an idea. But Tirians do love their bread and porridge."

"We may have to adjust our tastes to suit our supply. Though the peasants will take it as a personal affront and dislike me all the more."

Cameria didn't bother arguing this time.

Braith sighed. "It's not all they will want to discuss."

"The peasants?"

"The council. They will want to talk about Kharn." Braith had barely slept for two nights. Her sunset stroll in the garden with the young man had replayed over and over in her mind.

What did he want from her? He seemed so friendly. So genuine. She didn't know what to make of him.

"Yes, Your Majesty. They will want to discuss him. And it would be wise to decide in advance what you will say." Cameria looked at her closely. "What *will* you say?"

"I . . . know not."

"He is puzzling, to be sure."

"Yes. Just when I think I've decided what I'll—"

A knock at the door interrupted her. She raised an eyebrow.

Cameria moved quickly. "I will answer it."

Braith waited. This time, she did not pick up a book. She strained toward the door to catch any words she might.

Yes. It was his voice. "Good morning, Cameria."

"Good morning, Sir Kharn."

Cameria had certainly changed her stripes! Now he was *Sir* Kharn. Inexplicably, it made Braith smile.

"I've come to escort Braith to breakfast."

And then, there he was in the sitting room, bright as the sun. "Good morning! You look especially beautiful today. That color suits you."

Braith glanced down at her dress. "It's black. I'm in mourning."

"No one mourns quite as beautifully as Braith."

Braith rolled her eyes. She seemed to do that a lot around Kharn. "Honestly."

"Yes, honestly. You truly look lovely in black." He offered his arm. "Might I escort you to breakfast?"

Cameria nodded discreetly, and when Braith still didn't accept Kharn's arm, she spoke. "We were just about to go down to the dining hall."

Braith shot her a quick glare.

"Excellent." Kharn nodded to his arm. "Shall we?"

Braith stifled a sigh and took it. They moved from her front room into the hallway.

Kharn set off down the hall at a measured pace. "I'm afraid I've developed a liking for that tea of yours, Braith. If I spend all my fortune on coconuts, it will be your fault."

"Will it? I rather thought you would blame the coconuts for being so delicious."

He smiled. "Perhaps I should." He glanced over his shoulder at Cameria, then turned back to Braith. "Forgive me for the question, Lady Braith, but do you discuss politics with your friend?"

Braith frowned. "Pardon me?"

"Politics. I know you and Cameria are close, but that does not always mean one is privy to the queen's business."

"I hide nothing from Cameria. Though I'm not entirely sure Tir's politics or what my friends are privy to is *your* business."

"I didn't mean to pry. It's only because I wished to talk to you about council."

"Oh." Braith stopped and turned to face Kharn. "What about council? You may speak freely in front of Cameria."

"I thought perhaps you would like to discuss strategies for the food crisis in the Wildlands."

Braith blinked in surprise, then narrowed her eyes at him cautiously. "In the Wildlands, you say, but the crisis extends all over Tir."

"And your father's solution was to levy heavier taxes each year."

"That was not even an attempt at a solution, Sir Kharn, and we both know it."

"No, indeed. Personally, I am not concerned with your father's policies at present. I wondered if you had any ideas to solve the problem at hand. I do, and I would be happy to give them."

Braith paused and looked at Cameria. "We were just discussing the possibility of subsidizing some fishing endeavors. There is no shortage in the sea, and perhaps that could be enough to fill the gaps in our food supply."

Kharn considered this. "I think it has merit. But it is a temporary fix. It is possible to overfish the ocean. It isn't much of a problem here because our diet doesn't include much fish, but it is an issue for most island territories where they rely heavily on the sea and do little farming."

Braith eyed him. "And you learned of such things hiding on your secret farm?"

"No." He smiled. "I learned these things as the nephew of the king. The youngest son of the youngest brother doesn't get much training, mind, but I always did well with such studies."

"How fortuitous. And what are your ideas, Sir Kharn? You said you had some."

"Bellithwyn has some fascinating theories about crop rotation and nutrients. Different plants use different elements of the soil. The Bellithwynites have done extensive research and come up with planting schedules for all sorts of climates. Perhaps we might send an ambassador and ask for assistance in learning these methods and for a copy of their almanac. Or perhaps a thousand copies," he added lightly.

"That is an idea," Braith said.

Kharn's mouth twitched. "You sound surprised. The Minasimetese have farming machinery far more advanced than ours. Of course, there is the age-old problem of getting the reclusive Minasimetese to allow us on their island so that we might learn from them. But perhaps your emancipation will help that."

Braith regarded Kharn for a long moment in silence.

He waited, then grinned. "What?"

"You . . ." Braith looked to Cameria for help, but the maid seemed to have found something very interesting on the sill of the nearest window. Braith stifled a sigh. "Well, you're standing here in my palace."

"Yes, but also my palace, depending on how you look at it. Shall we duel for it?"

"That isn't funny."

"I thought it was a little."

"Honestly."

"My apologies." He gestured for her to continue. "Please, proceed."

"Well, you're standing here with me. Discussing the realm."

"Yes?"

"Is this appropriate?"

"Is it inappropriate?"

"I think it may be." Braith looked again to Cameria for help, but none was forthcoming.

"What about this is inappropriate?" Kharn inquired. "If I may ask."

"I'm the queen," Braith replied crisply. "You wish to depose me. You have a claim to the throne. We haven't sorted through that matter in the least, and yet you want to strategize solutions together. That seems appropriate to you?"

Kharn shrugged. "I respect your ideas."

She stared at him. "I don't know how to argue with that."

Kharn grinned. "Good."

"You . . . frustrate me."

"I've noticed." Kharn nodded down the hallway. "Shall we? I promise not to discuss any matters of state until after breakfast."

"How generous." Braith resumed walking toward one of the staircases.

"Or I'll wait until council, if you prefer."

Braith halted again. "What?"

"Council. I'll be there. I'll stand in the gallery if you don't want me at the table right away."

"I . . . no, you may sit at the table." Braith wasn't sure what she had just agreed to.

"Thank you—that's kind of you. I know we must get this sorted."

"Um, yes."

"But for now, we'll just have some tea and enjoy breakfast."

"You and the tea again." Braith shook her head. "You have an obsession."

They strolled in silence the rest of the way to the dining hall, and Braith's thoughts were a jumble.

Hopefully she could right them by afternoon council. Council. Where Kharn Bo-Candryd would be at the table.

And Braith had absolutely no idea how she felt about that.

CHAPTER THIRTY-TWO

TANWEN

MOR AND I NEVER DID HAVE TEA OR ANYTHING ELSE AT MHO'S, the pub on the Daflin docks. He and Jule had decided to dock for just a day before we made way again—just enough time to replenish our stores and make a few small repairs to the ship. Then we were off, down the Tirian coastline, around Meridione, a one-day stop in Bordino, then back into the open sea. We had charted a course for Minasimet, way out in the Menfor, and if the winds were in our favor, that trip would take ten full days.

The winds agreed with our plans, and Minasimet had been sighted now.

No one said it aloud, but I knew what was prompting the haste. In the four weeks since we left Paka, I had experienced one episode per week, and half a dozen little memory bubbles had popped. The rocks of my mind were beginning to slide all over the place.

And that was to say nothing of Gryfelle's ever-weakening state.

I avoided asking questions as though touching the answers might burn me.

How long had it taken Gryfelle's body to begin to fade? How many moons had the rocks slid from her mind before she didn't remember her loved ones anymore? At some point she had forgotten her feelings for Mor, but it seemed the unpleas-antness of her childhood remained. Would that be first to go for me?

Or had I lost it already?

Best not to ask. Best to keep moving forward on this quest and pray there would be hope for us both by the time we completed our task.

And as I stared up at the island that seemed to be one solid mountain, I wasn't sure we would be able to. No wonder the Minasimetese had been able to keep outsiders away for centuries. Instead of a beach, there was a wall. Instead of land, craggy peaks. Instead of a harbor, a huge sea gate.

With guards perched atop.

Though the Haribians hadn't met us with warmth, this island was infinitely more foreboding than Haribi with its wide-open, sun-kissed plains. We were well into the first moon of autumn now, and I could already see snow capping the Minasimetese peaks in the distance, beyond the barriers of the island.

"We'll never get in," I said to Father. "Unless you have an old friend lounging about that tower there."

He looked up at it grimly. "I doubt it. I've never set foot on this island. And that's only one of my worries." He glanced at me restlessly.

"I'm fine, Father." It sounded hollow, even to my own ears.

"No, you're not." He watched as the sea gate and the armed tower grew closer. "The list of concerns grows daily."

"Does it?" I frowned. Seemed we had been in the same spot for a while now.

"I sense something." His voice was distant. "Sometimes, I swear I can almost see it, then it's gone."

"See what?"

"I'm not sure. But I can feel it."

I shivered.

He cast a rueful smile my way. "Sorry. I don't mean to sound so grave. I'm not used to sharing my thoughts."

I almost hadn't noticed, so gradual had it been, but the rasp in his voice had lessened. His sentences were nearly always complete now. Least as complete as mine, anyway.

"You're doing better," I told him.

"It is a challenge." Then he stared into the distance again. "Do you ever feel we're being watched?"

"Well, I do now." My gaze darted all over, and I pulled my shawl tighter around my shoulders.

"General." Mor's voice preceded his arrival.

I turned to see him approaching with Jule. Jule nodded up at the tower. We were now close enough to count the men—and their arrows. "What are your thoughts, General?"

Father drew a long breath. "My Minasimetese has never been good. I have no friends here, but perhaps they know our names."

Mor nodded. "Perhaps they will take pity."

"Pity on us?" I folded my arms. "You know what we look like, don't you?"

The men turned to me but didn't answer.

"Exactly like a bunch of pirates."

"But we're not." Mor sounded a little wounded. "We're flying under the Tirian banner."

"But we're obviously not queen's navy. You've got women on your crew, and strictly speaking, we *have* been traveling around the world pillaging things."

Jule grinned. "Suppose that's technically true."

"Borrowing, more like," Mor insisted. "Borrowing for a very just cause."

"All right, Captain." I nodded up at the towers. "You explain that to them."

"My grandmam was Minasimetese, you know," Mor said.

"And mine was a fluff-hopper."

"I'm serious."

I eyed him. "Truly? I guess that's where your dark hair came from. I assumed you had Meridioni in your line somewhere. Do you speak Minasimetese?"

He snorted. "Do you speak fluff-hopper?"

I shrugged.

"I'll have to give it a try, then," Father said. He called up to them, "*Suru!*"

"*Tachi hanu!*" came the rather angry-sounding reply.

Already this wasn't going well, and my father's face confirmed it.

"He's telling us to go away. Where's Dylun?"

"Here." Dylun stepped forward. "But I don't know that my Minasimetese is any better than yours, General."

Father tried again. He called to the guards, but I could tell the language didn't sit comfortably on him. How would he ever be able to explain our situation? Where would he drum up the words for *curse* or *ancient cure*, or anything else that might inspire them to open their gates to us? And really, wouldn't they be a little daft to do so, even if we had the perfect explanation?

Dylun tried when Father seemed to be getting nowhere, but somehow, he made it worse. He looked at my father, eyes wide. "Did I say something insulting?"

"Seems so." Father shook his head. "But I'm not even sure what."

"*Sugatok kara koti!*" With that shout, the guard who had been speaking drew his bowstring and loosed an arrow.

Straight at me.

Time seemed to slow. Father turned with his arm extended, as if to knock me to the deck, out of harm's way. But before he could manage it, Mor grabbed my wrist. When we touched, a shell like a bubble of shimmering glass formed in front of us. It was only for a moment, but long enough to deflect the arrow.

It just missed Dylun on the ricochet, then sailed overboard and into the water.

After a breath of stunned silence, Mor whirled and yelled at the guard, "Hey!"

But he was still holding on to me. All it took was that one word, and a blast of hot energy shot out from our connection. It volleyed, faster than an arrow, toward the guard on the tower and smacked him in his armed chest. He toppled out of view.

I stared in horror, half expecting to see his body tumbling into the water off the other side of the tower. But he reappeared, clutching his chest and coughing.

He had only been knocked on his backside. Thank the stars.

Everyone aboard ship seemed to breathe a sigh of relief when the guard appeared to be fine. Everyone except Father.

A look of dread realization crossed his face.

"Father? What's wrong?"

"You're a weapon."

I stared at him. "What?"

"You and Bo-Lidere. The link. It makes you twice as powerful, and already you were formidable."

Mor looked as confused as I felt. "Are you saying they won't let us in because they think we're a threat? Because of our weaving abilities?"

"No." Father shook his head, almost like he wished he could just invite us inside his mind rather than having to find the words to explain. "Tannie, they've been following us."

"They . . . the guards?" The more he tried to explain, the more puzzled I grew.

But then he looked at me again, and something clicked.

"The presence you felt," I realized aloud.

"Yes."

"You think they're after me and Mor? Because of the link?"

"Yes."

Ice spread down my spine. "So, they *have* been watching us."

"Not just watching. Hunting." Father's mouth tightened into a thin line.

"How do you know?"

He nodded over my shoulder. "Because here they are now."

CHAPTER THIRTY-THREE

TANWEN

I SPUN AROUND SO FAST, I NEARLY FELL OVER.

Yes, there was a ship—far off, a mere speck on the horizon. But zooming closer was a wave of something. I strained to see it better and took a halting step toward . . . whatever grew nearer with each passing moment.

"Strands," I said, but I couldn't quite comprehend it. "Those are strands."

Indeed, the wave looked like it was made up of ribbons of night sky and tendrils of smoke and rivulets of molten metal. And they were racing across the ocean toward us.

Father didn't waste another second. He whipped back toward the guards. "*Miu? Sa, watachi ni rete kasai. Mohi anate kereba.*"

"What did he say?" Mor asked Dylun, watching the approaching wave of strands in disbelief.

Dylun glanced between the guards and the strands. "He told them we're all in danger if they do not let us in."

And the guards seemed to be considering it. They spoke among themselves, occasionally gesturing toward us or out into the sea. The torrent rolled ever closer.

"Please!" I called out helplessly.

"Tannie, stay close," Mor warned.

He pointed. One strand was ahead of the rest, just about to the rail of the *Cethorelle*.

Then the sea gate began to move. It was a wonder the hinges worked or that the guards even knew how to get the blasted thing open.

The gates began to open inward. But slowly.

Too slowly.

The strand in the lead—a perfect ribbon of starry-midnight sky—had reached us. And it was headed straight for my father.

He drew his sword, and so did Warmil and Aeron, but to what end? Would they cleave a ribbon of night in two?

"No!" Without thinking, I thrust my hand forward, and out came a beam of sunlight. It swallowed the night strand, and both disappeared with a pop.

Father grabbed my shoulder. "We have to get inside."

I looked back at the wave—nearly to the ship. There were too many strands. I could never hope to fight them all. Even with every weaver aboard battling them one at a time, we would be overtaken.

"Captain!" Wylie shouted. "Tannie!"

I spun. One of the crewmen had a strand of night wrapped around his ankle. Wylie and another sailor gripped the man to keep him from being pulled overboard.

I shot a ray of sunshine their direction, and the night retreated for a moment. Long enough for the crewman to reclaim his leg and scramble away. But the night strand didn't disappear this time. It was like I'd only hit part of it.

A crash on the deck startled me. Claws with ropes attached had anchored themselves to the ship. The Minasimetese had the gates open, and they were pulling us inside.

I turned to Father to reach for his hand. A tendril of smoke shot toward us and wrapped around his throat.

"No!" I launched a strand of wind at the smoke.

The wind did its job—the smoke puffed away. But it also knocked us to the deck and rocked the ship.

By the wheel, Zel rescued another crewman from a night

strand, and near us, Mor attacked another wisp of smoke that slithered toward my father. It darted out of the path of Mor's wind stream. I directed more wind toward the smoke, and the ship listed again.

I had no idea how to fight like this—strand for strand, battling evil of unknown intentions. A ship in unfamiliar waters didn't seem the best place to learn.

"Hurry!" I called up to the Minasimetese guards. "Please hurry!"

Dylun tried to remove a strand of night from the ship's railing with a stream of colormastery. The color splattered helplessly along the wood and didn't seem to touch the darkness. "My strands don't work!" he called. "What is this sorcery?"

Zel, Mor, and I seemed the only ones able to counteract the enemy strands. Were they coming from a fellow storyteller?

But thankfully, we didn't have to keep it up much longer. My fingers shot a band of ice toward a stream of searing liquid metal as it hit our ship. As soon as the strands met, the metal cooled—though not before burning a hole in the deck.

But a moment later, the *Cethorelle* was all the way through the gate, and the guards were reversing their machinery to get it closed.

Zel created a wall of wind and sent a half dozen strands tumbling backward, which gave us just enough distance. The gates settled back into their usual position. The wave did not attempt to clear it or follow us inside.

I collapsed to the deck and sat there, shaking.

Father knelt beside me. "Are you hurt?"

I had to think about it. "No. I don't think so. Is anyone else?"

Bruises. A few scratches. A lot of shock.

"I'll go check on Karlith and Gryfelle belowdecks," Mor said, hurrying past us.

"Father, what *was* that?"

"Whoever has been hunting us."

"They came after you."

"Aye."

I thought of the strand wrapped around his throat. "To kill you."

"Aye."

"Why? Who would do that?"

"I have no idea."

Comforting.

Father helped me back to my feet, and I took stock of our surroundings for the first time. The ship had been pulled into a small bay behind the seawall. Nearby was a dock. That's where the ropes that had hauled us to safety were attached to a wheel with large cranks. Two men worked each wheel, and at least six of those claws had been anchored to the ship. Beyond the dock, I could see that the water continued on—a river from the sea, cutting straight into the mountainous island.

"Well, well," a voice said from the dock as we approached. Very slightly accented, perfect Tirian, belonging to a man wearing the most beautiful studded leather coat I'd ever seen. It was dyed grass-green, somehow, unless they had green-skinned grazers here. Black and silver studs traced an intricate pattern along the front and down the arms of the coat.

If I had thought Dylun or Cameria's hair to be black, I was wrong. This man's hair was like purest ink, so black it almost shone blue.

"Welcome to Minasimet," he said. "I am Kanja, governor of Kyko. And perhaps now you will explain why you have brought evil to our shores."

"Sir." Father bowed formally. "Your servant, General Yestin Bo-Arthio. We thank you for your hospitality."

"It is not our custom." Kanja studied Father. "You know this."

"I do. We apologize. I bring good news and a request for aid."

"Perhaps the good news would ease your request for aid."

Father reached into his tunic and pulled out another of Braith's letters. "Alas, my Minasimetese is not good. I tried to speak to the guard, but I failed, I'm afraid."

"Indeed." The smile never appeared on his lips, but I could see it dancing in his eyes.

Father handed the sealed letter to one of Kanja's attendants. The governor took it and looked at the seal. "I do not recognize this. It is not the seal of Gareth Bo-Kelwyd."

"No. It is the seal of Braith En-Gareth."

"The princess?"

"The queen."

"Interesting. You do bring news. Is Gareth Bo-Kelwyd dead?"

"Yes."

"I cannot say we will mourn him in Minasimet."

"Nor we in Tir."

Kanja regarded Father another moment before sliding his finger under the wax seal to break it. He read the letter and looked up. "This is highly unusual."

"Indeed."

"I have never known a ruler to give back land without a fight."

"Our queen is an unusual ruler."

"What does she want?" Kanja inquired.

"Peace."

"Hmm." He folded the letter and tucked it into his coat. "I will pass the message to the other governors and the *kinshu*."

"King," Father translated for the rest of us, and added,

"Minasimet kept a ceremonial monarchy even after Gareth conquered them."

"The Minasimetese contest that we were ever conquered," Kanja said. "Gareth sank most of our fleet and killed off almost an entire generation of Minasimetese men. That is why the kinshu surrendered without a Tirian ever setting foot on Minasimetese soil."

Father bowed again. "We share a common enemy in Gareth Bo-Kelwyd."

"Or *shared*, as you say." Kanja looked skeptical. "This offer of sovereignty is genuine? Queen Braith truly means to emancipate the territories?"

"Yes. I swear it."

Kanja waved a hand. "Then I shall cancel my order to sink your vessel and take you hostage. As a sign of goodwill."

My breath froze in my throat.

But Father seemed unruffled. "Thank you."

"And the favor you must ask?"

He was told of the curse, after which Dylun detailed our specific request and his map.

"I believe what we need is hidden in the black-glass palaces—the *Kurgarasi*," he finished.

"I cannot recall if a Tirian has ever looked upon the Kurgarasi. Or a Meridioni, for that matter."

"Please, Governor Kanja." Father's tone carried urgency. "We are not here for idle sightseeing. This is life-or-death for two young women."

Kanja paused for an excruciating moment. "Very well. You cannot leave by the port you entered. That which is chasing you will await you there, and it is likely to get inside if we open the gate again. I cannot allow that. You will travel upriver. It is a three-day journey. The waterway is deep enough for your ship. Pray for wind, or else it will take thrice as many days, and you will have to use ropes and poles. The Kurgarasi is inland a short distance. When you finish, it will take you another day to reach the source of the river, the port at Azu. You may leave from there."

"The river cuts all the way through the island?" Father seemed surprised. I wondered how complete the Tirian map of Minasimet might be.

"Of course. Many of our rivers do. If one does not wish to have ports accessible from the ocean, one must be creative with rivers. The ancients made our rivers functional waterways—coast to coast, cutting straight through the land."

"Impressive."

"If Minasimet is anything, it is impressive. If you agree to this route, General Bo-Arthio, and if you agree to allow a party of my choosing to travel with you, I will allow you access to the river. Do you agree to my terms?"

"Yes, we agree. And we thank you."

"Indeed," Kanja said. "Ceremonial or not, the kinshu may have my head for this."

CHAPTER THIRTY-FOUR

NAITH

"Master, slow down, please," Naith pleaded. "I cannot understand you."

The Master's voice wavered, even more distorted than usual. "The distance is far. Sound must not be carrying well."

"That is a little better." Naith was relieved. "Perhaps if you speak slowly, I will hear you."

"The rebels made it into Minasimet."

Naith's mind reeled. "No! Even under the best of circumstances, the Minasimetese don't let anyone in."

"Indeed. The bay should have been the perfect place to trap them, and yet here I sit—on a ship with nowhere to dock."

"Were you able to—" Before Naith could finish the question, he was interrupted curtly.

"No. The general slipped away."

Naith swore. "And the others?"

"Can you not tell by my tone, Naith, that I failed both to capture our quarries or kill our targets?"

"I apologize, Master."

"The general lives, and perhaps he is most dangerous of all."

"He?" Naith said, surprised. "But he is not a weaver."

"No, but he suspects me." The Master's voice was clearer. "Even before I made my move, he had noticed my strands. They are nearly invisible, but he sensed them. Sensed my presence.

He needs to be removed before he figures out anything else and communicates it to his daughter."

"And the others?"

"We will never turn the old-timers. Any we gain access to must be destroyed. I will have to carve out another opportunity, for this one is now lost to me."

Naith was quiet for a moment. "Kill some, capture others, steal the strands. Your task is arduous, Master."

"Truly. Tell me, how goes it with the boy?"

"Bo-Bradwir's feelings for the girl are strong, but he is progressing." Naith was glad he had encouraging news. "He is growing more confident in his supposed abilities. I think he is beginning to believe he is the leader his people need."

"Good." The Master sounded pleased. "Will you have a session with him today? I shall need time to rest before directing any energy toward that channel."

"Yes, I planned to see him this evening. I thought—"

But just as Naith began to fill the Master in on the evening's plans, he heard the creak of his door's hinges. He whirled. Bo-Bradwir stood in the doorway with a puzzled look on his face.

"Your Holiness? Who are you talking to?"

"Brac, my son." Naith willed his heart to slow its frenzied rhythm. "You startled me."

"You were talking to someone." Bo-Bradwir looked around the room, as if expecting to find someone crouched behind the bedside table or hiding beneath the desk.

"Yes, of course. I was praying."

Although the conversational tone he used with the Master was nothing at all like the loud, formal prayers priests displayed in temple services.

Bo-Bradwir shrugged. "If you say so. Can't imagine ever talking to a goddess like that. Or at all, really."

Naith released an audible sigh of relief. "Well, son, that will be what we work on next." He crossed the room and put his arm around Bo-Bradwir. "I will help you discover the beauty of a prayer life."

The Master would not be pleased at having to expend more energy. Especially while redoubling efforts to apprehend the weavers. But it couldn't be helped. The boy would need some kind of answer when he prayed in order to be convinced.

Bo-Bradwir allowed himself to be steered from the room. "What were we to practice today, Your Holiness?"

"Well, your strands have been improving."

"Aye, it seems easier, somehow."

Naith almost laughed. Perception was such a powerful thing. The boy had not actually exerted any effort at any point.

"Yes, my son. Very good," Naith said. "I thought we would work on turning those strands into something real."

"I've seen Tannie do it." The lad paused and looked down at his feet. "I mean, the storyteller."

Naith flashed a carefully crafted smile—sympathetic at how painful it must be not to use her name, but approving of the effort. "Very good."

"She made my hat from strands once. After the battle in the throne room."

"So you understand how it's done."

Brac hesitated. "Not really."

"No matter," Naith assured him. "You just create the strands as you have been, then will them into something real." The Master would be listening, ready to perform the trick at the right time.

At least Naith hoped so. He had just been getting to those arrangements when Bo-Bradwir had interrupted them.

"Now, Brac, today we will turn your strands into bread." That would be enough for the Master to go on.

"Bread?"

"Ah, Brac." Naith flashed a fatherly smile. "Bread is a more powerful weapon than you realize."

"A weapon?"

"Yes. If you control the bread, you control the peasants."

"I don't want to control them." Brac sounded alarmed. "I want to help them." The lad was so earnest. So sincere.

He was perfect.

Naith touched Bo-Bradwir's shoulder. "Same thing, my son. Same thing."

CHAPTER THIRTY-FIVE

TANWEN

I HAD NEVER REALLY CONSIDERED WIND BEFORE. WHO DOES? Unless there's a mighty gale trying to pull the thatch from the roof or rip the grain from the field or topple all the fruit trees, there's little reason for a Pembroni to think about the wind much.

But the *Cethorelle* had taught me that, sometimes, wind is everything. And at the moment, our sails hung limp as a muddled marsh-grazer.

Dylun stared up at them and grunted. "We don't have time for this."

"We don't have a choice," Warmil countered. "Unless there's something in your studies that tells you how to control the weather."

Dylun shot him a look. "Really, you have been much more tolerable since Aeron affixed herself to your side. Don't ruin it."

Aeron, right next to Warmil, looked a touch embarrassed.

A thought struck me. "I can control the weather."

Dylun frowned at me. "Tanwen, you're very talented, but even you have limits. I'm quite certain something—or Someone—much more powerful than you controls the weather."

I rolled my eyes. "I know *that*. What I mean is that I can make strands of wind. I did before to fight the smoke strands. Couldn't I do it here?"

"Will it be enough?" Warmil asked, glancing up at the sails. "A strand is one thing. Those are large sails to fill."

"Maybe Mor and I could link. Or we could take turns—me, him, and Zel. I don't suppose colormastery would be much help with this. All your strands are so solid."

"Aye." Warmil turned to Dylun. "What do you think?"

He shrugged. "No harm in trying, I suppose. Between that and the poles, perhaps it would be enough."

"Aye," I said. "Nothing to lose."

And that might have been the dumbest thing I'd ever said. Perhaps it wasn't *harmful* to power a ship by windy story strands, but it sure was exhausting. Linking wasn't much help with this particular task. Links seemed to respond to emotion and instinct. Mor and I couldn't control it the way we could our individual strands. We created a lovely cage of golden light, a rainbow that bounced around the deck of the ship, and when we became frustrated, a rabble of painted-wings made of fire.

But no wind.

So he, Zel, and I took turns filling the sails with strands of wind. I was so exhausted after my turn, I was barely able to enjoy the Minasimetese scenery—crags, peaks, and mountains everywhere, some mossy and green, others jagged and rocky, capped in crystalline snow. The people had not cleared land to live on, as we might in Tir, but instead had carved towns and villages into the rocky face of the island. Villages spread up, not out, and I was desperate to step off the ship to explore or to meet some of the black-haired children with wide, curious eyes who waved shyly as we passed.

But we didn't stop along the way, and even if we had, I wouldn't have had it in me to do much exploring. After three days of filling those sails, I was ready to collapse on the deck and never get up.

"Tannie"—Wylie handed me a steaming cup of tea—"you could sell your services and make a killing. Sailors would pay your weight in gold."

"Aye, and I'd not live to see my eighteenth birthday."

"Isn't that in a few days?"

"Exactly."

He grinned. "Kanja says we're to begin the hike soon. They say it's not far."

The Minasimetese had been a strange and silent addition to the crew. It was clear they were along to make sure we didn't do anything nefarious, like desecrate their Kurgarasi or something. They were an armed guard more than a friendly accompaniment. They ate and slept and spoke in small, tight knots with each other. Only Kanja shared words with us, and even then, only with Father.

I couldn't blame them. They were breaking with their custom to even allow us inside their borders, and it's not like we had made the best first impression. I wouldn't take too kindly to someone banging on my cottage door, asking for favors, and bringing with them a cloud of danger.

I sipped the tea and hoped it would revive me. "I don't feel quite ready for a hike."

"Are you needed for this strand?" Wylie asked.

"Dylun says no. We need a colormaster and a songspinner this time. But I want to watch it, just the same."

"Don't blame you. Seems a once-in-a-lifetime chance."

"Does that mean you're coming?" It would be fun having him there.

"Aye, you bet your fish soup I am."

"I'll give you all the fish in the Menfor Sea for free. No betting needed."

"So generous."

I doffed my tricorn hat to him. "I'm going to go see if they need help getting Gryfelle up. She hasn't been above deck in at least a week."

Wylie nodded. "See you ashore."

I went down the stairs, gripping the cup of tea, and crept along the hallway toward Gryfelle's door.

I didn't know why I was creeping, except that I always tried to stay quiet around Gryfelle and not disturb her if I could help it.

Just as the door came into view, I halted. Mor's voice carried out to me—frustrated. And then Gryfelle's, more lucid than I'd heard her in at least two weeks. She must be having a moment of clarity. Those moments were fewer and farther between than ever.

"I remember, Elle," Mor was saying. "Even if you don't."

"Mor, I'm not the girl in those memories. That girl is lost. You don't love me in the way you think you do. You can't. I no longer exist. Not as I ought."

"You *do* exist. Why do you say things like that? You're sitting right here. You draw breath still, don't you?"

"You know very well what I mean."

"I'm tired of having this conversation with you every time you're awake and lucid. It's not what I want to discuss."

"I'm tired of seeing that pained look on your face every time I'm awake." Gryfelle's voice was soft but filled with resolve.

"I look pained because you're dying, Elle. You want me to be fine with that? Pretend like it doesn't kill me to watch you suffer?"

"You make it worse for yourself. And you make it worse for Tanwen."

"Stop."

"No. I'm dying, aren't I? You could afford me some consideration."

A moment of silence passed, and I knew I should continue on

to the kitchen. Return my cup and then come back like I hadn't heard a word. I was developing a nasty habit of eavesdropping on private conversations, and the twist in my gut chided me.

Yet somehow, I couldn't pull myself away.

"Elle, I'm never going to leave you." Anger colored Mor's words. "As long as you draw breath, I'm here."

"I'm not asking you to leave, Mor. I'm asking you to free yourself of your obligation to me."

"I won't listen to this. You draw breath. You still matter."

"And when I no longer draw breath, Captain Bo-Lidere? What then? You cling so to your self-imposed duty, you shall forever be shackled to it. You fail to see what you're doing to yourself. How will you ever find happiness with another while living in the shadow of my death? How will you ever want to?"

Mor's voice quieted. "If you could remember what you felt once, you would not be saying this."

"Perhaps. But I cannot. I cannot feel anything about us anymore. And truly, I must wonder. Have you built this up in your mind to suit your need to erase what transpired with your sister? Perhaps what we shared was nothing more than an adolescent flirtation and you've built it into something much greater. Mor, I'm not your wife, and I never was. Free yourself."

Another long stretch of silence, and when Mor spoke, his voice was choked with tears. "We're going to save you, Gryfelle."

"And if you do, then what? Mor, I don't say this to hurt you. But I do not love you in that way. And I know you honestly don't feel that way for me either. Whatever romantic feelings I had for you were the first thing to disappear. You *know* this because you saw it."

Mor didn't respond. And I thanked the stars I couldn't see whatever was happening on his face. I couldn't bear it.

Gryfelle's voice suddenly sounded distant. "I'm so tired.

Mother, I must rest. The ball is tonight. Please have the servants prepare my gown. Sir Gywas will be there."

She had slipped away again. I closed my eyes against the whole awful mess. The unanswerable question pinged around in my head—why? Why was this happening to any of us?

"Tannie?"

My eyes flew open, and the pewter cup tumbled from my hands and clanged to the floor.

Utter mortification doused me from head to toe. I braced myself for Mor's anger. I'd had no right to hear any of that, and surely he would tell me so.

But instead, he picked up my cup. He stepped closer and handed it to me. I took it back, but I couldn't meet his gaze. Too ashamed. Face too hot.

Slowly, his hand found the side of my face. His fingers wrapped around the back of my neck and tightened. He held me there, then brushed some hair away from my cheek with his other hand.

I closed my eyes again and felt the moment, because I knew what would happen next. I knew after a long pause, he would release me and disappear, wrapped up in his angst and his heartache and his duty.

He did.

I stood alone in the hall, my knuckles whitening around my cup.

CHAPTER THIRTY-SIX

TANWEN

I wandered through our hike in a haze of confusion. Wylie, bless him, didn't press me. He only helped me when I stumbled over stones in my distraction.

If only he could help me with the other things I was stumbling over.

"You're a good friend," I said suddenly.

He aided my climb over a large stone directly in our path. "I know." He grinned.

"You have a lass at home, don't you?" We hadn't talked about it before, but the moment I thought about it, I knew it was true.

"Aye. Back in Waybyr."

"I never even asked where you were from. I knew Eastern Peninsula, but . . ." I shook my head.

"You've had a lot on your mind."

Not really an excuse, but I was grateful he seemed to find it sufficient reason, nonetheless.

"What's her name?" I asked.

"Lafnys. It's not easy, having a sailor for a lad."

"I can imagine. You're gone moons at a time."

"Aye."

"Will you marry her?"

"Yes. It's set for the summer after whenever we return."

"Hmm. Autumn now, and I don't doubt we'll be back well before next summer. So that's less than a year."

He grinned again. "Aye."

It was nice to think of Wylie and his girl, a love that was difficult only because of distance. Otherwise, it was simple and uncomplicated.

"Tannie, look." Wylie's voice shook me from my musings.

I followed his gaze up to a peak of dark rock. Perched on the ledge was a fluff-hopper.

But it was lavender.

"Wylie!" My mouth dropped open. "Purple fluff-hoppers! I didn't know they existed."

"Who knows what else is here on this island."

I stared at the furry little beast, and it hissed at me. "I wonder if this is where the legend of the pink one comes from."

"The one that grants wishes? I'm pretty sure that's a myth."

"But you never know! Should we catch it? Does it grant wishes?"

"It grants finger injuries," Kanja said as he passed.

I frowned. Same as the white and brown ones in Tir. "But it's *purple*."

Kanja glanced at me with a look that clearly said, "So?" and continued on his way.

I sighed. "Sometimes, I just want to remember what it's like to be small and believe in fairy stories."

"Well, if that's not straight from a fairy story, I don't know what is." We had crested a rise, and Wylie gestured up ahead. I looked.

A fortress carved out of the island rose before us. Its Tirian name was well chosen, for it looked exactly like black glass. Setting sunlight reflected off mirrored stone. It resembled the palace at Urian but with sharper angles and deeper cuts. And it was carved right from the mountain, not built on top of it.

The sight stole my breath.

"What is it?" I asked.

"Volcanic rock," Warmil answered, and I was reminded that he, too, was well studied. Maybe not in languages like Dylun, but Warmil had read all the books in Urian, or so Dylun said.

"Volcanic rock?" I asked. "I'm not sure I know what that is."

"When a volcano erupts, the inner fire called lava cools and it creates rock like this."

"But it takes Minasimetese hands to shape it, polish it, and create something spectacular," Kanja added.

And I supposed he must be right, for I'd never heard of black-glass palaces anywhere else in the world. Though, if this trip had taught me anything, it was how little I knew of the world in general. Unless it existed on the Eastern Peninsula or in Urian, it was all new to me.

"Come," Kanja said. "Forgive me, but the sooner we can get you out of Minasimet, the better."

I knew he was speaking for our own good as well as his. And the thought was less than settling.

"Beware the *gurim*," Kanja said as he disappeared through the open doorway of the Kurgarasi.

I turned to Father. "The gurim?"

"Puff-prowlers."

I hadn't recalled hearing the term, but before I could raise a question, a small, four-legged beast stalked by. It looked to be at least three-quarters puffed-out red-orange fur. Its face was flattened and somehow still triangular, and two peaked ears sat atop its head.

"Aww." I bent to touch it. "It's so cute."

"Don't." Father snatched my hand away. "They do bite if you offend them."

The puff-prowler turned its narrowed eyes to me, then lifted its nose in the air and stalked away.

I watched it go. "I think I offended it."

"It's not hard to do."

"This way." Kanja continued inside briskly. "The central hall seems the best place to start."

He led us farther into the carved, polished structure. I couldn't help but notice puff-prowlers lounging among the black-glass ledges.

"It's emptier than I expected," Father said to Kanja. "I thought there would be others here."

"We consider these grounds sacred and do not enter them."

Only then did it really sink in for me what Kanja risked in bringing us here. He must have seen my thoughts on my face, for he said kindly, "Do not be troubled. It is a silly superstition." He turned back to Father. "Yet even if no supernatural power underlies the superstition, people who believe in it can be dangerous."

"Like our goddesses," I said to Father.

"Indeed." Father set his mouth in a grim line. "We will be gone as quickly as possible."

"I thank you for that," Kanja said. He stopped in the middle of the next room. "Here."

I looked up. The ceiling rose so high I couldn't see the top of it. It seemed to extend on in blackness forever.

Dylun scanned his notes again. He looked up. "Is Gryfelle awake?"

The four men carrying Gryfelle's litter brought her forward. Her eyelids fluttered.

Karlith nodded. "Sort of."

Dylun rolled up his notes. "I'll need her to sing." He knelt gently beside her makeshift bed. "Gryfelle?"

Her eyes cracked open. "Hello, Dylun."

He smiled. "It's good to see you, my friend."

"I cannot say it's good to be seen." She slowly returned his smile with just a hint of a wry twist. "What do you need of me?"

"I need you to sing. Do you think you can?"

"I can sing something. I'm not sure it will be pretty."

"It will be if you're singing it."

It was good to see her smile again. "You flatter me." She propped herself up on her elbows, then dragged herself to a seated position.

It really wasn't fair to ask anything of her right now—singing or sitting up or traveling all over the world. But we had no other songspinner.

Dylun worked quickly. We all watched, including Gryfelle, as he sent strands of golden color into the air. A moment later, Gryfelle began to sing. Her wispy bands of song followed the colormastery strands up toward the ceiling.

As she sang, the song circled the golden color, shaping it into a star with six points. The star and the song lingered in the air, then they burst into fragments. Through the cloud of strand pieces, a thick stream like deep-purple oil spiraled down from the invisible ceiling.

I unlatched the box and held it out. The purple strand approached but didn't coil into the box. It continued its dance around the box, around me, spiraling around every single person in the room.

I wanted to be annoyed. We didn't have time for this. The longer we stayed, the more danger we put Kanja and his men in. The longer we stayed, the sicker Gryfelle and I got. We still had another strand to collect before the cure would be complete. Something was hunting us, on top of that, and who knew when that something—or someone—would show up again.

And yet, as the strand swirled in gentle circles, peace wrapped around me like a blanket. Everything in our world was uncertain—like always—but in this moment, there was the kind of peace that carried through the uncertainty like a gift to your heart from someone watching over you.

The purple strand swirled back to me. It bowed. I held out the box, and it slipped inside and curled up beside the blue and gold strands. The three of them, coiled beside each other like three baby puff-prowlers, brought a smile to my face.

I closed the lid and latched it, still smiling. "Done."

But the next moment, Gryfelle groaned and fell back onto the litter. The men struggled to keep it righted under the sudden shift in weight.

"Set her down," Mor said quickly. "Now!"

They lowered her to the floor just in time for the lightning strikes to start. Karlith, Mor, and Father rushed to her side, and I knew they would be protecting her head from the polished black floor and keeping her as safe as possible.

But I turned away. I couldn't stand it. I couldn't stand what it looked like from the outside now that I had seen it from the inside. And I didn't want to know what she would lose next. Her voice? Her beautiful, songspinning voice? What else did she have left?

I passed Kanja on my way out of the Kurgarasi. "Thank you for helping us. You could be saving our lives."

He bowed, then cast a troubled glance back into the room we'd just left. "Creator help you both."

CHAPTER THIRTY-SEVEN

NAITH

COILS OF SMOKE SNAKED FROM BRAC BO-BRADWIR'S HANDS. In a heartbeat, the strands turned from wisps of smoke to loaves of bread.

"Excellent." Naith was genuinely pleased. "You are getting stronger."

"I feel like I'm almost ready." That oft-present frown appeared on Bo-Bradwir's face.

"What troubles you, son?"

"Well, when it's time to, you know, rally the peasants . . ."

"Speak, my boy. What is worrying you?"

"They won't hurt Braith, will they?" he blurted. "I know you say she's got bad blood, but I just can't believe that. She's only ever been kind, far as I've seen. And I understand that she shouldn't be queen and we're entering into a new age and all that, but she won't be hurt, will she?"

"You have a kind heart, Brac." Naith began to slowly pace the room. "There are casualties in war sometimes."

He looked startled. "Aye, but are we at war?"

Naith laughed, but he tried to tamp down the derision in it. "We are discussing an overthrow of the queen. What else would you call it?"

"I just don't want her to be hurt. We don't need to harm them."

"Them?" Naith stopped pacing and looked at Bo-Bradwir. "Who do you mean?"

"Braith and that new lord that showed up."

Naith stilled. "New lord?"

"You haven't heard? It's all the talk in town for at least a moon."

"I don't often leave the confines of my sanctuary, son. Please, tell me this news quickly."

"There was a man who interrupted council a while back. Marched right in, past the guards, and spoke to Braith. He said he wouldn't call her the queen, so he called her 'lady' instead."

"And the queen's guard did not remove his head? Dear Braith runs a more merciful court than her father, to be sure."

Naith saw Bo-Bradwir was uncomfortable. He glided over to the lad.

"Do not worry, my son. We will not storm into the queen's throne room and demand her crown. You will not lose your head in this. But please, tell me what else you know, and tell it quickly."

"Nothing, really. Except he came in, and now he's been meeting with the queen sometimes. They have tea. And he sits on the council in the afternoons."

Nothing? The boy considered this nothing? He truly was a fool.

Naith fought to keep the anger from his voice. "What is this lord's name, my son?"

Before the reply came, Naith's mind raced through a hundred possibilities. Sons of those who had been favored under Caradoc but had fallen into disgrace under Gareth. Those who had run afoul of the usurper king for one reason or a dozen. The one noble who had been a weaver of some sort and had lost his head because of it. Did he have a son?

"It's Kharn Bo-Candryd," Brac said. "Caradoc II's nephew."

Naith had not been expecting that. He lowered himself onto a bench.

"Your Holiness? Are you all right?"

"I need . . . a minute." Was the Master listening? Or had this news already traveled?

"I didn't realize this was important." Bo-Bradwir's face was concerned. "I'm sorry if I should have told you sooner."

"It's fine, my boy. It's fine." But it wasn't. A blood heir to the throne. "Is the queen inquiring after his claim? This could be some power-hungry throne-snatcher."

Please, let it be so.

"I can't say. I'm not livin' in the palace these days, so all I know is what I hear on the outside. And about that, I think someone recognized me today. My captain is looking for me. I've been missing from my post a long time now."

Naith waved away the concern. "We have far more pressing matters, son."

"Is this noble a problem?"

"He could be. If it is truly he, Kharn Bo-Candryd, he is the rightful heir to the throne."

"But Braith was voted in."

"It does not work that way." Simple dolt. "Blood is stronger than the vote. Always." Naith rose. "I shall retire for the evening. This has been quite a shock."

"But what about this noble? Shouldn't we talk about what to do?"

"I shall have a plan in the morning. I need a night's sleep to digest this matter." And a few moments alone to reach the Master.

"Aye. All right."

"I shall fetch you in the morning, my son." Naith scurried to his room faster than he had moved in many years.

✧

"Master, I need to speak *now*." Naith would not usually dare such a demand, but this matter was urgent enough to warrant it.

"I was sleeping, Naith."

Judging by the speed of the response and the Master's tone, Naith did not think it so.

"I have news."

"Then speak. Make the rude interruption worth its while."

"An arrival at court." Naith was breathless, since he had run the distance from the sanctuary to his chambers.

"Oh?"

"Kharn Bo-Candryd."

"Excuse me?"

"Kharn Bo-Candryd. The nephew of Caradoc."

"I know who he is," the Master snapped. "Or was. Is he not dead?"

"It would seem not. The farm boy told me he heard gossip in the street."

"And the identity has been confirmed? It is surely Candryd's son? I thought we killed them all."

Naith swallowed back his fear at the sharp tone of the Master's voice. "Bo-Bradwir wasn't sure. He had only heard gossip of the arrival, and now this lord sits on the council. Perhaps we ought to have kept the lad at the palace longer so that he was nearer the center of activity."

"The boy would never have been able to stay in the palace this long. As it is, the duplicity of conspiring against the queen is nearly undoing him. We were right to remove him."

Naith paused. "The boy said Braith and Kharn have been taking tea together."

"Taking *tea*?"

"That is what he said."

Silence.

"I only wish I had more information for you, Master," Naith said.

"As do I." The Master was still for a painfully long moment. "This changes everything."

"Tell me what to do, Master."

"Our timeline must be altered. We must act now."

Naith was taken aback. "The boy is not ready. He needs more practice. More refinement."

"We do not have time for it. Do you not understand what a blood heir means? What a courtship between Braith and this man would mean?"

The priest had no response.

"A united throne, Naith."

Complete and total dread washed over Naith. It invaded his every sense and drowned thoughts of all else.

"If Braith accepts him as a suitor and the two of them marry, it unites Tir. Those who supported Gareth will be pleased with his daughter on the throne. Those loyal to Caradoc will rest easy to see *his* heir on the throne. A marriage between Braith and Kharn Bo-Candryd will ease the unrest and lull everyone back into a sense of stability and calm."

"Their anger will fade." The full implication came into focus in Naith's mind. "And if that dissipates, it will be impossible to enact our plan."

"Yes, it is dependent upon unrest and the rage of the peasants."

"We must act now."

"Yes," the Master said.

"I'll need two weeks before the boy is ready to be put before the people."

"You have one."

Naith tensed. "One week?"

"And only that because Braith will resist a courtship."

"Why would she?" Naith asked. "It is a perfect solution to those who would challenge the legitimacy of her throne."

"Because she is Braith. It will offend her sensibilities to marry for a reason other than love."

"Stupid girl."

"Not so stupid as I would wish. If she were, we would not have to concoct such complicated plans."

Naith paused. What did the Master mean?

But he didn't voice the query. Instead, he said, "I will have Brac Bo-Bradwir ready in one week."

"Good. And in the meantime, we will hope Braith continues to be herself so that a marriage does not take place. It would be the permanent end of our aspirations."

CHAPTER THIRTY-EIGHT

TANWEN

Wind can also be the enemy of a ship. As we left the Kurgarasi, a storm began to brew. The rain and thunder were yet to come, but wind announced the impending arrival with a howl.

At least I wouldn't be half dead from making wind strands before we reached the port at Azu. But Wylie and the crewmen struggled to raise the sails and get them secured in the gale.

I pulled and tethered lines for a while, much greater help than I once was. But when the wind became too strong, Mor sent me belowdecks to get out of it.

I sipped bitter-bean brew beside Gryfelle's bed while Karlith knitted. Gryfelle had not woken up since her episode in the Kurgarasi, and I wondered if she ever would.

I buried my nose in my bitter-bean and tried to ignore the squeeze in my heart at Gryfelle's state.

"Ah!" Karlith said. "We're underway."

I paused and tried to feel what she felt, but I couldn't tell we were moving until the *Cethorelle* dipped to one side.

She returned to her knitting, smiling. "You get used to the slight movements when you're stuck belowdecks so much. Those little clues that let you know you're moving again."

"Has it been terrible down here?"

"Only because I have to watch Gryfelle worsen." Karlith paused and looked at Gryfelle. "But she needs me. Lass's mother should be here, but I'm happy to stand in that gap. She's a lass without a mother, and I'm a mother without her babes."

I stared at her. "Did you have children once, Karlith?" I had known she was married, of course. She was Karlith Ma-Lundir. But she hadn't mentioned children before.

Karlith returned to her knitting. "Some things never stop hurting to speak of, Tannie, love."

"Oh, I'm sorry."

"Doesn't mean we shouldn't speak of them." She knitted in silence a moment. "I had a son and a daughter. They would have been older than you now, but they were just wee ones when Gareth's guards and the priests came for them."

"The guards and priests came for them? Your *children*?" I kept waiting to find the end of the horror of Gareth Bo-Kelwyd, but I didn't seem to have reached it yet.

"They came for Lundir. He was a songspinner, and he refused to register, refused to sing those two crowned songs. He wrote and sang the most beautiful ballads of the Creator, and no threats from Gareth would stop him. He knew they would come for him someday, and he was ready. He was ready to die for the truth. But when the little ones got in the way, the guards didn't think twice, and I lost them all at once."

I was shocked. "And then you escaped and went into hiding."

"Yes, to the Corsyth," said Karlith. "I was the first. I never imagined I'd have company there, but I was glad of it. And glad to have a family again when Warmil and Aeron came along. Then Dylun. And the three young ones." She looked at Gryfelle.

I held Gryfelle's cold, limp fingers while I bit down on my lip to keep it from trembling. "Karlith, I'm so sorry."

"I'll see them again, lass." She smiled at me through sudden tears. "Mourning is for this life. I live for the next."

"You say strange things sometimes, Karlith."

"Aye." She returned to her knitting, her smile widening.

"But Tannie, my lass, just because something is strange doesn't mean it ain't true."

With the force of the storm behind our sails, we made it to Azu in half the time Kanja expected. But I won't lie. I was not looking forward to cruising through the sea gate out into open water in this wind. And what about when the rain hit?

Mor and Jule stood at the helm in deep discussion while the crew loaded up for our trip to the Spice Islands. I couldn't help wishing we had made it there during the summer moons and not now as the weather chilled and autumn blew shivers down our spines.

I hadn't spoken to Mor since our moment outside Gryfelle's room, and I wasn't sure if I should. Somehow avoiding him seemed to make things worse so that when we did finally speak or touch or make eye contact, everything exploded.

Maybe if I could talk to him about something normal, it would be like letting a little bit of steam from the kettle. Then there would be no explosions of strands we couldn't control. Or near-kisses in the belly of the *Cethorelle*.

I tightened my shawl around my shoulders and strode his direction with feigned confidence.

"Ho, Mor. How goes it?"

"Captain." Jule nodded to Mor and tipped his hat to me. "Tannie." He took his leave.

Mor stared after him. "We're hoping it will only take five days to get to the Islands, but this storm could slow us."

I grabbed at that thread of conversation. "Have you been to the Islands before?"

"Some of them."

"Some? How many are there?"

"About five hundred."

"Five hundred! How will we ever find the right one?"

"We have a name—Kanac. And I've visited it before. It's the major trading port of the Islands. The crown has an outpost there."

"Says the pirate who probably raided it a time or two."

"Or seven."

"Seven! You're a scoundrel."

"This is news?" His eyes twinkled. But then his expression fell, and he averted his gaze. "I may have some other business to attend to while we're there."

"Other business? What could you possibly have to do in the Spice Islands?"

"Family business."

I watched him. "Is this about Diggy?"

He waited a moment. Nodded slowly.

"You think there's a chance she could be alive." My mind jumped back to his strange phrasing—that he would give anything to see what she *is* like now, at seventeen.

"Unlikely." He shrugged. "I might be a fool for bothering with this at all. But before we left, I asked around in Urian to see what I could find out. When they took her from me, they said she was payment for my father's debts. That they would make her a palace servant. Then I ran off and sailed the world for two years. When I got back, I inquired after her as best I could without drawing attention to myself, but she was gone. She wasn't working in the palace anymore, and I assumed she was dead."

"But now you've found out something new?"

"While everyone was working on research in the palace libraries, I was caring for Gryfelle alongside Karlith. But I was also finding out everything I could about Diggy. A bit difficult, since so many people fled the palace when Gareth fell. But the head chef"—he thought a moment—"Ginia, I think. She remembered Diggy. Diggy had been a kitchen slave. She'd been mistreated pretty badly and become a favorite mark of some overseer servant there. So Ginia felt sorry for her and arranged a trade. Because of who our father was, she thought she might make a good cook on a ship."

I stared at him. "So Diggy ended up on one of the king's ships? And you think she may have made it to the Islands?"

"I'm almost sure she made it to the Islands—to Kanac, specifically, as that's where the ship docked. And I'm just as sure she never made it back. Like I said, she really can't be alive. She couldn't possibly be, for she would have been a valuable servant—a girl with sailing and kitchen experience. The ship's captain wouldn't have left her on an island unless she was dead. But I would at least like to find out what happened. A fever, or something, perhaps, but I'm just not sure."

"Of course you need to know."

"Aye. I've regretted not going after her for four years now. I owe it to her to learn what happened at least."

"There's a tiny spark of hope still." I took one step closer to him. "You don't have to pretend there isn't and insist it's a fool's errand. I know you. I can see it on your face and hear it in your voice. There is a chance she's alive."

He smiled a little. "Get out of my head, why don't you?"

"Do you want me to go with you?" I asked. "When you go on your search, I mean."

"Aye. It would be nice not to be alone."

Oh, that it would.

I smiled easily and nodded and pretended that this was normal. Said we would make arrangements as soon as we got our bearings on the island.

Just letting a little steam from the kettle.

TANWEN

THE *CETHORELLE* WAS A FINE SHIP, BUT I DON'T CARE HOW fine a ship is. When you're trapped belowdecks for five days because of driving rain and epic wind, every ship feels like a coffin.

I could have died of relief when I answered a knock at my cabin's door and found Wylie smiling and holding two cups of tea.

"Rain stopped. Want some tea?" He held out one cup to me and the other to Aeron, who stood beside me. "I know you don't care for the stuff, En-Howell, but we're out of bitter-bean."

Aeron smiled. "I'll take it. Thanks, Bo-Thordwyan."

"Glad I'm not a soldier like you two," I said as we all three made our way down the hall toward the stairs. "I still can't make your last name come out of my mouth right. Glad I get to call you Wylie instead."

"No offense, Tannie," Wylie said as he stepped back and let me and Aeron climb the stairs first, "but I think all of Tir is glad you're not a soldier."

I stuck out my tongue as I passed him. "That's right. Make your jokes. But who will you be calling when your sails go flat and you need some wind strands, hmm?"

"Tannie!"

"Exactly." But then my mind caught up to my mouth, and I realized someone was calling my name above deck—and there was a note of panic in the voice. I cast a worried glance back at Wylie, then took the rest of the stairs two at a time.

I burst into the humid air. Wylie had said the rain had stopped, but it felt like we were in the middle of a thick cloud.

I scanned the deck and realized it was Zel who had called me, for he was still shouting my name. But the sound was nearly swallowed in chaos all around us. Crewmen ran everywhere, and some corner of my mind registered Wylie sprinting past me.

But I couldn't make sense of what I was seeing. Warmil had his sword in his hands, and everyone was looking out at the sea, back the way we had come. I didn't need to see what they were watching for the whole scene to suddenly make sense. I knew.

The wave of strands had found us again.

"Captain, can we make it to Kanac?" one of the men shouted at Mor.

"They're coming too fast," Mor shouted back. "Get the rowboats loosed. We may have to—"

The first stream of fire exploded onto the deck. Wood splintered. I screamed and covered my face with my arms as shards burst toward me.

"Tanwen!" Father's voice, but I couldn't find him. The deck was aflame.

"Father?"

I looked around, but I still didn't see him. Instead, I saw a ribbon of inky night racing toward Warmil. I shot a beam of sunlight across the ship and intercepted it before it smacked Warmil in the face.

"Tannie!" Father again, but where was he?

Smoke curled all around me, some from the fire on the ship, some from strands that grabbed at me. I fought to collect my wits long enough to create some wind, but the smoke was everywhere. One strand snapped around my ankle and yanked me to the deck.

I screamed and kicked at it, but kicking smoke doesn't do much. I lifted my hand and loosed a blast of cold air. The smoke puffed away. The tension around my ankle released long enough for me to scramble to my feet and run.

But . . . where?

Tendrils snaked all over the ship. Everywhere I looked, a new hole was being punched in the deck. A ribbon of hot metal wrapped around the railing on one side and yanked. The whole rail came free and splintered to bits.

Realization hit me like a slap. We were going down. The *Cethorelle* was going to sink.

Gryfelle. Karlith. They were still belowdecks.

I blasted a strand of fire away from me with the thought of ice water, then ran for the stairs—to the right, I thought, unless I was totally turned around. But before I reached the steps, I saw Dylun and Karlith loading Gryfelle into one of the rowboats. Dylun had the box with the cure fragments and all his maps and notes tucked under one arm. Always thinking, he was.

But a coil of smoke was about to wrap itself around Dylun's neck from behind.

I ran toward them.

"Dylun!" I gave him half a breath of warning before sending a stream of wind toward him.

He gripped his papers just in time. The smoke puffed away as the papers fluttered, but he maintained his hold on them.

"Thank you," he panted. "My colormastery—"

"Doesn't work against this, I know. You take care of Gryfelle. I'll cover you."

He nodded, and I threw sunshine over his head to kill a ribbon of night.

"Who is doing this?" I yelled to no one in particular.

"Tannie!" Father emerged from the smoke. At last. "Are you hurt?"

"Get down!"

He didn't hesitate. He dropped low, and I sent a beam of ice over him. The fire had been a moment away from hitting him in the back.

"Tannie, you need to get away." Father stood quickly. "Captain's orders: abandon ship."

"But I have to fight the strands." I turned around. "Where's Mor?" I drove away a column of smoke with a puff of wind. "Where is Mor!"

"Tannie." Father put his hand on my arm.

I spun back to meet his gaze. "What?" But then I saw it there in his eyes, and somehow he didn't have to say anything else. I knew what he was going to tell me.

Captain goes down with the ship, fighting.

"No." I wrenched my arm away.

"Tannie girl . . ."

"No!"

"He needs to see to the safety of his passengers and crew. He will stay behind until everyone is safe."

"I have to find him. He needs my help." I gestured to Karlith and Dylun. "Help them get Gryfelle to shore. Take everyone you can in the boat."

"Tanwen!" Father's voice was sharp. "You need to get in that boat right now."

"I can swim," I said frantically. "I have to help!"

A huge stream of fire blasted into the starboard side of the *Cethorelle*, and she listed sharply. I stumbled into Father, and somehow he held us both upright. The *Cethorelle* started taking on water, swallowing great gulps of it onto the deck.

I pointed toward the boat again. "Gryfelle and Karlith are helpless in there. Dylun's trying to protect the cure. They need you right now. I don't. *Please* help them. You know only Mor, Zel, and I can battle these strands and give anyone else a chance. Help them. Please, Daddy." I hugged him quickly. "I love you."

I slipped away into the smoke before he could stop me.

"Mor?" I called. "Wylie?"

I stumbled into someone and realized it was Warmil. "War! Where is everyone?"

"Some of the crew were bailing water by the quarterdeck, but Mor's ordering everyone off."

"Do we have enough boats?"

"I don't think so. Maybe."

I glanced toward the shore. Kanac was so close. Swimming distance, probably, if we could get away from the strands long enough.

"War, can you swim?"

"Aye."

"Find anyone who can't, and get them to the boat on the port side. My father is there."

"I can't find Aeron."

Warmil would never leave without finding Aeron first. "She was with me and Wylie coming up the stairs." I shot a sunbeam into a knot of night strands. "Let's find them."

We splashed through several inches of water and bumped into a few crewmen.

"Jule!" I cried. He stood on the quarterdeck by the wheel. A cord of inky night was wrapped around his throat, and the color had left his face.

I prayed he would close his eyes, then I blasted a strand of sunlight into his face.

I hoped I hadn't ruined his eyesight forever, but the strand snapped away from his throat. Breath and color returned to him. In the next second, a strand of smoke wrapped around each of my wrists. Then two more around my ankles. I met Warmil's gaze. Gasped as the strands jerked me up into the air, high above the deck of the sinking *Cethorelle*.

As I floated above the ship in their grip, a strange thought passed through my mind: *They don't want to kill me.*

If they wanted to kill me, they would have gone for my throat or downed me with fire. Instead, smoke was lifting me up.

Why?

Who was it?

What did they want?

Before any of these questions found answers, all four strands of smoke were blasted away. I tumbled from the air, plummeting toward the watery deck. But before I smashed against the wood, a cushion of air caught me and set me on my feet. I looked up, and there was Mor, hands outstretched and eyes wild.

"Tannie, are you hurt?"

"I . . . I'm not sure."

I felt about and found a few sore spots, but I didn't care.

"Did the boat make it off?" The water was up to my knees now. We would have to climb toward the stern, now rising up in the air.

"Aye, I think so. I ordered the ship abandoned."

"But you'll stay?"

"Aye. Until everyone's safe. I don't run anymore."

"Then I'll stay too."

I expected him to argue, but he grabbed my hand. "Come on."

As we climbed for the stern, a sudden sadness overwhelmed me. I had come to love this dumb vessel with all its roasted fish and salty broth and green-faced seasickness. It had been home for three moons, and now it was sinking to the bottom of the Menfor Sea.

Wylie appeared through a cloud of smoke, clinging to the stern and holding on to a crewman being dragged overboard by a rope of night.

I gasped and thrust a ray of daylight toward them both. The night strand popped and disappeared, and the crewman smacked down onto the stern. But at least he was free. He dragged himself back on deck.

What was left of it, anyway.

I clambered toward Wylie, who looked just about spent. I wondered how long he had been keeping a hold on that crewman. I reached out my hand to help him back over the rail. He grimaced, and we grabbed wrists.

But then his eyes went wide, and his body jolted. Confusion clouded his face.

He had stopped climbing, and his grip around my wrist loosened.

I looked down and saw the strand of molten metal protruding from his chest.

"Wylie!" I cried out. "Wylie, no!"

He still looked confused. Puzzled. As though he wondered why his body had gone cold. Why his breath wouldn't come. Why he was slipping from the stern of the ship into the sea.

His entire weight dragged him backward, and I couldn't hold on. He slipped from my grip and tumbled into the ocean.

I screamed. And screamed again. I watched helplessly as Wylie sank below the surface, eyes frozen open. Blank. Unseeing.

I gripped the stern and tried to conjure something—an idea, a thought, a story—that might help. Sunshine to battle the night, or a rainbow of color to fight the gray panic overwhelming me. Anything.

But the only thing that came was another hollow scream.

CHAPTER FORTY

TANWEN

TWO HANDS GRIPPED MY SHOULDERS FROM BEHIND. "COME, Tannie." Mor's voice.

I couldn't move. I stared into the water where Wylie had been a moment before.

"Tannie, come away."

His voice was gentle, but it felt like a thousand needles under my skin.

"Wylie's gone." Grief smothered my words.

I felt as if I was floating over my body. I might as well be standing in the blackness with silvery memories fleeing my mind for all the reality I could grasp.

"Tanwen, look at me."

I turned and met Mor's blue eyes. "Wylie's dead," I choked.

"I know, Tannie. Come away with me."

"I feel sick."

"I know. Come this way now."

The water lapped at our legs, and I knew our situation was precarious. Life-or-death. Probably death. But I couldn't seem to shake myself from my haze.

"Mor!" Warmil shouted. "Both boats are loaded and pulling for shore, but I can't find Aeron."

"Can she swim?" I tried to focus on this new concern.

"I don't know." Warmil's agitation clipped his words.

"We'll look for her," Mor said. "And then we'll get as far as we can from these killing strands. We'll have to swim hard, or the ship will pull us under when she sinks."

The *Cethorelle* was mostly underwater now. It seemed only the three of us were left.

"Aeron?" Without thinking about it, I sent a strand of sunlight to obliterate a strand of darkness careening toward Warmil. "Aeron?"

Then I saw her hand—pale, fine fingers clinging to what was left of the railing of the ship as she went under.

"She's there!" I pointed.

We all splashed toward her.

Scraps of thought raced through my mind.

They won't kill her. They didn't kill me. We just have to get to her. Destroy the strands. Pull her aboard. Swim for shore.

We reached the railing, and I finally saw what had been constraining her.

One hand clung to the rail, but the other was gripping the hand of an unconscious crewman—one of the older sailors, Halen Bo-Tadau. He was bleeding from the head, and Aeron was barely keeping him above water. It seemed Halen was tugged by the pull of the sea alone, but a strand of night was wrapped around Aeron's ankle. Her scabbard was empty, sword gone, and burns and welts covered her body.

I shot sunlight her way and freed her ankle. But before Warmil could pull her back over, two more strands snaked from the water. She cried out as they snapped onto her wrists and yanked her into the sea.

My heart froze.

Not Aeron too.

Warmil dove in after her. I tried to shoot sunlight into the water, but it weakened before it reached the night ribbons around Aeron's wrists.

Warmil resurfaced, then was pulled under.

"They're both going to drown," I shouted to Mor.

He looked at me briefly. "Be ready."

Then he dove in after them.

I rested my head against the ship's damaged rail. My thoughts went dark for several moments. I couldn't seem to think or feel or do anything.

But Mor had said to be ready.

I forced myself up off the rail and watched the churning water. A patch of sea some distance away began to bubble as though a spring were working its way to the surface from the bottom of the Menfor. A moment later, a stream of water strands burst from the ocean, carrying Warmil and Halen.

Warmil's colormastery might be of no use against the sorcery strands, but this he could do. He gripped Halen around his chest with one arm and created water strands with his other hand. This kept them both afloat for now, but how long could Warmil possibly keep that up? Long enough to get to shore?

And where were Aeron and Mor?

I stared at the glassy patch of water where they should be. At the moment it seemed they would never resurface, Aeron's upper body broke through the waves. Her eyes popped wide as she sucked in great gulps of air. And then I saw Mor's hands holding her up as she fought to get her tethered left wrist above the surface. Her muscles rippled, and she screamed.

I realized what I needed to do.

Just as her wrist broke the surface, I shot a beam of sunlight toward it. The beam hit the night ribbon that twisted around her. The ribbon popped, and that arm was free. Then Aeron disappeared back under the surface. Mor came up a moment later, gulped air, and disappeared again.

This time, I knew what to watch for.

Aeron resurfaced. As soon as her other wrist appeared above the water, I sent sunlight toward it, snapping her free.

I could only pray more of this sorcery wouldn't find us.

The sea swallowed my legs as Aeron and Mor swam toward me. There was no time to waste. We had to swim away from the pull of the ship, toward the shore. Swim for Kanac and the last hope of the cure. Away from these evil, twisted strands before they pulled us down to the bottom of the ocean.

Down to where Wylie lay.

One stroke to the next. Hand over hand. Swim for the beach.

I blocked out all other thoughts.

An eternity stretched before me.

My lungs were ready to burst, and then sand was beneath my feet. But I couldn't make it all the way to the shore. I stumbled to my knees in the shallow surf.

Aeron's screams crested over the roar of blood in my ears. She was hurt. I heard Warmil's panic and a great commotion. More screaming from Aeron. But I just stayed there in the water, watching my fingers sink into the sand.

Mor appeared beside me. He stumbled to his feet, then scooped me up, out of the water and onto the beach. We both collapsed, coughing and sputtering salt water on each other.

I rolled onto my back, gasping in great breaths and trying to remind myself I was alive.

Though I barely felt it.

CHAPTER FORTY-ONE

TANWEN

MOR TOUCHED MY HAND.

But I couldn't move. Every ounce of me was spent. "Mor?"

"Yes, Tannie?"

"Wylie is dead."

"I know."

"Did everyone else make it?"

"I don't know."

"I can't breathe."

"Turn on your side. Face me."

I did, with effort.

He met my gaze. "You're alive, Tannie."

"Wylie is gone."

"Yes."

I heard screams again. Aeron was the toughest woman I'd ever met, and she screamed to pull the stars from the sky. What had those strands done to her?

Father's face came into my line of vision. Then his hand was rubbing my back. "We can go rest now, Tannie. Are you hurt?"

Everything hurt, but I couldn't tell if I was injured.

My father and Mor pulled me up. Jule's red hair registered in my mind at some point. He must have been there too. But the next thing I knew was a palm-leaf roof over my head, a woven mat under my aching body, and the deep sleep of utter exhaustion.

I woke. It must have been an entire day later, for the sunlight seemed that of early morning. Had I slept that long? My rumbling stomach said yes.

I could hear Mor and Jule talking outside about a new ship from the queen's navy. Jule would see to the preparations, but there were many docked here. Dylun had the good sense to grab Braith's letters along with his papers.

Instinctively, I reached for my mother's necklace. It was the only thing I owned that I truly cared about, and it was still there.

Was anyone hurt? Did everyone else make it? What happened to Aeron?

I wanted to ask, but I couldn't find my voice.

The scent of fish broth preceded the arrival of a plump Kanaci woman. She stared at me and clucked her tongue. I must look awful.

"You hungry?" she asked.

I nodded. "Aye." My voice came out raspier than Father's after thirteen years talking to rope-tails.

"Stay," she ordered as I tried to sit up. "I'm Narwat."

"Tanwen."

"You are sick."

Yes. I supposed that was true. Everything seemed so distant.

"We need the final strand," I remembered aloud.

"Strand. *Ya.*" She spooned broth into my mouth.

It wasn't half bad. For fish broth.

But the thought of how much I hated fish only made me think of Wylie.

"Why are you crying?" Narwat asked.

"A friend is dead." Tears trickled down my face.

"Your friends are outside. The injured one is alive."

I didn't bother explaining. Didn't have the strength. But Aeron was alive, and for that, I was grateful.

"Wounds heal," Narwat said.

I looked dully at her gray-streaked black hair, pulled into two braids and crisscrossed over the top of her head. Her eyes crinkled at the corners, and little wrinkles showed around her mouth. She had lived a lot more life than I had. Maybe she was right.

"Do we have to get the strand today?" I struggled to get up.

"No," she said. "You sleep. I will feed you. The strand waits."

She seemed to know what she was talking about, so I obeyed her. For the next three days, I let her spoon broth into my mouth, wrap bandages around my scrapes, and tell me stories about the Spice Islands between occasional visits from my friends.

"Narwat, why aren't you a storyteller?" I said with a laugh. "I want to see these tales in crystal."

"You speak nonsense."

I smiled, but the next moment, I froze. Mor, Warmil, and two Kanaci men walked into the hut carrying a litter. At first, I thought it must be Gryfelle's, but then my heart dropped. Black hair fell across the face of the woman on the litter.

Aeron.

I sat up on my mat. "Aeron?"

She didn't stir.

I looked up at Mor. "Is she all right? I thought she was going to be all right."

He glanced at Warmil, then shook his head.

"They did their best, but there was too much damage," Warmil said tonelessly. "They took her left leg below the knee last night."

"Cethor's tears." I stared at him, then turned to Aeron, still motionless on the litter as Narwat prepared a second mat on the other side of the hut. "Will she wake?"

"She's been given a sleeping draught," Mor answered as they lowered Aeron down to the mat. "She lost a lot of blood."

Warmil brushed Aeron's hair from her forehead. "Best thing for her would be to get back to the queen's infirmary in Urian."

"Karlith and War did what they could with their skills, and the physicians in town had good tools, at least." Mor nodded to the Kanaci men exiting the hut. "But we should get her home as quickly as possible."

"Then we need to get the final strand." I rose to my feet.

I was suddenly aware of the short, colorful piece of fabric tied around me like a dress. My face flamed. All the Kanaci women wore them, and Narwat had put it on me days ago. It hadn't occurred to me to be embarrassed in front of the others until I stood.

Narwat didn't flinch. "Tir clothes are here."

She grabbed my trousers, blouse, grazer-hide vest, and boots. She had laundered the trousers and blouse and tied everything into a neat bundle.

She shook her head as she handed the bundle to me. "So heavy, these. Tir clothes are not good for Kanac."

"I'll take them, just the same," I said, clutching the bundle close.

"We'll wait outside," Mor said. Then he put his hand on Warmil's arm. "War? Let's go outside, mate."

Warmil kept his gaze fixed on Aeron. "I should have saved her."

"You did." Mor pulled him gently toward the doorway. "You did save her." He glanced at me as they left. "Meet you outside, Tannie."

I tried to dress quickly, but I hadn't been off my mat for nearly four days. I stumbled, unsteady on my feet.

Narwat tsked. "You slow down. Be still. Don't need you falling over."

That was true enough.

I took my time, dressing as slowly as I dared. I sat to yank on my heavy boots. Narwat was right—these clothes were ill suited to the island, but it didn't matter. This was our last stop. We would be back on another ship as soon as possible, then home to Tir. Just as soon as we extracted that final strand.

I secured my braid with a piece of twine Narwat handed to me. She tucked a sunset-pink flower behind my ear. "Pretty."

I rather doubted it, but I suddenly felt the urge to kiss her cheek. "Thank you. Please take care of Aeron."

She nodded once. "Of course."

I stepped out into the sunshine, and Warmil immediately passed me as he headed back into the hut.

Mor and I were alone, staring at each other in silence.

After a moment, I spoke. "She's going to live, right?"

"I think so. Karlith was worried about infection. That's why they took the leg, ultimately. But they acted before anything could really set in, and I think Aeron will be all right, once she has a chance to heal."

That was the best news I could have hoped for, but still, my heart squeezed for her. Change of subject. "What does Dylun say about the last strand?"

"We're not needed to draw it up. Colormasters only, apparently."

Something unspoken swam in his eyes. I tried to read it. "Has Jule made progress on a ship?"

"Aye. He hasn't had much trouble at all. Thank the Creator that Dylun grabbed all our documents. I don't know how we would have proved our story otherwise. Now it's just a matter of getting the ship ready. The crew's been working on it."

His mysterious expression persisted, and I finally realized what it was. "You've found out something about Diggy."

"Aye." His face was pinched.

My heart sank. "Oh, no."

"There's a cemetery nearby. She's there."

"Oh, Mor. I'm so sorry."

He shrugged, but he wouldn't meet my eyes. "A fever. Knew she couldn't be alive."

"But still, there was hope." I reached for his hand.

And he almost gave it to me, but then he drew back at the last second. "Not wearing my gloves. It's too hot here."

"Right." I looked down at my boots, the toes sinking into the sand. "Lost my hat when the *Cethorelle* sank."

"Tannie."

I didn't look up right away. Not until I felt my hair ruffle in a slight, cool breeze. A strip of black grazer hide swirled in front of me. Then Mor flicked his fingers, and the strand formed itself into a hat—a tricorn sailor's hat, like my other, but this one didn't have a silky ribbon or fluffy plume. It was less ornamental and more functional. Like a real sailor's hat.

After a brief pause, Mor made another strand—sparkling blue—and it twisted into a silver hat pin with a glittering blue crystal at the end. The pin wove through one side of the hat. The whole thing dropped into Mor's hands.

He held it out to me. "There. It's the hat of a real sailor. But with a little something extra."

"I guess that's what we could call me." I took the hat. "Though the 'little something extra' might be a lack of sailing skill."

"You've improved." He smiled, but his eyes didn't crinkle quite the same as they used to. Everything Mor did, everything he said, everything he was, was now edged in grief.

"Do you want to visit her grave?" I asked.

"Aye." He looked away.

"Do you want me to come with you?"

There was a pause. "Aye." He started to reach for my hand, then stopped himself. "Blast. I forgot again." He nodded toward a grove up ahead. "This way."

Mor led me away from the hut by the shore, toward the

tropical trees. I had to wonder how much loss a person had to suffer before that edge of grief became permanent. I didn't want to find out.

But I wasn't sure I'd have a choice.

CHAPTER FORTY-TWO

TANWEN

WE STOOD BEFORE A FLAT STONE PRESSED INTO THE EARTH, just like the dozens around it. But carved on this particular stone was *Digwyn En-Lidere, fever*.

Just like that. One line. Three words. Her whole life summed up in her name and the way she had died.

What would mine say? *Tanwen En-Yestin, cursed*, probably.

"I'm sorry, Mor."

"It's as I expected." His reply was more to himself than me.

"But not as you hoped, and that's hard."

He gave a slight nod.

An intruding voice made me jump. "You. Come here."

I whirled around to find a woman about the same age as Narwat, half concealed by the trees of the jungle. She was staring at Mor, long and hard. Then she beckoned to us.

Mor placed himself between me and the stranger. "Who are you?"

"I am Ibu."

Mor studied the woman. "What do you want?"

She glanced over her shoulder. "Please, I will not hurt you. I must"—she hesitated—"must see your eyes."

Mor looked back at me, and I shrugged. She didn't look dangerous, but what did I know?

He moved closer to the woman and let her look at his face. She peered into his eyes, and hers filled with tears. "I have watched since you came to the island, and now, you come here. Are you . . . are you Digwyn's brother?"

Mor recoiled. "Yes. Did you know her?"

"I . . ." She looked over her shoulder again. "You have her eyes. And her name."

"Yes." Curiosity laced Mor's voice. "You knew her?"

"I know her."

I rushed up beside Mor. "You *know* her? Do you mean she's alive?"

Ibu looked around anxiously. "My son returns soon. Kawan will tell you. Please do not leave the island before you speak to Kawan."

"Speak to me about what?" A young man, taller and wider than Mor by a foot, approached. He frowned at us. "What is this, *apa*?"

She fired off some Kanaci words, then nodded to Mor. "Look."

The young man squinted at Mor, then drew back. "No. Cannot be."

"Is this your son?" Mor asked Ibu. She nodded briefly, and Mor turned to the young man. "Do you know my sister? Digwyn En-Lidere. I am Mor Bo-Lidere."

Kawan stared at Mor and looked at me. Then back to Mor. "Do you swear it?"

"Aye. I swear it. Please, tell me what you know."

Kawan's eyes churned with indecision. After a long pause, he said, "She is not there." He nodded to her headstone. "You will come to her island."

"Her island?"

"Yes. Oh, but she will not like this." He shook his head rue-fully, then strode toward the beach. After a few long paces, he turned around. "Are you coming?"

CHAPTER FORTY-THREE

TANWEN

MOR WAS FULL OF QUESTIONS WHILE HE HELPED KAWAN paddle the canoe. "Why is there a headstone?"

"Needed one," Kawan answered.

"But why?"

"They were going to take her back to the ship."

"She faked it?" I asked. "She faked her death to escape the ship?"

Kawan nodded.

My eyes widened. "Who else knows?"

"Me. Ibu, my mother. That is all. The bounty is great."

"She still has a price on her head?" I glanced at Mor.

"Ya." Kawan nodded up ahead. "Heliake is the island of Digwyn."

It wasn't far—just one of many tiny specks of land out in this tropical bit of the Menfor Sea. After less than an hour, we reached the shore.

The canoe skidded up onto the beach. Mor and Kawan pulled it until it was well out of the surf, and I sat on the canoe's bench, nearly as useless as I had been on the *Cethorelle*. But Mor had told me to sit, and for once, I listened. I'd barely gotten my strength back, and there was no use spending it on dragging a canoe when Mor and Kawan were capable of handling it themselves.

Mor helped me over the side and turned to Kawan. "Where is she?"

"I shall call her. You wait. Be patient." He walked a few yards into the thick of the tropical forest. Then he let loose a series of whistles that sounded very much like a birdcall. I'd not have realized they came from human lips if I hadn't witnessed it myself.

Several moments passed, and nothing happened.

Mor eyed Kawan, and I could see distrust swimming there. "Is she here?"

"She lives here. I do not chain her to the island."

"So she leaves sometimes?" A note of panic arose in Mor's voice. "Tell me the truth. Is she really alive?"

"Mor." I put my hand on his arm.

For once Mor looked at me like I was a stabilizing force, an anchor, and not like a complication.

I offered him a reassuring smile, then turned to Kawan. "Do you know where she dwells? Maybe we could find her there."

"I usually call."

"I understand, but she's not answering."

Kawan looked uncertain. "She does not like people to come without signaling."

"Yes, but it's her brother, after all this time. Please."

"Ya." He looked at Mor. "Follow me."

He disappeared back into the trees. Mor and I trudged through the sand after him. We'd walked for no more than three minutes when Kawan stopped and held up a hand.

"There," he said. "In that clearing over there."

I strained forward. I supposed there was a small area in the jungle that looked clearer than the rest, but I wouldn't call it a clearing. And I didn't see a dwelling anywhere. Maybe Mor was right. Maybe Kawan had led us astray. Maybe he meant us harm.

But then I remembered the Corsyth. There were means to

hide a dwelling if you didn't wish it to be found. Just because I couldn't see Diggy's home didn't mean it wasn't there.

Kawan stepped back. He held a few palm leaves out of our way. "Go."

Mor paused, then stepped into the clearing. I followed, but a twinge of fear drew me to a halt. The brush had rustled.

The sound of someone walking. And humming.

I saw Mor still his breath, as though he knew the hum. Or perhaps just the voice.

A moment passed, and there she was, stepping into the clearing with a basket full of water on her hip.

I almost did a double-take, so like Mor she was, and yet so different. Tiny, barely larger than a child, but with the corded muscles of someone who ate little and worked a lot. Her hair was dark, nearly black, and very long, but she had most of it tied up loosely. Her eyes sparkled seastone-blue. Black tribal tattoos snaked from her hands to her shoulders, and she wore something midway between Tirian peasant garb and the clothes of the islanders. A linen shirt with the sleeves sliced off. A pair of leather shorts that bared most of her tanned legs.

And strapped to those legs were half a dozen knives.

She froze like a statue. Blinked at Mor, then peered closer, as though she thought herself mistaken.

I couldn't see Mor's face, but his voice sounded choked with emotion. "Diggy."

She reared back, her eyes burning. "You!" she cried.

And she tossed her basket of water all over Captain Mor Bo-Lidere.

CHAPTER FORTY-FOUR

BRAITH

BRAITH SAT ON HER THRONE AND STARED IN SILENCE AT Cadwyth Bo-Balas, captain of the palace guard, as he finished reading his report for the council and gathered courtiers.

"Forgive me, Your Majesty. I wish I brought gladder news. But as you heard, we have completed our investigation into your father's murder and have made no progress in discovering the culprit. Nor were we able to confirm exactly how he died."

"But you told me he had been strangled."

"Indeed. And I believe he was. But there was nothing in his cell he might have been strangled with. The cell remained locked at all times, and all the guards swear no one passed through the dungeons that night and not one of them entered Gareth's cell."

Braith was puzzled. "Surely there must be an explanation."

Bo-Balas paused a moment. "I have only two theories, and I pray you'll forgive the absurdity of them both."

"Please continue."

"The first would be a conspiracy. Yet all the dungeon guardsmen would have to be participants, for they all swear they are telling the truth. I do not believe them capable of this deed."

"Because you trust them all implicitly?"

"No, but I do not trust that they could maintain such a united front or lie so convincingly for so long."

Braith sighed. "And your second theory?"

"Dark magic, Your Majesty."

Derisive laughter rippled through the court, but Braith did not laugh. She studied the captain, always so straightforward, serious, and honest. It was for that reason she had chosen him as captain.

These past four moons had shown Braith there was much about the world she didn't know. Weavers possessed abilities her father had tried so hard to stamp out. Could there be a different side to the weaving gift? Something that might be very much like dark magic?

"Captain Bo-Balas, thank you for your report."

He bowed.

"If there's nothing else," Braith said to her council, "we'll conclude for the day."

For once, no one seemed to want to linger with petitions or objections. Not even Sir Fellyck.

All Braith's councilors rose, and the courtiers filed out of the throne room. Braith was alone except for Kharn, who remained by the council table, and her personal guards at the back of the room.

Braith leaned her head back and closed her eyes.

"Are you well?" Kharn's voice twinged with concern.

Her eyes opened. "I'm just weary, I suppose. I had hoped . . ." Braith trailed off. What had she hoped?

"That you would get some answers, at least," Kharn finished for her.

"Yes. But this is worse, somehow."

"I'm sorry, Braith. Truly, I am."

"Thank you." She allowed a small, tight smile.

"These are not the ideal circumstances for this conversation, but I am afraid I cannot put it off any longer."

Braith frowned at him. "You cannot put what off any longer?"

Kharn was looking at her intently. "Lady Braith, will you marry me?"

She stared at him. "Kharn, that isn't funny."

"It wasn't meant to be."

"Are you honestly asking me to marry you?"

"You're surprised by this?" Kharn smiled. "I thought my intentions had been obvious."

"I thought you were seeking to depose me." Braith rose so they were at the same level. "History's politest deposition, perhaps, but a dethroning just the same."

Kharn laughed. "I should have been clearer, I see. No wonder you are so guarded with me."

"I am guarded with everyone, Sir Kharn. I have to be."

"But not with your husband, I hope."

"This isn't funny."

"Why do you keep saying that when I'm not jesting?"

"I'm not used to you being serious." Braith studied him. "But you are, aren't you?"

"Quite. We would rule so well together, Braith."

And the moment he said it, she knew it to be true. "I suppose it would be very convenient."

"Convenient?"

"To unite the throne." Braith's mind was filling with possibilities arising from such a union. "Now I feel foolish that it never occurred to me. I had always supposed it would be one or the other of us ruling, but never both together."

"Braith." Kharn reached out. "May I?"

After a pause, she allowed him to take her hand.

He held it tightly. "What you call convenience I call wisdom. But that is not the only reason I make this proposal."

"No?" Braith was startled.

"I have always admired you."

She laughed. "You dipped my braids in ink when we were children."

"I'm not above that now, you know."

Braith smiled at him. "I believe you."

He returned her smile, but as he watched her, it faltered. "You're going to say no."

"I . . . I don't know what I'm supposed to say. You're asking me to marry a stranger."

"That isn't entirely true."

"You've been out of my life for thirteen years," she protested.

"I've been back for two moons now. I have been trying to show you how well this would work. How well *we* would work."

Braith let go of his hand. "How can you possibly know that?" Ruling together was one thing. A personal relationship was something else entirely.

"Because I may have been gone from your life, but you were never gone from mine. The life you've led has been public, and I've watched from afar as you ruled better and more wisely than either of your parents. I watched a young princess fight for goodness—for mercy and justice. And that princess, this queen, was the same girl whose braids I dipped in ink. You have not changed, Braith."

Braith's gaze wandered to one of the Tirian banners hanging along the wall. "Do you know what my one private rebellion against my parents was?"

"I'm sure I don't."

"I always insisted I would marry for love. It drove my mother mad, though Father generally indulged the fancy."

"Royals don't often marry for love."

"No, indeed. But I did not want my husband to be selected for me because of his land holdings or the size of his country's army. I did not want to be loved for my father's empire. I wanted . . ."

"To be loved for your own merit, not your title."

"Yes. It is foolish, perhaps, and naïve. But it's what I always wished for myself."

"Braith." Kharn took her hand again. "That is what I'm offering you. Even if it doesn't seem that way to you, I will prove it. Don't answer now," he added quickly. "Think it over. Take a week and discuss it with Cameria or your councilors or whoever else you like. Just don't say no right away."

"Kharn . . ."

"Promise you will think about it. Or I'll dip your braids in ink next council meeting." He grinned.

"You're impossible."

"Impossibly handsome?" He bent and kissed her hand.

Braith smiled wryly. "You have your moments." She turned serious again. "I will think about it, Kharn. I promise."

"That's all I ask." He bowed, kissed her hand again, and took his leave.

Braith sank back onto her throne. Could this be the perfect solution?

Maybe, for once in her life, the answer really could be this easy.

CHAPTER FORTY-FIVE

NAITH

NAITH PULLED HIS HOOD FURTHER OVER HIS FACE, TILTING HIS head so that he might see the boy up on the wooden platform Naith had ordered constructed. He might not wish to show his face in the streets of Urian just yet, but there were plenty of people at his disposal. At least enough to build a platform.

Bo-Bradwir looked nervous. There was no denying that. But he also looked ready.

The young man waited a moment, looking out among the gathered peasants. Then he spoke loudly. "Friends, I bring you a message of hope. The crown has failed us all."

Even this simple statement garnered cheers.

"The number of Tirians isn't getting smaller, is it? Each year, more are added to our population. Babes are born, and that means more mouths to feed. Has the monarchy responded? Does the monarchy answer when these babes cry for food? When our farms are strained to the point of absurdity? No. They demand taxes."

A loud chorus of boos and jeers. Just as Naith planned when he wrote it.

"We must seize our power, friends. What powers exist in our world? Population? The nations of Haribi and Minasimet have as many people as we do. Meridione, though small, is not far behind. Tir no longer holds the power of population.

"Then maybe size? But, no. Tir is not bigger than Haribi.

The Bellithwyn continent is twice the size of Tir. What other source of power do we, the Tirian Empire, have?"

The boy was fouling up some of the language Naith had carefully crafted. But Naith had done what he was able to do with the time he was given, considering this boy had sounded every bit the Pembroni farmer when he had first come to Naith at the temple. The results weren't bad.

"The third kind of power relies on the strength of its people," Bo-Bradwir continued. "That we could have, friends. We *did* have once. But we let it die. We let it go to waste. As we scramble to meet the demands of the crown, we forget who we are.

"So what is our strength? Our Tirian race. Our Tirian heritage." Bo-Bradwir paused and looked at Naith.

The boy hadn't liked this part. In the end, the Master had needed to produce the most difficult of all strands, draining but effective. Ones that manipulated sentiment. The Master had showered Bo-Bradwir in them—wrapped them all around him like a coiled snake so that the words might come out the way the Master and Naith desired. Even so, Bo-Bradwir paused.

His will could be strong at times.

But after a moment's hesitation, the speech continued. "We need to remember the strength of our Tirian blood. The purity of it. The power of it. We must remember the purity of our race and the glory of the Tirian minds who conceived the great city of Urian, the Tirian hands that built it. Aren't we willing to fight for these things?"

A roar of approval from the crowd.

"Those who are not willing to fight will let our country— our pride and our glory—be stolen from us. Are you willing to fight, my friends?"

A louder roar than the first.

"Do you not want a leader you can believe in? Someone who is one of you? Someone who knows what matters?"

Naith's watchful look intensified. Bo-Bradwir held his hands out, and orbs of fire glowed in his palms. The crowd gasped.

"I am the one you can believe in. I will challenge the crown and restore Tir to its glory!" The fire turned to bread, and the peasants erupted.

The sound was delicious—the approval and rabid enthusiasm of those who didn't know any better and who couldn't see past their own stomachs.

Bo-Bradwir was passing out the large quantities of bread they had made in advance. Now was the time to slip away. Naith rounded a corner into an alleyway, pulled his hood lower, and spoke in low tones.

"Master?"

The misty strands appeared almost immediately. "Yes?"

"The boy is ready. And so are the peasants."

"Well done, Naith."

Relief. "A dozen more speeches like this, and the whole kingdom will be prepared. Tir is ready. It is time for you to collect your weapon, Master."

"Indeed. And this time, I will not fail."

CHAPTER FORTY-SIX

TANWEN

BEFORE ANY OF US HAD A CHANCE TO SAY ANYTHING, DIGGY disappeared inside her dwelling.

I could see it now, among the tree trunks, sprawled along the edges of the clearing, cleverly concealed by fronds and branches and the tangled underbrush.

It was the Corsyth, island style.

"Diggy?" a stunned Mor called after her.

Her head reappeared. "Why are you here?"

"I came for you."

The rest of her body emerged. She had set down the basket somewhere. "Let me rephrase," she said, every word sharp as a blade. "Why are you here *now*?"

"I . . ."

"Exactly." She shook her head and stormed past him, sparing me a glance. "You're pretty," she said. Then she kept walking.

Kawan and Diggy fell into step together, heading toward the beach, speaking in the island tongue.

Mor stared after her, flabbergasted and dripping wet. "Diggy, wait!"

She stopped so suddenly, Mor and I both almost crashed into her. "You're late."

Mor's voice faltered. "Aye, I know."

"Four years too late."

"Yes, that's true. Diggy, I want to apologize."

"You . . ." She laughed, mirthless and full of disbelief. "You want to . . . apologize? Well. Thanks. I'll take your apology and turn back time with it."

"Diggy, please let me—"

Diggy whirled, drew a knife from one of the straps around her legs, and hurled it end-over-end toward us. It thunked into the tree just to the left of Mor's head. I supposed she missed on purpose.

At least, I hoped.

"No, Mor, I will not *let* you do anything. You have nerve showing up here."

"I thought you were dead."

"Oh, that must be it, then. You waited until you thought I was dead, *then* you came for me."

"That's not what I meant."

"No! You're done speaking now." She pulled another knife and threw it. It, too, narrowly missed Mor and thunked into the tree right next to the other.

She had definitely missed on purpose. This girl could split huskbeetle eyelashes with her blades.

"You have to let me explain," Mor said, and a note of desperation crept into his voice. "These last four years have been full of hardship, I'm sure. But I'm here now. We're both alive, and that has to be a miracle."

Diggy was still for a long moment, regarding Mor. She grabbed another knife and threw it with a flourish. "You don't know what happened."

Mor took a deep breath. "I know it must have been bad if you left a headstone on the other island."

"Aye. You could say that."

Mor took a tentative step toward her. "You're right. I don't know. I only know everything I've feared. But you're *here*, and it's like a gift."

"A gift," Diggy repeated. She threw another knife.

"Diggy, I don't know what's happened to you. And I won't until you tell me."

She turned to face him, that strange, unhappy look on her face again. "Yes," she said finally. "I shall tell you now."

Mor waited.

"They made me a slave in the palace. You know that part?" she asked.

Mor nodded. "Yes. In the palace kitchens."

"Ah, you did know where I was. I wondered." She glared at him. "Because you never came!"

"I know. I'm sorry. I have no excuse. I was afraid."

"Yes. Poor Mor. I was a child. And my big brother never came."

"I'm sorry, Diggy."

Diggy shrugged off his words. "She beat me—the kitchen maid in charge of us all. She had a terrible temper. But I waited for you anyway. A whole year, I waited. But then I realized you weren't coming, and it was time to leave. I had help escaping. The others in the kitchens saw how she beat me. Ginia the chef wanted to help. Everyone knew who my father was, so they helped me escape to the sea. To one of Gareth's merchant vessels. It's what our family does, isn't it?"

She didn't wait for an answer. "I was such a *valuable* slave. I was only fourteen years old, but I knew how to cook and sail. And that's not all." Diggy threw another knife.

Mor's face stiffened.

"Do you know why they bring girls on ships, brother? Father never did that, so maybe you don't know." She threw her last knife. She had made a perfect circle of them on the trunk.

She strode to her knives and wrested them from the tree.

"Diggy." Mor approached her. "I'm so sorry."

"Are you? I am too. Sorry for my life, sorry I ever trusted anyone, sorry I was so happy to escape the palace kitchens at first. Aye, they beat me there, but that was better—better than the visitors to my cabin each night on the ship."

She clenched the knives.

"They come alone if they're sober. But in twos and threes and fives when they're drunk."

The horror of Diggy's words hung in the air. A strand of black silk curled from my palm unbidden. It looped toward Mor—a strand of grief and pain. I waved it away before it reached him.

Diggy stared at her knives. "For a while, I still hoped. Still waited for someone to come fight for me. But really, it was too late. I became less than human. Less than nothing."

"But that's not true," Mor protested.

"Isn't it, though? What am I?" She looked toward the tree. "Do you see, Mor? There's not enough soul left inside me to forgive anyone."

"Diggy . . ." Mor's face was ashen. "Digwyn, please don't say that." He reached a hand toward her. "I need you."

"We all need things we'll never get." She threw a knife.

And then she laughed. A hollow, joyless sound that dissolved into sobs. She turned to Mor, and the children of Lidere looked at each other, tears streaming down both their faces.

The sky darkened, and thunder rumbled. A moment later, a flash storm dumped warm, tropical water on us.

Diggy tilted her head back, and rain splashed her face. She laughed hollowly again. "And now you've come. Welcome to my island, brother. Welcome at long, dreadful last."

I looked helplessly at the broken shards of Mor's long-lost sister, and I wondered. Could she be put back together again?

CHAPTER FORTY-SEVEN

TANWEN

THE DRIVING RAIN SLOWED TO A SPRINKLE, AND DIGGY TOOK a deep breath.

Words poured from her again, quieter. Calmer. "I was on that ship a year. When we docked in the Islands, I ran away. I hid in a cargo crate and was delivered to the Kanaci dock. But as soon as they missed me, they sent out search parties. They rallied the islanders and offered a large reward. I mattered so very much to them, you see," she added bitterly.

"I'd made friends with Kawan already," she went on. "He said the islanders would hunt me to my end, because the offered ransom was so big. So we decided to fake my death. The captain was furious. He had made sure to let the islanders know I was to be kept alive. Because I *mattered*. But Kawan is a good actor. His mother was in on our secret, and her testimony convinced the captain and crew their valuable plaything was gone." Her gaze dropped. "Once their business was done, they left."

She turned over one of the knives in her hand. "But I couldn't stay on Kanac after that, of course. The ransom would still be delivered if I was returned to the captain alive, so I had to go somewhere else. I came here. It's been uninhabited for centuries because it floods terribly during the rainy season. Kawan visits me sometimes, but mostly it's me here alone." She looked directly at Mor, eyes dark. "This is all I want."

Mor again reached out toward her. "Diggy . . . come with

me. We've already made arrangements to acquire another ship. As soon as we get what we came for, we'll head back to Tir with you. There is so much more for you than this."

Diggy laughed. "I sincerely doubt that."

"Please," he begged. "We could be a family again."

"I have no need of family." She turned and headed for the trees. "Go home, brother. Enjoy your ship and your pirating and whatever else you do these days." She looked over her shoulder and smiled faintly at him. "Yes, I noticed the gold in your ear and those shark-leather boots. What would Father say about you turning pirate?"

"I'm legitimate now. Sailing under the queen's banner."

"The queen?" She stopped walking and turned. "There is a queen on the throne?"

"Braith En-Gareth."

Diggy's eyes narrowed. "The daughter of Gareth? You sail under her banner?" She snorted and turned back to the trees. "Why am I surprised? Go back to your queen, Mor Bo-Lidere."

"Diggy!"

"No, we're finished."

A bolt of lightning shot from Mor's hand in frustration. It snapped against a tree trunk at the edge of the jungle. But even at that, Diggy didn't turn back.

I paused a moment, then hurried after her. "Digwyn, please wait!"

The trees had swallowed her completely. I turned in a circle but saw no sign of her. "Diggy?"

"Is my brother your beau?" The sound came from the canopy of tropical trees above me.

I looked up, and there she was, perched in the trees like a little puff-prowler. "What?"

"Does he fancy you? Is he your beau?"

"Those are two separate questions."

"True enough," she said. "So?"

For some reason, I answered her plainly. "We fancy each other, but your brother is not free. Truthfully, I'm not either." I didn't suppose shoving my engagement band back into Brac's hands was an official-enough break. I certainly owed him an explanation when I returned.

"Interesting."

"Complicated, more like." I paused. "Mor has suffered, too, you know."

"Just when I was beginning to like you . . ." She pulled up her legs, preparing to jump to another tree.

"Wait."

She paused.

"I just meant . . ." I couldn't bring myself to speak specifically. "Diggy, you have been horribly hurt. I can't imagine what you've gone through. It must have been . . ." My mind couldn't find the words.

She tilted her head to the side and looked ever more like a wild critter.

I began again. "It would be easy to think that while those terrible, evil things were happening to you, Mor was off having a grand adventure on his stolen ship. That he abandoned you and lived in comfort because of it. But that's not true. He's been on the run as many years as you've been gone."

She sat, still listening.

"A lass he cares for very deeply is dying. We all care about her. That's why we're here in the Islands. We're trying to find the cure for her. It was important to Mor to stay with her and do everything he could to help her"—I hesitated—"because of his guilt over you. He knows he should have fought for you, and the regret and shame eat at him every moment. Everything he does for Gryfelle is what he so desperately wishes he'd done for you."

Nothing about her expression changed. "He abandoned me."

"But he's found you now. He had heard you were dead. But

he searched anyway. He came, hoping for a miracle. He wants to make right what went wrong four years ago."

"Nothing can make that right."

What else could I say to help her see? "Hope is not lost, Diggy."

"It's not?"

"No. At least I don't think so."

"Why?" She looked genuinely curious.

"Hope is never lost as long as you're willing to fight for it. And I do think there is hope for you."

Diggy paused like she might be considering it, really and truly. But then she shook her head. "Some ships are best left at the bottom of the ocean."

Before I could stop her again, she swung up and away, out of my sight.

I took in a big breath. I had failed too. She would live like this the rest of her days, hating the world, hating Mor, and I almost couldn't blame her. What she had endured was unfathomable.

But that was why she needed to be surrounded by people who loved her. Mor was right. We could be a new family for her.

As I stood there, feeling defeated and useless, Diggy's shriek pierced the air. "What have you done?"

She appeared in the canopy, swinging from branches and vines, and dropped before me with an accusatory glare. "What have you brought here?"

"I don't know what you mean." I took a step back. "Our ship was wrecked. We've barely brought anything."

"Wrecked by who?" Her gaze ripped through me.

"I . . . I don't know. It was some kind of magic." I hadn't given enough thought to who was behind the dark strands, for all those roads seemed to be dead ends. It was an unusual sort of magic no one understood. "They were strands," I told Diggy. "Like story strands, but warped, somehow."

Diggy turned and sprinted toward the beach where Kawan and Mor still stood.

"Mor!" she yelled. "What have you done?"

He looked too startled to respond.

"Look!" She pointed.

Mor turned. Off in the distance, a giant thunderhead rolled along the ocean toward us. As I watched it, I realized it wasn't a thunderhead. It was a colossal mass of strands, and they weren't headed toward us. They were headed toward Kanac.

"What have you brought here?" Diggy stared at the roiling strands growing ever closer.

Mor's face tightened. "We didn't bring them, Diggy. Not on purpose, anyway." He looked at me. "What do they want? They already sank the *Cethorelle*. Is it the cure they're after?"

"Why would it be wanted?" I asked as I stared at the mass, bewildered. "They seem able to twist strands however they want without the help of the ancients."

But then the memory of something Father had said struck me. "A weapon." The threads of thought came together slowly in my mind, muddled by all my memory loss, no doubt. "Remember, Mor? Father said whoever is behind the strands is hunting us."

"We have nothing for them anymore. Not even a vessel."

"The weapon." I whirled around toward Mor. "Us."

"What?"

"Remember what my father said?" I gestured between us frantically. "*We* are the weapon. Whoever is behind this . . . just look at what he's doing with these strands. They're story strands, but twisted. He wants storytellers. Linked ones. He wants to use us to do more of that." I pointed to the torrents of ill intent speeding over the waves.

"Cethor's tears."

The mass was too close for comfort. "Better start talking to the Creator instead."

"We have to get back to Kanac."

My heart tripped. "Father's there."

"And Gryfelle," Mor whispered.

Kawan was already at the canoe, dragging it into the ocean. "My mother!"

That was all the prompting Diggy needed. She bolted down the beach. "I'm coming." She spared Mor half a glance over her shoulder. "Well? Are you?"

CHAPTER FORTY-EIGHT

TANWEN

MOR AND KAWAN PADDLED AS THOUGH LIVES WERE AT STAKE. Which, of course, they were.

"Should have grabbed more knives," Diggy muttered to herself. "No, no time."

"I don't think knives work on strands," I told her.

"They kill those making the strands."

Couldn't argue with that, but still it chilled me to the bone.

She watched the mass move closer to the island. "Not sure we'll make it in time."

"We'll make it." Mor's arms strained with each stroke.

When we reached shallow water, Kawan didn't pause to pull the canoe to shore. He leapt out, splashed through the water, and sped toward the village, Diggy running after him. Mor and I followed a few paces behind.

"Where was the strand meant to be?" I shouted to Mor as we ran.

"There was a carved stone monument in the jungle somewhere. Dylun said they only needed a colormaster to pull it up."

Which was why they could spare us, of course. My mind was a muddled mess. I had no idea what we were supposed to do. The hail of dark magic had been too much to fight when we were on the ship, and now that we were here, beaten down and exhausted, I didn't see that we could fare any better. That mass of sorcery was rolling toward us, and we had run out of time to save Gryfelle.

Now we all needed saving.

"Tannie!" Mor's voice snapped me back. "This way."

We ducked into the trees, onto the jungle path, and somehow it was worse not to be able to see the strands coming toward us. They could overtake us at any moment without warning while we were in the jungle. But thank the stars there was a path, at least.

"Looking for your friends?" Diggy appeared beside me out of nowhere and nearly sent me jumping from my skin.

"Aye. What about Kawan and his mother? The other villagers?"

"Kawan's doing what he can to secure his village. If I really want to help them, I need to stop whatever that thing is before it gets to them." She paused, then raised her voice to address Mor. "You are going to stop it, right?" Her voice took on a frantic pitch. "You will not leave them to die, Mor. Don't you run away again!"

Which was a bit ironic because we were literally running.

Mor did not answer her, but I saw his shoulders tense. I hoped he could prove himself to her in all this somehow.

"Off the path here," Mor said, and he took a hard left into the trees. "This way."

"There are ancient stones here," Diggy said. "Is that where we're going?"

"Yes," I said between breaths. "We're unearthing some ancient strands. It's kind of a long story."

"For Mor's dying lass."

"Aye."

"Interesting."

What a strange choice of words. But no time to wonder over Diggy's oddities at the moment.

"Mor!" I called. "To your right, through those trees!" I could see my father's gray head.

And now I could see the others. They were huddled around a stone that looked to be a giant carved head, though the features had worn down so that it was barely recognizable as a face. Karlith sat on the floor of the jungle, Gryfelle cradled in her arms. Everyone else looked stormy and frustrated, especially Dylun.

"Tannie?" Father frowned at me. "What are you doing back so soon?" Then he turned to Diggy, and his eyes widened.

I could barely catch my breath to speak. "We—"

"Found Mor's sister." Father's intuitive eyes were focused on Diggy's face. "Remarkable. She's alive."

"Aye," I managed between heaving breaths. "She's alive."
Alive, though not well.

"Amazing."

"Father," I interrupted. "Did you get the strand?"

"No," Dylun said, impatience punctuating the word. "It won't come out. I can't understand why."

He touched the stone head, his fingertips glowing, and painted some sort of design in the divots that served as eyes.

"There!" I pointed. "The strand is right there!"

And sure as seastones, there was the tip of a red strand, just visible, poking out through the stone mouth.

"Box that strand and let's go," Mor said, "because we have trouble."

"Trouble?" Warmil asked. Lines of exhaustion etched his face. "What trouble?"

"Strands," Mor said. "A whole mess of them, like the ones that sank the ship."

"Coming here?" Warmil drew his sword, as if that would help.

I remembered Diggy's point about her knives.

"Yes, coming here," I said quickly. "So, grab the strand. We need to do something."

"But I can't get this one." Dylun looked like he was ready to punch the rock. "It barely comes out, and whenever I get near, it disappears again. We need all four strands for the cure to work."

"No." Warmil shook his head. "This can't have been for nothing. Think, Dylun. What did the scrolls say?"

Dylun closed his eyes.

I tried not to imagine the mass of dark strands flying toward us. How far away had they been? The ocean's horizon could play tricks of distance on you. Had they been closer than they appeared? Farther away?

"Diggy, will you check the horizon?" I asked.

She nodded once, then took to the tree canopy in her agile, critter-like way.

I was surprised to hear Gryfelle's voice. "Oh, that's strange," she said weakly. Her gaze fixed on Diggy. "What an interesting little person she is, up in the trees . . ." She blinked slowly. "She looks like a sailor I knew once."

Stars.

"Dylun," I said. "Is there something you're forgetting? Something we missed?"

Dylun's eyes popped back open, and at first, relief surged through me. Surely he'd had an idea. But then my heart plummeted. His eyes conveyed only anguish.

"We need a stoneshaper."

"What?"

"That's what I missed the first time. We need a colormaster and a stoneshaper."

"But we don't have a stoneshaper," I said.

Dylun ignored me. "How could I have missed this?" He shook his head in despair. "I've failed you all."

My gaze darted from weaver to weaver, then to my father. Panic flared. Tears welled. "Daddy?"

His voice was quiet, spent and exhausted. "If we had time. But this darkness . . ."

Diggy dropped into the circle from above. "A league off but moving fast," she reported. "You best hurry this up so we can get to the west beach."

A little life seemed to return to Mor. Perhaps the idea of failing his sister again spurred him to grasp at hope. "We have three colormasters here," he said.

I tried not to remember that we would have four if Aeron were with us.

"What are you thinking, Captain?" asked Father.

"Maybe War and Dylun could link. Try to double their energy. Karlith could help too. Maybe it would be enough even without a stoneshaper."

Father looked at Warmil. "Do you think you could link with Dylun?"

"Perhaps. He *is* like a brother to me. We should try."

And they did. Father handed me the box of strands, then took over caring for Gryfelle. Karlith, Warmil, and Dylun positioned themselves in front of the stone head. Dylun and War clasped each other's forearms. The fingertips on their unclasped hands glowed a little brighter, but it wasn't much. Definitely not like when Mor and I linked. Zel and Mor stood back far enough so as not to be in the way, but I stood nearby to capture the red strand with its fellows in the velvet-lined box.

With Dylun and War linked and Karlith doing her part, the head gradually transformed into a painted masterpiece with lifelike features of exquisite detail. I expected it to blink and start speaking to us. But the red strand barely showed another inch of length. It looked more like the head was sticking out its tongue at us, mocking our efforts.

"It's not working!" I heard the panic in Mor's voice.

Diggy fidgeted beside me. "There's no time."

And then she raised her hand. At first I thought she must

be holding a knife, and I almost dropped the box of strands to tackle her before she could attack the three colormasters.

But there was no knife. Lightning crackled across her palm, and then she thrust her arm forward, toward the colormasters and stone head.

A wave of unseen force pulsed from the head where Diggy's burst of energy collided with the colormastery strands. The colormasters stumbled back a step at its impact. Then the stone head shook, and the red strand whipped from its mouth. Diggy lifted her hand higher, then twisted it and made a flinging motion in my direction. The red strand, like liquid fire and blood, careened into the box with the others.

The force nearly knocked me from my feet. But I kept my balance and watched in amazement at the extraordinary scene unfolding before me.

The red, purple, gold, and blue ribbons met and melded, a kaleidoscope of colors swirling together in an ancient dance for the first time in centuries. For a moment, I held a rainbow in my hands.

Then the rainbow shot into the air beneath the tropical trees. It paused there, pulsing.

"Creator above." Karlith stared up at it. "It's beautiful."

"Magnificent," marveled Father.

Every gaze remained transfixed.

The rainbow exploded into white light. I threw my arm over my eyes to shield them. It was like the threads of white light that had appeared in my stories five moons ago—these past five moons that felt like a lifetime. But this was no mere thread, no tiny ribbon of truth to counteract the lies forced upon me by Gareth and Riwor and a society so far from truth that it could no longer recognize it when it stood in plain view.

No, this was a solid beam of the same stuff, and I knew I couldn't look at it. Not if I wanted to live.

But after several moments, the glow seeping through my

closed eyelids lessened, and I ventured a glance. The beam was gone, and in its place hovered an orb—clear, bright, with tongues of white fire licking the surface.

Diggy stepped toward it, hand outstretched. "There's no time."

"Stop!" I cried. It came out so forcefully, she obeyed.

Somehow I knew this was not a thing she should touch or command or manipulate. This was the cure. Its Source was something beyond my understanding, but instinctively I knew to respect it.

I carefully held out the box. The cure floated toward me, turned a graceful circle, and lowered itself onto the velvet.

We all looked at it, an orb of white fire full of promise, hope, and mercy.

If it worked.

But Diggy was right. We were out of time. That dark mass of strands must be at the shore, and we had promised to not run from those who needed help. It was time to try to save this island full of people.

I closed the box and latched it. "We need to get to the beach."

Everyone started to move, checking weaponry and flexing fingers and shaking our minds from the trance.

All except Mor, who stepped over to his sister. He put his hand on her shoulder and looked her straight in the eyes. "What was that?"

She shrugged off his contact with a shriek. "Don't touch me!"

He backed off, but his gaze didn't let up. "Diggy," he repeated. "What was that?"

Her defiant eyes darted around like she was looking for a way out. She didn't answer his question. "Kawan and his mother are on this island. Prove to me you've changed. Save them."

CHAPTER FORTY-NINE

TANWEN

WE SCRAMBLED TO THE WEST BEACH OF KANAC WITHOUT ANY idea what we were doing. Karlith limped behind with Gryfelle.

Were we sprinting to our deaths?

I skidded to a stop in the white sand behind the others. Warmil drew his sword. My father nocked an arrow on his bow. Diggy crouched like an animal ready to spring, a knife in either hand.

"Dylun? Warmil?" Fear seeped through my voice. "Father? What are we supposed to do?"

The black mass of strands was a heartbeat away.

"Try to think of them as strands like all others," Warmil shouted above the whip of the wind. "Fight them with yours like you did before."

Yes, except those strands had overwhelmed us on the *Cethorelle*. Fighting them one by one hadn't worked, and this gathering looked many times larger than the mass that had attacked us.

Mor stood beside me. The black cloud rolled closer. It blotted out the sun an inch at a time until the world turned gray.

We weren't going to make it through this. The certainty of death enveloped me, sorrow swallowing all my thoughts. It pressed in on me, squeezed until I couldn't draw a full breath.

"Tannie!" Mor was reaching out his hand to me across the whipping wind and the darkness and the terror.

"We were so close, Mor," I said desperately.

Everything we had been working toward, the cure we had sought, the desperate attempt to save me and Gryfelle, had been for nothing. We were all going to die on a Kanaci beach.

"Tannie." Mor's voice was firm but tender. He still held his hand toward me, and I saw my sorrow reflected in his eyes. "Together?"

Yes. Together.

I forced my mind to work through the problem. What were these twisted things? Stories? Ideas? Yes, ideas about pain, heartache, destruction, domination, greed. Who knew what else.

So we should counteract them with the opposite. Counteract them with the good.

I grabbed Mor's hand, and I felt that familiar click of our gifts linking. Our eyes met, and he nodded.

What was the best, most wonderful thing I could imagine?

A world with none of the evil things that comprised the mass of smoky strands now upon us. Not a world where good always won, but a world where good didn't have to fight because it was all that existed. A world with no sickness, no pain, no death. Only love and joy, flowing straight from the origin of goodness. People would live with each other and not grab for power or give in to selfish desires. Only love. Only joy. Forever.

White ribbons of light poured from me and Mor. Not quite as impressive as that beam from the cure, but close. Our white ribbons of love and joy were joined by splashes of color from the colormasters and streams of orange coils from Zel, the only other storyteller present.

I smiled to think of his wife, Ifmere, and her beautiful orange hair. This seemed to be becoming Zel's signature story strand, and perfectly so. Ifmere and their baby boy were never far from his heart, so what else would come out when it was time to fight for what he loved?

Our light and color and hope poured out down the beach toward the torrent. Strands of life to beat back those of pain and death. The mass retreated back to the ocean, and for a moment, I thought we had managed it, just like that. We had saved ourselves and the island and Diggy's friends, and Diggy herself.

But then it redoubled its strength and surged toward us.

I gripped Mor's hand as tightly as I could, but it didn't matter. A ribbon like liquid metal came straight for me. It wrapped around my waist, and I let out a scream. It didn't just *look* like burning metal. It *was* burning metal, and it seared my flesh.

"Tannie!"

"Tanwen!"

I couldn't tell Mor's shouts from Father's. I was twenty feet in the air, a searing stream wrapped around my waist. I screamed again and then went numb, unable to think of anything to counteract the pain or the fear. I just let the strand dangle me there, and again the thought flittered through my mind: Why wasn't it killing me?

Then I remembered. *We* were the weapon. The strands weren't there to kill us. They were there to capture us and bring me and Mor to their source. To use us.

But what about those who weren't useful weapons? What of Father? Gryfelle?

I came back to myself, pain and fear be blazed.

I didn't try to filter anything. I let my first thought of happiness form itself into a strand and made no apologies for it.

It was a future with Mor. Maybe a future telling stories together. Maybe one sailing around the world. Perhaps both. But no curse haunted this idea. No conflict or twisted-up feelings. Only happiness for everyone. Maybe it was the story of what might have happened if I had met Mor when we were younger.

Maybe Mor and I would have fallen in love before his ill-advised courtship with Gryfelle. Before Brac got it fixed in his mind that he and I should be husband and wife. Then Mor and I could have adventured on the seas in his father's ship. We might have entertained the crew together, and Gryfelle would never have been cursed or forced away from court life. She would have met a brave knight or wealthy nobleman and entertained the court and His Majesty, King Caradoc II with her beautiful songs.

And Brac would have his Pembroni farm girl, just like he wanted. She would love the hum of life in a small village, like he did. Or had, before he joined the guard. They would have a hundred little ones, and Mor and I would come to the naming ceremony for each and bring presents from around the world, and I would kiss those little babies and love them like they were my blood, because Brac and I shared a bond as strong as that.

Perhaps in this story, Mother had lived. She and Father never would have been separated. They would be enjoying the glow of having raised their child and gotten through their hardest years of work. Father would take Mother to visit his friends all over the world, and that world would receive them differently because there would not have been intervening years of war and oppression.

And then maybe someday, Mor and I would add a little babe to this world—this fantasy world that was happy and warm. One or maybe two or maybe even seven.

None of it was real, of course. But that didn't matter. The strands—azure, violet, rose, gold, pine, scarlet, and every other color one might imagine—swirled around me. Where it touched the molten metal, the metal sizzled, then disappeared. Like snipping one thread at a time until none remained and I was no longer bound.

Then I fell from twenty feet.

At the last second before I was about to hit the beach and break all my bones, something caught me, light and airy. The cushion held me a moment, then dropped me gently into the sand. I looked up, and there stood Mor, his hands out still, his fingertips pinked slightly where the strands had burst from them.

He pulled me up, and as I steadied myself, I surveyed the scene. My heart fell.

The mass was back over the beach now, and our efforts only drove back one small section at a time. It wasn't enough. We would never force the cloud of ill intent to retreat completely. Not at this rate.

"It's not trying to kill all of us," I told Mor. "I don't know who they're after for sure, except I know they don't mean to kill me and you."

"Because we're the weapon."

"Yes."

Mor looked out over the beach. I could see realization hit him. "The others . . ."

"Yes, anyone who isn't useful to whoever is controlling this mess will be killed."

"Gryfelle. Diggy." Mor's anger was growing—I could feel it in his words.

"My father." I grabbed Mor's arm as a thought struck me. "If they have any idea of what Diggy can do, they'll want her too."

Perhaps it hadn't occurred to either of us until I said that, but suddenly I wondered where Diggy was. Because even if she didn't care much about our mission, she did care about Kawan and his mother and keeping them safe on this island.

I spotted her, not too far down the beach.

She wasn't brandishing knives. Perhaps she had realized there was no person to target. At least not nearby.

Such intense sorcery done from a distance? I had never realized power or malice so strong existed in the world. Gareth's greed and self-serving deeds seemed commonplace by comparison.

But, though Diggy had sheathed her knives, she was still

in the thick of it, and I squinted to try to figure out what in the world she was doing.

Zel shot a ribbon of blue light toward the smoky mass. As the ribbon sailed over Diggy's head, she reached up and snatched it from the sky. Suddenly Zel's strand wasn't just blue light. It was blue fire. She hurled the blue fire toward the mass, and a big chunk of the dark cloud disappeared.

I should be running, helping, making my way back toward the strands, or at least I should be tending the searing flesh around my midsection. But instead, I stood stock-still, unable to take my eyes off Digwyn En-Lidere. I'd never seen anything like it.

Dylun fired off a splash of glowing green colormastery, and Diggy snatched *that* from the air and turned it solid, like a spear, except it glowed green and crackled with lightning. Diggy cried out and hurled it toward the mass. Another chunk retreated.

But even with Diggy's ability, whatever it was, we weren't making enough progress.

"Mor?" I had to shake him to get his attention, for he, too, was focused on Diggy. "Mor! It's not working!"

"I know," he said finally.

"We have to help! We have to save Gryfelle and the others."

He paused, looked at Diggy again, and said, "Aye. Let's go."

Mor and I ran with purpose, like we were going to single-handedly drive back the entire cloud of strands. But then we stopped. We saw the very last thing anyone had expected. Even stranger than Diggy and her strand-stealing.

Gryfelle was on her feet and walking down the beach, straight toward the cloud.

"Gryfelle!" Mor shouted.

"What is she doing?" I yelled.

We both ran. Toward Gryfelle as she glided toward this beast.

She must not realize its power. She must not know what she's doing. She won't survive.

We ran harder.

I could jump and throw my body over her. Shield her from the *thing*. Even if Gryfelle wasn't useful, I was. This mass of evil wanted me, and I could use that. I could cover Gryfelle and give Mor a chance to do . . . something. Anything.

And then a solution began to form in my mind. The cure. Of course. If we could just get half a minute to hold it in our hands the way we were supposed to, perhaps Gryfelle and I could be healed. It didn't always work, Dylun said. But it *might* work. If I could get to the box that held the orb, I could revive Gryfelle. She could help us fight. Maybe those ancient strands would even lend aid.

But the same moment the thought came to me, Gryfelle stopped and turned. She locked eyes with me, then with Mor. She was clear. Lucid. More than she had been in weeks.

She smiled sadly.

"No, Gryfelle!" Mor shouted. "No, no, no!"

He and I were almost there. Nearly close enough to touch her. Just about able to help.

But she smiled again, and her eyes sparkled with tears. "Good-bye, my friends."

CHAPTER FIFTY

TANWEN

I FOUGHT FOR MY VOICE. "GRYFELLE, STOP!"

Pale-green song strands swirled around Gryfelle, and only then did I realize she was singing. She didn't seem to hear me or Mor shouting.

Lavender, powder blue, sunset pink, sunrise yellow. Wispy tendrils of melody flowed over Gryfelle's body, and for a moment, her ashen skin, sunken cheeks, stringy hair, and skeletal form were replaced by what Gryfelle ought to have looked like. Young and rosy, with elegant, high cheekbones and piercing green eyes, pale-golden hair flowing down her back.

Her song strands glowed as she poured what remained of her life force into them. Brighter and brighter, until I could barely see her anymore. Then the glowing strands lifted her into the air. Up she rose, toward the haze of smoke penetrating deeper over the island.

"Gryfelle!" Mor's cry was lost in Gryfelle's song.

She lifted her arms around her and seemed to draw a deep breath. "I'm ready to do my part, at last. It is time to return home." There was music in her words. Gryfelle lifted her face toward the sky.

A burst a hundred times as strong as whatever Diggy had created at the stone head pulsed over the whole island. The next thing I knew, Mor and I were down in the sand together. The force of a windstorm surrounded us. I heard a tree crack and topple. Mor clutched me close.

Shouts swirled, as if on the wind. Sand pelted my bare skin. I tucked my face into Mor's chest to escape.

Another pulse rattled the earth. I closed my eyes against it. If we were about to die, I didn't really want to see what it was, anyway.

But a moment passed, and I still felt my heart pounding. Mor's arms held me. The wind was calm, the sand no longer showering us with stinging grains.

"Tannie!" I heard Father's voice calling me frantically.

I forced myself up and blinked against the sudden brightness.

The mass of dark strands was gone. Several trees were downed, and about a hundred fronds littered the beach. Warmil slouched against Dylun, dark blood spreading over his side.

I pulled myself up and stumbled over to Father. "What happened? Is everyone all right?"

But of course everyone was not all right. And the moment I spoke it, I knew. I turned to look, and there she was.

Gryfelle's body lay crumpled in a heap on the beach.

I pushed away from my father and ran toward her.

Mor, Karlith, and I reached her at the same time. I dropped to my knees in the sand. Tears choked my throat.

Karlith was crying, too, as she touched Gryfelle's face. "Shh," she whispered. "Be at peace now, my dear girl."

Mor looked like he had taken a whole sheaf of arrows to the gut.

Karlith positioned Gryfelle so her limbs weren't splayed strangely. So that she did look at peace. At long last.

"But—" My sobs overtook my words. "The cure. We *have* it. We have it!" I wanted to hurl curses at the blasted black swarm that had swallowed the time we needed to heal Gryfelle.

Karlith was stroking Gryfelle's hair. "So beautiful she is."

And she was. All traces of the curse had left her body.

Gryfelle didn't look haggard and ill anymore. She looked like herself—lovely, young, and perfect.

My heart broke into a dozen pieces. "We were supposed to save her."

"She saved us instead," Karlith said gently. She laid Gryfelle's head back on the sand. "And if her sacrifice isn't to be a waste, we need to go."

"Why?" I stared out over the peaceful ocean. All signs of the black cloud were gone.

"It will be back, won't it?" Karlith looked up at me. "They won't retreat forever, and if I'm not mistaken, that'll be the end of us all except you and Mor. I think you know they want to capture you."

So she knew too. They would kill everyone else.

"Yes, Karlith. I know."

"Tannie, if they catch you, they'll use you just like in ancient times."

"We won't let that happen," I said.

Karlith nodded. "Then we have to go."

Mor was whiter than milk.

So I turned to Father. "Is the new ship ready yet?"

He held a hand over his heart and looked at Gryfelle's body like it hurt him. But he had heard me. "Jule has been working on it, but I don't know if the ship is ready to set sail yet."

"Digwyn." We all turned. Kawan was running down the beach toward us. "Diggy, you must go."

Diggy looked at him sharply. "What is it?"

"You were seen. Recognized." He glanced at the rest of us. "And they're saying you brought it."

"Brought what?"

"Whatever that was. The dark."

Diggy's eyes hardened. "And now they want to kill me. Again. Always."

"Yes."

"I can't go back to my home. They will follow."

"Yes."

After a long moment, Diggy turned to Mor. "I guess I'm coming with you."

Mor nodded. But not even Diggy joining us could bring joy back into his face.

"Warmil." I looked at his wound. "Is it bad? Can you make it to the docks?"

"If Dylun helps me, I can make it."

I was suddenly aware of the searing burns around my middle.

Karlith could help, but only if she had the supplies. I prayed Jule and the men had stocked the new ship well.

"And Aeron? Is she back in Narwat's hut?"

Warmil closed his eyes and shook his head, still clutching his wound. "She's with Jule and the crew. I thought to move her to the ship in case something went sideways."

Good planning, that.

Father knelt beside Karlith. "I will carry Gryfelle."

"Don't forget this." Zelyth jogged toward us, box in hand. "I think Tannie still needs it."

I nearly *had* forgotten it—the cure we had traveled around the world to retrieve. I'd almost left it lying on some Kanaci beach without using it.

"Kawan." Diggy looked up at him, and it was plain to see the friendship that passed between them. There was still something very human, very fragile about Digwyn En-Lidere, whatever she tried to make the rest of us believe.

"Good-bye, Dig." He brushed her hair back, then kissed her on both cheeks, like they did in the Islands. "You will come see me someday." He kissed her forehead.

She winced. Pulling away from this man—the only man she trusted—physically hurt her.

Father scooped up Gryfelle. "Let's hurry."

We ran as fast as we could manage, carrying our injury and death, dismay and heartbreak with us.

IF THERE WAS ONE LUCKY BREAK THIS WHOLE DAY, IT WAS that our new ship was nearly ready.

Commander Jule must have had the remaining crew working around the clock to get the *Lysian* prepared.

Jule looked both relieved and dismayed when he saw us limping toward the docks. "I expected we would have to make a fast departure, though I wasn't sure why. But when I saw that cloud of . . . whatever it was, I didn't know if you would make it back at all." Then he noticed Gryfelle. He removed his hat and held it to his heart. "Oh, no. Poor lass."

"She saved us," I said. I wanted to shout that from every rooftop across all of Tir. So everyone in the kingdom would know of Gryfelle En-Blaid's final act.

"Jule," said Mor. "We need to get underway immediately. I don't know how long those strands will stay away."

"Aye, Captain. Right away." Jule started shouting orders, and the men scurried into action.

"Karlith." Mor's voice hitched, and he cleared his throat. "Let's place Gryfelle down in the captain's quarters. Would you and the general see to that? I need to get my sister settled. And then we'll see to the injuries, once we're underway."

"Of course." Karlith had been crying steadily since Gryfelle's final moments on the beach, but somehow, she looked the least shaken of all of us.

Gryfelle was like a daughter to her. Karlith had spent moons by her bedside, barely away for a moment at a time. Her calm amid her tears didn't make sense.

But I couldn't ask her because she and my father took Gryfelle's limp body aboard ship and belowdecks. And something told me Mor needed my help.

Diggy stood at least half a dozen paces from the rest of us, shifting her weight back and forth on her feet. Mor approached, and she jumped a pace backward. She jabbed her finger toward the ship. "I can't go on that thing."

"Diggy . . ." Mor looked twice his age. "Please."

"I can't." She seemed to be struggling to draw breath.

"Diggy." I held out my hand before taking another step toward her. "It's all right, lass. Do you want to come with me?"

She shook her head. "I can't."

"You can. You'll be with me. All will be well." I forced a smile, despite all the danger and grief. "You'll be fine."

The pained, jerking breaths continued. Tears streaked down her face, tracking lines through the dirt on her cheeks. But then she reached out and grabbed my hand—so tightly, it was as if she'd fall from a cliff if she let go.

I closed the distance between us and smiled again. A little easier this time. "We'll go together."

She stood frozen for so long that I began to wonder if she would ever respond. Then she surprised me by clutching my elbow and moving closer to my side.

We slowly passed Mor. I made a point not to look at him. I wanted Diggy to forget he was there so she could focus on walking. No ship, no brother, no leaving her home behind. Just walking. Because walking is easy, right?

It felt an eternity. Any moment, I was sure a knot of angry islanders would burst from the trees to come for her. But it didn't seem they had tracked us to the dock just yet. Hopefully Kawan had led them on a wild chase. But even if the islanders didn't find us, surely those threatening strands would return in the interminable time it took me to shuffle Diggy aboard ship.

The islanders never came.

When Diggy and I hit the planks of the deck, I put my arms around her. "You did it. You made it."

Her breathing still came in ragged gasps, though not quite so fast now. But as her gaze darted around the ship, her chest rose and fell more rapidly again.

"You're safe here, Diggy. I'll stay with you the whole time. No one will harm you."

"I'm trapped." She sounded nothing like the Diggy of her own island. A sharp note of panic laced each word.

"No, you're safe. Here with me, and here with people who care about you. No harm will come to you."

Not from us, anyway. I turned to Mor, who had followed us aboard ship and was watching wordlessly. "Are we about underway?"

"Aye."

But he didn't jump into action the way I expected him to. He trudged over to the mast and slumped against it.

Should I talk to him? I couldn't leave Diggy. Not until she felt safe.

Which might be never.

Commander Jule shouted a final order, and we eased away from the dock.

Diggy's breathing had evened again. "Where are we going?"

"Physgot. I think." I glanced at Mor. He nodded once but didn't offer anything else.

"Home?" Diggy's eyes begged me to say I was wrong.

"I . . . yes, I suppose."

"I've never been back. I . . . I can't do this." Her eyes darted everywhere again, as if she might jump overboard, swim back to her island, and take her chances with the locals.

"Diggy," I said, "after we dock in Physgot, we will move on. We won't stay there."

"Where?" At least she was looking at me and not into the water. "Where will we go?"

"Urian, probably. That's where we've been living."

"I'm not going to Urian!" she hissed.

"But you need to meet the queen," I said, keeping my voice steady. "Gareth is no longer king, you know. We have a queen instead, and she will want to meet you. The queen gave Mor his ship."

She frowned. "Why?"

"Because the queen is our friend. And because we helped"—I searched for words—"do the right thing."

It didn't make sense to say "overthrow her father," even though that was technically true.

"Diggy, let's find somewhere to sit." I coaxed her toward a bench near the quarterdeck of the *Lysian*.

"I know what you're doing," she said, even as she let me lead her to the bench.

"Aye? What's that?"

"You're trying to make friends with me."

"Not really. I'm just trying to make sure you feel safe, because you are. And I'm also trying to make sure you don't jump overboard."

"And what if I did? What would it matter to you?"

"You're Mor's sister, and he loves you. That's enough reason for me to want to keep you safe." I sat beside her. "But that's not all. I care about you, and I want to make sure you're looked after."

"You don't even know me. And I don't need looking after."

"Not on your island, you sure didn't. But out here, I think you do."

She rubbed her forehead. "I don't understand what's

happening. This morning I was harvesting coconuts and spearing fish. And now *this*."

"Believe me, I understand." I leaned back. "A few moons ago, I was a story peddler, traveling around with my mentor, selling stories. Trying to work my way to Urian."

"Can't imagine ever wanting to go there."

"When you've been starving half your life and Urian sounds like a place of plenty, it makes more sense." I paused a moment. "I was like you in some ways, you know. I had to fend for myself too young."

Diggy frowned. "But you had your father."

"I didn't." And then I told her the tale of Tanwen and Yestin, the daughter and father who had been separated by thirteen years and the stone walls of the palace at Urian.

As I told my story, strands flowed from my fingertips. Fine brown leather and tiny tendrils of ink for Father. Sparkling seastone-blue for me, and this time a little purple satin found its way in. I smiled. Strands for me always seemed to come out blue because of my eyes, but purple was my favorite color.

"Why are you smiling?" Diggy asked.

The ribbons paused. "My strands are reflecting me in different ways these days, and I guess it makes me smile. Maybe I'm growing into who I'm supposed to be."

At that, my strands crystallized into solid form—a tiny journal, pages filled with the musings of Yestin Bo-Arthio, and a pen with a fluffy plume of purple and blue. Yestin and his feather-headed daughter. I looked at it fondly.

"When you talk of your strands, it reminds me of Mor when we were little."

"Aye?"

"He used to tell stories to the crew on Father's ship. They would all gather around at night and put on dramas, and Mor's story strands made the whole thing magical. He makes stories that are like . . ." She trailed off like she couldn't quite think of the word.

"Tapestries," I supplied.

"Yes! Tapestries. When that usurper started cracking down on weavers, Father wouldn't have it. He said, 'Mortimyr, don't you ever be anyone except who you were created to be.'"

I swiveled on the bench to look at her. "Mortimyr?"

"He didn't tell you? That's his full name."

And then we were both laughing. It wasn't *that* funny, but we were laughing good and loud. And then we were crying. It was silly, but sometimes things are just too much. So many feelings at once after being in danger so long, suffering so much pain, and you need to let yourself laugh and cry over something silly.

If anything could shake Mor from his trance and pique his curiosity, it was me and his sister laughing and crying our heads off. He moved from his spot near the mast and approached us. At the same moment, Karlith and Father came up from belowdecks.

"Gryfelle's been seen to," Father said. "For the time being."

Our laughing ceased, but the tears lingered. At least for me.

Karlith looked at Diggy and smiled in her motherly way. "How about some tea, lassie? Commander Jule knows me well enough after all these weeks at sea. He's seen the *Lysian* stocked with some lovely teas."

"Spike-fruit?" Diggy asked tentatively. "It's my favorite."

Karlith laughed. "Somehow, I don't doubt that. Come here, my girl. Let someone look after you for a bit."

Before Diggy disappeared belowdecks, she paused and stared at Mor. "Maybe you have changed."

His gaze fixed on her, but he didn't say anything.

"If that lass—what was her name?"

"Gryfelle."

"Gryfelle. If she thought you were worth dying for, yes, maybe you have changed."

Then she disappeared down the stairs, Karlith trailing after her. Father stayed with me and Mor.

Mor lowered himself heavily onto the bench beside me. Then he dropped his head into his hands. "We were so close to saving her."

"Yes," I said. "She loved you, Mor." I took a breath. "She loved all of us. Even if she couldn't remember it all, I think she knew in her heart how much she cared. She wanted to save us."

"But we were so near. We *had* the cure."

"Son." Father laid a hand on Mor's shoulder. "Gryfelle was too sick. She's barely been alive for weeks—perhaps only hanging on so you could finish the quest."

Mor looked up. "What do you mean?"

"She knew she was going to die unless there was a miracle. Even the cures of the ancients have limitations. This journey has always been for *you*. Gryfelle told me so herself."

Mor's chest heaved, and I couldn't bear to look at his face. "Why wouldn't she tell me? Why did she let me have hope?"

"Because you needed it. You needed the hope. You needed to do something. Gryfelle had peace. And then Tannie came aboard, and there really was someone who could be saved. Gryfelle desperately wanted that."

A wave of guilt, colder than the sea, washed over me—doused me from my scalp to my toes. "She let us drag her half-way around the world in her final days for me."

Father's voice was gentle. "For you, for Mor, for Dylun, Warmil, and Zel. And Aeron."

I suddenly understood something. "Not Karlith, though. Because Karlith knew."

"Karlith knew the best way to help Gryfelle was to make her comfortable and to ease her soul into the next world."

Karlith's sad but serene face made sense now. She had been

preparing for this day. She had been praying to the Creator for Gryfelle. With Gryfelle. These last weeks had been a sacred time to her.

"I haven't used it yet," I said numbly. "The cure. I suppose I should."

"Aye." Father reached over and took my hand, then looked puzzled as he touched the crystallized story I was clutching. "What is that?"

"Oh." I smiled and opened my palm to show him. "Our story."

"That's one of my journals." He returned my smile.

"And the blue and purple thing is me, I guess. All fluff and fuss."

Mor rose. "I'll go get the box. Zel secured it somewhere."

"Thanks," I said. And then I was alone with my father.

He eased onto the bench beside me.

"Daddy, I don't want to be a mountainbeast anymore."

"Have you been? You hide the fur well."

I chuckled. "You've been hanging around the salty sailors too long." And then the thoughts crashed in unbidden.

Wylie.

I put my hands to my temples. "No, no, no. I can't think about him right now."

Father put an understanding arm around me. "Your friend, Bo-Thordwyan."

The tears welled in my eyes again. "This must have been what it was like for you when you were a soldier. You must have lost so many friends."

"Aye." He looked down. "Many friends. Many men under my command. And I served mostly in times of peace."

"How do you bear it? How do we make it so it doesn't hurt?"

"It's supposed to hurt. Because people matter. And when we lose them, it hurts. They leave a void."

"I'm beginning to feel so full of voids, I'm like a piece of holey cheese."

Father smiled and guided my head to his shoulder. "But you're not a mountainbeast."

"Sometimes I am," I mumbled into his shoulder.

"You are a daughter and I am a father, and we were kept apart a long time."

"Aye." I slid the crystallized journal into his hand. "Let's never do that again, all right?"

"Agreed."

A moment later, Mor and Dylun traipsed up the stairs, the cure box clutched in Dylun's hands.

"Are you ready, Tanwen?" Dylun said. "You have been waiting a long time for this."

And though my burns still smarted, I rose. "Yes. Let's see what the ancients were made of."

I stood at the forecastle and felt like I might as well be onstage.

Not everyone had crowded around me. Warmil was below-decks with Aeron, having his wound tended.

Diggy was below with Karlith still, and Jule and the men strode about the ship. Yet somehow, I felt like everyone in the world was watching me.

"What if it doesn't work?" I stared at the closed box.

"What if it does?" Dylun put his hand on the latch.

"I don't want to let you down if I fail somehow."

"Tanwen." Dylun opened the box and held it out to me. "Whatever happens, you aren't letting anyone down."

My gaze dropped to the cure. The orb was so perfect, so clear, it might as well have been made of air. But that white fire . . .

"I'm afraid to touch it."

"I don't think it will burn you."

I remembered the strands of white light that had blown up my life half a year ago. Master Insegno had said this was of the same power. "I think it already has burned me."

But truly, was that fair? Sure, those white light strands had upended an existence I had thought was comfortable. Passable. But in getting uncomfortable, fighting for the truth and chasing after what was right, I had discovered more. And I had found family in more than one sense. More than one wrong of the world had been righted.

And if this worked, it meant those white light threads that overturned my life had actually saved me.

"I guess I have to just trust it."

"Yes," Dylun said. And he held the box closer to me.

After a deep, slow breath, I reached out and took the orb before I could lose my nerve.

Instantly, the ship vanished. The ocean disappeared. I stood in a dark room. Alone.

"Hello?"

"Don't worry. It's just us, Tannie." A candle flamed, and Brac's grinning face appeared beside me.

"Brac!" I threw my arms around him. Then I paused, frowning. "You're not really here, are you?"

"Dunno. You tell me."

I looked around at the blackness. "I think . . . I think we're in my mind."

"Or your heart?"

"Depends on what you mean by that."

For once, this didn't seem to bother him. Truly, we must be in my imagination somewhere.

"So, what're we doing here, Tannie? Got something you want to say?"

"I've got lots of things I want to say. But to real you. Not imaginary you."

Brac frowned and looked around. "I don't think this is your imagination."

"No?"

"No. It's all dark in here."

"Maybe I've finally run out of stories."

He snorted. "Not likely." But he still looked puzzled. "Also, I feel something."

"What do you mean?"

"Something real. Something I should tell you."

"And if this were my imagination, I would already know." Somehow, I knew I'd normally feel a sense of dread, but nothing seemed unpleasant here. "What is it?"

"I think I'm in trouble, Tannie."

"What kind of trouble, Brac? Do you need help?"

"Aye."

I touched his shoulder. "I'll always try to help you."

"I know, but . . . something doesn't feel right."

I turned away and looked into the blackness. "Lots of things don't feel right. Maybe we can sort it out."

"I hope so. They might be tricking me somehow."

Whatever that meant.

"Well, well." Another candle flamed, and Mor stood on my other side. Not pinched, grieving, downtrodden Mor who tried to carry the weight of the world on his shoulders. Smirky, jesting Mor with his twinkling blue eyes. "I didn't know if I'd be invited."

"Ho, Mortimyr." I grinned.

"Oh, great. I'll kill Diggy."

An unexpected voice floated from one pitch-black corner of the room. "Rude," Diggy said.

Mor raised an eyebrow. "Diggy, come out of the shadows,

will you? However much you might wish it, you're not a night-flier or a rope-tail."

"I'm fine here, thanks."

I released Brac's shoulder and put my hand on Mor's arm. "Let her be."

"She's probably hanging upside down over there or some-thing . . ."

"She's fine."

"I suppose."

We sat still. Then I said, "What are we supposed to do?"

Mor shrugged. "Wait, I guess?"

"I wonder what's happening to my body," I said. "Don't let me hit my head, all right?"

"Yeah," Brac said, "drop her on her face instead. Might improve the look of things."

I punched him. "I didn't know this was a place where we returned to all the jokes we thought were hilarious when we were twelve."

He laughed, but I'd been struck with an idea.

I gasped. "Maybe this *is* a place like that."

Mor's eyebrows rose. "Where we tell childish jokes because we can't express ourselves plainly?"

I shot him a glare. "Look who's talking. No, a place for memories. When I had my episodes, this is what it was like. A black room like this. And things would fly by me. Like silvery strands of memory. Sometimes there would be pictures. It's a bit fuzzy."

"So we're looking for those memories?"

"Maybe."

"Look on the floor, Tannie girl." Another candle, and there was my father. "You never did like to pick up your things off the floor."

I really wanted to argue with that, but he wasn't wrong. And even worse, I looked down and saw a silver strand of memory sitting right at my feet. As though I'd tossed it there like a piece of dirty clothing.

I bent to snatch it up. "Fine." I made a face at Father. "What do I do? Shove it back into my head?"

"I'd wager not." Father didn't offer anything else, but he didn't need to.

The next moment, the strand seemed to wake up. It rippled, then snapped to attention and wrapped itself around my arm. A second passed, and my skin absorbed the strand.

I held up my arm and turned it this way and that in amazement.

Suddenly, strands appeared everywhere, like silver snake hatchlings. Had I really forgotten so much? That's the strange thing about losing your mind. You can't remember what you've forgotten.

I scooped up strand after strand, and each snapped to attention, wrapped itself around some part of me, and melted into my skin.

"You've got them all now," Mor said. "I'm pretty sure."

"I don't see any others," Father confirmed. "Though I did find the Digwyn lass in the corner."

"Brac?"

He stopped scanning the floor for escaped strands and looked up at me. "Aye, Tannie?"

"Remember that time when I was six and we chased a white fluff-hopper? The newborn one that was trying to eat your puppy?"

"Aye."

I grinned. "Me too."

He returned my grin at first, but after only a moment, it fell. "Tannie?"

"Yes, Brac?"

"Promise you won't forget that day."

"I just told you. I got it back. I won't let it go again."

"I mean don't forget it, even if you might want to."

Now *my* expression fell. I took a step back. "Brac . . . what's happened?"

"Promise you'll remember all those good times from when we were children."

"I will, but—"

He disappeared before I could finish. I turned, and it was only Mor and Father in the black space with me. And Diggy, shrouded in a corner somewhere.

"Well, I guess that's it," I said. "Time to go back to the—oh." And I held a hand to my heart, because even in this place where nothing seemed quite as troublesome as it did in the real world, the sight before me just about shredded my soul.

A shimmering form of Gryfelle stood on one side of Father. And a shimmering wisp of Wylie on the other.

"Oh, my friends." Tears didn't come. Maybe they didn't exist here. But I felt them in my heart. "My friends, I'm so sorry."

They didn't seem to hear me. Or anything at all.

Gryfelle, looking whole and very young, wore a dress like the ladies at court wore, and I realized this was what I imagined Gryfelle looked like before she was banished. Wylie had rope in his hands. His mouth moved. He was teaching me at knots and laughing over how my supposedly gifted fingers couldn't manage a task sailors learned as cabin boys.

"It's not really them," I said. "These are just my thoughts. My memories and my imaginings of them."

"Yes." Father ran a hand through the arm of the Gryfelle figure. "They've moved on, Tannie."

Mor took my hand. "Time for us to move on. Back to the *Lysian*."

"We're still there on the deck. I think. This place is strange."

"Aye."

"But I guess real life is strange sometimes, too." I looked down at our interlocked hands.

I closed my eyes and kept them closed until the feel of Mor's fingers disappeared. My eyes stayed shut until I could taste salt in the air, hear the lapping of the waves against the hull, and feel the hard wood of the deck beneath my body.

Then Dylun's voice. "Tanwen, are you all right?"

I cracked one eye open. Mor was on one side, Father on the other. It looked like they had broken my fall. The orb was still clutched in my fingers. "This thing needs to go back in its box."

"Did it not work?" Dylun asked curiously.

"It did." I sat up and placed the orb back onto the velvet lining of the box. "But you weren't kidding about the power of those strands."

I tried to stand, then tumbled back over. "Oh. Maybe not yet. I tell you, having a rush of memories fly back into your head isn't as peaceful as you might think." In fact, my head was throbbing pretty badly.

"Take your time, Tannie girl." Father supported me as I sat.

I glanced down at my midsection. My blouse was still tattered where it had been burned, but my flesh had healed beneath it.

I was just about ready to make another try at standing when a sudden remembrance smacked me back down. "Oh, stars."

Mor crouched beside me. "What is it? Are you feeling sick again?"

"No. I just remembered something." I looked up at him. "A lost memory from the battle in the throne room. The high priest. Naith Bo-Offriad."

"What about him?" Father's concern clipped his words.

"That halo-head creature I made. Well, it went after him, but before it could get to him, he vanished. It was like he made strands of night. That's what I thought at the time, until the memory disappeared with a pop." I looked from Father to Mor.

"But the strands he used to escape during the battle looked an awful lot like the ones we've been fighting."

Mor and Father shared a look.

"We need to get back to Tir," Father said. "Immediately."

CHAPTER FIFTY-TWO

TANWEN

THE AWFUL THING ABOUT HAVING SOMETHING URGENT TO attend to when traveling by ship is that a ship goes as fast as it goes. You're at the mercy of the wind and the rigging and the skill of the sailors and the whims of the currents.

Wylie would have corrected me. Currents don't have whims, he'd say. They obey the laws of the sea, just as we must.

But that didn't change the fact that they seemed against us. Stalling our return to Urian, just for fun.

We took turns pacing the deck. Father, Karlith, Dylun, and Warmil had talked over my recollection about Naith. I heard them talking about weavers in general, too, and how the rules of our strands seemed to be bending all over the place. There was the appearance of the truth strands in my stories that were beyond my control, the reawakening of the ancient curses, the dark strands of malice being manipulated in ways the Creator surely never intended.

Then Dylun casually mentioned "other" strange uses we had witnessed lately, and all eyes turned toward Diggy.

She had come back above, but she huddled in a dark corner near the quarterdeck, sipping yet another cup of spike-fruit tea. Karlith had furnished her with a near-constant supply since Diggy first learned it was on board. Truthfully, it seemed to soothe her nerves, and that was a good thing.

I eyed the others and felt a spark of protectiveness for Diggy.

I knew what information they hoped to get from her. We all had seen it. That thing she had done. And Diggy had not mentioned being a weaver. So what was this trick of hers?

We all wondered.

But could it not wait? She was panicked and defensive. We had practically forced her onto a ship, the one place in the world she didn't want to be. Yes, we were saving her life, but still, she needed some space to breathe.

"Don't," I said to the others. "Let's not ask her about it now. She's exhausted."

"We're all exhausted," Dylun pointed out. And he wasn't wrong.

"Aye. But her more than us. Her life has exhausted her."

Dylun didn't know the whole extent of it, of course. And I'd not be telling him. That was Diggy's story to share, if she chose to.

"Tanwen," Dylun said, "if she knows something about all the strange occurrences we've been seeing, we need her to tell us. It's a piece of the puzzle."

"I understand that. And I know how you love puzzles. But she's not *just* a puzzle piece. She's a person, and I'm telling you, we need to give her some time. And space, if you're wise."

Dylun sighed. "Honestly, she's a tiny lass. You make her sound most dangerous."

"You didn't see the knife-throwing."

"The what?"

I shrugged. "Suit yourself. Go ask her."

He strode over to her darkened corner. "Hello, Digwyn."

She looked up at him but didn't move, smile, or speak. She cupped her mug of tea in both hands, her palms covered in curious leather gloves—they had no fingers at all.

Diggy seemed to notice Dylun looking at them. "For climbing trees," she said. "Harvesting coconuts."

"Oh. Of course."

"It's cold on board. I don't like it."

She wore the same outfit she'd worn each day since I had met her, but Karlith had knitted an oversized sweater so she might wrap up against the wind of the ship and the sea and the Tirian autumn she had not felt for three years. Mor was rather dismayed she insisted on her shorts and wouldn't wear a proper pair of trousers or a skirt. Perhaps the chilly Tirian air would eventually inspire her.

"Yes," Dylun said. "It does get rather cold aboard ship." He cleared his throat. "Digwyn, I would like to ask you a few questions, if you don't mind."

"I do."

"Pardon?"

"I do mind. Stop talking to me."

Dylun swiveled around to look at me. I held up my hands. I'd tried to tell him.

"Well, it's very important that I ask you these questions," Dylun said.

"Then why even bother asking me if I mind?"

Dylun looked unnerved. Not sure I'd ever seen that before. But he forged ahead. "I need to ask you about what happened on the beach."

"We fought a black cloud, and the sick lass died. Now we're here."

"I mean what you did."

"I fought with you." Diggy frowned at him.

What looked like genuine confusion settled on her face. Then again, I knew I was already developing a soft spot for the lass, prickly though she was. Maybe she was just giving Dylun a hard time.

"There was something particular you did. Something with Zelyth's strands, and then mine. You did it at the stone head, too."

"Aye."

"What is it, that thing you do?"

Diggy shrugged. "I don't know."

"You don't know?"

"I. Do. Not. Know." She pulled her mug closer. "I don't like you."

"I'm sorry."

"Because I don't like you?" She almost smiled. "That's strange."

Dylun sighed. "Can you explain to me what you did?"

"Nope."

"You can't or you won't?"

"Both. I don't know, and if I did, I don't think I'd tell you."

"Has it happened before?"

I moved closer now. "Dylun, I think that's enough. She says she doesn't know what happened."

"But she did it. She grabbed strands out of the air with her hands. Changed them into other things. It was as if lightning crackled in her palms. She did something to *our* strands."

"I couldn't use my knives," Diggy said. "There wasn't a person making the dark strands. I couldn't use my knives, so I did something else instead."

"But how?"

"I don't know."

Dylun sighed again.

"Dylun, really," I said. "Do we have to figure it out now?"

"Tanwen." He turned to me. Grave, but not unkind. "She grabbed strands from the sky and turned them into weapons."

When he said the word "weapons," I remembered our situation a little more clearly. This girl—this abused, shattered, frightened girl—could amplify others' strands. She could grab the strands of any weaver straight from the sky and use them for whatever she wanted. Her will alone seemed enough to accomplish . . . anything.

And some unknown pursuer wanted to use me and Mor as

a weapon because we were linked. What would that thing do when it found out about Diggy? Perhaps it already knew and was chasing us all the more intently.

I sank down beside Diggy on the deck.

Dylun tried again. "Has this ever happened to you before, Digwyn?"

She shrugged. "Once or twice."

"When?"

"A long time ago. And if you ask me any more questions, I promise to remove your eyeballs in your sleep."

Dylun's brows rose, and his mouth opened.

Diggy turned to me and held out her cup. "Spike-fruit, Tannie?"

I forced a smile and accepted a sip of the tea, but my thoughts raced.

We had to protect her. And protect the world *from* her.

CHAPTER FIFTY-THREE

TANWEN

SLEEP ELUDED ME THAT NIGHT. WE HAD TO BE GETTING CLOSE to Physgot now. And then what? Would there be some evil strand sorcerer waiting on the dock for us, ready to kidnap me and Mor? Or worse, Diggy? I had promised to keep her safe. Was I about to break that promise, after just a couple weeks?

I rolled over on my bunk and stared at Diggy's back, watching her breathe for a while. Then my thoughts wandered to Wylie and how I wished I could have asked him for advice or reassurance, or even just talked to him about nothing at all or shared a jest. My heart pinched.

Grief is like that. It crashes over you in unexpected waves.

I needed air. I slipped my feet into my boots and wrapped up in a shawl. Bless Karlith and her knitting. She was the only reason I hadn't shivered to death on this trip, so fond I seemed to be of jumping aboard ships with nothing except the clothes on my back.

I creaked my way up the stairs to the deck.

And really, I'd almost been expecting him.

"Ho, Mor."

"Ho, Tannie."

"Couldn't sleep again?" I asked.

"I don't think I've slept in moons."

"I'm sorry for that. You must be so weary."

"Aye."

I wrapped the shawl tighter around my shoulders and leaned my back against the rail so I could see his face better. "Do you want to talk about it?"

"Which part?"

"Any of it."

He sighed wearily. "I don't know, Tannie. I just—" He broke off. "I tried to do the right thing. And somehow, I feel like it made everything worse."

"That's not true."

"Isn't it?"

"No. You didn't make anything worse. Everything is better because you tried to do the right thing."

"Gryfelle is gone. Diggy seems to despise me."

"Gryfelle being gone isn't because you tried to save her."

Mor looked past me to the sea. "I didn't succeed."

"That's not the same as making everything worse. You did right in trying to save Gryfelle. And, hey, you accidentally saved me in the process, so there's that."

He gave a half-smile then. "I'm sorry, Tannie. I didn't mean to make it sound like that didn't matter. It *does* matter to me, and it wasn't an accident."

"Mor, I know. Of course I know. I was teasing you." I smiled. "And Diggy will come around. I'm sure she will."

"I'm not so sure. But she's taken to you, that's certain."

"I like her." I grinned. "Even if she is a little unraveled."

"Do you suppose the awful things that happened to her made her that way?"

"Perhaps. Living alone on an island for three years sure didn't help. Imagine what my father would be like if he hadn't had Cameria to keep him sane. Or sane-ish. Diggy needs a lot of love. And honesty. And trust."

"I'll try. If she'll let me."

"I think she will. Even if not right now."

There was silence for a long moment. Then he murmured, "Wylie is gone."

"Yes," I said, and I managed it without tears for the first time. "He is." I realized suddenly that Mor shared my heartache about the crewman he'd lost. "But you didn't do that either."

"Aeron lost a leg."

"That wasn't your fault. Aeron lost her leg because she fought for the people she loves. She fought for what she believes in."

"Thank you for not saying she would want it this way."

I snorted. "Well, that's a load of rubbish. Who would want it this way? We all want to fight for what we believe is right, but we all would like to make it out on the other side alive and in one piece, if we can help it. Anyone who says otherwise is trying to sell you something."

"Aye. Like a tragic romance story crystal. Those romances seem to disagree with your sentiment. They revel in the misfortune and heartbreak of death."

"Fie on them."

Mor chuckled. He leaned toward me, and I stilled

But he tucked a strand of loose hair behind my ear and leaned away again. "It's never going to be all right, is it? You and me."

I regained my composure. "I hope it could be. Someday. You're still drowning under a tidal wave of grief, so maybe we don't have to think about all that just now."

He gave me a look, then took my hand. A blend of colored lights arced from our connection into the blackened sea. "Sure. We'll just ignore that for a bit. Should be easy."

I smiled and gently unlaced his hand from mine. "Well, ignore isn't the right word. Maybe we just don't have to talk about it right now. But I do want you to know—as soon as I can, I'm going to talk to Brac. I'm going to be honest with him and end our engagement, good and proper. I love him too much to carry on like this. I know I should have told him before, but everything was such a mess. I was so terrified of what was happening to me, and I didn't want to admit it. It just felt like too much to handle at once."

"I understand," Mor said quietly.

"I just hope Brac does." I sighed. "Something tells me he won't." I stifled a yawn.

"You should head to bed. Sleep while you can." He traced the line of my jaw with his thumb. "Night, Tannie."

The tiniest crackle of lighting sizzled where our skin touched.

I smiled up at him. "Good night, Mortimyr."

CHAPTER FIFTY-FOUR

TANWEN

THE EASTERN PENINSULA WAS SO CLOSE, I COULD TASTE THE hathberries.

I had to restrain myself from waving to Pembrone across the bay as we neared Physgot.

"Never thought you'd be so excited to see Tir," Father said. He'd caught me grinning at the coastline.

"Home."

"Indeed."

"I appreciate it more than I used to, now that I've been around the world, raiding strands from foreign lands."

"With Braith on the throne, there is opportunity to make Tir more than it was, besides."

"You speak in riddles."

"I'm an old man. Allow me my riddles."

I laughed. "You're not old. Forty, maybe?"

"Forty-five."

I whistled, just to tease him. "Never mind. You must be one of the ancients Master Insegno talked about."

"Impertinent." He kissed me on the forehead and went to help the crew.

"Tannie?"

That small voice stirred me to immediate action.

"It's all right, Diggy." I turned and found her wrapped twice around in the sweater Karlith had knitted. She had pulled it so tightly that the yarn was stretched. "It's all right. Come here by me."

Diggy scooted next to me. Her breathing was a bit irregular, but not galloping yet.

"Look." I pointed. "There's Pembrone over there. That's where I'm from. And I'm sure you remember Physgot. You must have sailed into this harbor a thousand times with your father."

"Aye."

"But this is my first time."

She looked at me funny. "Can't be."

"I'd never been on a ship before this trip," I said. "Farm girls don't often take to the sea."

"Fishermen's girls do."

"Yes."

"Do you have a farm up there?" Diggy nodded to Pembrone.

"I have a cottage. My mother's family home."

"Is your mother dead?"

Diggy was consistently abrupt, but I was growing used to it. "Yes, she's dead."

"Sorry. Mine is dead too."

"Yes, I know. I'm sorry too."

Diggy looked at the approaching coast. "Tannie?"

"Hmm?"

"I'm afraid."

She let me wrap her in my arms. "I know you are, Diggy. But I'm going to keep you safe. I'll do everything I can to protect you."

"Will you leave?" This childlike side of Diggy squeezed my heart.

"Never."

"Will you be my friend?" Her strong island façade had faded to frailty as we moved closer to the place where her life had begun to unravel.

"I will always be your friend, Diggy."

"Then let's go home."

I knew something was amiss in Physgot before we set foot on the dock.

I had only been there the one time, but the hum of the town had been a balm to my hurting heart. I knew what that hum sounded like.

This Physgot did not sound like the one imprinted on my heart.

"Mor," I called.

He was busy getting the *Lysian* secured to the dock, but he looked up anyway. "Aye, Tannie?"

"Something is wrong." I glanced back out over the rooftops. "The city doesn't feel right."

"Doesn't feel right?" Mor clomped down the deck toward me. "What does that mean?"

"It's the middle of the day."

"And it's dead silent," he realized aloud. He nodded toward Diggy. "Stay here with her, will you?"

"Yes."

"Warmil, General, Jule. I need you," he called. "Sword belts on."

The men and several crew members made their way down the dock, hands on hilts and ready for danger, should it rear its head.

They disappeared among the shops and homes, and anxiety crept over me.

But nothing happened. It was only a few long moments before Mor appeared again, his hands spread out. "No one is here."

"No one?" I headed down the ramp onto the dock. "How is that possible?"

Mor folded his arms as I began to inspect locked and boarded shops and homes. "Well, I didn't make it up, Tannie."

"I believe you. I just don't understand. Did something happen?"

I didn't want to say it out loud. Could they have all been killed? That seemed a terrible and unlikely prospect. *But how else does a whole town full of people disappear?*

"They're not dead," an unfamiliar voice chimed in beside me.

I nearly screamed.

"Sorry, lassie." The old man was so tiny and shriveled, I hadn't seen him in his rocking chair on one of the front porches. "Didn't mean t'scare ya." He smiled a toothless grin.

"Sir." Mor strode up to him. "Can you tell us what happened?"

"Aye. They's gone."

"Yes, I can see that, but where? How?"

"They marched."

"Marched?"

"To Urian."

Mor and I turned to look at each other.

"They marched to Urian?" I asked. "Why?"

"Guess they marched *on* Urian, more's the like."

My heart stuttered. "Marched *on* Urian—as in, to take it over?"

The man nodded and chewed on the end of a pipe. "Aye. Got thar revolt goin' good and proper, finally. You's lucky they gone. You'd've been taken prisoners for sailin' under tha queen's banner thar."

Mor looked like his heart had skipped a few beats. "When did they leave?"

"Least a week's time. Maybe more." He shoved his pipe

back into his mouth, then leaned against the back of his chair and appeared to fall asleep.

One awful moment of silence passed, and then we were both moving and shouting. Mor snapped out orders, and the men began to grab the supplies they had just unloaded.

"Warmil!" Mor shouted. "We need to get to the river. Immediately."

I was sprinting back toward the boat. "Diggy! Karlith! Come quickly. We're heading for the river."

"The river?" Karlith held an armload of forest-green yarn. "What's happened?"

I grabbed the yarn from her. "We have to get to Urian now. They've all gone to overthrow Braith."

CHAPTER FIFTY-FIVE

BRAITH

Braith sat on the garden bench beside Kharn, but she was not comfortable. Tension filled the air all around them. Kharn was unhappy. It was plain on his face.

"Braith . . ."

"Don't ask again." She gripped the stem of her wine glass more tightly.

"Then give me an answer. I only persist in asking because I've never received a proper answer in the first place. It's been ten days' time."

"I know. And I'm sorry. I truly am."

He took a long sip of wine. "Braith, I did not want to have to approach it from this angle. I wanted to sweep you off your feet, to convince you of my love and get you to believe in the possibility of loving me. Because I believe that is possible for us in every way."

Braith stared at the ground. "I know. I don't doubt your intentions."

"Then please understand my intentions when I tell you this."

She looked up.

"You have councilors and nobles who support you. But surely you understand that I have them also. I have those who have been pressing me from the moment I stepped foot in Urian to take what they see as my rightful place on the throne."

"I'm sure that's true." Braith looked down into her wine. Imagined drowning in a big sea of it.

"They are pressing me ever harder to make a move for the throne. And I don't want to do that to you."

"Is that a threat, Kharn? Are you telling me that if I don't marry you, you'll take the throne from me?" But Braith couldn't even muster convincing indignation because, of course, he wasn't saying that at all.

"You know that's not true."

Braith sighed. "Yes," she told him. "I do."

"Unlike my supporters, I believe you *also* belong on the Tirian throne. We could do this together. They will accept it. If only you'll say yes."

Braith signaled a nearby servant to retrieve their empty goblets. Her gaze lingered on the guardsmen lining the perimeter of the garden. "It's a pity this is what it takes these days."

"Pardon?"

"An entire armed guard, just for an evening in the gardens. Do you remember when we used to play here as children?"

"Yes, I do."

"You and that nobleman's son—what was his name? Jay-something?"

"Jaylith Bo-Joffrey." Kharn smiled for the first time that evening. "He was fast."

"He was the worst. He caught the girls and shoved our faces in the mud."

"As I said, he was fast."

"He ruined more than one of my dresses in that mud."

"I wonder what became of him."

"No, don't," Braith said. "It's best not to."

Kharn looked at her. "Best not to wonder? Why do you say that?"

"So many from the old days—from Caradoc's days—are

dead. And it's easier if you accept that fact without naming them."

"But wasn't Sir Joffrey loyal to your father?"

"Yes. But many nobles' sons died in my father's wars." She still recoiled at the thought. "They were knights, a great many of them."

"Yes, of course." Kharn paused a moment. "It must have been dreadful for you to lose so many friends, Braith."

"I wouldn't call Jaylith Bo-Joffrey a friend." She glanced at Kharn wryly. "But all the same, it is always hard to lose those with whom you have shared your life."

"Indeed."

A long silence passed between them. Braith stared at the velvet-petal bush across the path—deep indigo flowers in their final burst of beauty before their winter sleep.

"Kharn?" Braith turned toward him and looked him in the eyes. "I need you to listen to me. I never want Tir to have another era like my father's reign. If I can help it, Tir and her neighbors will live in peace and prosperity forever. I know that is just a dream. This is the real world, and it is ugly—a playground for man's darkest desires. But I don't care. I want to hope for something better. I want to spend the rest of my life doing what I can to bring something better to my people—a better way of living and thinking and believing."

"I don't think it's just a dream. I think we *can* live better."

Braith searched his eyes. "That's what I want from my reign." She had made her decision. "From *our* reign."

Kharn stared, eyes wide. Then a smile blossomed on his face. "Does that mean . . . ?"

"If you share my vision for Tir. If you will support my goals, then I will agree. And I will endeavor to support your goals and be a good queen to my people and a good wife to you."

He touched her face with his hand. "Braith, our goals are the same."

"Then you will not try to dissuade me from my vision?"

He laughed and gently pulled her closer. "You're not listening."

"I confess, I'm nervous." She smiled. "And suddenly quite aware that there are at least a dozen men in this garden with us."

Kharn laughed again. "You needn't be nervous. Ever again, for you will have me by your side always."

Their lips edged closer, and Braith was near enough to smell the shave oil on his beard when sounds of chaos erupted.

They started. Kharn jumped to his feet, and they both watched in horror as a volley of arrows cascaded into the garden. A guardsman was struck in the face and fell to the ground.

Braith screamed.

"Braith!" Kharn pulled her to her feet and tried to shield her from the arrows.

But they were everywhere. Wave after wave. More guardsmen were collapsing around them.

"Get inside!" a remaining guard shouted. "Get the queen—" But his command was cut off by an arrow to his throat.

Braith covered her mouth, muffling her cry.

"Braith, come!" Kharn hid her in his shadow and pulled her toward the gate.

But that gate led to a courtyard, and then through that courtyard was another garden. The palace seemed so far away. And where were the arrows coming from? Oh, why had they taken their wine so far from the safety of the palace halls?

Kharn led her toward the gateway, and they passed the body of a young servant, the tray of wine goblets toppled next to him. Braith cried out. She knew this boy. His mother was a palace bread maker.

Tears streamed down Braith's cheeks. "Kharn." She stopped him and reached for the servant boy. "Let me close his eyes, at least." She moved her hand over the dead boy's face.

"Come, Braith," Kharn said after a moment. "We must go." He pulled her to her feet and past the fallen boy.

In the courtyard beyond the garden, the arrows were fewer, and her hope was rekindled. Perhaps they could make it if they ran.

But the hope died quicker than it had arisen. For now a rabble appeared on the path that led from the front of the palace. At least two dozen of them, armed and angry. They clearly recognized Braith and seemed to have expected her to be here. Of course, that must have been the plan. To flush them from the garden with arrows and slaughter them here. At close range, to be sure their deed was accomplished.

Braith's heart sank. These were not the soldiers of a foreign army. They were not distant conquerors, come to take Tir. They were peasants and merchants and farmers and fishermen. They were Tirians. Braith and Kharn's own people. And they were here for their queen.

Braith and Kharn stopped. Kharn pushed her behind him again. "Stay back."

"You're unarmed."

"I have my fists. They're not much, and I'm rather attached to them, but they'll have to do."

Braith wanted to laugh and cry at once.

Kharn called out to the peasants. "You will not harm her! You will not harm your queen! You'll have to kill me first."

Shouts arose from the crowd of foot soldiers, and by the sound of them, they seemed perfectly willing to comply with this request.

"Shall we run?" Braith whispered in Kharn's ear.

"We wouldn't make it in time. But I'll hold them off as long as I can, and you run."

"But you—"

"Promise me."

"Kharn . . ."

"Promise!"

"I . . . I promise."

He kissed her. Not tender and sweet, as their kiss might have been just a few minutes before, but hurried and desperate and determined. "Go!"

Braith picked up her heavy skirt and tried to obey. She sighted the next gateway and ran toward it. But she had only managed a dozen steps when a man seemed to come from nowhere and forced himself directly into her path.

"Oh!" Braith crashed into him.

"I'm sorry, Your Majesty. But I can't let you do that." His voice was vaguely familiar. "You need to come with me."

And then his hands were on her. Rough, calloused, strong. Shoving her arms behind her back.

"No!" She fought against him. "Kharn!" she screamed. "Kharn!" She looked up into the stranger's eyes and found he was just a young man. One she knew.

"I'm sorry," he said. "Truly. It ain't like I wanted it this way."

"Guardsman Bo-Bradwir?" Braith stopped struggling. "What are you doing? Why are you here?"

"Forgive me, Lady Braith. But it's time to go." He looped a rope around her wrists.

"No!" Braith thrashed against his grip and the rope and the horror of what was happening. The yells of foot soldiers filled her ears. Shouts reverberated through her bones. "Kharn!"

She twisted so she might look back the way she had come. So she might see Kharn one last time and cry out to him. But she looked just in time to see a man hit Kharn in the head with the hilt of a sword.

Braith screamed.

Kharn stumbled to his knees. The man delivered another blow to Kharn's temple.

"No!" Braith screamed again.

Kharn Bo-Candryd collapsed to the cobblestones and lay still.

Guardsman Bo-Bradwir pulled her away. "Come on, now. You have places to be."

"No!" Braith poured every ounce of her will into her struggle and screamed the whole way out of the courtyard. As she went, she saw peasants stream into the castle. In a moment of sheer desperation, she prayed to the Creator that those inside would be able to hide or run.

Though how could they?

The servants and the councilors and their families. All the women and children and the sick who lay in the infirmary. Even the condemned in the dungeon.

Dray.

And, Creator above, Cameria.

Braith's voice finally failed. She gave a strangled gasp and began to weep.

"I'm very, very sorry, my lady," Bo-Bradwir said, but his words were undercut by the bonds around her wrists. "They've said they won't harm you. I hope—" But he didn't finish his ambivalent thought as he pressed a rag filled with a strange, medicinal scent over her mouth and nose.

All Braith knew was blackness.

BRAITH

BRAITH'S HEAD POUNDED.

The medicinal scent lingered in her nose, and she sucked in air to clear it. She opened her eyes, but it made no difference. Blackness was everywhere.

She tried to take stock of her surroundings—not what she could see, but what she could feel. The ground was hard beneath her. Stone. She was slumped against a wall. She tried to put a hand to her aching head and met with strong resistance and a metallic clang.

She tried the other hand with the same result. She was chained to something. The wall? Yes. She was shackled to the wall. She tugged at the chains once more, but they snapped her wrists back.

A stream of fire lit the darkness and sailed toward the side of the room. A torch flared in a bracket. Then another stream and another torch. And another and another.

Braith blinked.

A figure stood in the center of the room, shrouded head to toe in black fabric.

The figure chuckled. "Here we are at last."

Braith squinted in the firelight, but the figure was obscured, the voice strange and distorted. "Who are you?"

"The truth?"

"Of course."

"Very well."

The figure stepped forward and began to unwrap the black fabric. Yards and yards of the material pooled on the floor, and a human form took shape.

Braith looked into the eyes of the person staring at her—so deeply familiar as never to be forgotten. She strained forward, for she must be mistaken. But then she sank back against the stone wall.

She spoke with difficulty, disbelief rising in her throat. "Mother?"

Continued in
The Weaver Trilogy: Book 3
The Story Hunter

ACKNOWLEDGMENTS

D RAFTING *T HE S TORY R AIDER* WAS ONE OF THE MOST DIFFI- cult things I've done in my career. I wouldn't have made it through in one piece without the support of some excellent people.

Always first, my husband, Dave. Without your encourage- ment to pursue my creative efforts, none of my stories would be told. Thank you for believing in me.

To my children: Shane, Jared, and Keira. For making your- selves dinner sometimes while I was trying to make my dead- line. I'm so proud of the people you've grown into. Never change. Except your socks. Please change those.

To my agent, my shield-maiden, Rachel Kent. Thank you for always having my back.

To my team at Enclave: my "marketing lovelies," Jordan Smith and Katelyn Bolds, whose enthusiasm and support for *The Story Peddler* kept me going while I was trying to launch it and write *The Story Raider* at the same time; and to Steve Laube, my fantastic editor, who did not throw me out the window when I changed the title of this book midway through drafting. Sorry about all the tea, Steve. Hopefully no kittens will die.

To Ashley Mays, for being a constant, even when my world is filled with chaos. You make life better, and I'm so lucky to call you friend.

To Dana Black, who is the world's best assistant, handler, and friend—the one who remembers to pack snacks, never lets me forget my purse, and was the first to shout, "More Mor!"

To my Wonder Women: Avily Jerome, Catherine Jones Payne, and Sarah Grimm. Thank you for carrying my sword when I couldn't.

To Chris, whose GIF game is unrivaled.

To my street team, the Corsyth Crew. While I was typing enough words each day to make my fingers fall off, I fled to our Facebook group to hang out with you guys more times than you know. You are *the best* and I'm so blessed to have you as my team. For my "Hay, Brac" girls . . . I'm sorry. I'll make it up to you somehow!

To Kirk DouPonce, for this cover that made me gasp in delight the moment I saw it. You're still the literal best.

To my dad, Doug Powell, for lending his colormastery skills to my map and for always adding a little something fun in the process.

To the readers who have discovered Tanwen's story—to those who have written to me, internet-yelled at me for having to wait so long for this book, who have gushed on your blogs and your Instagram accounts and in your reviews. You have no idea what your support has meant to me. Thank you for imagining with me.

And as always, all glory goes to God, the Source of all good things and the one who rescues from even the darkest circumstances.

Lindsay A. Franklin is a bestselling author, award-winning editor, and homeschooling mom of three. She would wear pajama pants all the time if it were socially acceptable. She lives in her native San Diego with her scruffy-looking nerf-herder of a husband, their precious geeklings, three demanding thunder pillows (a.k.a. cats), and a stuffed wombat with his own Instagram following.

Connect with Lindsay!

Website: *lindsayafranklin.com*
Facebook: *facebook.com/lindsayafranklin*
Twitter: *@LinzyAFranklin*
Instagram: *@linzyafranklin*
Pinterest: *@linzyafranklin*